ECHOES OF YOU

NEW YORK TIMES BESTSELLER

MARGARET McHEYZER

Echoes of You

ISBN: 978-0-6483670-7-9 (ePub)
ISBN: 978-0-6483670-8-6 (Paperback)

Cover Design: Book Cover by Design
Editor: Debi Orton
Interior Formatting by Tami Norman, Integrity Formatting

email: hit_149@yahoo.com

ECHOES
OF YOU

New York Times Bestseller
MARGARET MCHEYZER

Find Your Courage

PROLOGUE

The palms of my hands are sweating.

Standing in front of an unassuming building, I look up to see its sheer size. Still, it's inconspicuous because it looks exactly like all the other buildings surrounding it.

The sun breaks out just behind the brick building, casting the entrance into shadow.

Funny, that. Because I've been living in the shadows all my life. Now is the time for me to come out of the shadows, and speak my truth.

Speak our truth.

There's a line of cars in front of the building, all marked with the same lettering.

My heart beats quickly as a shock of finality runs through my veins.

This is where part of me will die and another part of me will live.

All my life I've been worried about what people think of me. But I can't continue on in a life where I'm only breathing. I need to learn to live.

I take several deep breaths, ready to cross the street and take the leap I've been longing for.

"You can do this," I say to myself. The sun is moving higher, the shadow becoming smaller.

Yes, you can.

I look to my left, and to my right, checking for oncoming cars.

I keep walking, crossing the street. I know if I stop for even a second, I'll talk myself out of going.

You can do it.

I walk until I come to the automated doors that slowly slide open.

Hopefully, they'll believe you.

I head to the counter, where a woman with dark hair pulled back in a severe ponytail and wearing a uniform is working on a computer. She looks up, but remains seated. "Can I help you?" she says in a flat voice.

My hands tremble, so I knit them together to stop the emotion bursting to come forward.

"I, um," my voice quivers with uncertainty.

"Are you okay?" She stands and comes closer to the counter. She looks behind me, searching for a hint as to why I'm so edgy.

"I, um, need to talk to the police unit that deals with sexual abuse."

Part One

Past

CHAPTER 1

"Thank God it's finally over," I say to AJ, who's lying on his bed.

"School's not that bad," he replies.

"For you it's fine. For me, it's only ever been…" I look away, hoping he doesn't see how I'm really feeling. "…hard," I finally say.

"School's fun." AJ sits up on his bed, and flexes his arms, checking the mirror to admire how he looks. He stands, walks over to his dumbbells, and starts pumping them.

"Don't you ever get sick of working out?"

He looks down at his body, and gives me a cheeky smile. "Not when the end result is me being so strong and so hot."

"Ugh, how can we be friends when you're so full of yourself?"

"We're friends, *because* I'm full of myself." Rolling my eyes, I shake my head. "What are you going to do now you've finished school. College? Work?"

"I have no idea. I suppose I'll just hang back, and you know, do nothing."

"Great aspirations."

AJ huffs. He places the dumbbells down, then drops to the ground, doing pushups effortlessly. "You know, you're gorgeous. Why don't you try modeling?"

"Modeling? Really? When have you ever known me to want to be a model?"

"What about an actress?" I shake my head at his ridiculous suggestions. "A politician?" I curl my top lip, questioning his bizarre work suggestions. "Astronaut, professional wedding guest. You know, I once watched a thing on YouTube about a guy who was an earwax cleaner. They had this little hook, and they'd get the wax out of…"

"Stop!" I say before he finishes the sentence. "I don't want to hear anymore."

"Suit yourself." He keeps doing his pushups. "What about a pimple popper?"

"Really? Are you trying to gross me out?"

"I'm giving you career options."

"And pimple popper is a career?" I question with lifted brows.

"Thirty," he says as he springs up to his feet. "People make an absolute fortune from popping pimples on social media. Truthfully though, I've never really been into social media." He walks over to a bar above his door frame, and starts doing pullups. "One, two, three," he continues.

"But you've watched things on ear wax cleaners? Yeah sure."

AJ laughs. "You gotta figure out what you're going to do."

"We both know that's impossible. Until M can deal with the demons, I can't do anything."

AJ slows his pullups, and hops to the ground. He runs his hands through his hair, then steps back, leaning against the door jamb. "M has a long way to go." He lets out a long breath.

"Do you think M will find peace?"

AJ sighs again. This time his mood is darker, more tortured. He looks away from me. "I um, don't ever want to go through that again."

A knot forms in my stomach. I know the pain he's gone through. And still, to this day, he struggles with the horrors he's had to face. We all have. All for M. What I went through was bad, but what AJ had to do… no one should have to endure that.

The room is heavy with sadness. AJ is wrestling with his own demons, his own memories.

"What about a bee keeper?" I say, trying to break the massive weight that's crushing both of us.

AJ's staring at something invisible. It's what he does when his pain gets bad. He's fixated on one point, not hearing me.

"AJ," I say a little louder, trying to snap him out of his misery.

"Yeah?" He flicks his glance to me, and I see the bitterness. He moves forward, picks up his dumbbells again, and starts working his arms. "What did you say?"

He's completely distracted now. But I can see if he doesn't distract himself, the pain will eat him alive. "I said, maybe I can be a beekeeper."

A small smile tugs on one side of his mouth. "Beekeeper? I like my idea for a professional ear wax cleaner better." His muscles flex beneath his white t-shirt. Sweat beads on his forehead as he pushes himself.

"Maybe I should try to get in shape."

"Nah, you don't need to. I'll protect you," he says as he keeps the repetitions up.

"It's not about protecting, AJ. It's about being healthier."

AJ smiles. "You're fine the way you are." I look down at my too-skinny legs. "I know what you're doing," he says.

"What's that, Mr. Smart-Ass?"

"You're looking at yourself, and telling yourself you're too skinny. Right?"

Damn him. "No," I snap.

"Aha! I don't believe you." He places the dumbbells down, and comes over to me. "Come here." He crooks his finger for me to walk toward him. His hands are big and rough, with cracked skin around the knuckles. They can be frightening. Yet I know he'd never hurt anyone. Not without cause.

"What?" I say as I stand close to him. He has a distinct smell. One that always puts my mind at ease when I'm stressing. It's a mix between sunshine, and sweat. Not that repulsive sweat that makes you hold your nose, more the sweat that's bordering on ash from a fire, but with a twist of warmth from the sun. I love his smell. He always makes me feel safe, like it doesn't matter what's going through my mind, he'll be there to protect me.

He places his hand over my heart, his eyes locked with mine. "This is beautiful," he says with a gentle tone. "And because this is beautiful, this is beautiful too." He moves to place his palms to my temples. "And if these are beautiful, you're beautiful." He leans in and gives me a tender kiss on the forehead.

"I have ugly hair," I say trying to fight him.

"It's luscious, dark, and long. I wish you'd wear it down more often." He smiles.

"My legs are too skinny, my body's too long, and my face looks like a fairy's."

Stepping back, he shakes his head before he bends to pick up the dumbbells again. "Nope," is all he says. I wait for more. But I don't get anything else.

"Well then, I've got a joke for you," I say, not really knowing where to go from here.

"Yeah? What is it?"

"What's the best thing about Switzerland?" I ask.

"What?"

"Don't know. But the flag is a big plus." I giggle at the stupid joke, and AJ raises his brows while he continues working is arms. "Oh, come on, that was funny."

"For who?"

I roll my eyes. "Alright then, what about this one? Did you hear about the claustrophobic astronaut?"

"You're killing me, Kate. Don't tell me, he needed a bit of space?"

"Oh, no fair! You already knew that one." I sulk, and AJ smiles cheekily. "Hang on," I say thinking about his response. "Why did you say *he* and not *she*?"

"Huh?" AJ looks over to me, confused. "What?"

"You said *he* needed a bit of space, why didn't you say *she* needed a bit of space? Are astronauts all male? Or are you sexist?"

"What?" He looks over to me again. This time, his mouth is screwed up and his eyes narrow in question. "When have you ever known me to be sexist? And, I don't know why I said he and not she. It's just…I don't know." He shrugs his shoulders.

"So you think only men can go to space?"

"Really, Kate? Really? Anyone can go to space. You just have to be fit and smart."

"That means you'll never get there," I tease.

AJ stops his arm reps, and turns his head. His mouth is open with shock. "Now I'm hurt," he says. But the corners of his lips quickly twitch with a smile.

Suddenly, he stops. He straightens his shoulders and puffs out his chest. He glances sideways, and arches a brow. The palms of my hands become clammy, as I watch AJ go from fun-loving to rigid with dread anticipation. "Hey, want to play a game of Tic-Tac-Toe?"

AJ doesn't acknowledge me. As he moves closer to the door, he clenches his hands into tight fists. I can see his knuckles turning white from where I am. "You have to leave," he says, his voice low but firm.

A lump sits in my throat. I can't leave, not now. I have to be here for AJ. "I was thinking we could put a movie on. What do you want to watch? Your choice. Anything. I'll even watch one of those stupid action movies you love so much."

AJ's eyes close, as he hangs his head down low. His lips draw into a pursed thin line. He shakes his head. I'm not sure what he's saying 'no' to. "You have to leave."

I breathe quickly through my mouth. My insides are going crazy. My stomach is knotting as my blood cools. I know what AJ is going to have to do. "AJ," I say as I stand.

"Go away!" he shouts at me.

"AJ," I say again in a softer voice.

AJ walks over to his cupboard, opens it, and slides out a box with an overstuffed bunny rabbit. When I first saw the bunny, it was pristine white. It's been through a lot, and now has a gray tinge to it. He holds the bunny by the paw, the bunny stares at me. "Kate, you have to go," he says again, this time in a low, pained voice.

"Let me stay and help you."

He shakes his head, and wipes at his eyes with his free hand. "Kate, get out. Get out before I throw you out. I don't want to, but I will if you force me." He stands, fixed to the one spot. His head drops as he holds the bunny.

"AJ. Please…" I can tell how much this is hurting him.

He throws the bunny on the bed, stomps over to me, grabs me by the shoulders and lifts me off the ground. I should be scared of him, but I'm not. I know his mind and body is screaming with pain. He doesn't want to do this, but there's no other way. "Get out," he yells in my face. His mouth is scrunched, but his eyes tell a story of fear and agony. He shoves me, and I fall back against the wall. He takes a step closer to me, but stops and backs up. Tears well in his eyes. "Just go," he says as he holds back a strangled cry. I don't see AJ cry often, but when he does, it breaks my heart.

I pick myself up, and move closer to him, wanting to console him, ease the pain he must be feeling. But AJ backs away from me, his hands up in a position of surrender. He turns, grabs the bunny up off the bed, straightens his shoulders and marches toward his door. He leaves the room, slamming the door shut so hard, it rattles.

My soul grieves, knowing what AJ has to do.

I fall to the floor, curl into a ball, and weep.

CHAPTER 2

Walking back to my room, my head is swimming. Back in my room, I open the cupboard, take the box out, and shove that stupid bunny in it. I thrust the box back in the cupboard and slam the door.

I plunge face down onto the bed, and let out the tears that I've been holding in. I don't cry in front of the others, I can't. If they see me falling apart, then they'll know I'm not strong. And if they think I'm not strong, they won't be strong either.

My throat is tight, and my stomach is gurgling. Not from hunger, but from sadness and rage.

I hate being the enforcer. Really hate it. There's nothing admirable or strong about being the enforcer.

It takes me a long time to calm down, maybe an hour, maybe even a day. I don't know, but I eventually stop feeling sick, and stop crying. This is what happens every time I have to take that damn bunny out of the box. I hate this part of my job.

Turning my head, I see my dumbbells laying on the floor. I push off the bed, grab my dumbbells and start pumping my arms. I push hard. I keep going until my arms burn. The fire coming from my muscles distracts from the agony I feel in my heart.

I keep flexing my arms; I have to. I have to hurt myself to atone for my role in this. I can't *not* hurt myself. I deserve to be in pain. I deserve the misery for what I do.

My arms are weak, like I am. Although they struggle to keep lifting. I have to do this. The sweat rolling down my back only reminds me to push harder. My hands clenched around the dumbbells are becoming slippery from the sweat gathering. I know I'm about to drop the dumbbell out of my right hand. I don't care. It can fall on my foot. Hopefully it'll break the bones. I deserve to be handicapped. I deserve the wrath of Satan to come down on me, to exile me to Hell. I deserve this, and more.

The dumbbell slips out of my right hand and falls. I don't even try to move my foot. But the dumbbell doesn't fall on my foot. It lands with a deafening thud and bounces once before it stops. "Why?!" I scream. "Why couldn't you hurt me? I deserve it!" I yell at the stupid dumbbell.

Bending to pick it up, I sink to the floor, just staring at the stupid weight. What good is being muscle-bound, if I can't use it to protect the ones I love?

I let out a deep breath, and try to push it to the back of my mind. I have to be strong, especially for the others. They need to see me strong, so they know that they'll be okay.

"AJ," I hear Kate's sweet voice calling me. Closing my eyes, I take a few seconds to regain myself, get back the control I've lost. "AJ," she says again, this time in a softer tone. I feel her beside me, feel her warmth desperately attempting to reach me.

"I'm okay," I say.

"You sure?" I open my eyes, and turn my head to look at her. It takes all my strength, but I muster a small smile for her. Kate lets out a sigh the moment she sees me smiling. She leans her head against mine, and closes her eyes. "I was scared," she says.

"I'm sorry for being angry at you." I wrap my arms around her and draw her in close. I need her. I need to feed on her positivity. I need it so bad. "I'm really sorry," I say again, leaning in to give her a kiss on her forehead.

"You didn't mean it." She's letting me off too easily. I deserve her anger. But I know Kate's not like that. She refuses to hold on to the bad. "What you have to do is…" She gulps and then breathes out heavily. "It's not easy."

"I hate myself so much."

"You look out for us," she says.

"Kate, I'm not sure I can keep doing this. I don't know how much longer I, or any of us can survive. It has to stop."

"It will."

"When?" I feel myself choking on my words. But I have to be strong, for all of us. I pull away from Kate, and hop up to my feet. Pacing in front of her, I try my hardest to push the monster, this demon version of myself, as far away as I can. The weight bar shines over on the other side of the room. I walk over to it, load it up with two fifty-pound weights on either side, and begin lifting.

"AJ, that's pretty heavy," Kate says as she gets to her feet and heads toward me.

"I like it heavy. It helps me deal with it all." A hundred pounds on each side isn't enough. I lower the bar, then add another fifty pounds on each side.

"AJ!" Kate snaps. The shock in her voice is undeniable. "AJ! You're going to hurt yourself." She walks over, and stands in front of me. Crossing her arms in front of her chest, she looks angry at me. Good. I deserve her anger. "Put that down," she insists.

"No. If you don't like it, go away." The moment I say the words, I already regret them. I shouldn't be so hard on her. She's just trying to help me. But I have to deal with my atrocities.

Kate's eyes fill with tears. I've made her cry, too. It's not what I want, but she has to let me deal with this.

Kate takes a step backward. Then another. Her knees find the edge of my bed, and she flops back on it. "Well, if you're going to be an ass, then you owe me," she says.

"Fine, I owe you. Can you go now?" I pump the bar, my arms

are stinging, and I have sweat running down my back. I feel drips of sweat clinging to the short hairline across my nape.

"So, you admit you owe me?"

"Yeah, yeah. Whatever." Can't she see I'm trying to get rid of her?

"And I can call on that anytime I want?"

"Yes. Jeez, Kate, you're a pain in the ass."

"Yes, I am." She smiles cheekily. "Then I call on what you owe me, now." She stands, stomps one foot, and holds her head high.

Man, she's cocky. I can't help but smile at her. "Not now," I say trying to not allow her infectious, bubbly personality to distract me from my own demons.

"Yes, now. You said you owe me, and you agreed that I can call on the favor any time I want. You said those words, AJ." She points to me.

"Ugh," I grumble, setting the bar down and taking the weights off the ends. "Fine, what do you want to do?"

"I want to play Monopoly," she says as she rummages around my book shelf, and brings out the board game.

"Okay, but I'm throwing you out in half an hour so I can keep beating myself up."

She places the game on the bed, looks at me and flicks her hand. "Whatever," she says.

When I finish putting the weights away, I flop on the bed beside the open game. The pieces she's taken out jump up, then land on the board in the wrong spots. "I'm the race car. I'm always the race car." I put back the dog, and get the car.

"I'm the car!"

"No can do, sister," I tease. "I'm the car. And your puppy dog eyes aren't going to work on me this time."

"You suck," she grumbles. "Then I'm the banker." She slides the money over to her.

"No way in hell are you the banker. You cheat."

"I do not," she replies indignantly. But her cheeky smile gives away the truth.

"Then how did you end up with an extra two-thousand dollars after one round of the game the last time we played?"

She flicks her hand at me again. "I did not."

"You're not the banker." I slide the money over to me, and far enough away that Kate can't reach out and take it.

"Fine. Be the banker. I'll still kick your butt."

We start playing the game, and Kate's intent on winning. She's concentrating so hard her tongue sticks out the side of her mouth as she rolls the dice. "Ha! I'm passing go. Hand it over, bank man." She holds her hand out for the two-hundred dollars.

I give her the money, and we keep playing. Although Kate's doing the best she can to distract me, my mind is still playing events over and over on repeat. But I have to forget them. "Hey, how did you get that?" I ask as I point to one of the best properties on the board.

"I bought it," Kate says.

"Oh man, you're a cheat. We've only had two rounds of the game, and you haven't given the banker any money."

"What?" She crosses her legs in front of her. "I also bought these." She points to another three properties.

"Cheat!" I call her out.

"No. You must've gone to the bathroom."

"I haven't moved." Truthfully, I know she cheats. She always does at games. But I don't mind. I never have.

"Yeah, you went to the bathroom."

"You can insist all you want. We both know, you cheat."

She smiles at me. A cute, perfect dimple appears on her cheek when she smiles. I love Kate for so many reasons. I love her infectious laugh, and I love her bubbly personality, but most of all, I just love her for the person she is.

"Okay," she says with an eye roll. "I will neither confirm nor deny I cheated."

"Which means you cheat." I point at her.

"I am merely an expert at sleight of hand."

"So now you're a magician." I can't help but chuckle. She always makes me happy whenever she's around.

"Oh man," Kate says and looks toward my door. "Can you smell that?" I look behind me at the door, and after a moment, shake my head. "You never can smell it. But it's like a beacon to me. Like a lighthouse in the middle of the night. It's intoxicating."

"I can't smell it." I inhale deeply in case I get the smell she does.

"Hmmm, popcorn. Yum. I've gotta go." She hops up off the bed, and four other property cards fall out of her pockets.

"Hey!" I grumble as I pick up the cards and wave them at Kate.

"Yeah, sorry about that." She winks at me, as if to say, *I'm not really sorry.* "Popcorn." She wipes at her mouth and leaves my room in a hurry.

I pack up the game and put it away. Kate always makes me feel better. Even when she disappears at the smell of popcorn. "Can't believe you chose popcorn over me," I mumble.

I grab my dumbbells, and start working on my arms again. This time, not to punish myself, but to improve myself. To be stronger, because they deserve for me to be stronger for them.

CHAPTER 3

The moment I saw him huddled on the floor I knew I had to do something. I can't stand seeing AJ like that.

AJ is tough and strong. But seeing him a crumpled mess just screws with my head. It hurts me to see him so broken.

When he shoved me against the wall, I knew how bad this one was going to be. Usually he can hold it together enough to get the job done. I shouldn't have tried to interfere. It's not my place to hinder his work. He has a responsibility, and he has a commitment to it, regardless of how we feel.

Standing outside Neve's bedroom door, I take a few deep breaths before I go in to see her. I hate having to come in here, but I know Neve needs me. Especially in these times.

I creak the door open, and Neve is sitting in the corner on the floor, hugging her knees, crying.

"Hey, Neve," I say, taking in her appearance.

Neve is the youngest of us. She's eleven, but she's lived a hard eleven years. We all have. Neve looks up to see who's in her room, the moment her gaze falls on me, she lowers her head again and draws her knees in tighter.

"Do you want to play a game?" I ask as I slowly approach her.

"No thank you," she says in a small voice.

"Do you want to color?" I sit cross-legged beside her.

Neve doesn't answer. Her tears seem to have stopped. "Okay," she replies after a long time. I stand and hold my hand out to her. She shakes her head. She pushes up off the floor and follows me to the desk in her room. I open a drawer, and take out a coloring book and some pencils. "I like this one," she says and points to another book.

I smile as I look at it. "It's my favorite one," I say. The coloring book has stars, planets, and the universe in it. I empty the pencils on the table, and Neve flinches when they hit the hard wood. "It's okay," I whisper.

She reaches for the yellow, and begins to shade in a scene that has the sun shining, and tall flowers among thick grass fields. "I want to lay with the flowers," she says in a small voice.

Her limp hair is hanging over her face. Smudges of dirt darken her cheeks. Her young eyes are so hollow. "Can I lay with you?" I ask. "We can look up at the clouds, and watch as the birds fly over us."

"No. I don't want you there," she answers candidly. "I want it to be just me. I want to be somewhere where I'll never hear *that* song again."

My stomach churns as I listen to Neve. I can completely understand that she wouldn't want anyone there. "What would you do if you were in the flowers?" I pick the red pencil up, and color in a flower.

Neve's head is down, she's coloring on the edge of the page. She shrugs her shoulders. The room is quiet, and tense. The curtains are drawn, so the only light is what's coming from the overhead bulb. "I'd stay there until I became a flower."

"But flowers die," I say as we continue to color.

"I want to die," she says in her soft voice.

I stop coloring, and lift my head to look at her. She doesn't understand the heaviness of what she's said. Or maybe she does, and she actually wants to die. "Do you know what my favorite food is?" I ask, trying my hardest to get her thoughts away from the burden she must feel like she's bearing.

"No."

My heart breaks for Neve. She's so young, and gentle. And her voice is anything but angry or sad. It tears my heart into two, watching her color while she talks about dying. "I love popcorn," I say.

"I'm not allowed popcorn. One time I was allowed ice cream." Her face remains stoic, unchanged despite the emptiness she must be feeling.

We both reach for the pencils, and my fingers accidently touch the back of her hand. She swiftly pulls it away and looks up, her face filled with fright. She stares at me for a split second before she begins screaming. The ear-piercing noise she makes is filled with horror.

"I'm sorry," I say, jumping back. "I'm sorry, Neve, I'm sorry." I hold my hands up, showing her how I'm not a threat. "I'm so sorry."

Neve's eyes are still wide with terror. She's breathing rapidly, as her hands tremble in clenched fists.

"Neve, look. Can you help me color?" I move forward quickly, pick up another pencil and color the grass green.

Neve stops screaming, but remains in the same spot. I can hear her breathing heavy as she settles herself. Her little shoulders are slumped as she stands, not really sure what she should do.

"I'm so sorry," I say again, and I mean it every time I say it. Tears well in my eyes, but I hold them in. I can't have Neve see me crying for her. I hate how I made her scream. I hate that I caused her pain.

"It's okay," she says in a tiny voice.

"I know you don't like being touched. I was careless."

"You didn't do it on purpose. It was an accident." Neve has a beautiful heart. She's so forgiving of everything around her.

"I won't do it again. I'll be more careful."

I hear her crawling along the floor, coming back to the table. Out of my peripheral vision, I see her pick up another pencil and continue coloring. The safest thing for me to do is slide most of the pencils to her side, so I don't mistakenly touch her again. I see her cheeks puff up, like she's trying to smile. "Thank you," she says.

"You're welcome."

"Maybe next time you can bring me some popcorn and I can try it."

"I can ask AJ to bring some."

She shakes her head. "I don't like seeing AJ. I know he has to be here, but I also know what happens when I see him. He never visits me unless it's to tell me it's time."

My heart is squashed. My entire body feels crushed. I pick the pink pencil up, and color one of the flowers. "Which is your favorite color? I like yellow," I say.

"Purple is mine."

"Why purple?"

"When I look at purple, I see so many possibilities. Like, if it's dark, I see strength. When it's a light purple, I see happiness. But I don't like red. When I see red I see pain." She shakes her head, like she's dislodging a particularly unpleasant image. "I hate red." She picks the pencil up, stares at it for a moment, before she snaps it in half and throws both pieces on the table. "There's too much red around me."

While she continues coloring, I quietly take the two red halves, and slide them into my pocket. If red is a trigger of hate, then I'll remove it so she doesn't have to look at it any more. I look around her room, and can't see any red anywhere. Actually, her room is quite sterile, bleak even. The bed is small, with a beige blanket and beige pillowcases. Her walls are all a pale blue color. The curtains are a heavy, dark blue. Other than a cupboard, and her desk, there's nothing to give this room personality.

"Do you want to watch a movie?" I offer.

"No." She shakes her head. "I like to color."

"You don't want to do anything else?"

"Just color."

"Want to listen to music?" I'm trying to get her to interact with me more, but Neve has all her walls up.

"I don't like music."

Who doesn't like music? Obviously, Neve. "Do you mind if I stay for a bit longer so I can color with you?" I ask. Neve needs someone around, and I want to be that someone who's here for her.

"I want to be by myself."

"How about a friend from school then? I can call them."

"I don't have friends, Kate."

I want to lean over and hug her, I want to tell her that I'm her friend. But I know how much she hates being touched. "I'm your friend," I say.

"You're here after I hear the song and come back from *him.*" I slump my shoulders, grief-stricken and utterly sad. She looks up at me, and must see the hurt in me. "Kate," she says. I lift my chin and plaster a fake smile on my face. "It's okay that you come after the song. I don't want you here any more than you want to be here."

My entire soul splinters at the thought of poor little eleven-year-old Neve, who's so kind and forgiving.

"I tell you what, Neve. I'm going to come back tomorrow. Because I want us to be friends. I want you to know that I do want to be here. Not just after that song, but whenever you need me." It's the least I can do, considering everything she does for M.

Her lips pull up into a half-smile. "I'd like that," she says.

Standing, I walk toward the door. "I'll see you tomorrow, okay?" I say.

"Can you bring some popcorn?" she asks with hope in her voice.

"If I can, I promise I will."

She continues coloring as I walk away.

I have to try to be better, especially for Neve.

CHAPTER 4

"Neve, are you in there?" I say as I knock on her door.

"Yeah," she calls from inside.

"Can I come in?" I want to give her as much control as possible. It might make her feel safe around me.

"Yeah," she says again.

I open the door, and find her laying on her bed, reading a book. "Whatcha reading?" I ask as I make my way slowly into her room, and sit on the end of the bed.

"A book."

I smile. "I can see that. What's it about?"

She moves the book so I can see the cover, and I'm surprised to see it's a picture book on frogs. "Do you like frogs?" I ask.

"Not really. But they're part of nature, and I want to be part of nature too."

Her hair is fanned out on the pillow, and she's got one leg crossed over the other as she keeps turning the pages. "Want to draw?" I offer.

"Nope. I want to look at my book. Did you know frogs absorb water through their skin, so they don't need to drink?"

"I didn't know that."

"Did you know a frog can live up to about twelve years? Unless people are cruel, and kill them. People can be so cruel and heartless." Her tone is even, like she's talking from experience. "Kate?"

"Yeah?"

Neve doesn't lower the book she's looking at. She talks as she keeps looking at the pages. "Do you think I'm like a frog, and I'll die by the time I'm twelve?"

I gasp at her casual words. "Don't say that, Neve. Life is beautiful."

She lets out a small, mirthless chuckle. "For who? You? AJ? Me? Because we know life is anything but beautiful. It might be for some, but not for us...me," she quickly corrects. "Not from what I've seen, and...," she immediately stops herself before she says anything else.

"I know that's how it feels right now, Neve. But I thoroughly believe that change is coming, for all of us."

She chuckles, then clicks her tongue to the roof of her mouth. "That change can only happen when my life ends."

A huge lump forms in the pit of my stomach. "Neve, let's color." I stand and walk over to her desk.

She lowers the book and looks at the door. "AJ is coming," she says.

I look to the door too, but can't see him. "I don't think so."

"I can feel him. He's close." She sits up in bed, and places the book next to her. Standing, she heads to the door, and stands just inside, staring out.

"He's not coming."

Neve turns to look at me. Her eyes brimming with tears. "I can't keep doing this," she says. "This isn't life. This is a slow, painful death. It's slowly killing every part of me."

"He's not coming," I say again, trying to reassure her. I'd hug her, but I know what she's like if she's touched.

Suddenly, AJ appears at the door. As if he's materialized out of thin air. He's standing in front of Neve.

"Oh," Neve says and looks down at her bare feet. "You brought the bunny."

"It's time, Neve," he says in a harsh tone.

"I can't hear *the* song. It might not happen." She backs away from AJ, and backs herself into the corner of the room. She curls up, trying to make herself as small as possible.

"Neve," AJ says with a sigh. "You know what has to happen."

"No, please don't make me go, AJ. I'll be good. I won't cause you any problems. Please, please don't make me go. I promise, I'll be good."

I watch as Neve struggles with what she has to do. My breath is short and labored, coming in pants as my heart aches for what she has to go through.

AJ looks down at the ground. His own chest heaving rapidly. "Neve," he says in a smaller voice.

"Please," she begs. "Please don't do this."

He steps forward, and she pushes herself against the wall. "Neve," he says again. AJ looks at me, and shakes his head. "You have to go," he says.

"I want to be here for Neve."

"That song…" Neve whispers. I can't hear a song. "It's starting." She unwinds herself, and steps forward.

AJ holds the bunny rabbit out to her. She takes another hesitant step forward and reaches for the bunny. She holds the bunny to her face, and sniffs it deeply. "You'll be okay, Neve."

"I used to love this bunny," she says in a small voice. She heads to the door, turns, and looks at me. "But I hate it now. Will you be here when I return?"

"If you want me to, I'll stay right here."

She shakes her head, and lowers her saddened gaze. "I don't want you to come back, Kate. You try to help me forget, but what happens here is too much for anyone to forget." She turns her little body around, and slowly walks out of her room.

The air is thick with sadness.

Neve is like a twenty-five-year-old woman trapped in an eleven-year-old's body. She's wise, and smart. But so damn sad.

"Kate," AJ says bringing me back from the brink of hopelessness. I look over to him. "We have to go."

I nod my head, and step toward him. "What if I stay, and help her when she gets back?"

"She doesn't want you here."

"She's a kid, AJ. She doesn't know what she wants."

"She's the most mature one out of all of us. She's the one who's on the frontline. If she says she doesn't want you here, then get out." He runs his hand through his hair.

"Don't be so rude," I snap at him.

"Then don't be so disrespectful to the girl who's helping us all get through this," he yells back. He takes a deep breath, and runs his hand through his hair again. "I'm sorry. I shouldn't be so bitchy toward you. But Neve said she doesn't want you here. We have to respect that. For her."

I head toward the door, and stop just short of the exit. "She's the strongest person I know. I just wish I could do something for her."

"Come back tomorrow, Kate. I'm sure she'll be better by then. You know, this." He makes a twirling action with his finger, indicating this scenario we're all in. "This is hard. It's hard for all of us, but especially Neve. It's my job to protect all of us, including M. But especially Neve."

I hate how he's right.

I hate how this is our life.

I vow to myself to try and make Neve's life better in whatever way I can.

CHAPTER 5

I'm worried for Neve. Outside has become dark, and Neve has yet to return.

I stand in her room, pacing. I'm also contemplating going out and searching for her. She's never been gone this long before. What's happening? Why is this taking so long?

Standing in the corner, all kind of worries are jumbling in my mind.

Does she know how to get back?

Is she okay?

Is she dead?

The hair on the back of my neck stands to attention. My skin crawls as I become hyper-aware of everything happening around me. Every sound, every smell, every feeling. I know something's not right with Neve.

I shouldn't have let her go. I knew something was off. I knew the moment she was called. There was a darkness when he said her name. A darkness so black, and so consuming, that I just had a gut feeling something terrible was nearing.

My stomach tensed the moment he whispered her name. I should've stopped him, should've done something to stop this happening. But how can I stop him? Who'd believe me?

I'm powerless to do anything.

I'm such a bad person. I send Neve to go into the slaughterhouse, and all I can do is feel sorry for myself. I should protect them. I should do everything in my power to safe guard them. Why can't I be better? Stronger? Not so evil?

"AJ," Neve whispers.

I open my eyes, and leap forward to hug her. But she holds her hand up, stopping me from touching her. "Are you okay?" I know the answer, but I still have to ask.

She looks up at me and slowly shakes her head. "I will be, one day." Neve drops the bunny by the door. She carefully walks over to her bed and gingerly lays down, her back to me.

"Can I get you anything?" I offer.

"Yeah, peace." My heart bleeds. "Can you leave now? And take the bunny. I don't want to see that thing until the next time."

"I'll come back and bring you some coloring books. I know how much you like them."

"I need pencils. Take the red one out though. I don't like red. I found another one, and I want it gone."

I'm not sure what she's talking about. "Okay. Do you want or need anything else, Neve?"

I step closer, but catch myself before I reach out to rub gentle circles on her back.

"I want to be left alone."

"Okay." I walk to where she's dropped the bunny, bend, and pick it up. I look at it in disgust. "Bye."

"AJ?" Neve calls before I leave.

"Yeah."

"Do you think M is okay?"

I shrug. "You were gone for a while. A lot longer than normal. Actually, you were gone for too long."

"I'm worried for her."

And she still has the compassion to be worried for M. But, if I'm being honest, I'm really worried for M too. It's never been this long before. It's usually done quite quickly, but Neve was gone for a lot longer than that. "She'll be okay," I say trying to give Neve some comfort.

I stay in the room for another moment, and when Neve doesn't reply, I know she doesn't want to talk any more. I look at the stupid bunny, and leave her room.

CHAPTER 6

EVE

I hate being the person I am.

This is why I refuse to have a mirror in my room. I'm too scared of what I'll see in its reflection. My life has never been easy. From the moment I can remember, all I've ever been is nothing. Nothing at all. Not a person, not a child, not a God damned thing.

As I lay on my bed, I can hear AJ's footsteps becoming further and further away.

This is how I like it. I hate having AJ here, and hate it even more when Kate comes. What they don't understand is how much I hate me. To my very core, I can't stand me. I hate everything about me. Nothing about me is worth saving, nor am I worth anything.

But I don't stay because of what I think of myself. I stay for M. M needs me. And if I left, if I disappeared into nothing, then M would suffer. And I can't have that on my conscience. I wouldn't be able to live with myself.

I have to protect M.

I'm left alone, and this is the way I like it.

When Kate comes to visit, she looks at me with such sadness in her eyes. I hate the way it makes me feel, which is why I barely look at her. She tries to cheer me up by doing things with me, but I just want to be left in peace, without her looking at me like I'm damaged or broken.

My head is heavy, and all I can think about is *that* song, and what happens when I hear it. I don't like what happens. No, "like" isn't a strong enough word. I hate what that song symbolizes. Because while *that* song plays, it means I'm no longer myself. I have to become someone else. I have to be quiet, and take the punishment for M. I can't say anything.

I never do, because I don't want to wake M. If I wake her, she'll be hurt instead of me. And if she screams, then we don't know what can happen. I fought once, which woke M and she screamed. It turned out to be so much worse for all of us.

So now, when AJ comes to my room holding the bunny, I know what I have to do.

I know how I have to prepare myself.

AJ doesn't want this anymore than I do. He hates having to be the one to do that, but he's the only one strong enough to do it. The first time he did it, he cried more than I did. It broke my heart, knowing he was here, waiting for me, and in so much pain.

I hate to think how he's coping.

My role is straightforward, his isn't. It's much harder than mine.

"You'll be okay, Neve," I say to myself as I swing my legs over the bed, and sit up. I look out at the inky sky. It's a moonless night. A starless night too.

There are no clouds, though the sky isn't clear either. A thin veil of haze hangs in the air. It makes everything foggy, barely visible.

I heard Kate and AJ talking once, a long time ago. And Kate told AJ I'm so mature for my age.

I feel like I've lived a thousand lifetimes. Each more painful than the last.

"One day, you'll no longer be needed," I say out loud.

It's funny, because if Kate or AJ were here, they'd feel sorry for me.

But to me, the mere thought of not being needed, makes me the happiest I've ever been.

One day, I won't be needed.

Smiling, I choose to hold onto that hope.

CHAPTER 7

"What are you wearing?" AJ asks as I stand in his room.

"Like it?" I twirl, letting the multicolored tutu fluff out. "Oh, and I have this too." I reach into my bag, and take out a yellow rubber clown nose. Sliding it onto the end of my nose, I give AJ a huge, cheeky smile.

"Why are you dressed like that?" He eyes my attire, before turning back to his weights.

"I'm going to see Neve. And I'm hoping she lets me do some face painting on her."

"When did you learn to do face painting? And why isn't the clown nose red?"

"Because Neve hates the color red. And, I have a lot of hidden talents. Face painting is one of them. So is bubble making." I hold up the big wand of soapy water that makes large bubbles. "And, if I put my mind to it, I can also make balloon animals."

"You can make balloon animals?" He eyes me sideways while continuing his reps.

"Making balloon animals may be a bit of a stretch. I can blow up a balloon. And I call it a worm."

AJ laughs. "So what you're saying is you actually have no idea how to make balloon animals."

I clutch my hand over my heart. "I take offense at that, AJ. I know how to make a balloon animal—a worm. Do you know how much talent it takes to make a worm?"

AJ rolls his eyes. "Well, what's the purpose of you looking like a fairy clown? Are you trying to make me smile? Because if you are, you've succeeded."

"I told you, I'm going to see Neve. I want to see her smile."

"Kate." AJ stops, and places his weights on the ground. He walks over to me, and gently places his big hands on my shoulders. His body shines with a thin layer of sweat forming over his defined muscles. "It's not a good idea for you to see her."

"Why? She of all people really need some happiness in her life."

"Yeah, she does. But this isn't the way to make her happy." He steps back, shaking his head. "She needs more than a tutu and a yellow nose." He walks over to his bed, and sits on the edge. "We can't help her, Kate."

"We might not be able to help her, but at least we can try to lessen the pain."

"There's nothing we can do to make her pain less. Nothing."

"We can support her," I explain. "We can make it more comfortable for her." AJ's brows fly up in surprise. "I know this is hard, but for now, we have to work with what we've got. We can't do anything about this." My arms go out to indicate our surroundings.

AJ stands, walks back to his weights, and starts lifting again. "My job is to protect you and Neve. That's what I can do about this."

"It's frustrating, AJ. I want to help, and this is the only way I know how."

AJ shrugs and breathes out a deep breath. "Then try and go to her, but I doubt she's going to want you there. I hope you can convince her to change her mind. But Neve isn't like that. She likes to hide. Hide away from the world, hide away from us. Hide away from everyone."

I want to cry, because he's right. He's so right that my entire body aches. "I'm going to try. She's worth that at the very least."

"It's up to you."

"You're right; it is. See ya." I pick my bag up, and head out to see Neve.

"Heya, can I come in?" I knock on Neve's door.

She's sitting at her table, coloring in her book. She doesn't turn to acknowledge me or even look at me. "Suppose," she says.

I walk in, and my tutu makes a rustling sound as it swishes against my legs. Even the sound isn't intriguing enough to make Neve turn to look at me.

"What do you think of me practicing my face painting on you, Neve?" I ask as I carefully approach her, making sure I don't frighten her.

"No, thank you," she replies in her cold, lifeless voice.

"How about I make a balloon animal for you? I'm skilled in the art of worm making. So skilled, I could win awards for it."

"No, thank you," she says again, not raising her head from coloring.

"Please? I really want to do this for you."

Neve turns her head, and sees my silly yellow nose, and puffy, multi-colored tutu. She runs her gaze the length of my body, and I see the tiniest smile tugging at her lips. "You look funny," she says. "I like the nose. Maybe you should keep it." This is the closest thing to fun I've ever heard from Neve.

I squeeze the nose, then pose like a clown. "I made it myself," I say. She turns her little head, and proceeds to color. "What do you think? Can I paint your face? I can paint a butterfly."

"Butterflies come from ugly caterpillars. I don't care much for them."

"What about a frog? I know you like frogs," I'm trying my hardest to convince her.

"No, thank you. You can go." And just like that, she flicks her hand at me, dismissing me like I don't even matter.

"I want to stay with you, Neve. I want to do something with you."

Slowly, she turns her head, staring at me. Her eyes are soulless. Her face, expressionless. "I'm here for one reason, and for one reason only. I don't want to be friends, Kate. I don't want to be anything. I'm here for M and only M. This is how I have to be, in order to get through this. I can't have a connection with anyone, or this won't work. Not for me, not for you or AJ but mostly, not for M."

I feel sick. Sick to my absolute core. "But you don't have to be alone."

"I know, but I want to be."

"But," I begin to protest.

Neve stands with force, knocking her chair over. It makes me step back, almost afraid of this side of her. She's not angry, it's an emotion I haven't seen before. It's more than anger, it's more than sorrow, it's like she's rejecting me and isolating herself. "There's no 'buts,' Kate. I have to find a way that I can survive this. And for me, it's about abandoning all hope, and living with what I have, *now.*"

She completely stuns me. Her insight, and her wisdom is well above any eleven-year-old. She's severing all ties, all connections, so *she* can outlive the circumstances thrust upon us. "I understand," I whisper, still nearly speechless at her maturity.

Neve returns to her table, rights her chair, and sits. "Please, don't come back," she says.

What paralyzes me most, is her cold, spiritless voice. She seems burdened by merely breathing.

I walk away, and respect the fact that even though I think Neve needs me, she doesn't want me. My entire soul grieves for a little girl I once knew.

Part Two

Present

CHAPTER 1

"Can you believe tomorrow is our eighteenth birthday?" I ask Tina.

She swings her arm around my shoulder, and squeezes. "Who would've thought when you came to live with us, that our birthdays would be on the same day. Still blows my mind."

I give her a big smile. I'm so glad we both ended up in the same family.

Mom and Dad adopted Tina when she was six, and me when I was seven. Tina and I might not be sisters by blood, but we're closer than sisters could ever be.

"Dad wants us to get tomatoes and a head of lettuce," Tina says, reading her phone as we walk toward the mall.

"Did he say what he's making?" I ask.

"Nachos."

My stomach grumbles, and my mouth instantly salivates. "You know how Dad always fishes for compliments with his cooking?" I ask.

Tina chuckles and shakes her head in jest. "Oh, man! He's always saying, 'I'm so good at this cooking thing,' every night through dinner."

"You know, I think we should say tonight, 'I've had better.'"

"Oh no, that's so mean. But yeah, let's do that. You say it first, and I'll agree." Tina is so cheeky. "So, we need tomatoes and a head of lettuce. I've got to try to find a dress for tomorrow night. What are you wearing?" Tina asks.

I shrug my shoulders. Fashion and me don't really mix. "Whatever's in my closet. I don't know."

"Mom and Dad are taking us out to celebrate our birthday, and knowing them, it'll be somewhere nice. Can't you dress up, just a little?"

"Tina, you know I'm not into fancy clothes and shit. I'll just wear jeans, and a shirt."

"No, you damn well won't. If Mom and Dad are going to take us out somewhere nice, you're dressing up." She grabs onto my arm and starts dragging me toward the closest fashion store.

Slumping my shoulders, I follow. I know when it comes to clothes, Tina's going to win every time. I've learned over the years to just go with it. Put up a bit of resistance, and if she backs down, yay. If not, suck it up and go with it. "I don't want to do this," I whine.

"Too bad," she snaps back. "Oh, I like this." She picks up a floral dress, and holds it up against my body. "It's cute. Flirty even. Off-the-shoulder, fitted to the waist, then slightly flared to the knees." She thrusts the coat hanger in my hands, and I stand like a mannequin holding the stupid dress. "Hmmm. Nah, I don't think it's going to work. You have nice size boobs, we have to show them off."

"Now we're talking about my boobs? Really?" I grumble.

"Yep. And you have really nice legs. Your ass is flat though. Like a guy's butt. So we don't want to show that off." I shake my head.

"Hi, can I help you?" the young shop assistant asks.

"No, we've got it, thanks," Tina replies.

"Help me. Save me," I joke. The assistant smiles at us both, then quickly leaves to help another customer. "Can we just buy this and go?" I really hate shopping.

"Nope. I don't like it." She takes the dress, puts it on the rack, and continues browsing the store. "Oh, I really like this." She holds up a black dress. One that doesn't look like it would fit my thigh, let alone the rest of my body. "Yep. You're trying this on."

"Are you kidding? There's not enough stretch in the material to get it over my head."

"Why do you do that? You're smoking hot. And you dress like you're a fifty-year-old grandmother. You're going to try it, and I know you're going to love it. Excuse me," she calls the assistant over. "Change rooms?"

"At the back of the store, around the corner." The girl points.

"Thank you," Tina happily chirps. She's way too happy for me to try on clothes. I detest clothes shopping. Hate it with a passion, so the quicker we can get this over and done with, the better. "Go, and I have to see it. Because I know you, you'll go and stand in the change room, not try it on, and say you don't like it."

I try to hold in the smile, but I can't. "Fine." I snatch the dress from her, and head to the change rooms. Closing the loose curtains, I quickly slip out of my jeans and t-shirt, and hold the dress up in front of me. "Ugh," I grumble. "My pillowcases have more material than you," I mumble at the dress. I slide it over my head, and glide it down over my hips, to my thighs. "Hell no!" I look at myself in the mirror, in shock at what it reflects back at me.

"Let me look!" Tina draws back the curtain. Her eyes widen and her mouth falls open. "Hell yes!" she says. "You look hot! Man, your boobs look so good. I wish mine looked like yours." She reaches out and cups her hands around my breasts. She lifts them slightly, then steps back. "Yeah, you don't even need a push-up bra. Turn around." Why do I feel like her own personal doll? "Shit, man. Even your butt looks rounder than what it is."

I turn to look at myself in the mirror, and I can't help but like how my butt looks. "It's too short though," I whine as I try to pull the dress down.

"You can't see your vagina, so why are you complaining?"

"If I bend over, everyone will know I've had toast for breakfast."

"You over-exaggerate everything. Here, step forward." I do. "Turn around, and bend in front of me."

"I'm not bending in front of you, Tina." I roll my eyes and let out a sigh.

"If you can't do this stuff in front of me, then who can you do it in front of? Just trust me. Bend," she demands. I groan, but do as she asks. "Stay there." Her fingers go near my bottom. About three inches down. "This is where the dress ends. So no. If you bend, we won't know you had toast for breakfast. This is a hot dress. It makes your legs look longer, and your boobs don't need assistance. Your butt looks really good. We're buying it."

"Tina," I argue as I straighten and turn.

"We're buying it," she says over her shoulder as she leaves.

Just go with it, Molly. If rolling eyes was a national sport, I would've already won a gold medal. I close the curtains, and quickly change back into my comfortable jeans and t-shirt. I place the dress on the coat hanger, and pray I can sneak it back to the rack before Tina sees. No such luck, she's waiting outside at the entrance of the changing rooms, leaning against the wall. She holds her hand out to me. "Ugh," I grumble.

"Whatever. And I have the nicest pair of red high heels you're going to borrow."

"Can't I wear my Converse?"

She turns and shoots me a dirty look. "I'm going to pretend you didn't just say that."

"I can't walk in heels. I'll look like a baby elephant on rollerblades."

Tina smiles. "Then you're going to have to practice when we get home."

Can this get any worse? "Are we done playing dress-up?" I drag myself to the counter, where Tina takes her charge card out and hands it to the girl so she can pay for this stupid dress.

"Now I have to find something for me. But, I saw this cute dress on-line. So we're going to one of the stores down the other end." Tina keeps walking as she talks. I kind of tune out, not because I don't care, but because when Tina starts talking about clothes, she can go on for hours. We walk to the other end of the mall, and Tina disappears inside a boutique dress store.

Dragging my feet, I follow her into the store. "That's cute," I say as I hold up the first thing I see.

Tina turns to see what I'm holding, and her nose scrunches as she grimaces. "That's horrific. How are we related?"

"No need to say anything, your face gives away how you're feeling. Maybe I should grab something, make you try it on, then feel your breasts. See how you like it."

"One." She holds up her finger. "I don't care. And two." She holds up another finger. "I don't care." She smiles cheekily, swings on her heels and keeps perusing the racks of clothing. "I have no idea why you don't like fashion. We are sisters and all."

"Wow, are you two sisters?" the sales assistant asks.

No one ever picks us as sisters. We've been asked if we're a gay couple, or cousins, but not sisters. Not that we look like each other. Tina has short blonde hair, with pale skin and the biggest blue eyes. My hair is long and brown, and my complexion is more olive. My eyes are a dark brown so dark, you could be forgiven for thinking they're black.

"We are," I say to the assistant.

"Adopted," Tina echoes in.

"Oh," the girl replies as her brows fly up. I bet she's wondering which one of the two of us is adopted. Everyone always asks. But she doesn't. "Can I help you?"

"There's a dress I saw online, and I want to try it on. It's red, it has a really low-cut front, comes to here," she points to between her breasts, "thick straps, and a low-cut back."

"Oh, yeah. This way." The assistant heads toward the side of shop.

"I'm going to go buy a coffee, want one?" I ask Tina.

"Nope. Don't go too far, you need to give me your opinion on how hot I look in the dress."

I shake my head, but smile. Tina is full-on. It's the only way to describe her. She's like a battery that recharges when she's asleep, and she wakes with so much energy. She's also always intense about everything. She loves with her whole heart, and hates with it too if you wrong her.

I head over to a small coffee shop, and order my latte. As I stand and wait for it, I get knocked forward by someone. "Hey," I say as I turn to see who the culprit is.

"I'm so sorry," says this tall, young guy in a fitted shirt, and dress slacks.

I want to snap at him, but he looks genuinely apologetic for knocking into me. "It's okay." I turn forward again, waiting for them to call my name for my latte.

There's a tap on my shoulder, and I turn to see the same guy. "I really am sorry," he says.

"It's okay. Don't sweat it."

"Let me buy you a coffee. Just to say I'm sorry. I feel so bad."

"Molly," the barista calls and slides my coffee along the counter top.

"I've already got one. But thank you." I pick my coffee up, and start heading back to where Tina is.

"Dylan," the barista calls as I walk away, and the guy steps forward to get his coffee. He grabs it and catches up to me quickly. "Hey, Molly?"

"You were eavesdropping. Or stalking. Which one?' I ask.

"Oh my God. I'm not a stalker. I promise. Oh crap, only a stalker would say they're not a stalker." His face reddens. "I should go. I'm so sorry." He steps back, and just by the pitch of his voice, I can tell he's worried about what I think of him.

I turn to see him walking away from me, while he's shaking his head. He must be upset with himself. "Hey, Dylan," I call before he gets too far away. He turns, and waits for me to say something. I flick my head at him, indicating he can come back.

He jogs a few steps, which looks awkward considering he's wearing office clothes. "Hang on. Are you stalking me?" he asks.

"Well, obviously. I know your name's Dylan. And you work in the office over there." I tip my head to the side, not really having an idea where he works.

He turns to face the direction I gestured. "You think I work in the female bathrooms?"

I look over, and sure enough, there are the female rest rooms. "I was reaching. I have no idea where you work."

He smiles, and I'm drawn by his enigmatic charm. There's something about him. He's old-school, but in a young guy's body. "Well, I can tell you, I don't work in the female rest rooms."

"Does that mean you work in the male bathrooms? Are you a janitor? Hey, if you are, no judgment from me."

"What? No." He lets out a soft chuckle, and even the deep pitch of his voice invites me in. "I'm a security analyst over at Collins and Partners," he clarifies.

"Collins and Partners? As in the lawyers?"

"Yeah, that's them. But I'm not a lawyer, so please don't hate me."

I let out a laugh. Dylan's goofy, but fun. "Why would I…"

"You were supposed to help me, oh, hello," Tina says as she approaches me. She stops in mid-sentence when she sees me talking to Dylan. Men love Tina. She's outgoing, and funny, and drop-dead gorgeous with her long legs, perfect figure, and big blue eyes. "Who are you?" she asks as she eyes him up and down.

"Hi, I'm Dylan." He holds his hand out to shake hers.

She takes his hand in hers, and turns her head to look at me. Her arched eyebrow tells me she's silently pushing me to ask him out. I look at her, and give her a small head shake, pursing my lips together. "Fine. I'll do it then."

"Stop it!" I say, trying to stop Tina before her speedy mouth gets me into trouble.

"Um, I'm sorry. Are you two a couple or something?" Dylan steps back, ready to flee.

"No, we're not. We're sisters," I reply.

"Oh, right. Okay." He looks confused.

"Are you going to ask her out?" Tina blurts.

"Now it's my turn to apologize." I grab Tina's hand, and pull her away from Dylan. "Can you, for once, not do what you usually do?"

"What?"

"You steamroll over everyone. It's embarrassing. Please," I beg. I let out a sigh, and avert my gaze. "Don't worry about it," I say, losing all hope of a possible date with Dylan. He probably isn't even attracted to me now that he's seen Tina.

"Hey, I've gotta go to the shoe store upstairs. I'll be back in about ten minutes, okay?" Tina asks. This is her apology. Her way of saying, she's sorry for being so forceful. She leans in to give me a hug. "He's cute, go for it," she whispers. And just like that, my frustration is quickly replaced with a smile.

"Think so?"

She pulls away, and winks at me. "See ya around," she says to Dylan before flittering away like beautiful butterfly.

He steps closer, and turns to look at Tina. "Wow," he says as he focuses on me. "Is she always like that?"

"You mean a live wire?" He nods his head. "Yep, that's my sister."

"Wow," he says again.

My stomach churns with the thought of him being attracted to her, and not me. It makes perfect sense. She's really special, whereas, I'm not. I'm just me. Plain, boring, quiet Molly. She's vivacious and intoxicating. I'm mild and reserved. She makes friends everywhere she goes. I prefer to stick my headphones on and listen to music. I'm a homebody. Other people don't really interest me.

"I can give you her number," I say.

"Why do you think I want her number?" He gestures to a bench seat, and waits for me to walk ahead.

"Because you've said 'wow' twice in the moments since you've met her."

"I'm sure your sister is great, but I prefer brunettes." His lips turn up into a cheeky grin.

"Oh, right," I feel my cheeks turn pink. "Anyway." I sit on the bench, and turn my body toward him. "Tell me about your job as a security analyst. Is it exciting?"

"It's interesting, and complicated. But I'd like to get to know you better. How about dinner?"

What? He wants to take me out for dinner? "Wh-what?" I stammer.

"You know. That thing people have anywhere between six and nine at night. You sit at this magical invention called a table."

A goofy smile tugs at my lips. He makes me smile. "Dinner would be nice." I've never really been out on a date before. Unless you consider Hank Reed a date in freshman year. All he wanted was to kiss and grope me. He made me feel really uncomfortable and kinda freaked me out.

A shiver runs up my spine with the mere thought of Hank Reed.

"You okay?" Dylan asks.

"Yeah, sorry. Just..." I shudder, and push the thought of Hank as far down as I can. "It's okay." I flick my hand, dismissively.

"So, what about dinner tomorrow night?" he asks, eagerly.

"I can't."

"Oh." Dylan looks away. "Well, nice talking to you, Molly." I think he thinks I'm blowing him off.

He goes to stand, but I place my hand on his firm arm. "I meant I can't have dinner tomorrow night, because it's Tina's and my birthday."

"You're twins?" He cocks his head to the side.

"No, nothing like that." I chuckle, because I understand the confusion. "We're both adopted. But our birthdays are on the same day, in the same year."

He looks in the direction of Tina, then back to me. "I know I shouldn't ask a lady her age, but how old are you?"

"We'll be eighteen tomorrow."

"Um. Okay then." He nervously wipes at his brow. "Um."

I recognize that emotion right away. Surprise at my age. "It's okay," I say as I stand. "I get it. I'm too young, or too old. I'm too something. Whatever." I offer him a smile.

"No. It's not that," he adds.

"What is it then?"

He stares at me. "I can't lie to you, Molly. I think I'm too old for you."

I shrug. "Okay then. If you say so."

I take a step back from him. "Wait, don't you want to know how old I am?"

I turn to face him, and find he's now standing a little bit too close to me. I shake my head. "You've made up your mind about me and *for* me, there's no use in trying to convince you otherwise. Have a good day, Dylan." I smile again to hide the pain of his rejection.

Crash and burn.

"No, wait."

I hold my hand up over my shoulder as I walk away.

I head toward the store Tina said she was headed to, and don't look back.

Truth be told though, I'm hurt.

But I'm not going to let him ruin my day.

CHAPTER 2

"Are you going to tell me what happened yesterday with that cute guy?" Tina asks as she looks through my closet.

"Nothing to tell." I shrug my shoulders.

"Nah, there is. You've been quiet since we got back from the mall. I mean, more quiet than normal."

"If there's nothing to say, then why talk for the hell of it?" I fidget with the hem of my t-shirt.

"Hmm," Tina mumbles as she turns to give me the stink eye. "I know there's more to what you're saying."

"Are you excited about dinner tonight?" I ask, trying to change her focus from me.

"Am I ever! I think I want to put make-up on you. A full face. What do you think?"

Ugh, no thank you. But I know if I don't say yes, she's going to continue asking questions about Dylan. I'd best distract her by agreeing to whatever she wants to do. "Sure, that'll be nice. Just nothing too dramatic. Subtle."

"Subtle. Yeah, okay, I can do subtle. Maybe some vivid eye color though. That dress is gorgeous, so what if I do smoky eyes and red lips, and I've got to get my shoes. Hang on." She leaves my closet, and runs to her room which is on the other side of my wall. Mom's and Dad's suite is at the other end of the hall upstairs. "Here you go. Put them on, and walk in them." She hands me a pair of red, extremely high heels.

I hesitantly reach out to take them. "Oh, I see. You want to visit me in the hospital tonight, do you?"

"They're not that high," Tina teases. "Try them on."

There's no way in hell, I'll be able to walk in these shoes. Nope, impossible. But, if Tina doesn't see me try them, then she's not going to believe me when I say I can't walk in them. I slide them on. Damn it, they fit perfectly. Standing, I try to balance on the thinnest heel I've ever seen on a shoe. "I can't wear these," I say as I shuffle forward. "I can't even lift my foot. How do you walk in these?"

"Easy." She leans against the wall, watching me walk like a baby giraffe on ice.

"I'm not wearing these." I stumble back to my bed, where I collapse, and kick off the heels. "Sorry, Tina. But there's no way at all."

"You're right. You can barely walk in flat shoes, so high heels aren't going to cut it." She pushes off from the wall, bends and sweeps the shoes up in one fluid movement. "What shoes have you got?" She heads to my wardrobe, walks in and looks at the rows of shoes. Mine are all practical, and comfortable. "You don't have anything here you can wear."

"I can wear them." I point to a red pair of Converse.

Tina's mouth falls open, as if she's disgusted with my suggestion. "You aren't wearing Converse with that dress. I told you that already. Let me go to Mom's closet."

"Mom's foot is also two sizes smaller than ours. So no, that's not going to work. Let me wear the Converse. I think it'll be really nice. Especially if you make me up too, no one will be looking at my feet."

"Hmm. I know what you're doing," she says with narrow eyes as she walks toward the door. "You're trying to distract me so I don't make you wear these shoes." She looks me up and down while she drums her fingers on the red, shiny high heels. "But you're right. You need to be able to walk, and not break your neck. But I'm doing whatever I want on your face."

"Can you just go, and let me relax before you make me into your own personal Barbie-doll?"

"Hey, I'm allowing you to wear your Converse. You should be happy." I lower my chin, and raise my brows. "I'm going, I'm going." She walks out, and closes my door behind her.

I lay down again on my bed, and stare up at the ceiling. Reaching over, I get my Air Pods, switch my music on, and close my eyes.

Zhen has been curled up at the foot of my bed, sleeping this entire time. Zhen's my chocolate Labrador. He's our family's dog, but for some reason, he really gravitates toward me.

Meditation starts and I instantly relax as I listen to the cool drawl of the woman who's narrating. There's something about meditation that helps me calm down when things get to be too much. It takes me away from the now, and allows me to live in a harmony.

"Wow, you look really nice," Mom says as I make my way down our grand staircase.

"I did her make up," Tina proudly says as she looks up at me.

"You both look amazing," Dad says as he slides his suit jacket over his shoulders. "I can't believe my girls are eighteen."

I get to the bottom of the stairs, and Tina looks at my shoes. "They actually look good," she says, though I can tell it's killing her to admit it.

"See, told ya."

"Are you two ready?" Mom asks as she slings her bag over her shoulder. Mom always looks beautiful. She has this old-world glamor about her. Like she's a black-and-white movie star. Mom's fair features are truly breathtaking, but her heart is even more exquisite.

"We're ready," Tina answers for us both.

"You be a good boy, Zhen. We'll be back home soon," I say to my boy, who's wagging his tail. I know he'll disappear upstairs to my room and go to sleep, waiting for me.

"I'm the luckiest man in the world, to have such a breathtaking wife, and two perfect daughters." Dad hugs both Tina and me together, then places gentle kisses on our heads. "Come on; I'm hungry," he says.

"You're always hungry," Mom teases.

Mom locks the front door, as Dad reverses the car from the garage. We all get in, and Dad starts driving toward the restaurant they picked. I'm never fussed by extravagant things, they're simply objects. I'd be just as happy going to The Cheesecake Factory for dinner, as I am going to Chapter, the two Michelin star restaurant we're heading to.

Mom, Dad, and Tina talk, and I look out the window. Distant from the happy, animated conversation they're having. Going to fancy places isn't my scene, but I know Mom, Dad, and Tina love going.

I take my Air Pods out of the charging case, and slip them into my ears. Turning on some gentle, easy listening music. No one talks to me, or if they do, they know I've got my headset in, which means, I'm zoning out.

Another easy song comes through the headphones, then another, and I close my eyes and relax.

I feel a soft whack on my thigh. Looking over, I see Tina smiling. I can faintly hear her over the music. "We're here."

I take my headphones off, and slide the small charging case into the pocket on the back of the passenger seat. "I was listening to music," I say.

"We know," Mom says from the front. Dad pulls up to the curb, where there's a valet waiting to park our car.

Dad takes Mom's hand, and they walk ahead of us. "You okay?" Tina whispers as we approach the doors to Chapter.

"Yeah, I'm good."

"Cool." She smiles. "You look so hot."

"Thanks."

We're quickly shown to our seats, where a waiter in a full tuxedo approaches us with a bizarrely flamboyant glass pitcher of water. He doesn't say anything, only pours the water and leaves.

"This is way too fancy for me," I say as I look around the room. There's another two families sitting on the far-right hand side of the restaurant, and several couples who are all eating, and enjoying quiet conversation.

"We wanted to make it special," Mom says. "It's not every day our girls turn eighteen."

I feel awkward, way out of my comfort zone. That's funny though, because Mom and Dad always give us nice things, and take us to expensive places. I just don't know if I'll ever get used to it.

"Thank you for bringing us here," I say to them.

"Yeah, thank you. This place is sick," Tina says looking around at the simple, stylish décor.

"This is why we work hard, because we want you both to have the best we can give," Dad says.

They've never made us feel like we're just two adopted girls. They've never talked about us like we aren't part of their family. But I often wonder why they chose me. As for Tina, I understand that. She's so bubbly and warm, it's easy for anyone to fall in love with her. But I'm not like Tina. I'm more reserved, and introverted, the total opposite.

A different waiter approaches us. She's dressed in smart black clothing too. She tells us the specials for the evening, without even reading it from a menu. Her voice is controlled and calm as she says words like, 'truffle, lobster, kobe beef and caviar.' Of course, they all sound delicious, but the moment she said lobster, my mouth began watering.

She stands and waits for our order.

She doesn't write anything down, which blows my mind. If I worked in such a fancy restaurant, I'd want to write it all down to make sure I don't screw anything up.

"I've got to go to the rest room," I say as I stand. I look around the room, and quickly spot where the bathrooms are.

"Hurry back. We want to give you our presents," Mom says with a huge smile.

Once I'm out of the restroom, I head back to our table. "Latte girl," I hear from beside me.

The voice is familiar, and the hair stands to attention on my arms. Turning, I see Dylan. "Dylan." I smile. "You already forgot my name? It's good we're not going on a date then." I step away from him. Before I do, I quickly glimpse at his table. I'm half expecting to see a gorgeous woman sitting opposite him, but I don't. I see an older man, who looks exactly like Dylan, only older.

"She got you good, son," his father says as he chuckles.

"You're supposed to be on my side." He gives the man who must be his Dad a pointed annoyed look. His Dad flips his hand, and adds a chuckle. "Can we talk?" Dylan asks.

"Nothing to say." I take a step away, but Dylan reaches out and puts his hand on my upper arm. It's not hard, or forceful. "I'm sorry about yesterday."

"What part? The fact you heard I was eighteen and you made the decision for me that you're too old for me? Or was it something else?"

"Damn, she's got you again, son," his Dad comments.

"Dad," Dylan says in a strained tone. His father gives me a little wink, and I instantly like him. "For all of it. I shouldn't have done that."

I shrug, and turn to see Tina looking over at me. I shake my head slightly at her. She appears to be ready to come over and rescue me. I don't need rescuing. If anything, Dylan does. "Apology accepted. Have a nice night."

"Please, don't go," Dylan begs. "Just hear me out."

"I did. You said your piece, I accepted your apology and now I'm going back to my family."

"You're a damned fool if you let her go," his Dad mumbles.

"Molly, please," Dylan says again. *Good,* he remembers my name. "Please," he says again, giving me a pleading gaze.

"Okay," I say sassily, stepping closer to him. "What is it?"

"All I could think about yesterday was you." I lift my brows, surprised. "I'd still like to take you out to dinner." I smile, waiting for him to continue. "Anytime you want. Can I give you my number? Will you give me yours?"

I wait five heartbeats before I say anything. "I'd like that," I say.

Dylan visibly lets out a sigh. He pulls his phone out of his pocket, unlocks it, then hands it to me. "Can I have your number?"

"You can." I take it, and put my number in under Latte girl. He sees me put in that name, and chuckles. "There you go."

"Do you want my number?" he asks, looking at my empty hands.

I shake my head. "If you want to take me to dinner, you can call me. I'm not chasing you." I've never said anything so assertive to anyone in my entire life. It's shocking, but so damn freeing too.

"Son, marry this one," his father eagerly adds.

"Sorry, sir. I'm only eighteen, and marrying isn't on the agenda for me." I shock myself again. I've never considered marriage. Never really thought of spending my life with anyone, other than myself.

"I'm Harold Walker." His Dad stands, and extends his hand. I take it, and smile. I really like him.

"Pleased to meet you, Mr. Walker."

"Pish posh. It's Harold."

"Well, it's been a pleasure. I hope to hear from you soon, Dylan."

"You will," Dylan says to my retreating back.

"She's a keeper," I hear Harold say to Dylan.

I go back to my seat, and the conversation at the table instantly dies. Mom, Dad, and Tina are all staring at me.

Here we go.

"Who's the young man?" Mom asks.

"Young man? He was drooling all over her. He could barely contain himself," Dad says, definitely irritated.

"She met him yesterday at the mall," Tina replies.

"Did you tell him we were coming here?" Dad asks.

"How could she tell him, when she had no idea we were coming?" Mom snaps at Dad.

"What happened?" Tina asks leaning in, but looks over to Dylan and Harold.

"Is everyone done speculating so I can actually tell you what happened?" I ask.

"He's too old for you," Dad says again. "How old is he?"

"I have no idea," I answer truthfully. "But I met him yesterday when he accidently knocked into me. He asked me out for dinner, and when he found out my age, he freaked out."

"How did he freak out?" Mom asks.

"Yeah, how?" Tina's voice drops, as she turns to give Dylan the stink eye. "I think I'll go have a word with him."

"Tina," I say sharply. "No, you won't. Leave it alone."

"No one hurts my little sister."

"We're the same age." I shake my head. "Anyway, he said he was too old for me. So I left. I thought, no use in trying to change his mind. It was already set. But just then, as I was coming back from the rest room, he stopped me. Apologized," I pause before adding, "a few times. And he asked me out again. I didn't make it easy for him. His Dad told him I was a keeper." I smile.

"He's here with his father?" Mom asks. "That's a good sign. Means he's not a total loser."

I laugh a little too loud then snort in error. I cover my mouth as I try to contain the laughter. "No, he's not a loser. He's a security analyst and works at Collins and Partners."

"Oh, he's just moved up on the shit list," Dad says.

"He's not a lawyer, Dad."

"I meant he's moved up in a good way. He has a decent job, and works for a good firm. I'm still not liking him yet." Dad holds up a finger at me. "But I'm not as upset as I was. But I'd like to know how old he is."

"Would it make you feel better if I go ask him?" I slide my chair back.

"No, not now. We're here to celebrate," Mom injects. "Oh, look, our dinner." Four waiters bring all our dinners out at once, and place them in front of us in unison. Now that's fancy.

My phone buzzes in my clutch. I reach for it, and see there's a message. Sliding my phone unlock, it's from Dylan. **Love your shoes** is all it says.

This makes me smile. Instead of replying, I put my phone away and enjoy dinner with my family.

I try not to look over toward Dylan as we enjoy dinner, but out of the corner of my eye, I notice he and Harold swap seats, so Dylan can watch me and I can watch him. I have to say, it's cute and it makes my stomach flip flop with excitement.

Talk around the dinner table is about everything. Dad's work as an aircraft mechanic, Mom's a financial manager, even the college Tina is planning to attend. I'm glad I decided to take a gap year, because I don't yet know what I want to do with my life.

Instead, I'll work for a year, and see where that path takes me.

Our dinner is finished, and the plates are all taken away.

Mom reaches over and takes Dad hand. "Your father and I want you both to have the best birthday ever."

"I already have," I say.

"Well, we'd like to give you this." Dad lets Mom's hand go, and takes out two identical boxes. Both are black with a blue ribbon tied around them. Dad slides one over to me, and one to Tina.

Tina is already excitedly trying to tear off the ribbon. But I want to savor every moment.

She lifts the lid, and screams. I look over to her, and she holds up a car fob.

I open mine, and have the same car fob. They bought us a car to share. I look down at the box, overwhelmed with happiness. Our parents are always generous, but to get us a car…that's amazing.

"Thank you," I whisper as tears fall on the pristine tablecloth. I'm so moved by their kindness, and can only hope I'll grow to be half-as-good a person as they are.

"Mom, Dad," Tina says as she flies up to hug them.

I stand, and hug them too. "Thank you," I say again.

"Thank you so much," Tina says. We sit down, and Tina turns to me and says, "We'll work out how to share."

"Share?" Dad says. "Why would you share? We got you each a car."

I stare at my parents, unable to verbalize what's going through my head.

"Are you kidding?" Tina shrieks. Half of the restaurant patrons turn to look at us, including Dylan and his father. Tina's excitement is infectious. Everyone's smiling. "Thank you." She launches herself into Mom's open arms, nearly knocking Mom off the chair.

Standing, I give our parents another hug. There aren't many words I can think of other than two. "Thank you," I say.

Mom and Dad are beaming. They're so proud of themselves. I'm so proud of them, too.

Tina sits again, and she wipes at her eyes. "I think I can speak for both of us, to say we never expected this."

"That's what makes it the best present. Neither of you had any idea your father and I had plans to buy you girls a car each."

"We appreciate this so much," I say.

"We know. Now, don't go thinking it's a BMW or anything. You got a Toyota Corolla. One's white, and the other's black. We'll leave it up to you two to decide who's is whose. But we wanted to make sure you're both safe when you're driving."

"What color do you want?" Tina asks.

My forehead crinkles, as I stare at Tina. "Are you actually asking?" That's not like Tina, she usually tells me, and I go along with it. I know she's always got my back so something like the color of a car is inconsequential.

"Shut up," she playfully grumbles. "And yes, I'm asking." I'm about to tell her which one I'd prefer and she cuts me off. "Actually, I want the black one."

"There it is." I point to her.

"Fine, which one do you want?"

I let her sweat on it for a moment. Tapping my chin, and looking out at the distance (by distance I mean Dylan). "Um, I think I want…" I tap my mouth with my finger. I can see Tina jumping out of her skin, not able to contain her excitement. "I think…"

"I want the black one!" Tina snaps, unable to control her impulse.

"Wait." I hold a finger up to her. Mom and Dad are chuckling to themselves. Tina's like a kid in front of a candy case. She's shaking from the excitement. "Yeah, I think I'll take the white one."

"Yes!" She fist pumps the air.

"I was happy with whichever color. I just wanted to make you sweat."

"Grrr." She narrows her eyes at me, grinding her teeth together. But I know Tina, she doesn't mean anything nasty. She's just impatient. "Well, I'm taking the black," Tina announces dramatically.

"Okay," I say.

"You can't stop me."

"I won't."

"You can't beg me later to change."

"I won't."

"Last chance."

"No need."

Tina gets up, and gives me a hug. "Thank you, you're awesome. And I have something for you." She goes back to her chair, and takes a little box out of her bag. She hands it to me.

"I didn't get you anything, Tina." I feel so bad. We never exchange gifts.

"Good. Because I don't want anything. Well, except the car." She blows Mom and Dad a kiss.

"You bought me something, and I didn't get you anything. That's not fair." I don't want to accept the present, because I feel like I'm not contributing to our relationship.

"When have I ever said you have to do something for me because I do something for you?" she questions.

She's right. She may be impatient, bossy, and generally a pain in the butt, but she's not greedy or selfish. Not with me. "Thank you." I open the little box, and inside is a gold pendant on a gold chain. The pendant is two rings entwined. One has my name on it, and the other has Tina's. "Wow," I say in a breathless voice. "This is beautiful, Tina."

"I want you to know, that no matter where our lives go, I'll always be with you. If you need me, just call, and I'll be there."

I smile again. Tonight's been really overwhelming for me. I've been showered with so much love. I take the chain out of the box, and signal for Tina to help me put it on. I don't need to say anything. She stands, comes around to my back, and clasps the chain around my neck.

I pick the pendant up, staring at it. "It's perfect, thank you."

Tina leans down and gives me a kiss on the cheek.

Tonight, is the best night of my life.

"Who's ready for dessert?" Dad asks.

"Me," Mom and Tina answer in unison. I nod my head, too overwhelmed with all the emotions running through my body to verbally answer.

What a night.

CHAPTER 3

"Are you taking Zhen or do you want me to?" I ask Tina as I stand leaning against her door.

"Can you? I've got a date, and I want to get ready."

"Who's the date with?" I walk in further to her room, and sit on her bed. She's sitting at her table, cleaning her face with a make-up wipe. Zhen follows me, and lays with his legs spread behind me on the floor. "You hot, boy?" I ask as I lean down and pet his back.

"I swear, that dog doesn't give a rat's ass about anyone else in this family. Anyway, it's with Preston," she says.

"Oh yeah, that's the guy you met when you went out with Gabriella and Willow last month. You've been seeing a lot of him. When am I going to meet him?"

"I'll set something up," Tina says, smiling at me in the mirror.

"You two going out today? During the day?"

"No, not during the day. We're going out tonight. Dinner, then a movie."

"And you can't take Zhen to the vet for his vaccinations, why?" If she's going out tonight, she can take Zhen to the vet.

"I have a very valid reason."

"Which is?"

"I don't want to. I'm getting ready for our date."

"Now?"

"It takes time to look this good." She waves her hand over her body, and I can't help but let out a laugh. "Anyway, he doesn't listen to me." She looks back, and sees Zhen laying on the floor. His eyes staring at her. "Zhen," she calls him. He doesn't budge.

"Go on," I say to him.

Zhen gets up, and takes a few steps to Tina. She lowers her hand, and gives him a few pats before she returns to her beauty regimen. "See? He doesn't listen to any of us."

"Come here, boy," I say to Zhen. He slowly trots back to me, and sits on my foot. "I'll take you to the vet." His tail wags and flicks my ankle. Zhen stands seconds before I do, it's like he can anticipate my moves. "Have fun tonight."

"I'll see you before I go. Oh, hey, can I borrow that black shimmery top?"

"Which black shimmery top?"

"The black one. The one you wore to Dad's forty-fifth. Remember?"

"Yeah, sure. Do you want me to get it?"

"Nah, I'll get it after my shower."

"Be safe tonight, Tina. If I'm asleep when you get home, wake me so you can tell me about it."

Tina swings around to look at me. "I was going to." She waggles her brows at me.

She always makes me smile. She's so honest and raw. But she's kept her relationship with this Preston under wraps until now. I wonder why.

"Come on, Zhen." I snap my fingers as we walk out and down the stairs. Zhen's behind me, only by a few steps. "Mom," I call."

"In the living room." I head in to find her streaming a movie. "What's up?"

"I'm taking Zhen to the vet for his vaccinations."

Mom looks at her watch, and back to me. "Oh crap, I was supposed to do that." She quickly stands.

"I can do it. Stay here and relax. I might take him to the dog park afterward."

"Are you sure? I can come with you."

"I'm okay, Mom."

"Hang on, let me give you my card." She dashes out of the room, then comes back with her purse. "Here you go." She hands me her charge card.

"I'm not sure what time I'll be back."

"Okay, sweetheart. Just drive safely," she says.

Zhen follows me out, and I head to the mudroom to get his lead. He walks beside me without it, but I know when we take him out of the house, we have to put it on him. For some reason, it makes people feel safer.

We head out to my new car, and I open the back door for him. "Do you need to pee?" I ask him. Zhen runs over to one of the low bushes in front of our home, and pees against it before running to the car and jumping in the back seat.

I head out of our gates and down the road toward the main part of town. We live in the suburbs of a fairly large and bustling town.

Zhen's in the back, breathing heavily, and slobbering all over my back seat. "You're the first person in my car, and you're drooling everywhere." Zhen closes his mouth and tilts his head. Then opens his mouth and pants. "Great, more slobber."

We get to the vet's office, and I park right outside. Going in, Zhen walks beside me as I loosely hold the lead. As soon as the lady sitting at the counter sees me, she smiles. "Hey Zhen," she says acknowledging him before me.

Zhen wags his tail, but stays close to me.

"Michael shouldn't be too long," she says to me. Michael is Zhen's vet.

"Thank you." Zhen and I take a seat in the waiting room. He jumps up on the bench beside me, and places his head in my lap. "You okay?" I ask him. He blinks several times.

I zone out, petting Zhen. But it doesn't take long for Michael to call us into an exam room. I tap Zhen's head, and he jumps off the bench, following me into the room.

"How are you?" Michael asks.

"Good," I smile.

"What can we do for you, Zhen?" he bends, and grunting, picks Zhen up to place him on the table.

"It's vaccination time," I say.

Michael is a fantastic vet. He treats Zhen like he's his own. "Let's check you out, and make sure you're all good." Michael works his hands down Zhen's body and gives him a thorough examination, even checking his temperature. "He's good. Come on, buddy. Let's check your weight." He carefully places Zhen on the floor, and watches as we walk out to the large scale they have in the waiting room. "Perfect, seventy pounds. Let's go back in the room, and I'll get his vaccinations ready. He's a perfect weight for a dog his size."

I lift Zhen and put him on the table as Michael gets the vaccines ready. He comes back into the room, and closes the door. "Do you think these will affect him at all?" I ask.

"They've never posed a problem in the past, have they?" Michael asks.

"He tends to be a bit sleepy the day after, but other than that, nope."

"He'll be fine."

"Will it be okay to take him to the dog park after we leave here?"

"I can't see why not." He pinches the skin on the back of Zhen's neck, and injects the vaccines into him. He hands me a small manila envelope containing some tablets. "He needs to take one of these tonight with his dinner, and the other tomorrow with his breakfast. It's to prevent heartworm." He lifts Zhen and places him back on the floor.

Zhen finds my legs, and leans against them. "Thank you," I say, and lead Zhen out to the reception area to pay for our visit.

Once we're in the car, Zhen lays on the back seat, just keeping his eyes open. Thankfully, the dog park isn't too far away.

"Come on, boy," I say to him as I open the back door, and take his lead.

I open the gate to the dog park, and unclip his lead. Zhen runs to the other side, then comes back to find me. There's a coffee cart along the side of the fence. I head over, order a coffee and wait while it's prepared. I watch as Zhen runs around the dog park, playing on the dog obstacle course. I can't help but giggle at him. He's acting so free.

"Your coffee," the guy says and hands me a cup.

I take it and go sit on one of the bench seats inside the fence.

There are four other people here with their dogs. All the dogs seem to be doing their own thing, which I find entertaining, except for one guy who's throwing a ball for his dog. The dog runs off to retrieve it and brings it back.

I sip on my coffee, and watch everyone.

"You stupid fucking mutt!" I hear.

The aggressive tone has me swinging my head to the side to see the guy who was throwing the ball punch his dog. The dog yelps, and backs away from him

Zhen must sense something's not right, and runs straight back to me, positioning himself protectively in front of me.

"Hey!" I yell, as the guy draws his fist back to hit his dog again.

"Mind your own business!" he yells at me.

No one else says anything to him, even though they're all watching.

I stand, but stop before I can take a step. I blink. The words are caught in my throat. A vivid picture of a discolored, stuffed bunny rabbit, with big floppy ears, forces itself into my mind. I blink again, and the bunny is gone.

Pushing the image back, I charge over to him before he has a chance to hit his dog again. "Don't you dare hit this animal," I say, standing in front of his dog. Zhen is standing in front of me.

"Fuck off. Out of my way, you nosy bitch!" the guy spits angrily.

"If you want to hurt that dog, you'll have to go through me." I stand firm, crossing my arms and refusing to budge. I have no idea what happened for him to become so aggressive with this poor, innocent animal.

He moves to step around me, but Zhen maneuvers to confront him, baring his teeth so the guy can't get close to me, or his cowering dog.

"I'm going to beat the shit out of you when we get home." He points to the dog. "Move out of my way," he spits at me.

"That dog isn't going anywhere with you."

"He's not yours, he's mine. Move, before I smash you like that useless fucking mutt."

My adrenaline is running high. My heart's going crazy in my chest. The bunny pops back in my head for split second, catching my words in my throat.

"We've called the police," one of the other dog owners calls to me.

The guy looks around at everyone, and calls his dog over. The dog cowers on the ground, but won't go to him. "Come here, boy," I say as I crouch toward him. Zhen stands still between the man and me, and the other dog comes to me. "Have him, he's a dumb mutt anyway." The guy turns, and jogs out of the park, obviously trying to get out of here before the police show up.

The dog whimpers beside me as he lays on the ground.

"Hey there. Are you okay?" I ask softly, patting him on the head.

The guy takes off quickly, spinning out his tires as he leaves.

"Oh my God, that was so brave of you," a woman says.

"I couldn't just stand there watching him beat his dog," I reply. But the delayed shock of it is making me tremble.

Zhen smells the other dog's butt, the other dog smells Zhen's. "Looks like you have a new dog." She looks over her shoulder, and sees her husband waving his phone at her. "Good. My husband got that guy's tags. We'll report him to the police when they arrive."

"He shouldn't have any animals. Why would you do that?"

She shrugs. "We'll wait with you until the police come."

"Thank you. I appreciate it."

Zhen and the other dog walk together around the park. I have a little laugh. "Don't they look like they're friends who are talking?" she asks.

"They do. I'm not sure how my parents are going to take me bringing another dog home. I suppose we'll soon see. I think I'll take him to the vet, get him checked out first. He looks a bit underweight."

"Makes you wonder why that guy would bring his dog to a dog park if he would publicly mistreats it. What makes people do that? Probably drugs."

I gasp, and look around me. Placing my hand to my heart, I can feel it fiercely throbbing in my chest. That damned bunny comes forward again.

"Are you okay?" the woman asks.

I'm stuck, unable to think a coherent thought, let alone a sentence.

Zhen appears beside me, and he nudges me with his head. The other dog, sits on my other side.

"What was that?" I whisper.

"Hey, are you okay? You've gone all white," the woman asks. "Do you need some water?"

"No, I'm um, I'm okay." I shake my head, trying to dislodge the image of the bunny.

It wasn't pleasant. The bunny was old and tattered. Darkness surrounded it, not happiness. It's probably impact from the shock.

"Police are here," the woman says.

The image has left a sour feeling rumbling in my stomach. There's something sinister about it, but I can't put my finger on it.

The police walk into the dog park, and I stand back, letting the woman and her husband explain what happened. Zhen and the other dog are now playing together.

I give my statement to the police, but keep an eye on the dogs, still being distracted by that image of the bunny. I don't know what's happening. It's like a blur. Everyone's talking, the dogs are having fun, and I'm under a veil of heaviness I can't explain.

"We'll follow up with this, and if there's anything we need, we'll be in touch," one of the police officers says. They both walk out of the park.

"You were so brave," the woman says again.

"Thank you." I smile. Turning, I whistle for Zhen, and both dogs trot toward me. "Come on, new guy. I'll take you to the vet and see what he has to say."

Both dogs walk together brilliantly, like they're life-long friends. Zhen jumps in first, then the other dog. I get in the car, start it and head back to the vet.

Once inside, the receptionist looks up and does a double take. "You're back?"

"I've got an extra dog."

She peers over the counter and smiles. "Where did you come from, buddy?"

"I kind of rescued him. Long story short, there was a guy at the dog park who was beating him."

"Oh," she gasps, her mouth falling open in shock.

"I know. Anyway, do you think Michael has time to check him out, please?"

She looks at the computer, checks her watch, then back to the computer. "Yeah, he's got a patient in there with him now, but he should be able to squeeze you in straight after."

"Thanks, you're a life saver."

She looks at me and smiles. "In this case, I think *you're* the life saver."

I hear the door open to Michael's room, and a woman walks out holding a pillowcase. I see whatever is inside the pillowcase, moving. Or should I say, slithering.

"Yuck," I grumble as a chill runs over my spine. Zhen turns to look at me. "It's okay," I say and pet him.

"Molly, you're back already?" Michael asks.

"I have someone I'd like you to look over to make sure he's okay."

"Then come in." The other dog is so placid, and gentle. He just follows Zhen, and Zhen follows me. "What's happening?" Michael asks.

I give him a rundown on how I came into possession of this dog.

"Poor, dog. But, I'm glad he found you. Alright, let's get you up on the table." He picks the dog up, and gives him a thorough examination. He takes some x-rays and checks everything.

It feels like we've been in here for an hour by the time Michael has finished. "Is he okay?"

"He's fairly healthy, considering what you told me. He's definitely underweight though, so he needs some tender loving care, and a lot of food. I have no idea if he's had his vaccines though."

"Can we give them to him again? Will that be too much if he has had them?"

"No, not really. But judging by what you've said, I doubt he's been taken care of. He needs a wash. He's got fleas, and he stinks." Yeah, he does. I have to agree on that.

"What kind of dog is he?"

"He's definitely got boxer in him, but as far as the any other breed, I have no idea. He's not a pure bred. I hate to say it, but he could've come from a puppy mill."

My stomach churns with disgust. "I hate when people are cruel."

"What do you want to do? You can surrender the dog to me if you don't want him, but I can't guarantee we'll find him a home."

"No, I'm taking him. Give him his vaccines, and I'll get him cleaned up."

Michael smiles, and heads out of the room. Zhen is relaxed beside me, while the other dog anxiously pants. Michael returns and places the kidney tray on the counter. "So what are you going to call him?"

I shrug. "No idea."

"He's a pretty good boy, considering I assume he's come from a fairly hard life." He pinches the skin on the back of his neck, and injects him with the vaccines. The dog whimpers. "It wouldn't surprise me if the guy who hurt him was some kind of drug addict. I see it a lot with abandoned or mistreated animals. Some are even given drugs or used for target practice. The things I've seen are horrible. Unfortunately, not all can be saved."

"Please, don't say any more. I don't think I can take it. Animal abuse is a… it's…" I shake my head, my heart bleeding with sorrow. "It's beyond disgusting. I wish I had a stronger word for it."

"I think that's a fairly accurate description." Michael finishes with the other dog, and lowers him to the floor. "I think you've got yourself a good home now, my friend," he says as he scratches him under his chin. "Let me know if there's anything I can do to help," Michael offers.

"Thank you." I've attached Zhen's lead to the other dog, and Zhen's walking beside me without one. We head out, and I pay for the second vet visit.

I get both dogs in the car, and head home.

On the drive home, I go over the conversation with my Mom in my head. I try and get every possible combination of answers for why we should keep the dog.

I drive through the gates, up the rounded driveway, and park under the four-car carport on the side of the two-car garage.

Opening the back door, Zhen jumps out first, and runs to one of the poles holding the carport up. The other dog does the same thing. Zhen sniffs, lifts his leg, and pees. The other dog waits until Zhen is finished, then does the same thing. "There's another three poles. You don't have to wait. And look, there are shrubs and trees everywhere."

I head in, with both dogs following closely behind. Opening the door, I listen for where Mom is. I can't hear her. "Mom!" I call.

"Bathroom," she shouts. Judging by where her voice came from, she's in the bathroom down stairs between the guest room and the den.

I walk into the large, bright kitchen, and get some dog food out. Placing it on the floor, the new dog pounces on it, like he hasn't seen food in days. He probably hasn't. Zhen stands beside me, watching the newcomer.

"Honey, your ho…who do we have here?" Mom asks as she enters the kitchen.

"Well, it's a bit of a long story." I proceed to tell her the whole thing while I pour myself some water.

Mom sits on one of the dining room chairs as she keeps looking over to the dog, then back to me. She places her hand to her chest, as I continue to tell her about what happened. Her shoulders slump forward, and she shakes her head. "What did Michael say when you took him to the vet?"

I continue to fill her in. "So now, we have to make a decision as to what we're going to do with him," I say.

"What?" Mom turns her head, her top lip turned up in a semi-scowl. I'm not sure if she's mad, or angry or something else. "We're going to keep him." She stands and walks out of the kitchen, only to return a few seconds later with her phone. "I'll call Izzy the dog washer, and get her to come wash both Zhen and him today." She points to the dog who's now lying on his stomach, his hind legs stretched out behind him. "What are you going to call him?"

"We can keep him?" I ask. I was ready to try to convince her why we shouldn't surrender him.

"Look at him." We both turn to see how comfortable he is in front of the large floor to ceiling glass doors overlooking our backyard. "Even if I wanted to get rid of him, which I don't, he wouldn't want to go."

I run to Mom and throw my arms around her. "Thank you," I say.

"He's your responsibility though, Molly. You better come up with a name." She flicks through her phone book, then brings her phone to her ear. "Izzy, it's Paris Dawson." She listens for a few seconds. "No, I know Zhen isn't due yet. But Molly has brought home a stray, and he's really hard on the nose. Any chance you can…" She listens for a few more seconds. "Five? Thank you, I owe you." Mom hangs up.

"She's coming today?"

"Five o'clock."

"Wow." I lean against the kitchen counter, and think about the bunny rabbit. "Mom, I have a question for you."

"What is it?"

"When I came to live with you and Dad, did I have a stuffed bunny rabbit?"

Mom's shoulders stiffen. She visibly swallows. "You came to us with the clothes you were wearing, and a small bag with a few articles of clothing," she says. Mom's told me little bits and pieces, but nothing substantial.

"I know you've told me you didn't know a lot about my life before I came to you, but do you know anything about it at all?"

"Only what we've told you, sweetie. You came from a broken home, your birth mother wasn't on the scene, and you lived with your father. Authorities were called when the neighbor heard you crying. You'd been left alone in the house." I nod my head. This stuff I've heard before. "Why, what's bothering you?"

"Something happened today, and I don't know what it means."

"The guy at the dog park?"

I nod. "When I saw him hit his dog, I stood up to go and confront him, but I just got this vivid picture of a mangy stuffed rabbit. It's like I had a connection to it, but I have no idea from where or how. It made me feel uneasy. My stomach churned, and it was like a warning or something. I was hoping you'd be able to tell me if I came to you with a white rabbit. It had big, floppy ears. It was supposed to be white, but it was discolored." Mom's shaking her head. "Nothing?" I'm desperate to try and find out about this bunny.

"No, I'm sorry. I can tell you about Tina's adoption though. But that's not useful considering your birthparents are different."

"Okay, well…I don't know." I shrug. "I wish I knew what this rabbit meant."

"I'm sorry, I can't help you."

I walk over to Mom, and give her a kiss on the cheek. "That's okay. I'm going to head up so I can do some research on dog names."

"Okay. Izzy will be here at five. We'll get both dogs washed. I'll call you down when she arrives."

"Thanks, Mom." I head out of the kitchen, both dogs right behind me. I take the steps two at a time and get to my room quickly. Again, both dogs right by my side. "Right, let's find a name for you." I sniff, and get a waft of the dog. "Stinky wouldn't be nice, would it, boy?" I pet him. Zhen lays beside me.

Opening my laptop, I search dog names for courageous males.

CHAPTER 4

"Zhen, Zorro," I call both boys. They're outside, playing in the backyard. Both ignore me. "Dinner," I say, louder. Just like magic, they stop playing and run toward me. "So you come when I say dinner? Traitors." I run my nails through Zhen's short hair, then pet Zorro.

"He needs fattening up," Dad says as we sit at the dinner table.

"Yeah, Michael said he's underweight."

"You can see it," Dad says. "He's a good dog, though. I'm surprised he's as well behaved as what he is. Especially if he came from a home where he was abused. I'm really surprised he's not cowering every time we put our hands down to pet him."

"He probably feels comfortable around us," I answer. "Even Tina likes him, and we both know she's not a fan of animals."

"Who's not a fan of animals?" Tina asks as she comes in and sits beside me at the dinner table.

"You," I answer.

"They're alright." She shrugs. "I mean, I wouldn't ever purposely hurt an animal, but they're not really my thing." She reaches down to pet the dogs. Both clamber to stand beside her.

My phone vibrates on the kitchen counter, and I get up to see who it is. I smile like a goof, because it's Dylan. He hasn't messaged me since our birthday a few nights ago.

> I haven't heard from you, are you okay?
>
> *Yeah, I am. Eventful couple of days.*
>
> You can tell me all about it over dinner, tomorrow night.
>
> *Maybe I don't want to go out with you.* I jokingly tease.
>
> Now that's a load of BS. Of course, you want to go to dinner with me. I'm funny, and charming, and my father really likes you. It's a no brainer.

I look at my phone, and chuckle.

"Oh, someone's made Molly happy. Is it the boy from the restaurant?" Mom asks.

"Yeah, it is. He's asking me to dinner tomorrow night. I'm not sure if I should go."

"Why not?" Mom asks.

"Let the girl be, she doesn't need to date," Dad chides her.

"Dad, you're being overprotective," Tina responds.

"We don't need two teenage girls dating." He pointedly looks at Tina then me.

"It's just dinner, Thomas," Mom says.

"Are you done discussing if I should or shouldn't go?" I look to the three of them.

Dad makes a grumbling sound. Mom and Tina both smile. "I think you should go, it's only dinner. Not sex, or marriage," Tina says.

"Hey, I don't want to hear about that," Dad says.

Mom's holding in a smile. Tina rolls her eyes and shakes her head. She reaches for another slice of pizza.

"Do you think I should go?" I ask all of my family.

"No," Dad responds with conviction.

"Yeah," Mom and Tina reply together.

A small smile tugs at my lips. Dad's reaction is exactly what I thought it would be. "It's just dinner," I say trying to justify it, more to myself than to Dad.

"Yeah, and make him pay," Tina says.

"No, these days you go halves," Mom protests.

"If you're going out with him, you make him pay," Dad chimes in, having lost his earlier fight.

I stare at the message and try to think of what I can say. *Seeing as your Dad likes me, then I'd better let you take me to dinner.*

I smile. Then add, *I'm only doing it for your dad. As a favor to him.*

I place my phone face down on the table, and sit back. "Okay, I'm going out on a date with Dylan tomorrow."

"When do we get to meet him?" Dad asks.

"Maybe never. I don't know. We'll go for dinner tomorrow, and I'll see how things turn out."

Dad points at me with his slice of pizza. "No funny business."

"No funny business," I echo. "Trust me."

"It's not you I'm worried about. How old is Dylan?"

"We've gone over this. No idea," I candidly answer. "I assume he's at least twenty-five judging by the way he acted when I first met him."

Dad grumbles. "If he hurts you, I'll end his life."

Aww, I think every father has said that to his daughter at least once in their life. Dad says it to Tina every time she finds a new boyfriend. Usually it's Tina who ends up doing the hurting.

My phone vibrates again, but I don't rush to get it. Dylan can wait. Family dinner is way more important than setting up a date.

"Hey, Tina, what are you doing?"

"Listening to music. You okay?" She sits up on her bed, crossing her legs. "You look worried."

"I'm kinda second guessing myself about tomorrow night."

"Your date?" I nod. "What's the problem?"

"You know I'm not like you, right?" I sit on her bed, Zhen lays beside me. Zorro is nowhere to be seen. He's taken a liking to Dad, so he tends to be where Dad is when he's home.

"What do you mean?"

"I mean, we're complete opposites. You're so bubbly and outgoing, and I'm really not. I'm nothing like you."

"So? What are you getting at?" She shrugs one shoulder.

I wring my hands nervously. "I'm not sure if I'll be able to talk to him. Or what to talk about. What if he wants to try something, you know?"

"Like a kiss? Or something more?"

"I'm not having sex with him. If he thinks he can try that on me, then it's not happening." My stomach jumps with uncertainty. Sex isn't something I've ever really wanted to do. Well, not yet.

"Listen, you're meeting him there, right?"

"Yeah, he said he'd pick me up, but I don't want him knowing where I live. Not yet. You know he might turn into some crazy-ass stalker guy." Tina laughs. "What?"

"Not everyone is nuts. But he might be."

I throw a pillow at her. "Why, 'cause he asked me out?"

"You're such a dork. If he makes you feel uncomfortable, text me, and I'll be right there. Actually, I can come along if it makes you feel better."

I let out a laugh. "Yeah, good thinking. No!"

"How about I meet up with Preston at one of the cafés close to where you're having dinner? If anything happens, then I'm close."

Just the thought of having Tina nearby eases my shaky thoughts and feelings. "I don't want to put you out. Don't worry about it." I feel like I'm a burden to her.

"Don't be a dumb-ass, Molly. You'd do it for me, wouldn't you?"

"In a heartbeat," I answer candidly.

"Good, 'cause that means I get to go out with Preston again. I really like him," Tina says. She runs her hands through her hair, then twirls some around her finger. I've never seen her so hung-up on anyone.

"Then you should go for it. When do I get to meet him?"

"How about we double-date?"

"Not tomorrow?" I ask a little too forcefully.

"No, not tomorrow. What about Sunday? If it all works out for you and what's-his-face, then you can ask him if he wants to double-date with Preston and me."

"Dylan." I tilt my head as my brows arch.

"Yeah, yeah, him. What do you think? I can suss Dylan out, and you can suss Preston out. Then we can compare notes."

"Yeah, that'll be cool. Thank you." I lean over and give her a hug. "I'm going to bed, I'm so tired."

"It's nine o'clock. Since when have you become a grandma?"

"I'm not a grandma. I think the last couple of days have really caught up with me. You know the guy at the park, our birthday. All of that."

"Night, stinky butt."

"Really?" I say as I turn to look at Tina before I leave her room. "Stinky butt?"

"I was referring to the dog," she teases.

"No, you weren't."

"No, I wasn't," she giggles at the same time.

Zhen and I head back to my room. I take a quick shower, get changed into my pajamas, and crawl into bed. Zhen's already asleep on my bed by the time I'm in. I grab my Air Pods, and turn on my meditation music. It doesn't take me long before I'm sound asleep.

CHAPTER 5

Walking into the restaurant, I half expect for Dylan to not be here. We decided to meet at Cracker Barrel, a popular restaurant where there are always a few people. You can never be too safe.

I head inside, and look around for Dylan.

"Table for one?" the woman at the front asks.

"No, I'm meeting someone. For two, please."

She picks up two menus, and I follow her while keeping an eye out in case Dylan's already here. I should've told him I'd meet him outside.

A few moments pass, and I begin to worry when he doesn't arrive. I check the time on my phone, and frown. He's only five minutes late, I say to myself.

Tapping my fingers, I look around Cracker Barrel. There are families and couples all sitting and enjoying their meals. I feel self-conscious being the only person sitting on their own.

I check my phone again. He's ten minutes late.

It makes me feel better to know Tina and Preston are only a couple of streets away and can be here in a moment.

Rejection takes over from the worry, and I'm feeling hurt and abandoned. I wish Zhen was here with me. He'd put his head on my lap, and the hurt would instantly melt away.

Twelve minutes late.

I'm not going to sit here like a fool. I'll give him three more minutes, and then I'll delete his number and block his ass.

I look up and see Dylan standing at the hostess counter. He looks around, sees me, says something to the waitress, and walks toward me.

Right away I see a black smudge on his face. And then the same black is on the front of his jeans too.

I'm not sure what to think. Why's he so dirty?

He approaches the table, sets his phone and car keys down on it and says, "I have to go to the bathroom. I'll explain when I get back. I'm so sorry I'm late."

He doesn't give me a chance to respond. He dashes off behind me, leaving only his belongings on the table. I don't feel rejected now, but I have no idea what's happening.

Am I being punked? I look around the restaurant in case I see a camera inconspicuously placed somewhere.

I look over the menu, but my mind is traveling so fast, I can't concentrate on it. I'm in a whirlwind of emotions.

"I'm sorry," Dylan says as he slides into the chair opposite me. His face now clear of the black smudge. "I was trying to get here earlier, so I'd be waiting for you. But on the way, my car had a flat tire and I had to change it."

"Oh," I say. "Explains the black marks down the front of your jeans."

"I couldn't go home to change. Well, I could, but you would've been sitting here for another fifteen minutes. And I didn't want that."

"Right." I look down at the menu. I fidget with my hands under the table.

"I'm really happy you agreed to come to dinner with me." I smile, but don't say anything.

My stomach is going nuts, and my pulse is hammering through my veins. How awkward. I'm such a mess. I want to say something, but I have no idea what to say.

"Tell me about what's been happening. Last night you said you've had an eventful few days. What's happening?" he asks.

"Other than your *eighteenth* birthday." He says eighteenth in a strained way, almost like he's embarrassed way.

"Okay, let's do this," I say. He looks at me questioningly. "You're still hung up about my age. So, how old are you?"

He gives me a small smile. "I'll be turning twenty-seven soon."

"Ew," I say and scrunch up my nose. "I really shouldn't be having dinner with such an old man."

"I'm not that old," he snaps.

"Then why are you hell bent on having an issue with my age, when you just said, *'I'm not that old'?"*

"You know, you're nothing like anyone I've ever met before, Molly."

"Good, because everyone else you've ever met hasn't lasted."

"How do you know?" he asks, defensively.

"Because you wouldn't be sitting here with me now."

Dylan says nothing, instead he stares at me. Looking hard into my eyes. I keep his gaze, refusing to back away. It takes him to the count of fourteen before he says, "You're remarkable."

"Yes, I am," I agree.

He gives me another smile. This one tells me something else. It tells me the whole age gap thing isn't going to be a problem for him for long. *Hopefully.*

"I know you turned eighteen. And I know you said you were adopted. What else can you tell me?"

I half shrug. "What do you want to know?"

"When were you adopted?"

"I was seven when I came to live with Thomas and Paris, but I call them Mom and Dad. They're the only real parents I've ever known. What about you? You introduced me to your father. Where's your mom?"

"She's somewhere, with someone and her new family. By "new," I mean I think I have two half-brothers. But I have no idea. She couldn't handle being a mom, so she left."

"And started a new family?" Dylan nods. "Ouch, that's got to hurt."

"It did when she left. But after a lot of therapy, and Dad stepping up and being not only my Dad but my Mom, too. I think I turned out okay."

"Jury's still out," I say in a small voice. Dylan chuckles. "And you decided to be a security analyst? How did that happen?"

"I fell into the job. And thankfully, I love doing it. What do you want to do when you graduate? What college are you wanting to get into?"

"I'm not going to college, yet."

"What? Why?"

"I'm taking a gap year."

"What are you going to do? Travel? See the world?"

"I don't do well if I'm out of my comfort zone, so no travel for me. I'm going to work. I teach yoga one day a week at one of the gyms' to kids under sixteen."

"You like yoga? That's cool."

"Yeah, I find it keeps me grounded."

"Do you like movies?"

"I prefer music to movies. I fall asleep watching them. I also have two dogs. Zhen, he's my Labrador. And as of very recent, I have another dog, Zorro."

"Zhen and Zorro. What type of dog is Zorro?"

"The vet said he's a Boxer cross with who knows what."

"What about where you got him from? They couldn't tell you what breed he is?"

"Yeah, that's a story in itself."

"Hi, welcome to Cracker Barrel. Are you ready to order?" the waitress asks.

"I'll have the Barrel Cheeseburger, and a side order of fries, please." I hand her the menu once I've ordered.

"And I'll have the grilled sirloin steak with house salad and fries. I'll have my steak well-done, please."

The waitress takes the menus and leaves.

"You were telling me about Zorro."

I recap what happened at the dog park. I watch as Dylan's jaw tightens, and his brows furrow together. When I finish, he clicks his tongue to the roof of his mouth. "Are you okay?" I ask.

"Ha," he huffs. "Am I okay?" He shakes his head. "No, not at all."

"I know, it makes me sick to the stomach to witness animal abuse."

"Molly, can I be honest about something?"

I blink twice before I talk. "The only thing I want is honesty. Please spare me any bullshit."

He lets out a humorless chuckle. "The animal cruelty is sickening, but the fact you were in danger, that makes my blood boil. No woman—no, I'll correct that – *no person* should ever be made to feel unsafe. There's no need for violence."

"I had Zhen. There was no way Zhen would've allowed him to put his hands on me."

"I'm grateful you have a dog that's so protective of you, but it still makes me very angry."

"At me?" I'm confused.

"Not at you. At the monster who punched a defenseless dog, and threatened you."

"It's in police hands now."

"I'd still like to know who he is," he says under his breath.

I shake my head. "You don't solve violence with violence."

He looks amused. "You're wise beyond your years." He huffs.

I sigh heavily. "Okay, I'm going to tell you something. This whole age thing is getting old. If you keep referring back to my age when you think I've said something insightful, I can't see us going any further than tonight. You keep bringing my age up, and eventually it's going to cause a rift. So either stop, or thank you for tonight, please don't contact me again." I'm sick and tired of him having an issue with my age.

He sits back in his chair, and crosses his arms in front of his chest. I can spot a defensive maneuver anywhere. "Okay." He nods his head. "I don't want whatever we have to start off on the wrong foot. I'll be more conscious of what I say."

"Thank you."

"I'm going to say this, and I hope it doesn't offend you. But you are so unique. You have a fire inside you that I don't think I've ever seen in anyone else. And I like it. I like it a lot. You're quiet and humble. But there's an inferno burning hot beneath the surface that everyone sees."

I cock an eyebrow, surprised. Licking my lips, I try to distract myself from the beautiful, perceptive man sitting opposite me. His words resonate deeply within me. I'm not sure why, though.

"I'm just trying to be the best version of myself. I'm not hiding anything."

"Molly, I like how you keep me on my toes. You aren't afraid to call me on my crap. The women I've dated before, they laugh in all the right places, but they don't have substance."

"You're the one picking them, not me."

He laughs again. "Ouch. You're not afraid to tell me what you're thinking either. I like that."

"I'll be honest with you, Dylan, as long as you're honest with me."

"Always."

"Good, then tell me about Dylan. Has he ever been married?"

"God, no. I'm not keen on marriage. Nor kids. Kids don't do it for me. What about you?"

"Well, considering I live at home with my parents, I think they'd kick my butt if I told them I want to get married. But marriage isn't something I can see me doing. Not yet. I'm too young, unlike you who's an old man."

"Hey, who's playing the age card now?"

"That would be me. Obviously."

Dylan laughs.

"Here are your meals," the same waitress returns and places two incredibly large, full white plates in front of us.

"Yum," I say looking at my mouthwatering burger. "Just an FYI, I love my food. And I will eat it with gusto. If I make a mess, I don't care."

"I think this is real love. A woman who loves her food."

"Not only do I love food, I'm not going to share. However, at any point if I want to have some of yours, it's written in the rule book that you have to share."

"Is it?" he asks as he nibbles on a fry.

"It's state law. Hell, I'm pretty sure it's federal law too." I lean over and steal a fry from his plate, chewing on it happily. "Now if you tried that, I'm fairly sure there'd be secret-food riot police waiting to drop from the ceiling to arrest you. You can try it, but I don't like your chances."

Dylan looks up, and I sit watching, smugly. "I think I'm going to have to follow the rule book. I wouldn't want to be arrested by the secret-food riot squad. Man, how would I explain that to my Dad?"

I shrug my shoulders. "That's what you have to ask yourself. Is it worth the criminal record? I think not."

Dylan cuts into his steak, leans over and places it on my plate. He's given me a piece before he's even tasted it. "It's the law."

A huge cheesy grin tugs on my lips. "You know. You may have my approval, but I'm not the one you have to worry about."

"Your sister?" he asks

"Tina? She'll be happy as long as I'm happy."

"Your father?"

"Dad's the same."

"Your mother? Mom's usually like me."

"Oh no. Mom's easy going. You have to worry about Zhen. If Zhen doesn't like you, then I'm sorry, but this is where the train stops."

I know he's a good guy. I can feel it deep in my stomach. There's something soothing about Dylan. He looks up from cutting his steak. "If your dog doesn't like me, then we're not going out again?" he asks with a blank expression.

"Zhen is protective of me. He might sense something in you that I can't."

He cuts into his steak and eats it, then takes another bite. "What treats does Zhen like? I want him to let me stick around."

I let out a laugh a little too loud. "Zhen can't be bribed with treats. If you like though, the next time I take the boys to the dog park, I can let you know and you can meet us?"

My heart beats way too fast. I want him to say yes, but who knows if he will.

"I'd like that. You know, I'm not working tomorrow, and I happen to be in town near the dog park."

"What time are you heading wherever you're going?" I ask as I take a huge bite of my burger. I feel the juice squirt out the side of my mouth and cling to my chin.

"Whatever time you'll be there."

I chew my food, quickly swallow, and wipe my chin. "Do you live with your dad?" I ask.

He shakes his head. "No, I have my own apartment. Dad lives six streets away from me."

"That's nice. You stuck close to where he lives."

"Actually, he bought there after I moved into my apartment. He's following me."

"Awe, that's cute. Are you close?"

"Yeah, really close. It's just been me and dad, I relied on him a lot growing up. I still do."

"Yeah?"

"Yeah, you know, he's always there. If I need something, he's there." I take another giant bite of my burger. "You're loving your food."

"I warned you."

"A woman with a hearty appetite is refreshing to see. That's it, Molly, I'm taking you to a Japanese steakhouse."

"What now? What's a Japanese steakhouse?"

"Hibachi?" he asks as if I should know what he's talking about.

"No idea."

"We're so going. Are you allergic to anything?"

"Not to my knowledge. I'm not a huge meat fan, but I love my burgers."

"I can see." He makes a gesture, wiping at his cheek. "You've got sauce everywhere."

I flick my hand dismissively at him. "It's only sauce."

"You eat with gusto." I shrug, I suppose I do. "Tell me about yoga. What made you get into yoga?"

"I like meditation. And I found yoga and meditation work well together. It relaxes me and keeps me grounded. Have you tried it?"

"Uh, no. Yoga isn't for me."

I roll my eyes. Here we go, another 'it's not a man's thing.' "Why not?"

"I'm not flexible. I think it could, um." He runs his hand through his short hair and looks around to make sure no one's listening. "I think it could hurt me in the groin area."

"You'd be surprised."

"Maybe you can teach me."

"Are you just saying this so you can score extra brownie points with me?"

"Is it working?" he asks, enthusiastically.

"Hmm." I take my napkin, and wipe my face. "I'll let Zhen decide if I should be impressed with you."

He holds his hand out to shake mine. Hesitantly I extend my hand and shake his. "Deal. We'll let Zhen decide. Tomorrow."

"Tomorrow," I say.

I like Dylan. I've got a good vibe about him. He doesn't make me uneasy. I feel safe with him near.

Hopefully Zhen and Zorro will like him, too.

CHAPTER 6

The dogs and I get to the dog park, and I see Dylan standing in front of the entrance. I can't help but smile.

He came. Yay!

I park my car, and open the back door. Both Zhen and Zorro are eager to jump out. I take their leads, and let them out of the car.

Walking up to the entrance, Dylan sees me. A huge smile lights up his face.

He's really, *really* handsome. A baseball cap covers his dirty blond hair. While a pair of sleek sunglasses shield his brown eyes.

"Hey," I say when I approach.

"Hi." He leans down and gives me a brief kiss on the cheek. He pulls away quickly, not making this awkward. Though it's just a peck, something happens to me. My skin tingles, and I feel nervous butterflies fluttering in my stomach. "Here are the infamous Zhen and Zorro. Let me guess." He points to my Labrador. "Zhen, for sure. Which means you must be Zorro." He doesn't hesitate, he gives both dogs a scratch on their back.

"Yeah. Should we go in? I brought two balls. Thought maybe you'd like to throw one."

"Sure." He opens the gate, and waits until we're in, before

closing. He walks beside me with his hands in his pockets. "Um, are you okay?" He must be sensing this weird feeling.

"Yeah, I am. I wasn't sure if you'd show up." It's a partial truth. I wasn't, but that peck on the cheek is kind of making feel jittery and excited. Ugh, these are unknown feelings. I shake my head, trying to push that feeling away. There's no logical reason why I'd be feeling like this.

We sit on one of the bench seats, and I let the dogs off their leads. They both run together. "Why wouldn't I show up? I like you."

"Have you got pets?" I ask.

"God, no. I had a fish once, when I was about twelve."

"Yeah? What was the fish's name?"

Dylan casually slings his elbow up on the back part of the bench seat. He starts laughing. "You're gonna think it's stupid. And it was."

"The fish or the fish's name?"

"The name."

"Okay, let's start with an easier question. What kind of fish was it?"

"It was a goldfish." He turns his head, and laughs again. "And his name was Sushi." He tries to contain his laughter, but his broad shoulders are shaking. "Man, I'm going to Hell for that one, aren't I?"

"Sushi?" I ask, and laugh too. "As long as you didn't eat him, then I don't think Hell is the place for you."

"I didn't eat him. But I did kill him."

"What?" The smile on my face fades fast. "How?"

"I gave him an entire container of fish food."

I clasp my hand to my mouth. "Why?"

"'Cause I was a dumb kid."

"Please tell me you've never had another animal?"

Dylan's expression says it all. He screws his nose up, then quickly nods. "Yeah, I did."

"Oh no. What did you have?"

"I had a bird. He was nice. He'd sing all the time. And when we didn't want him to sing, we'd put a sheet over his cage, and he'd go to sleep."

"He sounds nice."

Dylan screws his nose up again. "Yeah he was. A really nice bird, actually. He was pretty. Blue and white."

"Should I ask his name?"

"Oh man." Dylan cringes as he looks away. "Roadkill."

"No! You're nasty with names. Tell me you didn't overfeed him too?"

"No, no. Something far more sinister."

"Oh god. Do I want to know?"

"I don't have to tell you."

"You can't say that. Now I want to know. Just rip the Band-Aid off and tell me."

"I cleaned his cage, and I hadn't clicked in the top wire part properly. Roadkill stuck his head under to try and get out, but he got stuck, and snapped his own neck."

"Dylan. You suck at looking after animals!" I'm completely shocked at how bad he is with animals.

"I know. To this very day, I still feel bad. But I promise you, I'll do better with your dogs."

"Nope. You're never looking after my boys. Not knowing you have the touch of death." Zhen runs back to me, and wags his tail. I give Dylan a sideways glance. I can see he wants to put his hand down for Zhen to sniff him. This must be a big deal for him, because he knows how important Zhen and Zorro are to me. "I'm trusting you. Dylan. Put your hand down slowly, and let Zhen come to you. If he likes you, he'll smell you, rub himself on your leg, maybe lick your hand. If he doesn't, he'll just smell you and walk away. But he's really protective of me, so if he thinks you're trying to hurt me, he won't back down."

"I'd never hurt you, Molly," Dylan says even before I have a chance of finishing my sentence.

"Zhen, this is Dylan. Dylan, this is my best dog, Zhen." Zhen wags his tail. Dylan slowly drops his hand down, waiting for Zhen's reaction. I keep scratching Zhen's back, and when Zhen takes a step toward Dylan, I stop.

Zhen takes a good minute to smell Dylan, maybe even longer.

He gives Dylan's knuckles a small lick, then goes back to sniffing him. I raise my gaze to look at Dylan. He's watching Zhen as Zhen inspects him. Zhen finally gives his hand another lick, then rubs his torso up against Dylan's leg before returning to me.

"He likes me!" Dylan says too loudly and excitedly.

"He does." I say while Zorro runs toward us. He's only been with us for a few days, but he's like a different dog, a carefree and happy dog. He runs straight over to us, lifts his leg and pees on the bench leg closest to Dylan. Some of his pee splashes on Dylan's shoes. "Of course." Dylan lets his head fall back.

The laughter inside bursts through. "They do say if a dog pees on you, they really like you," I say.

"Do they?" Dylan asks.

"No idea, I just made that up to make you feel better."

"I didn't like these shoes anyway." He shrugs.

Dylan's being too much of a gentleman to admit that his shoes look relatively new. "I have a question for you, and feel free to say no."

"You're already giving me an option to back out. What if I don't want to back out?"

"Then you can say yes."

"What if, now we've talked about it, I don't want to say yes, but I'm being forced to because we know I can't really say no?" He smiles cheekily.

I rub my fingers over my temple. "You're overcomplicating everything. It's either a yes, or a no. My sister wants to go on a double-date."

"The sister I met at the mall?"

"I don't have any other sisters so yes, Tina."

I wonder what he's thinking. Is he ready to bolt out of here, or is he thinking of a way to let me down nicely? "Okay," he says after a few seconds of pause.

"What?" His reply shocks me. "Why would you say yes?" Is there something wrong with him?

"Why would I say no to spending more time with you? I told

you, I like you. And if your sister wants to put me through the proverbial wringer, I'm fine with that."

"But you're so calm about it."

"You know what was really obvious to me the day I met you at the mall?" I shake my head. "You and your sister have a tight, special relationship. You both adore each other. Which means she's protective of you, and I want you to be comfortable around me. So I'll show up for inspection."

I want to pinch myself. Dylan is not only incredibly nice looking, he's also charming and understanding. I just hope he's not saying what he thinks I want to hear. I mean, he has passed the Zhen test, now he has to pass the Tina test.

"We are. Fiercely protective. We've both been given a privileged life, and neither of us want to see it go to waste on something irrelevant."

"Are you calling me irrelevant?" Dylan's tone is slightly off. I think I've hurt his feelings.

I have to think what to say to tell him, it's not personal. "Every night I lay in bed, and think to myself, was I the best version of myself today? The nights I can't sleep, I know I wasn't. I wasn't meaning that *you're* irrelevant, I'm meaning, *I* don't want to be."

Dylan nods his head. "I like that. That's actually very deep. It's something even I wouldn't think of."

"Mom has always said I've lived a thousand lives already. For some reason, I tend to believe her."

"I'll make you a deal. After we double-date with your sister, I'd like to take you to dinner with my Dad. He likes you, and I think it's important for him to meet you."

"I'm okay with that."

"My Dad's opinion matters a lot to me, just like your family's opinion matters to you. Dad's straight up. He tells it like he sees it. He doesn't sugar coat anything at all."

"I'm not into bullshit, so I guess your dad and I will get on great."

"I'm hundred percent sure I'll be the one walking into the lion's den."

"Hey, my family isn't like that."

"I wasn't referring to your family. I was referring to my father." He laughs. "Just an FYI. He will embarrass me as much as he can."

"That's what family does." Zhen and Zorro got bored with us talking a few moments ago, and went to play. Both come back, but Zhen is limping. "Shit," I say as I stand and run over to him. I fall to my knees, as Zhen sits. Zorro sits beside me. "What did you do?" I pick Zhen's paw up, and see he's got a small twig penetrating his paw pad. "Hang on, let me see. Can I take this out or do we have to go back to Michael?"

"Is he okay?" Dylan asks as he squats beside me.

Zorro swings his head to look at Dylan, but doesn't move. "I'm not sure. There's a small twig stuck in the edge of his paw." I scratch under Zhen's chin. "Let me see if I can pull it out." Zhen's panting heavily. "If he cries, I'm taking him to the vet."

"Do you want me to do it?" Dylan asks.

"Chivalrous, but no. Zhen probably won't let you touch him."

"Okay."

I tug on the twig, and it has a lot of give. Slowly, I pull it out. The moment it's out, he starting licking his paw. "I've got to get you home so we can put some ointment on it and bandage it up." Dylan and I both stand. "I have to go, I'm sorry."

"Don't be sorry. Go, take care of Zhen."

"Thank you," I smile, glad he understands. "Um, tomorrow?"

"We'll talk later. Call or text me after you've taken care of Zhen."

We walk toward the bench seat where the dogs' leashes are. Zhen's still limping, but not as bad. It must be sore. Dylan walks us to my car, and opens the back door for the dogs. They both jump in and Dylan closes it.

Fumbling with my keys, I don't look up to Dylan. "I'll text you later," I say stiffly. I'm not sure what happens here.

"Molly, is it okay if I kissed you?"

I know we have a connection. I can feel it. It's easy and light, and we just meld into each other. I'm not sure I'm ready for this, though. Other than Hank Reed, I've never really been kissed. Kissing is so intimate and personal. I imagine souls can connect with a perfect kiss.

"It's okay," he says stepping away, obviously affected by my hesitation.

I've over thought it. I've created this huge monster ready to destroy the thought of being kissed. "I'm sorry," I say embarrassed. Lowering my head, I refuse to look at Dylan. What a fool. I can't believe I self-sabotaged what could be with Dylan. "Um, I'll message you later." I jump in my car fast, not looking back at Dylan. I've made a total mess of this.

I'm in my car and out of there so fast, Dylan is but a mere distant memory.

What an idiot.

What happened?

Frustrated and angry at myself, I drive home.

CHAPTER 7

I messaged you last night, and you didn't reply. Is Zhen okay?

Ignore.

Is everything okay?

Ignore.

I'm looking forward to our double-date.

Ignore.

I didn't get any more messages last night. And I didn't sleep well either. I wasn't the best version of myself. I was an ass. An ass who let her head get in the way. I roll over, and try to move the blanket up, but Zhen's sleeping on it, making it hard to shift him. "Move over, Zhen." That doesn't work. He's sleeping hard.

Reaching for my phone, there's another message from Dylan. *Good morning.*

I want to reply, but I think it's best if I don't. What can I offer him? He asked to kiss me, and I froze. What the hell was that?

I throw the covers back, sit up in bed. Scrubbing my hand over my face, I try to stop thinking about my bizarre behavior yesterday.

Instead I focus on the class I have to teach at eleven. I head into the bathroom, and have a quick shower before getting ready for class.

Turning, I see Zhen's still asleep on my bed, although he's moved and is sleeping on his back with his hind legs spread apart, but his front legs are making the motion of running. How cute, and funny. "Zhen," I say. He jumps up and looks around him. He must've been dreaming. "Come on." I hit my thigh twice, and he jumps off the bed and casually strolls toward me. "Today would be nice." He takes his time as he walks toward me.

I rush down the stairs, heading into the kitchen, and pour out Zhen's and Zorro's kibble. "Do you have a class?" Dad asks from his usual chair at the kitchen table.

"Morning, Dad. I do." I walk over and give Dad a kiss on the cheek. "Where's Mom?"

"Still asleep. And your sister's at Willow's, so she won't be back until much later." Zorro's lying beside Dad, watching us, but the moment he sees me pouring the kibble, he jumps up happily.

"Yeah, I knew she was there." I pour myself a coffee, and pop two pieces of bread into the toaster.

Dad's got his laptop open, and is typing on it. I butter my toast, and take it and my coffee to sit with Dad. He closes his laptop, and pushes it to the side. "Tell me about this boy."

"Dylan?" I ask and take a bite.

"Are there any others?'

"No." I chuckle. "And I don't think there'll be anything to tell of him, either." I avert my gaze, knowing Dad knows what I'm saying.

"Did something happen?" He shuffles in the seat and crosses his arms in front of him.

"No, nothing."

"Did he do something to you? Try to force you to do something you're not ready for?" Dad clears his throat. This is uncomfortable, for both of us.

"No, again, nothing like that. I just don't think we're, you know… It's nothing." I look out the glass back door, to the large, luscious green lawn beyond the patio and the pool. "I, um, it's just. I don't know, Dad."

"What don't you know?"

"I saw him yesterday. And he's really great. We get on so well. He gets my dry sense of humor, and we spar against each other. He's so nice. And Zhen likes him."

"So, what's the problem?"

I sigh, lift my mug, and take a sip of my coffee. "I think I am."

"Why? What happened to make you feel like this?"

I don't want to tell Dad. I know he's protective of all of us. And the fact is, I've never had a boyfriend before, so he'll be extra protective of me. "He asked me if he could kiss me."

"And what happened?" Dad asks in a cool, controlled voice.

I shrug, and slightly shake my head. "I froze. He asked, and I froze. That's it." A stupid tear rolls down my cheek, and I quickly wipe it away. My soul feels tender, and bruised. "I think I'm broken."

"Darling, you're not broken. You're scared. And that's okay to be scared. We can't always be fearless. Sometimes, we have to let our guards down."

"I don't know how, though."

"First thing you have to do is tell him you're scared."

"What if he laughs?"

"Then you lift your chin, you hold your head high, and you get out of there. Because if a man laughs when you tell them you're feeling vulnerable, they're not for you. They're not worthy of you."

Dad surprises me. His advice is logical and sound. "I might reply to his texts."

"How many texts has he sent?" his tone is harsh and cold, again.

"Three yesterday after the dog park, and one this morning."

"Okay, that's doesn't qualify as crazy-ass stalker. If it was double-figures or more, I'd be telling you to delete his number and run. But four, that tells me he cares." He takes a sip of his coffee. "Talk to him. Tell him how you feel. If he's good for you, then he'll understand. If he's not, he won't."

Dad's right. If Dylan is sincere, then he'll have to understand that I'm not ready for intimacy the way he may be. "Thanks, Dad. I've got to get to work. I'll see you later, okay?"

"I'm taking your mother out to lunch, so we may not be home when you get back."

"Okay." I grab my car keys, give Zhen a quick scratch and leave.

Jumping into my car, I head to work.

It's a good fifteen minutes' drive, so I turn the volume up, and get into the rhythm of the music.

I find parking around the block from the gym, and pass by the café on the corner. It always smells amazing when I walk past. They make the best muffins. Their apple and cinnamon is my favorite. They've got a few tables and chairs on the sidewalk, and those seats are usually occupied.

When I head into the gym. Sky, one of the owners, is standing at the front desk. She's an absolutely beautiful woman. When she was younger, she was a model and even had been on the cover of *Vanity Fair, Vogue,* and *Elle.* Her striking blonde features, and amazing big eyes make her a head turner.

"Hi, Molly," Sky says and gives me one of her perfect smiles.

"Hi, Sky" I look around to search for Sky's wife, Charlotte. "Is Charlotte here today?'

"Nah, she's got a family emergency. I didn't need to be there, so I'm here and she's there."

"Cool."

"Actually, before you go to class, I wanted to talk to you about something."

"Sure, what's up?"

"Before you finished school, you asked if there were any extra classes you could teach. Are you still interested?"

"Yes!" I cry enthusiastically.

Sky smiles. We stop talking for a moment as Sky has a quick chat with one of the regular members who uses the gym facility. "Great. As of next week, we're changing the class you run. It's now an under eighteen class, and it'll be every Monday, Wednesday, and Friday. Do you think you'd want to teach it?"

"Oh my god? Really? You want me to teach three days a week?"

"Yeah, it seems the kids like you. And we've had a lot of calls about taking the class. The classes are yours, if you want to run them."

"Yes!" I shout again. This time I run around the desk, and give her a big hug. "Thank you. I'm speechless, just...thank you!"

"You're welcome. I know you're reliable and hardworking, so it was an obvious choice for us. You'll get a pay raise too."

This is a dream for me. I'm so happy Sky and Charlotte have asked me to take the classes. I head up to the classroom, give it a quick vacuum, and get ready for my class.

No one can wipe the smile off my face.

Walking out of the gym, I feel wonderful. I had a great class, and the kids I teach are really respectful and chill. They want to be there; they're not forced to come. I sling my yoga bag over my shoulder and head toward my car.

But something stops me from taking another step. Every morsel of happiness is sucked out of my body.

I see Dylan at the café, sitting at one of the outdoor tables and talking to a woman with long, brown hair that falls to just above her waist. She's leaning into him, but he's sitting back in his chair holding his cup as he laughs at something said in their conversation.

I knew he was too good to be true. He's not anything like he's pretended to be. I should've known. He stares straight at me.

I can't move; my feet are grounded to the spot. I can't believe my eyes. This isn't real.

Dylan smiles and lifts his hand to wave, but he quickly lowers it. His eyes become large, and his mouth falls open. I've caught him in his deceit.

Lowering my head, I find my strength and walk past him.

"Molly," he calls. I ignore him. I'm so mad at me. I was allowing myself to feel something for him, and he's with someone else. "Molly." I have no right to be upset with him. We've only gone out twice and we haven't discussed being exclusive. But it still hurts. It hurts so bad. "Molly!"

I can hear him running behind me. He grabs my arm and swings me around to face him. "Please, no need to explain," I say trying to remain diplomatic, though really I'm kicking myself internally.

"Explain?" He tilts his head to the side. "Are you upset?"

"No, I'm not." I muster all my willpower and smile at him. "I have to go." I try to duck past him, but he stops me again. "Please," I silently beg for him to spare me.

"Would you like to meet my cousin Gemma?"

I close my eyes, instantly feeling like a fool. "Your cousin."

"My cousin," he echoes.

I had jumped ahead and thought the worst of him, when he's given me no reason to react like this. "I'm sorry," I say, embarrassed. "I feel like an idiot."

"Don't be sorry. I get it, really I do."

"You do?" I look up at him, still too ashamed to meet his eyes.

"I do. I was seeing a woman two years ago, and I had a gut feeling she was hiding something. It was niggling away at me. I asked her, and she said it was all in my head. It was sending me crazy. Until…" He closes his eyes and shakes his head. Opening them, he struggles to continue, but he does. "Until I saw her having sex with another guy in my car."

"Oh man," I say, clutching at my chest.

"Yep." He screws his mouth up and looks away. "The point is, it devastated me, and I vowed to never make someone else feel like that. If I want to leave, I will tell the person I'm with. I wouldn't ever cheat on you. I couldn't do that because I know how much it hurts." I nod, still avoiding his eyes. "Please, come meet Gemma. I was just telling her about you."

"You were?"

"I was." He holds his hand out, and even though my internal voice is still telling me he's lying, I know he's not. Self-sabotage at its best.

Hesitantly, I reach to take his hand. Linking our fingers together

I notice how warm he is, and how well we fit together. "I'm sorry." I know he told me I don't need to be sorry, but I behaved like a crazy stalker.

"I know. Come, meet Gemma." He leads me over to where he was sitting, and he pulls a chair out for me. "Gemma, this is Molly. Molly, my cousin Gemma."

Gemma isn't as blessed in the looks department as Dylan. She's got a crooked nose, loads of freckles, and her teeth are a little wonky. Her smile is large, and she instantly comes across as really friendly. "Hi," she says with the biggest smile I've ever seen.

"Um, hi."

"Latte?" Dylan asks. I nod my head. He holds his hand up, getting the attention of the waiter. "Can I get a latte, and do you want something to eat?" he asks.

"Have you got the apple and cinnamon muffins today?" I ask.

"We do," the waiter replies.

"I'll have one of those please."

The waiter writes down my order, and leaves.

"This is probably super awkward for you. So let me tell you a bit about myself. I'm Dylan's cousin on his dad's side. My dad and his dad are brothers. Dylan and I grew up together, and hung out a lot when his mom took off. I love long walks on the beach and reading." She starts laughing. "Romantic movies, and sharing my life with the perfect person." She sounds like a personal ad.

I can't help but laugh as well. "Do you live around here?"

"I don't live far from here. But Dylan and I have brunch once a week."

"And you picked here?" I point to the café.

"I'm local to here, Molly," Dylan says.

"Really? How local?"

He points down the street. "See that tall brown building?" I turn my attention to where he's pointing and nod. "Third floor. I'm one of the apartments there."

"Wow, that's close. How have I never seen you here before? I love this café. The muffins are delicious."

"I don't know," he shrugs. "We've probably crossed paths many times."

"Kismet," Gemma says. "You two could've walked past each other many times, and never known it."

"Kismet? I like that," Dylan says. "And I think you're right, Gemma." Gemma smiles and sips on her coffee.

"Latte, and apple and cinnamon muffin," the waiter says as he places the cup and plate in front of me.

"Thank you." I pick my coffee up and savor every drop of it.

"Dylan was saying you rescued a dog."

"Yeah, from a guy at the dog park. The guy was playing with him, then snapped and punched him."

"I wonder why he'd do that?" Gemma asks as she continues her coffee.

I take a huge bite of my muffin, and lift one finger as I chew it as quick as I can. "A few people think he could've been drug affected. But in reality, who knows? So now I have another dog. I already had one, Zhen, and he's now got a friend, Zorro."

"Oh my God! I love those names." She laughs and crinkles her nose. "Zorro. What a cool name. Does he respond to it yet? Because this only recently happened, didn't it?"

"Zorro's been with us for about a week. But he's fitting in so well. Actually, he has a strong attachment to Dad."

"Awe, that's so cute. You know, I'm glad you rescued him. I bet he's getting spoiled now he's with you," Gemma says.

"He is." I finish off my muffin in a bite, and drink the last of my latte. "Crap!" I say.

"What is it?" Dylan asks.

"I meant to make food for the dogs this morning. I have to go, I'm so sorry." I stand and pick my bag up.

"Make the food for your dogs?" Gemma asks.

"Yeah. I cook rice, peas, and carrots, and add either chicken or ground beef. I make enough for a week, but seeing as we have

Zorro now, this week's food is gone. I need to make a new batch."

Dylan stares at me. "You cook for your dogs? That's why people go to the supermarket to buy canned food."

"Nope. Not for my dogs. Nothing but the best. Keeps them healthier."

"Molly, you are impressive. I hope we can hang out more," Gemma says as she stands. She steps toward me, and gives me a hug like we've been friends for years. I like Gemma. Her heart is big, and she's honest. She gives me a good feeling.

"I hope so too. Anyway, I've gotta go."

"I'll walk you to your car," Dylan offers. "Back in a few minutes?" he says to Gemma, but it's more of a question.

"I'm not sitting here like a complete loser, twiddling my thumbs, waiting for you. Give me your keys, I'm going back to your place." She holds her hand out, waiting.

"I've got some dirty dishes in the kitchen sink." I barely know Gemma, but I doubt she's going to wash them for him.

She walks away, but turns and walks backward. "Get a maid!" She then turns forward and keeps walking.

"I like her. She makes me smile," I say.

"She can be too much sometimes, but I'd do anything for her."

I reach for Dylan's hand, linking our fingers together. Oh crap. Did I do that? Did I initiate us holding hands? Or did he do it? He's not pulling away, which means he's okay with it either way. Am I okay with it?

"You're doing it again, Molly."

"What?" I'm completely consumed in my own head.

"It's the same thing that happened yesterday."

We reach my car. I unlock it, and place my bag on the back seat, before closing the door and leaning against it. "What happened yesterday…" I know exactly what he's referring to, but I don't want to verbalize me being a jerk.

"You're fighting with yourself." I swallow hard, knowing he's right. "But I'm patient."

"I…um…" I look away for a second to gain strength. I have Dad's words stuck in my head. "I'm terrified, Dylan. I'm so scared I can't give you what you want."

"If you're talking about sex, then I'm going to stop you right there. I'll tell you this. Do I want sex from you? Absolutely. But I refuse to make you feel like you have to do something you don't want to do. I'm not putting an ounce of pressure on you. We can take this as slow as you're comfortable with."

I lean forward, and slide my arms around his waist, hugging him close to me. He smells like fresh coffee. Placing my head to his chest, I can hear his strong heartbeat. "I don't know what I'm doing," I admit.

"Neither do I." I feel his lips on the top of my head.

Pulling back, I look into his brown eyes. "You might get sick of being patient."

He shrugs and breathes in deeply. "I might. But I probably won't."

"What if it doesn't work out?"

"Then it doesn't work out."

"What if I hurt you?"

"Then I'll pick myself up, and try to mend the hurt."

I gaze past him, staring at our reflection of the store front glass. "Okay," I say.

"Okay," he says.

We'll try. And I'm not going to argue with myself anymore.

"Can I kiss you?" he asks.

My head wants to argue, but I push the crap down. "You can."

Gently he slides his hands up my arms, making my skin quiver from his warm touch. He tenderly lets his fingers skim over my neck. My body is on fire. I can feel sweat beading on my hairline. Slowly he leans down, his wicked lips only a hair's breadth from mine. The warmth of his breath touches my lips. "Is this okay?" he whispers, his voice confident.

"Yes," I sigh. Closing my eyes, I allow myself to lean into him.

His supple lips graze mine. The kiss is fragile, as if he's kissing glass. He's barely making contact with me. He softly sweeps his tongue on my bottom lip, gently asking for permission for more.

I'm overtaken by so many feelings. Excitement being the one that's coming through hardest. But I pull away, unable to continue kissing him so tenderly and seductively.

"I'm sorry," I say, and lower my hands to clutch at his t-shirt.

"Why are you sorry? I loved every single second of that. It was perfect."

"You wanted more, and I couldn't..."

"I want what you want, Molly. And truth be told, I really like when your arms are around me."

He makes my body shiver with happiness. He's just so perfect. I lean into him again, hugging him as tight as I can. His hands slide around me, embracing me to him. "Dylan?"

"Yeah."

"Can we go on that double-date with my sister?"

"Tonight?"

"Not tonight, but tomorrow."

He kisses the top of my head. "It's a date."

I step back, and give him a quick kiss on the lips. "I have to go."

"Okay. Drive safe. Text me when you're home."

"I will." I get in the car, and pull out onto the street. Dylan stays watching until I can no longer see him. I drive home on cloud nine. Maybe even above cloud nine. I can't wipe the smile off my face.

Yeah, he's a good guy and I *really* like him.

CHAPTER 8

There's a boy, no not a boy, he's a young man. Maybe my age; I don't know. He's standing in my door staring at me. "What do you want?" I ask.

He stares at me. The white t-shirt he's wearing showcase his rippled muscles.

"It's time," he says.

"Time for what?" I sit up in bed and rub at my eyes.

"You know what you have to do. It's time."

I shake my head, and rub at my sleepy eyes trying to wake myself. "I don't understand," I reply.

The boy looks at me, and tilts his head to the side. "Please, I don't want to have to do this either. But it's time," he says again.

"Time for what?" I snap at him.

He holds up an overstuffed, once-white bunny. A rumble of nausea swirls in my stomach. I know the bunny means something. But I'm not sure what.

"Can you hear it?"

"Hear what?"

The temperature in my room falls to icy, causing my skin to

pebble with goosebumps. Something's not right, I have this gut feeling something sinister is lurking nearby.

The boy-man steps forward, holding the bunny out for me. But I don't want to take it. I know that bunny is much more than it seems. It's darkness. It's hate. It's evil.

"No," I say. "I won't take it."

The boy sighs letting his shoulders fall forward. "This is what you have to do. It's your job." Has he had this argument with me before?

I blink several more times to make sure I'm not still asleep, then run my hands through my hair. "I don't even know who you are, or what you're doing in my room. So you can take that stupid rabbit, and leave." I reach for Zhen, because he always makes things better, but he's not here. I look around at the floral sheets, and the tiny bed. This isn't my room.

What's happening?

I try to gauge where I am and what's happening.

"Zhen," I call desperately trying to find him. Panic overtakes my body. My heart is beating fast, and my hands tremble.

Sitting up in bed, I reach for Zhen. He lifts his head from the mattress and stands protectively over me. I pet his head, trying to calm myself.

"I had a dream, Zhen," I tell him.

Zhen relaxes into me as I lay back down. I try to find a new comfortable position, but it doesn't matter how many times I turn, that dream remains disturbing.

I flick the covers back, and sit up in bed. Zhen jumps off the bed, and sits beside me. "You okay, boy?"

It's pitch black in my room. There's no moonlight shining through the window. There's no light at all, not even a glimmer of the stars. My eyes take only a few seconds to adjust to the dark.

"I had a dream," I say to Zhen. He wags his tail and yawns. "I saw that bunny again. It's got to mean something." Zhen turns his head, and gives me a lick on the hand.

Standing, I head into my bathroom, and splash some water on my face.

This dream felt so real. Like I know the boy from somewhere. That damn bunny, ugh. It gives me the creeps. The boy-man, not so much. But the bunny makes my skin crawl and my stomach churn with dread.

I leave the bathroom, and head down to the kitchen to get some water. Zhen hangs his head, and follows me down the staircase.

I grab a glass from the cupboard and turn on the faucet. I stare at the running water; my mind is consumed with the vivid memory of that discolored bunny.

"Are you okay?" Mom asks as she walks into the kitchen. Her hair is a mess, and she's in her mis-matched pajamas. She wipes at her eyes, and leans against the counter.

"I had a dream."

"Yeah, you okay?"

"It was actually a nightmare. I think. I don't know."

"What happened?"

It's all fuzzy now, except for the sharp image of that damned bunny. "I don't remember all of it. Except, I saw that rabbit again."

"What rabbit?" Mom walks around behind me, and takes a glass from one of the top cabinets. She fills her glass with water, then returns to lean against the counter. All the while, I keep seeing the bunny. The big, floppy ears. The discolored body. The beady little blue eyes. I know it's a children's toy, and stuffed animals make kids happy. But this one is making me anxious, and I have a sick feeling in my gut. "What rabbit?" she asks again.

"Remember when I rescued Zorro?" Mom nods. "I told you, just before I confronted that guy, I saw an image of a bunny. Remember? I even asked you if I had a bunny when you adopted me."

"Oh, yeah. Can you tell me anything else about the dream?"

"Nothing else." I rub my fingers across my eyes, trying hard to remember what I can. "Um, I think there was a guy in my dream. I don't remember, Mom. But this damned rabbit." I walk over to the table, and drag out a chair before sitting. Zhen lays down on the floorboards, and within a moment, his paws are moving like he's running.

Mom comes to sit beside me. "I don't know how to help you. All I can tell you is you didn't have much when we adopted you."

"I know." I exhale a long-drawn-out breath. "I just wish I knew why I keep seeing this rabbit. What does it mean? Mom, is there something wrong with me?" I hate feeling so hopeless.

"There's nothing wrong with you," she assures me.

"Is there nothing you can tell me about my life before I came here? Nothing at all?"

Mom looks away and shakes her head. "What I know, I've already told you."

I'm so frustrated. I wish I knew more. "Do you think I could research where I came from?"

Mom's head whips back to look at me. "I don't think that's a good idea, Molly."

"Why?"

She averts her eyes, and chews on the inside of her cheek. Does she know more than she's ever said? "I think you should leave the past where it belongs."

"But this dream...and the rabbit. Maybe it's trying to tell me something. Maybe I should try to figure this out. What if all this is meant to be a warning or something? I don't know, Mom. I don't know what to do."

"How about this." She pauses, and I wait for her to continue. "Leave it for now. You never know, maybe this rabbit doesn't mean anything at all. You're going through a lot of changes and this rabbit has only appeared since your life has taken a turn."

"What do you mean?"

"Dylan, and Zorro, and now work. Maybe they're triggering something that you've buried. Or possibly, maybe the change is what's causing this. You know, like things are uncertain and not solid. You've always been someone who blossoms under routine and structure."

Mom's right; I do like routine. "Yeah, you're probably right. I'll wait for everything to settle and see if I keep seeing this rabbit."

"Maybe start writing it down. Over time, you can see if there are corresponding events that happen around the time you see this stupid rabbit."

"That's a really good idea. Thanks, Mom." I let out a huge yawn. And that very moment, Zhen farts. He doesn't even move, but Mom and I both turn to look at him. The waft of his fart spreads fairly fast. "Oh my God!" I say as I cover my nose.

Mom balks. "That's rancid," she says. "I'm going to bed to get away from that smell. What are you feeding him, Molly?"

"Just his normal food."

"I suggest you sleep with your door open tonight. Because if he farts like that again, you'll die of suffocation."

"'Night, Mom."

She blows me a kiss from the other side of the kitchen.

I'm sure Mom's right. A lot has been happening, and this is probably my brain telling me things are changing and I'm not a fan of change.

CHAPTER 9

"Are you okay?" Tina asks as we drive to meet Dylan and Preston. Zhen and Zorro are secure in the back, and the picnic basket is in the trunk of the car.

"I'm fine. I didn't sleep great last night. Had a stupid dream."

"What was it about?"

"I can't even remember most of it. Except this stupid white stuffed bunny. Anyway. It doesn't matter. What's Preston like?"

I quickly glance sideways at her before turning my attention back to the road. "He's nice, I think. I don't know. I want you to give me your honest opinion."

"I will."

"He's a bit older, but not like Dylan old. Preston's twenty-two."

"Zhen's the best judge of character."

"Maybe for you, because he's super protective of you. Everywhere you go, he's right behind you." Tina looks out the window and sighs. "I really like Preston. I think I could love him."

"I'm happy for you."

"Promise me, Molly. Promise me if you get a bad vibe or anything from him, you have to tell me."

"Promise." I hold my pinky out to her to make her a pinky-promise. She hooks her little pinky around mine, and we shake on it. "You have to tell me what you think about Dylan too."

"Pffft, like I wouldn't." We get to the park, and I park the car. There's few other cars here, and I have no idea which is Dylan's. "Do you see Dylan?"

"I don't know which is his car."

"I can't see Preston either. Man, what if we've been stood up? I'm so nervous." Tina says as she opens the door.

"Then we've over catered." I know Dylan won't stand me up. Not after that amazing first kiss, or even the fact he texts me all the time. I open the back door, and put a leash on both dogs. They jump down, and stand beside me. "Come on, boys." I encourage them to pee before we head down to the clearing to set up for lunch.

"Preston's here," Tina says in a low voice. I look around and see a guy walking toward us. He's holding a picnic blanket, and has a giant smile for Tina. He's cute, I suppose. He walks over to us, and gives Tina a scorching, hot kiss before he even says "hello." That's not exactly what I expected to see or happen before they even speak to each other. They've only been dating a few months, and it seems a little intimate.

"Okay then," I mutter as I look away.

"Molly, this is Preston. Preston, this is Molly."

"Hey," he says in a casual, almost dismissive way, and slings his arm over Tina's shoulder.

My gut is telling me something isn't quite right with him. But I can't make a decision based on first impressions. He may be nervous about meeting me.

"Hi," I say, trying to call up a genuine smile.

He looks down at Zhen and Zorro, and steps back a small step. "I'm not a fan of animals. Sorry, but I don't pet them."

"You don't like animals? Who doesn't like animals?" I ask.

"Don't get me wrong; I wouldn't hurt an animal. I'm just not a fan. I know they serve their purpose and all but, you know. For me…meh." He shrugs coolly. I think he looks like a pompous ass, but like I said, I can't determine if he's a good enough guy for Tina, not yet.

"Hey, there you are," I hear Dylan calling from behind. Zhen turns, and with his tail wagging, steps toward him. "Hey, buddy." Dylan squats, and gives Zhen a good scratch behind the ears, and Zorro trots over. "You're not going to pee on me again, are you?" he asks Zorro.

"Dude, did he really piss on you?" Preston asks.

Preston is either a jerk, or he's trying too hard. Dylan stands and steps forward. "Hi, you must be Preston."

"Yeah, I am. Dylan, right?"

"Yeah." Dylan holds his hand out to shake Preston's. Preston extends his and they shake. "Hey you," he says to me, leaning down and giving me a soft kiss on my forehead. "Tina, we meet again." He moves forward, and gives Tina a quick kiss on the cheek.

I keep an eye on Preston, and can tell he doesn't like Dylan's familiar gesture. He puffs his chest out slightly, and hugs Tina closer to him.

Maybe my gut reaction isn't off.

Tina seems oblivious to his behavior. But to me, something is certainly not right.

"Should we head down to the clearing?" I ask.

"Wait, I forgot." Dylan holds a finger up, before running back to the car. Zhen watches him.

"I suppose we're waiting," I say.

I see Dylan jog up to his car, open the passenger side, grab a bunch of flowers, and what looks like a half-gallon plastic bottle. He jogs back, and Zhen starts wagging his tail. "These are for you," he hands me the flowers. It's a beautiful arrangement of lilies and roses with various shades of greenery. "And this is for us." He holds up the bottle.

"What is it?" I ask as I place the flowers in the picnic basket.

Dylan puffs his chest out, all proud. "It's homemade limeade."

"You made this? For us?" I ask.

"I did."

"Why?" Preston asks.

The smile on my face immediately disappears when I hear Preston ask that question. I'm trying really hard not to form a negative opinion about him, but his attitude isn't helping. "Because I wanted to," Dylan replies.

"Cool. Well, I brought a picnic blanket." He holds it up, as if he's earned praise.

"Thank you, Preston," I say.

"Let's go, guys. I'm hungry," Tina says, as she slides her hand into Preston's and they walk ahead of us.

Zhen and Zorro walk on my right, and Dylan walks on my left. "Let me," he says as he reaches to take the picnic basket.

"Thank you."

Tina and Preston are a good twenty feet away before Dylan says, "You look beautiful."

"And you've won brownie points with me by bringing flowers and limeade. Did you really make it?"

"I'll have you know I can cook. And I can cook well, too."

"Can you? What can you make?"

"I can cook enough meals that you won't go hungry for a month. And, if I might add, I like cooking too." He's pleased with himself.

"Well then, I think you should cook for me one night so I can judge these supposed cooking skills you claim you have for myself."

"I would be happy to cook for you. Just name the day, and I'm all yours." He quickly looks over at me, seeing if I caught what he said.

"All mine, huh?" I tease.

He clears his throat, and turns his head. "I…uh…you…um."

I can't help but giggle at how uncomfortable Dylan is. "It's okay." I place my hand on his arm, then slide it down so our fingers entwine. He looks down at our hands. "Is this okay?" I ask.

"I was about to ask you the same question. I don't want to rush you, Molly. In anything. However long it takes you to be comfortable with me, I'll wait."

He makes my heart swell with happiness. There's something

comforting about him. He makes me feel grounded and safe whenever he's close. He's kind of like a security blanket.

"Is this spot good?" Preston calls.

It brings me back to the now, and I nod my head. There are four other groups of people picnicking at various places in the park. We're far enough away from the others that we're isolated, but can still see each other.

"Yeah, this is great," I say again, confirming the spot is good.

Preston lays the blanket down, then sits before anyone else. "Tina." He pats the blanket next to him.

"I'll help Molly first," Tina says.

"Molly and Dylan can do that."

Man, I'm really struggling to find anything good about Preston. "Want to go for a walk?" I ask Dylan.

"Sure, let me put these down." He places the plastic bottle, and the picnic basket down, and turns to me.

I take Zhen and Zorro off their leashes, then reach into the picnic basket to get a couple of plastic bags. "What's with the bags? Preston asks.

"In case the dogs poop," I reply.

"Just leave it, no one is going to know."

"I wouldn't want to step in dog shit, and I'm sure you wouldn't either," I snap a little too forcefully.

"I just meant it really doesn't matter. Others do it." He tries to backtrack.

"I know." I smile, but inside I'm angry at him. "But I'm not like others, I'm responsible for my dogs."

"Yeah, right." He nods.

Talk about awkward.

"How long do you think you'll be. I'm getting hungry," Tina says.

"Not long. I'll take the dogs for a walk, then we'll be back. Ten minutes?"

"Okay, cool."

Dylan and I start to walk away, Zhen and Zorro follow behind us. "I know it's not my place to say anything, but that guy is a jerk," Dylan says when we're far enough away that Tina and Preston can't hear.

"I'm trying to keep an open mind."

"I'm sorry, I shouldn't have said anything."

"No, it's okay. I'm struggling to find anything nice about him too. I'm not sure what Tina sees in him. But he may be nervous around me. I don't know."

"So you're giving him the benefit of the doubt. I get it. But usually first impressions count for something. I won't be going out of my way for him."

"I know." I swallow back and watch as Zhen runs ahead to pee. Zorro stays beside me.

"He's really well trained." Dylan points to Zhen. "And I'm surprised how easily this little guy has slotted into your family. I can only imagine the horror he would've come from, what with the guy who hit him. If he hit him in public, likely chance is he did worse to him in private."

"Animal cruelty angers me. It makes me see red. People who hurt animals should get the same treatment as they gave their animals."

"You should do something with animals. It's blatantly obvious you love them. And look how these two are. You can see they love and respect you. You've got a certain way with them."

"Animals are easy. They need attention, and boundaries. And if you have their attention and respect, you can set boundaries for them. We've been lucky with Zorro. It's almost like he was looking for a family like us." I duck down and pet Zorro's head. He wags his tail. "I've got to get him neutered soon."

"Buddy." Dylan turns to Zorro. "You're only going to be a half man." I laugh out loud. "No grandchildren for you then?" he asks.

"Not from my fur babies."

"Do you want kids?"

"I've never thought of having them. Maybe, one day. But it wouldn't be for a long time. You have to remember, I'm not in my twenties, like you, grandpa."

"Hey!" He playfully knocks his shoulder into me. "I'm not that old." We keep walking to where Zhen has left a lovely present for me to scoop up. Yuck. "I'll do that." Dylan reaches for the bag.

"You don't have to get my dog's poop. I do it all the time."

"Poo doesn't bother me. I'm good." He walks over, puts his hand inside the bag, and shovels the poo into the bag. "See, natural."

"You're definitely in my good books now." Zhen wags his tail, proud of his deposit. "Good boy." I pet Zhen. Zhen gets a pat from me, then goes to Dylan. He waits for Dylan to give him a scratch. Oh my God. Zhen likes Dylan. Not a little bit, but quite a lot.

"Hey boy." Dylan scratches Zhen, and gives him a gentle slap on the stomach. "Your poo stinks." Zhen's tail hasn't stopped wagging, proud of his smelly poop.

We head toward a trash can so we throw the bag away. "Do you?" I ask.

"Do I what?"

"Want kids?"

"Yeah, I do. One day. I'm in no rush though. I'd like to travel first."

"You haven't travelled?" I ask.

"I've been to a few states, but never overseas."

"What country would be your first stop?"

"The land known as 'down under.'"

"Oh, Australia. Really? I hear it's hot. And every dangerous animal in the world lives there."

"Gemma went two years ago. She loved every moment of it. She said she felt safe, and saw no dangerous animals anywhere, unless she was in the outback, or at a zoo. She can't wait to get back there. She said she loved Sydney and her favorite was climbing on top of the Sydney Harbor Bridge, and she'd go back in a heartbeat. I want to go with her." I smile. I like the relationship they have. It's what I think family should be. "You're smiling."

"I am. I would love to go to Australia one day. But most of all, I love how you and Gemma are close. Tina and I aren't close with our cousins."

"Why?"

I shrug my shoulders. "We get on fine, it's just, they're kind of snobs. All they talk about is what they're doing, and how wonderful their lives are. They'll ask us a question, and find a way to direct the conversation back to them. My aunts are exactly the same."

"How many cousins do you have?"

"Four on my Dad's side, and two on my Mom's. I like one cousin, Jeffery. He's nice. He's cool, but we don't see him much. They live up north. It's really just us."

"Can I ask you a question? It might be too personal though."

"If I don't want to answer it, I won't."

His face instantly cracks into a huge smile. "You're refreshingly different, Molly. I like how straight up you are. Do you know anything about your birth parents? Where you came from, anything?"

I lift my shoulders. "Mom told me a bit, but she didn't know much. All I know is I lived with my birth father, and my birth mother was nowhere to be found. I don't know who she is, or even where she is. I have no recollection of or contact with my birth father. Actually, I don't want to have contact with either of them."

"I don't know how you do it. If it was me, I'd want to know where I came from."

"Why? For whatever reason, he couldn't keep me safe, or even offer me something as simple as food. Why would I want to know about that? There's nothing for me there."

"I might want to know one day, but for now, I don't. I actually don't think I'm in the mindset to find anything out. I don't know how I feel about them, and I don't want to feel like shit."

"I get it. You're incredibly strong, Molly. I will say this, I'm glad you're here, and I'm even happier that I met you."

"Hurry up! I'm hungry!" Tina yells from where she and Preston are sitting.

"Sounds like we'd better head back," Dylan says.

Dylan, the dogs, and I all head back to the picnic blanket. Zhen sits beside me, and Zorro lays down beside him. "Preston, what do you do?" I ask as I hand Dylan the hand sanitizer after I squirt some on my hands.

"I'm about to graduate."

"What were you studying?" Dylan asks.

"Food and drink production. I want to make my own beer. Top of the line, expensive beer."

"Wow, making your own beer. That's cool," Dylan replies.

"Yeah, it is."

Tina leans in and gives Preston a kiss on the cheek. "I'm so proud of him."

"Are we eating or what?" Preston asks.

He doesn't try to find out anything about Dylan or me. Instead, he turns the conversation back to himself. I don't like this.

"Sure." I hand out the plates and cutlery, and take out the various foods I've prepared.

"I've made some fried chicken, coleslaw, beef and cheese wraps, a pasta salad, and a potato salad." I bring everything out and take the lids off.

"Wow, you did all this?" Dylan asks.

"I did."

"Hmm, it appears I might have competition in the cooking department." He picks up a piece of chicken, and bites into it. "You made this?" I nod. "This is very good. Wow."

"Molly, this chicken is really good," Tina says as she finishes the first piece, and reaches for a second.

I can't help but notice the look on Preston's face. He catches me staring at him, and softens his hard features.

"Come here, Sven," he calls Zhen over.

"It's Zhen," Tina corrects.

"Oh yeah. And Zorro, right?" He points to Zorro. "Come here, boys."

Zorro stands, and wanders over to Preston, Zhen refuses to leave my side. He pets Zorro, but it's more for my benefit rather than from wanting to touch Zorro. Preston's lips are downturned, and he looks like he's repulsed and holding in vomit.

"Zorro," I call.

Zorro obediently returns to me.

"Can I have some of that hand sanitizer? You never know where dogs have been."

"The boys are super clean," Tina replies. "Come here, Zhen." Zhen goes to Tina, and I notice Preston roll his eyes.

Zhen doesn't like Preston. And that in itself speaks volumes to me.

When lunch is finished, Preston and Tina go for a walk leaving Dylan, the dogs and me.

"I have to say it," Dylan says.

"Say what?"

"I don't like him. I'm sorry, Molly, I know it's not my place. But he's arrogant, and self-centered." He holds his hand up as he speaks. "If Gemma brought him home to meet me, I'd be telling her exactly what I thought of him. But like I said, it's not my business. But he's..." He shakes his head, tightening his jaw.

"What is it?"

"I saw the way he looked at Tina when she reached for more food. I struggled not saying anything."

"Funny, because that's exactly what I saw, and what I think. And Zhen doesn't like him. He gives me the creeps."

"You have to talk to Tina." I look at him, raising my brows. "I don't mean you have to, ugh, that's not what I meant. I mean I think you should. I don't want to tell you what to do. I just get a bad feeling about him, Molly. He doesn't treat her right."

"I'll talk to her on the way home. I'm not thinking highly of him at all. Anyway, enough about him. I don't want to let him spoil our time together."

"I've got to go interstate for work next week. Why don't you come with me?"

"Ah, what?"

"Yep, I did just say that out loud. I was thinking how nice it would be if you came with me, but it seems my filter is broken around you."

I can't help but laugh. "Thank you for the invitation, but no. How long are you going for?"

"Only two nights. I'm going on Tuesday, and I'm flying back Thursday."

"Wait? This coming Tuesday?"

"Yeah." He packs the last of the plates into the picnic basket. "What do you think of my limeade?"

"Damn delicious. Now I'm looking forward to you cooking for me."

"Name the night."

"Did I tell you the owners of the studio I work for offered me extra classes? I'm teaching Monday, Wednesday and Friday now."

"Are you trying to avoid answering my dinner invitation? Sneaky."

I was. I don't really know what to say. "I'd." I look down, avoiding his beautiful face. "Really like that." My stomach flips with happiness when I look up to see him smiling.

"Good. How about when I return on Thursday night? I'd like to see you then, if that works for you." His confidence is suddenly wavering.

"That's perfect for me." I want to lean in and give him a kiss. But I stop myself when I see Tina and Preston heading back.

"Hey, Preston and I are going to go to a movie. He'll bring me home. Can you let Mom and Dad know?" Tina asks. Preston snakes his arm around her waist, and draws her close to him.

"Why don't you come home, and meet Preston at the theater?" Even to my ears, it sounds ridiculous.

"Movie starts in half an hour," Tina says.

I wish I could talk to her about him before she does something stupid, like sleeps with him, or gets in too deep. "What time do you think you'll be home?" I ask, trying to gauge a timeline so I know she's home safe.

"I don't know, maybe about ten."

"Twelve," Preston corrects her.

I have to think quick on my feet and get her home at a more

reasonable hour, so I know she's safe, and so I can talk to her. "Crap. I forgot. I need help tomorrow morning with the boys. Do you mind helping me?"

She huffs, annoyed. "What time?"

"Eight-thirty."

She rolls her eyes, but turns to Preston. "I'll have to be home early tonight. Can you get me home by ten?"

"Sure thing, babe." He gives her a kiss on the cheek.

Babe.

Ugh. I despise the way that word rolls off his tongue. It's gross. Just like him.

"Bye." Tina blows me a kiss. "Bye, Dylan. Be good to my sister."

"Bye, Tina." Dylan says as they start to walk away.

"See ya," Preston says over his shoulder. The fact he doesn't even turn around to acknowledge us separately, or even try to pet my dogs really grates on my nerves.

I lay on the picnic blanket and look up to the sky, watching as the fluffy, white clouds move rapidly through the vivid blue sky.

"You okay?" Dylan asks.

Zhen lays down and puts his head on my stomach. "I don't like him, Dylan."

"I know."

"I'll talk to her tonight."

"I think that's the best thing."

"But I'm worried. And a part of me wants to follow them to the movie to make sure she's safe. I've got a bad feeling. A real bad feeling."

"This is difficult, because you don't want to alienate her so she won't tell you anything. I think you need to give her space, and talk to her when she gets home tonight."

Dylan's right, I can't bombard her when Preston is near. I need to approach this cautiously. "I know. Maybe I should talk to Mom and Dad too."

"You don't want to betray her trust. You two are really tight, right?"

"Aha," I mutter.

"Unless you have something really concrete, I wouldn't spill anything to your parents yet. You don't want them worrying if there's nothing to worry about. Just talk to her. I'm sure you'll both sort through this."

Zhen's face is over mine, and he's panting. Drool falls on my face. "Zhen, did you really have to slobber on me?" Zhen wags his tail. His entire body moves when he's happy and wags his tail. "Alright, boy." Sitting up, I don't want to leave. "What'll you cook for me on Thursday night?"

"What do you want?"

"I'll get my PA to email you a list of my do's and don't's. And I only drink Evian water, chilled at a precise sixty-four point four degrees. It must contain three round ice cubes, not melted, and must be in a tall, blue glass."

Dylan laughs. "I'll get on to that right away. Does one also require twenty feet of red carpet?"

"Don't be ridiculous," I humorously play.

"Phew, here I thought you might be difficult."

"Twenty feet is way too long. Fifteen will do." He laughs, and quickly slides his arm around my waist, rolling me over so I'm on top of him. He stares into my eyes, and lifts his head to kiss me. "I have dog slobber."

"And I picked up dog poo."

"You win." I lean down, his head relaxes on the picnic blanket, and I place a gentle kiss on his lips. He snakes his hand up to the back of my head, and entwines his fingers into my hair. He deepens the kiss. It's not an elicit take it behind closed door kiss, more like a Disney movie kiss. Quite a bit more than a peck, but not quite carnal.

"I like kissing you," he mutters against my lips.

"I like you kissing me," I reply. Placing my head to his chest, I can hear the regular rhythm of his heartbeat. He draws lazy circles on my back. "I think I really like you," I admit.

I feel him chuckle. "That's a good thing, because I wouldn't be too impressed if you went around kissing random guys."

"So I shouldn't tell you about the guy I kissed yesterday? Or how about the guy I kissed three days ago? Oh, there was that other guy who…" I don't get a chance to finish my sentence, because his hands go from my back to my waist. He finds every ticklish spot I have, and keeps going until I'm laughing so hard I swear the other picnic goers would be looking. "Stop…" I try to say through gales of laughter.

"How many guys have you been kissing?" he teases as he continues his deadly assault on me.

"Heaps," I manage to say. He keeps tickling. I'm laughing so much, that Zhen decides to join in and climb on top of us both, trying to nip at us. Zorro looks at us, and turns back to sleeping on his side. He doesn't care. "Don't…stop."

"Don't stop? Oh, okay," He flips us, so he's over me. Zhen is now play barking. He stops tickling, and I calm down. My cheeks hurt from laughing so much. "Now, about those guys."

"I promise, I haven't been kissing random guys."

He ducks his head down, plants a big kiss on my lips, then jumps up to his feet. "That's all I wanted." He holds his hand out, and I grab on to it. "I've got a project I have to finish up, and if I stay any longer, I won't get it done. Do you want to come back to my apartment?"

I look at Zhen and Zorro, and I know they wouldn't like it. "I'd better not."

Dylan picks the picnic blanket up, and shakes it out. "It's an open invitation. Any time you want, you're officially invited."

He takes the basket, and I clip on Zhen's and Zorro's leashes. We walk back to our cars. "Apart from Preston, I enjoyed today. Actually, I'm glad Preston was here. It showed me the kind of man he is. He's arrogant, and selfish, and I don't like the way he looks at my sister."

"If you need anything, you can call me, okay?"

"I will."

We get to our cars, and I open the back door. Both boys jump in, and sit. I open the trunk, so Dylan can place the picnic basket in. He walks around to me, and blankets me in a hug, close to his body.

I feel him kiss the top of my head. "You're so short. What are you, five foot nothing?" he laughs.

"I'm five-foot-six. I'm not that short. You're just freakishly tall. What are you, eight feet?" I put on a deep voice, mimicking, and teasing him.

"No, I'm six-foot-four."

"Freak."

"Short-ass," he counters instantly.

"I'm not short!"

He laughs, and bends to give me a kiss. "Okay, you're not short. But I have to go."

"I know. Message me later?"

"You better believe it." He steps away, and I already miss him. He walks backward toward his car. "In case you're wondering, I'm etching every detail of you in my mind."

Oh, how beautiful. I don't want him to go at all. But he has to. "Bye." I get in my car, and drive away, refusing to look at him. I can't torture myself like this. I like hanging out with Dylan, but he has work to do.

At least today taught me a few things.

Biggest thing was that Preston isn't a good fit for Tina.

I'll talk to her tonight when she gets home. I'm worried for her; my stomach gurgles with concern. Turning onto the main road leading to my home, I get a quick glimpse of something that's dirty white. That bunny. It startles me. Pulling over to the side of the road, I blink a few times, and look around. "What was that?" I say aloud to myself. It was there, vivid in my mind. I take several deep breaths, and calm myself.

What is it with this damn bunny?

CHAPTER 10

Ten comes and goes.

Eleven comes and goes.

Midnight comes and goes.

I send a text to Tina. *What time will you be home?*

I anxiously wait with my phone in my hand. Pacing in my room, I'm worried about her. Something isn't right. Why hasn't she texted me back? Zhen sits beside my bed, watching me circle my bedroom floor.

My stomach churns with uneasiness, and my skin is covered in fine goosebumps. This isn't like Tina. She always replies to my texts. The turmoil within tightens, coiling tighter, ready to snap and strike.

I look at my phone and it unlocks with facial recognition. I tap on the green phone icon, and hit favorites. Tina's number is third on my list, beneath Mom and Dad. I dial her number. It rings out.

Crap.

I dial it again.

It rings out.

I don't have Preston's number, or I'd be calling him too.

I dial for the third time. This time, Tina answers. "For fuck's sake, Molly. What do you want?"

"Are you on your way home?"

"You don't have to check up on me. Mom and Dad trust me; why can't you?" she snaps angrily.

"I do trust you. I was just worried. I thought you may have gotten into an accident or something."

"I'm fine." She's short with me. She doesn't say anything else. "Is that it?"

"When do you think you'll be home?"

"I'll be home in time to help you with the dogs, okay?"

Man, she's so angry at me. I hate this. I have to fix it. "Just…I'm sorry. Be safe, okay? Call me if you need anything."

"Whatever." She hangs up on me.

I walk over to my bed, and sit on the edge. Zhen moves and places his head on my lap. A tear trickles down my cheek, and I try to hold in the hurt and sorrow. I can't believe she hung up on me.

Wiping away my tears, I stand and head into the bathroom. Turning on the light, I look at my reflection. I've got dark circles beneath my eyes, and my skin looks blotchy. I turn on the faucet, and splash water on my face.

"Okay, stay awake until she gets home, then talk to her," I say to the girl with sad eyes in the reflection. Turning off the light, I head back to bed, and lay down. I like falling asleep to meditations, but I don't put one on, because I want to stay awake for when Tina comes home.

I drop my arm, and feel for Zhen. He's right there, almost like he knows I need him.

"It's time."

"Time for what?" I ask.

He slumps his shoulders and looks down at the floor. "We can't keep doing this. You know what has to happen. Here." He holds the stupid, ugly rabbit by its ears and thrusts it out to me. "Take it."

My throat tightens, as panic claws its way through my veins. "No, I'm not doing this," I say, as if I know what this all means.

The boy-man steps closer. "This is why you're here. It's your role, your job. We all have to protect her. It's the only reason why we're here. All of us," he says through a clenched jaw.

"I'm not doing this anymore."

"I'm sorry, Neve, but you have to."

"Molly, don't take the rabbit," Dylan appears beside my bed.

"She has to. If she doesn't, we can't protect her."

"Who are you protecting?" I ask looking between Dylan and the boy in the white t-shirt. "Who are you? Why are you here?"

The boy steps forward as he moves closer to my bed, ignoring Dylan. "You know who I am, and you know why I'm here. Take the rabbit, please." He holds it out again. He looks defeated.

"No, don't," Dylan begs.

I reach for the rabbit, my fingers only an inch away.

"What the hell is your problem, Molly?" Tina's angry voice startles me awake. "Do you know how embarrassing it is to have your sister check up on you?"

"You're home," I say still trying to wake up and decipher the dream I had. That rabbit was back, and I think Dylan was here, too. Wait, was he?

"I told you I was coming home. I can't believe you and what you did. Do you know what Preston said? He said you must be bored and you have nothing better to do than to meddle in my business." Her footsteps are heavy as she walks out of my room. Tina slams the door to her room, making me startle. I hope she didn't wake Mom and Dad.

I tiptoe out of my room, and look in the direction of our parent's room. I wait a few moments, expecting them to come out. But they don't. I head to Tina's room, and knock on the door. "Tina."

"No, go away. I'm pissed off at you so bad. I can't even look at you."

"Tina, let me in!" I try the door handle, but she's locked it from the inside. "Tina," I call again in a low voice, loud enough for her to hear, but not loud enough to wake Mom and Dad.

"Go away."

"Fine, I'm going to wake Mom and Dad. Maybe they can get you to open your door." I turn to find Zhen sitting outside my door. I take two steps, and hear the door opening.

"I'm already angry at you. Do you want to make it worse?" she snaps.

"No, I don't. But I want to talk to you."

She crosses her arms in front of her chest, but steps aside. Phew, at least she's allowing me into her room. I head in, Zhen's right behind me. "Go back to bed, boy." Zhen turns, and walks into my room. "Can I sit?" I ask.

"Knock yourself out." Tina's still standing by her door, looking down at her fingernails. "What was so important that you had to keep calling like that?"

"I wanted to talk to you about Preston."

"Ugh." Tina rolls her eyes and shakes her head. "He was right," she mumbles.

"Right? About what?"

"That you're bored, and have nothing better to do."

"That's not true. He gives me a bad feeling, Tina. The way he talks and acts, he's really… I don't know how to describe him. It's like he's possessive, or trying to control you.'

"I'm not an idiot, Molly. I can judge people for myself.'

"You asked me to let you know what I thought. And I'm not saying you're an idiot. I just want you to be careful, okay."

"There's the patronizing bullshit you always get away with. You've got this sweet and innocent thing down pat, don't you? I'm having fun, Molly, and I suggest you do the same thing."

"Tina, I'm worried. Preston creeps me out. The way he talks, how he interacted with me today, it's not right."

"Oh, and Dylan is the perfect guy, right? He was patronizing Preston. Did you hear how he was talking to him? And what's with the best chicken he's ever eaten? It wasn't that good; even Preston said he's eaten better."

"Huh," I say as I stand. "Well, it appears you and Preston now share the same opinions. Careful, Tina. Next thing you know, he'll be telling you that I can't love you like a real sister and only he understands you. Classic move from a predator. Isolation, then control."

"You have no idea what you're talking about. Now, get out." She points out the door.

I stop in front of her as I leave her room. "This is exactly what he wants, for us to fight and drift apart. But is it what you want?" I don't give her a chance to respond. I leave before she can say a word.

Walking into my room, I find Zhen asleep on my bed. He's on his back, his legs up in the air. "Zhen," I say as I try to slide into bed. He moves over, making room for me.

I lay in bed awake, going over everything that just happened.

I need to get sleep. I'm tired, but I don't think I can. The nightmare and Tina's anger have left me shaken. Preston isn't a good guy. I know it. I've read plenty of books, watched enough real-life documentaries to know how a predator works. Isolation, manipulation, then total control. Images of Preston's judgmental face when Tina reached for more food flashes through my mind. I can't shake the bad feeling I have. I have to try and talk her out of pursuing any kind of serious relationship with him.

My eyelids become heavy, and before I know it, Preston is the last thing on my mind.

CHAPTER 11

My hands tremble as I reach for the buzzer on the outside of the building. I hope Dylan doesn't expect anything from me tonight. My nerves are dancing. In my head, I suspect that something has to happen, regardless of the fact Dylan keeps telling he'll take it slow. I believe him, I do. But I'm also conflicted as to how slow I'm going to be for him.

I press the buzzer and wait.

"You're right on time. I'll meet you down stairs."

"Okay," I reply through the intercom. The door buzzes, and I walk into the foyer. Ahead of me are two elevators side-by-side. On the left wall is a door that has a sign which reads 'stairs,' there's also a hallway that runs the length of the building with two apartments. To the right, there's another hallway, again with two apartments.

One of the elevators descends. When it reaches the ground floor, the doors open and I catch my first glimpse of the beautiful man, Dylan. He's leaning against the hand railing wearing loose fitting jeans, and a green t-shirt. His dirty blond hair is combed back neatly. He is truly stunning, so much so, he takes my breath away. "Wow," I whisper.

He pushes off the hand railing and walks toward me. "Aren't you a sight for sore eyes." He sweeps me up in a hug, and gives me a kiss on the lips. "You have no idea how much I missed you. Just the thought of us spending this time together kept me going through all those boring meetings."

"Believe it or not, I missed you too." I wrap my arm around his waist as he presses the button to wait for the elevator. God, he smells so good.

"I hope you're hungry. I've been cooking since I returned from the airport. I've made an Indian curry for you. I hope you like it spicy."

"A curry?" Not what I was expecting at all.

"A chicken curry." I grimace and groan.

Dylan looks at me, as the elevator doors open. "What? You don't have to eat it if you don't want to. I can order pizza."

"Did I forget to tell you, I'm vegan."

"Oh shit. Really?"

I can't hold the smile in. "Nah, just messing with you. I don't think I've ever had a spicy curry before. That's really weird. Why'd you pick a curry to make?"

"Well, when I was younger my Dad and I used to try all kinds of foods. It was like a bonding time for us. And my Dad had never had a curry before, obviously neither had I. There used to be a small family-run curry restaurant in the town where we were living, and we thought we'd give it a try. It was always busy. I mean you could go there on any day of the week, and there'd be a half hour wait. Dad and I went knowing nothing about curry, but being really excited to try something new."

"How old were you?" The doors open on the third level, and Dylan grabs onto my hand as we walk down the hallway.

"I was about ten, I think. Anyway, Dad ordered a chicken vindaloo, and I ordered butter chicken. Bear in mind, neither of us had ever had a curry."

"What happened?" Dylan reaches into his pocket and grabs his keys, before unlocking his front door. He opens the door, and I'm assaulted with unfamiliar, but delicious smells. Of course, I can identify the scents of garlic and fried onion, but the other odors, I have no idea. If I'm being honest, it smells amazing in here. "Yum," I say as I close my eyes and inhale deeply.

"Dad had no idea his chicken vindaloo is one of the hottest curries. Not the hottest, but up there. He scooped up a huge serving, and shoved it in his mouth. His face went red, he had snot coming out of nose, and his eyes were watering. But he loved it. Loved it so much, he asked for it every time we went back."

"Your dad likes spicy food?"

"Ordinarily, no. But when it comes to curries, the hotter the better."

I look around his apartment, and see his kitchen. "We're having vindaloo I take it?"

"First, the grand tour. Come." He leads me down the hallway. "My bedroom." He points to the right, where I look in and see a room that's neat and tidy. A huge four poster bed stands against the back wall. "There's a bathroom in there." He points to a door in his bedroom. "Walk in closet." Points to the door next to it. "This is the second bedroom." He pushes the door open, and I find almost a mirror image, but with only one door."

"Bathroom or closet?"

"Another bathroom. This one has a built-in closet."

"Wow."

"And living room. Dining room, and kitchen." We're back to the front door. It's not really large, but it's certainly comfortable. The dining room has a spacious six-person table, with plenty of room to move around it. Nothing's cramped, or cluttered.

His apartment is impeccably clean. Everything is in its place, there's nothing out of line. "Are you a neat freak?"

"No, I just like everything organized. Then I know where everything is."

"Now this is scary." I gesture around his apartment. He tilts his head to the side, questioning my statement. "Are you a serial killer? If you are, I have it on very good authority, I wouldn't make a very good victim."

"If I was a serial killer, then I wouldn't say I was, obviously, I'd deny it. And I think you'd make an excellent victim."

"No way." I wag my finger in front of his face. "Wrong girl to pick to be a victim. I'm a survivor. I'd find a way to turn the tables, so then I'd be the serial killer, and you'd be the victim."

"But I could overpower you."

"I see," I say as I head into the kitchen to taste whatever he's cooking. "What you're saying, is because you're so big, you'd have the brawn."

"No, I didn't say that."

"But I have the brains." I tap my head. "You see, in just the moments I've been in your apartment, I've secreted several different weapons around it. And you had no idea, I'm actually well prepared for any of your attacks. Not to mention, I've slipped a sleeping tablet into your glass over there."

"Obviously, I'm aware of these things now, because you've told me." He chuckles. "So I can adjust and attack you without your knowledge."

"I don't see this being successful for you, because now *I* know you're going to change your tactics."

He walks into the kitchen, smiling. "Would you like a drink?"

"Sure. What are you offering?"

"What would you like? Wine?" Dylan lifts the lid of the saucepan, and stirs dinner.

I stand leaning against the counter of the kitchen. I remain silent. He places the lid back on the saucepan and looks over at me. "What?"

"Wine? I'm not twenty-one."

"Shit, sorry. I forgot." He walks over to his fridge, and opens it. It too is immaculately clean and organized. "I have a wide choice of water or juice. I can go to the store to get soda if you like."

"Water is my go-to drink, I'm fine with that."

"I'm sorry, Molly. I didn't consider your age."

"Good. I'm glad my age didn't impact you. It means you're okay with the difference now."

"The fact you don't behave like any eighteen-year-old I know plays a major part." He lifts the lid again, stirs, and tastes it. "Yum."

"Wait, how many eighteen-year-olds do you know?" I question.

"No! I don't know any except you, and your sister. Speaking of which, how's she been?"

My shoulders slump, and I look down to the floor. "She's still not talking to me. She's coming home for dinner, but during the day she's at Preston's. I haven't spoken with her for days."

"Give her time. She might need to, I don't know, cool down a bit."

"I've got a bad feeling, Dylan. I think Preston is filling her head with bullshit. She's not even talking to Mom and Dad. She's so quiet. I know something's wrong."

"What do you want to do about it? Can I help?"

I drag out a chair from under the dining room table, and sit. Dylan brings me a glass of water. "I don't know what to do. I suppose, I'll have to wait until she's ready to talk to me. But I don't want to wait too long, and end up losing her to him forever."

"It's a tricky situation. I don't have any brothers or sisters, so I can't comment from experience. Well, I do, Mom's new family. But they want nothing to do with me, and I want nothing to do with them. I don't really consider them family. In all honesty, I don't even know for sure if I have just two half-brothers now, or more." I remember him telling me about his *maybe* half-siblings.

"Do you hear from your mom?"

"Sometimes she'll send me a Christmas card, and a few times she's sent me a birthday card, but usually in the wrong month."

Ouch, I wince. "How can she forget when your birthday is? She gave birth to you."

He shrugs his shoulders. "I don't know. I gave up blaming myself for her lack of interest in me or my life."

"Is there a reason? Has she ever tried to explain it to you?"

"You know, I used to beat myself up over her leaving. If I was smarter, if I was a better kid, if I listened to what she said, but then, after a lot of therapy, I discovered something."

"Yeah, what?"

"It really had nothing to do with me. All of her choices are *her* choices and not mine. I'm not going to waste another moment crying over what could've been, when I have the best Dad in the world."

"See, now we have a problem."

"Why?"

"Because I'm afraid, I have the best Dad in the world."

"Them's fighting words, lady." He lifts the lid to a different saucepan, and tastes whatever's in it. "Hmm, yum. Yeah, dinner is ready."

"Great, what can I do to help?"

"Nothing, but make yourself at home." He brings over two deep bowls, and cutlery. Then starts bringing the food over. "I know it looks like I've made a lot, but I make up containers for my Dad too. And I take some to work. So really, it's not that much. Speaking of which, you've probably noticed Dad's not here. He's not feeling great, so he decided to stay at home to rest."

He brings over a large pot, a bowl of rice, and something that resembles bread, but it's flat. "Wow. Did you seriously make all of this?"

"Except the naan bread, I bought that. But yes, I made the curry from scratch. And obviously, I cooked the rice."

"The rice is yellow."

"It's how I made it. Mustard seeds, turmeric, cardamom pods and a few other things."

I nod my head, impressed with his skills. "You sure you didn't buy it?" I tease.

"You know, I am a grown-ass man. I should hope I know how to cook. I actually took some cooking lessons when I was in high school. Food is important to me and to Dad so I wanted to make sure I was able to do it for myself. Eating out is expensive, and I'd rather spend my money on more important things."

"I like that." I look down at all the food on the table. "Since this isn't something I usually have, can you put my first bowl together and show me how much of each to add."

"Your first bowl. Nice. I already know you're going to like it."

"I'm game to try anything."

"Good to know. Nothing worse than a picky eater." I hand him my bowl, and he heaps in some rice, and then the potent, aromatic dark curry. He rips a piece of naan bread in half, and places half on the plate to the side of the bowl. "To soak everything up. Although, I like to eat it like this." He picks his naan bread up, piles on the curry, then adds a little bit of rice. Folding the naan bread, he shoves it in his mouth.

I copy him, and when I taste the curry, there's a flavor explosion in my mouth. It's spicy, really spicy, but the heat doesn't overpower all the different spices. "Oh my God," I say through a mouth full of food. "The chicken just melts in my mouth. Wow." Before I know it, I'm having a second, third, and fourth mouthful.

"It's good, huh?" Dylan asks with a huge smile.

"So good."

I finish my first bowl, and my stomach screams for more. Settle down, I hear ya. I dish up more, not as much rice this time. I use the naan to soak up the curry. "See, I can cook," he says proudly.

"You can cook for me any time you want."

"Challenge accepted."

As my eating slows down, a thought crosses my mind. One that I think needs to be asked. "I have a question, and it might sound judgmental, but it's not."

"What is it?"

"You're twenty-seven soon, right?" he nods his head. "Why aren't you engaged, or married?"

"Um." He swallows his food, and places his fork down. Picking up his water, he has a gulp. "I was with someone for about three years. She turned out not to be the person I thought she was." I can tell this is difficult for him.

"How?"

"She cheated on me. She was cheating on me with her brother's best friend. Cliché, right?" I don't reply, I don't know what to say. "She was cheating on me for nearly the full three years. She also maxed out one of my credit cards. And she was in a car accident with my car, which incidentally, she caused because she was drunk driving."

"Is this the same one you caught having sex in your car?" He nods. "Why'd you stay with her?"

"Blinded by love. Or so I thought. But as it turns out, I had this overwhelming need to fix her, so she wouldn't abandon me."

"How long ago did all this happen?"

"I broke up with her three years ago. And since her, I decided to casually date." I can read between the lines to decipher what he means. "Until now."

"You're not casually dating anymore?"

"I don't consider what we have as casually dating. I don't cook for my casual dates. And I'm not a fan of bringing them here."

A shudder rolls up my back. He's making himself sound like a man-whore. "Right," I say as I sit back in my chair, done with the food, and nearly done with tonight.

"What's wrong?"

"Do you want me to be truthful?"

"It's the whole casual date thing, right?"

"Yeah, I'm struggling with it. You've made yourself sound like casual dates is a really common thing. And you're some kind of male ho. And I'm not… um… comfortable with that."

"Before my cheating ex-girlfriend, I was with one other woman in a semi-long-term relationship. Since my cheating ex, I've been with three other women. When I say 'casual dating,' I don't mean an abundant amount of sexual relationships. I mean casual relationships that for whatever reason, haven't worked out."

Five women at the age of twenty-six is not as many as I thought. "Have you tried to make them work?"

"One, straight up no. The only thing compatible about us was the fact we were happy to keep it very casual. With one of the others I tried, but it didn't feel right. We both knew by our second date that neither of us were very excited about seeing the other. And the third, well, it started casual, and she was seeing someone else at the same time. They ended up getting married. I could see a future with her, but it didn't work out."

"Are you still seeing any of them?" He furrows his brows

together, almost like he's offended I'm even asking. "I want to know if I'm on that list. I need to know where I stand."

"I haven't seen any of them in months. The married one, we cut it the moment she told me she'd fallen in love with the other guy. The casual one, we barely speak, and the other one, we've drifted apart."

"And what happens if the casual one decides she wants a booty call one night?" I'm asking hard questions, but I think I deserve honesty. And that's exactly what he's giving me. Complete, transparent honesty.

"I'd tell her, thanks, but I'm seeing someone I think I could fall in love with."

My mouth gapes open. The hair on my arms stand to attention. I can't believe he said the L word. "I don't know what to say. But I like the fact you'd say no to her."

"I'd say no to everyone, except you. I want to make this as clear as I can, Molly. I like you. Way too much for such an early stage of our relationship. I like how you're kind, and generous, and caring. You challenge me, and I really like that. I want more. I want as much as you're willing to give me."

I feel a goofy smile tug on my lips. I think Dylan and I can be more. But I'm not going to jump into bed with him yet either. "If we're being completely honest, you have to know, I don't have any past relationships."

"That's okay," he replies. The blank look on his face is priceless. It's almost like he wants to say something, but doesn't.

"Do you want to add anything to go with the indifferent stare?" I ask, almost frightened at his response.

"This isn't foreign to me. I get it. Neither of us want to get hurt. And neither of us will, if we're honest with each other. I gather that you haven't been with anyone before. And I have no right to feel anything about it. It would be hypocritical of me to say I'm happy you haven't and I have no right to ask why you haven't either. I don't care about why you have or haven't. The only thing that matters is the now, not the past."

How can he be so perfect? There's no human in the world who

has no flaws. And so far, I haven't seen anything I don't really like. "Slow, okay?"

"Turtle slow."

I lift one shoulder in a half-shrug. "Then okay."

"Good." He leans over and gives me a kiss on the lips. "Tell me about Zhen. How long have you had him?" The atmosphere is much lighter now. And Dylan seems more at ease, too.

"My parents got him when I was about ten or eleven. They got him because I was struggling with school and couldn't make friends. I had terrible anxiety. I couldn't look anyone in the eyes. I wouldn't talk to anyone. I was a mess of a kid."

"Because of the adoption?" He scoops up some curry with his naan, and eats it.

"Not from the adoption. I bonded really quickly with Tina, but I couldn't deal with things. I didn't know how to express it."

"And you don't recall much of what happened before your adoption?"

I shake my head. "No, not really." I think for a moment. "Actually, not anything. I think if I remembered, it might explain the rabbit."

"Rabbit?" Dylan asks as he finishes what's in his bowl.

"It's gonna sound really dumb. But I've had these…" I sigh, frustrated at my lack of words. I don't want to say 'visions,' because it sounds stupid.

"What? What is it?"

"Like dreams. Some guy tries to hand me a rabbit and tells me it's time. But the worst thing is, I've had flashes of this rabbit while awake a couple of times. It's dumb, right?" I lean my elbow on the table, and rub at my temple. "Just forget I said anything."

"It's not silly, Molly. It may be nothing, but it may be something. I don't believe in psychic stuff, but maybe it's some kind of repressed memory or something. I don't know. Have you thought of seeing someone?"

"Like a shrink?" Does he think I'm crazy?

"Exactly like a shrink. I have one who I call on from time to time."

His revelation stuns me. "You see a psychiatrist?"

"No, not a psychiatrist, a psychologist. I find him to be really helpful when I find certain times in my life challenging."

"Do you see him all the time?"

"Nope. I started seeing him when Mom left. And then when Dad got really sick and we didn't know what it was. And sometimes with stuff at work, I need someone to talk to, and he's really helpful. There's only so much stress I can get out at the gym."

"Your dad got sick? What happened?"

"He was diagnosed with type two diabetes. He got really sick, and was in the hospital. They tested his blood sugar, and found it was crazy high. They ran some more tests, and found he had type two diabetes. It doesn't seem like a lot, but for someone whose Mom walked out, and whose Dad was so sick that I had no idea if he was going to live or die, it was too much for me, you know? Like the weight of the world was on my shoulders."

"You're surprisingly candid about the fact you see a psychologist."

"Why wouldn't I be? I'm an open book. And I hate when people label people who need mental health help as crazy. There's a little crazy inside all of us."

I laugh out loud. "Preach it." I smile.

"And besides, we all need some type of mental health help from time to time. There's nothing to be ashamed of. Stigma be gone." He flicks his hand dismissively.

"You constantly surprise me."

"So, back to you. Maybe you should see someone, try to figure out where this rabbit came from."

"Yeah, maybe. But first, I have to try and mend what's happening with Tina."

He stands and takes his bowl over to the sink. "I'm here for you, whatever happens."

I take my empty bowl over to the sink, and start clearing off the table. "Where do you want these?" There's quite a bit left over, even though we both managed to eat a lot too.

"I'll get some containers." He opens one of the cupboards, and takes out some containers. "Dad loves food. And he loves this curry, so I have to make sure he has some. If he finds out we had curry, and I didn't make enough for him…well." He shakes his head, then makes the motion with his thumb of cutting his neck.

"Your dad's pretty cool. Does he work?"

"Not so much anymore. He used to do work on airplanes a long time ago."

"No way! My Dad's an aircraft mechanic."

"Wow, that's what Dad used to do. He retired about two years ago. He likes to help people though, so he mows the lawns of a few old people he knows. They pay him next to nothing, but he doesn't do it for the money. He actually donates the money."

"I don't think I've ever known anyone as perfect as you and your dad."

"Perfect? Far from it. Dad's brought me up to not be a strain on society. We get into some pretty huge fights. Massive. Dad became an alcoholic when Mom left. The bottle was his coping tool. He's been sober for about twelve years now. The alcohol made him an asshole."

"Wow." I lean against the kitchen counter and watch as Dylan divides the remainder of the food into various containers. "You're a good son," I say.

"I may not be a good son, but I'm definitely not an asshole." He divvies it all up, places the lids on, and places them in his (crazily organized) freezer. I catch him yawning, which instantly makes me yawn too. "I have dessert, and a movie," he says.

"Hmm, I think I'm going to have to go."

"But it's only…" He takes his phone out of his pocket and looks at the time. "Crap, it's eleven. Have you really been here for hours?"

"Oh, sorry?" I question skeptically.

"Oh my God! I didn't mean like that. I meant, I love having you here, and time goes by so fast when I'm with you."

"Nice save. But I'm still going to go. Thank you for dinner."

"I'm thinking I'll make pizzas Saturday night."

"Is that an invitation?"

"An open invitation. I'd really like it if you come for dinner Saturday night."

"Okay."

He moves in close to me. His body heat rolls off him, and onto me. He towers over me, and I love how his body is like a blanket over mine. He makes me feel safe. Tilting my head up, I watch as he closes the gap between us. He brings his hand up, and gently trails his fingers up and down my neck. "Can I kiss you?"

I don't have the courage to say yes. Instead, I nod.

He lowers his head, and kisses me softly on the cheek. My heartbeat goes into crazy mode. He lightly brushes his warm lips from my cheek, to my ear, then down my neck. Jesus, it's getting hot in here.

I push my body into his, wanting more.

"You're beautiful," he whispers between delicate kisses to my lips.

Our kiss is sensual. He breaks away, leaving me breathless and wanting. I look down at the kitchen counter, trying to focus on anything but his mouth. I take several deep breaths, straighten my back, and hold my head high. "Thank you for dinner," my voice cracks. Stepping away, I gather my bag, and take my keys out.

"I'll walk you out," he says. Taking my hand, he walks me to my car. Every moment together makes my head spin. I can't help but love how I feel around Dylan.

CHAPTER 12

"This boy, Dylan, you've been hanging out with him quite a bit. You also have a stupid smile whenever you talk about him. Serious, huh?" Mom asks as I prepare salads for us for lunch. I can't help but smile when she speaks his name. "Like that." She points to my goofy smile.

"Yeah, I like him. I think I like him a lot."

Mom moves so she's leaning against the counter. "Your father and I think it would be a good idea to invite him to dinner."

"Yeah?" I turn to look at her. "You want to meet him?" I'm so excited.

"We want to make sure there are no red flags." I crinkle my brows together, thinking about Preston. "What's wrong?" Mom asks.

"Tina's boyfriend."

"What's wrong with him?"

"I don't know. I've got a bad feeling about him. I don't think much of him."

"Has Tina said something?"

"No, no. Nothing like that. But have you noticed she's a bit more distant lately? She's not talking to me. It's been over a week. We've never gone this long without talking."

"Hmm," Mom huffs. "Maybe we can have Dylan and Preston over for dinner." She purses her lips tightly together. "Do you think Dylan would like to come to dinner tonight?"

"What? Tonight? Um, I don't know." I'm not going to lie, a bit of panic courses through me.

"Can you ask? I'll have Preston come too. I want to meet this boy, and see what kind of vibes I get from him."

"Preston or Dylan?"

"Both. But more so Preston. Tina doesn't always make the best decisions when it comes to the opposite sex."

"I suppose I can ask Dylan, see what he has to say."

"Good. Do that for me, Molly." Mom walks away, heading out of the kitchen.

I reach for my phone sitting on the counter, and send Dylan a message. *I've got a bit of a favor to ask.* I go back to chopping the vegetables. Dylan doesn't reply, instead he calls. I answer, "Hey. You didn't have to call. I know you'd be busy at work."

"Any chance to talk to you is good. Anyway, I'm having a shit day at work, and I need the distraction. What is it?"

Now I feel bad. Putting the pressure on him to come to dinner tonight. "It's okay, don't worry," I say. My voice deceives me though, it breaks with disappointment.

"Come on, what is it?"

"Ugh. I'm sorry to ask this, but do you mind coming for dinner tonight? My parents want to meet you. Actually, it'll be you and Preston too."

"Um," there's a slight pause. "Sure. What time?"

"Are you sure? I can tell my parents you can't make it."

"Of course, I'm sure. I'd love to meet them."

I smile like a fool. "Thank you. It means a lot to me."

"I know. You wouldn't have asked if it didn't. Speaking of meeting parents. Dad's coming to pizza night, is that cool?"

"Yes! I'd love to officially meet him."

"Great. I'm sorry, Molly, I have to go. I've got this problem I'm dealing with and I have to get back to it."

"Anything I can do to help?"

"You already have. You've made my day better just by hearing from you."

Stupid smile. "Alright, I'll text you my address and time."

"Bye."

I hang up, staring at my phone like a goofball. I finish the salads, and set the table for Mom and me.

It doesn't take Mom long before she heads back into the kitchen. "Did you speak with Tina?" I ask.

"Yep. She and Preston are coming to dinner." Mom doesn't sound happy. She's chewing on the inside of her cheek as she stares out the back door.

"You okay?" My gut tightens with worry. Zhen gets up from where he was sleeping, and rubs up against my leg. Zorro lifts his head, then lowers it again.

"Yeah, I'm fine." She forces a smile. I know she's not, but she's hanging onto whatever's bothering her. "Thank you for setting the table, I did have intentions of doing it."

"It'll be okay, Mom."

She nods and takes a deep breath. "Yeah, I'm sure it will."

"I've missed you," Dylan says the moment I open the door. He's holding flowers in his right hand. "I'd give you a hug, but I know I'd crush these. And no, they're not for you, they're for your mom." The bouquet is fairly large, consisting of a range of white flowers, with some pops of yellow and green.

"They're beautiful. She'll love them."

He steps inside, leans down and gives me a soft peck on the cheek. He takes a deep breath in through his nose, closing his eyes to savior the aroma. "I could smell that from outside. What is it?"

"Mom's made beef and bacon meatloaf, garlic knots, and roasted vegetables."

"Yum. My stomach just growled. It's almost like you were speaking with it directly." He chuckles.

"Dylan, right?" I hear Mom approaching.

"Hello Mrs. Dawson, I'm honored to be invited for dinner." Mom nears us, and goes in for a cheek kiss. Dylan, being the man he is, obliges. "For you, ma'am." He hands Mom the flowers.

"They're beautiful. Thank you, and please call me Paris."

"Dinner smells amazing."

"Dylan, right?" Dad asks as he makes his way toward us. He holds his hand out to shake Dylan's.

"Yes, sir. Thank you for the invitation to your home." Dylan's nervous. His voice is shaky, and I can tell he must be edgy because he's meeting my parents. I grab hold of his hand, and give it a small, reassuring squeeze.

"Drink? Scotch? Beer?" Dad offers.

"No, thank you. I'm not a drinker by nature. Occasionally is fine, but not usually."

Dad gives him a nod, but he doesn't say anything. "Molly, can you set the table please?" Mom asks.

"I'll help," Dylan offers.

"Thanks." I smile. Dylan follows me into the kitchen where I get plates, glasses, and cutlery out. He walks over to the table, and begins to set it up. "Thank you," I say.

"Darling, set up in the..." Mom walks in and sees Dylan setting the table. "This'll do."

"Oh, I'm sorry," Dylan says. I cringe because I know he'd be feeling super awkward at the moment.

"We'll eat out here, that's fine." Mom walks over to Dylan, and gently taps her hand on his.

"Mom, Dad, we're here," Tina calls from the front.

My stomach drops, and I feel sick. She hasn't talked to me in over a week, and I don't have anything nice to say about Preston. I feel uncomfortable knowing they're here. But I want Mom and Dad to see him for themselves.

Mom scurries out of the kitchen, and I gaze over to Dylan. I worry my bottom lip between my teeth, troubled by the thought of Preston and my sister together.

"It'll be okay," Dylan quietly says. "We should go out too." He finishes setting the table, and we head out to the foyer.

Tina looks different. She's lost weight. How's that possible in only a week? Her eyes look sunken, like she hasn't been sleeping or eating. She doesn't even look at me. My heart breaks. "Hi Dylan," she says.

"Tina, nice to see you again." Dylan gives her a kiss on the cheek, then holds his hand out for Preston. Preston shakes it. The whole thing is forced on both parts.

"Tina." I don't even wait; I go in for a hug. Tina resists then quickly melts in around me. "I miss you," I whisper.

"I'm sorry," she replies in a hushed tone. "Let's not fight again." I hug her tighter.

"Preston, right?" Dad asks from behind me.

"Pleased to meet you, Thomas," Preston says.

This grates on my nerves. Preston's cockiness annoys the hell out of me. Dad's brows lift, and he doesn't extend his hand to shake Preston's. Preston steps forward, and extends his. Dad takes it a few seconds later. "Drink?" Dad offers.

"What are you offering?"

Mom gives me a sideways glance. The hair on my arms stand, just the sound of his voice irritates me.

"Soda, wine, scotch, whiskey?" Dad suggests.

"A whiskey would go down nicely, thank you."

"One whiskey coming right up. Why don't you come into the den?"

Preston follows Dad and they both disappear into the other room. Mom heads into the kitchen, and Dylan nods his head. "I'll go see if your mom needs help." He's leaving Tina and me alone for a moment.

"Are you okay?" I ask.

"Yeah, why?"

"Are you eating? You look like you've lost weight."

"Yeah, all the time." The conversation is strained. It's nothing like how we usually speak.

"Tina, what's happening? Talk to me, please," I beg. "This isn't like you. You've always been full of life, and you look so down."

"I'm fine. Honestly. I'm just tired. You know?"

"You've been coming home late every night. You're up early and gone before I even get a chance to talk to you." Her smile is lifeless, her eyes are the same. "Is it Preston? Is something happening with you both?"

"No," she says, but it's a rehearsed, strained reply.

"Whatever it is, I'm here for you, Tina. Don't shut me out, okay? Please," I beg.

"I promise, if there's anything to tell, you'll be the first to know."

"Girls, can you help?" Mom calls.

Tina and I hold hands while we walk into the kitchen. Dylan's standing by the oven with oven mitts on. He looks at us, then back to the oven. "Nothing to see here, ladies, nothing to see," he says.

Tina and I both laugh. "Dylan was telling me how much he likes to cook," Mom says.

"He does. He's making pizzas tomorrow night, and I'm officially meeting his dad."

"Really?" Mom's voice breaks with a higher pitch. "Meeting your parents?"

"Just my Dad," Dylan corrects.

"Whose dad?" Dad asks as he and Preston come into the kitchen and make their way over to the table. Preston sits, a glass in hand with some amber liquid in the bottom of it.

"Dylan likes to cook, and he's making pizzas tomorrow night. Molly's going to meet Dylan's father. What's his name?" Mom asks.

"Mark. He's looking forward to getting to know Molly, and to my pizzas."

"You cook?" Preston asks condescendingly.

"Yep, and very well too," I say before Dylan gets a chance to reply. "He made us a chicken curry last night. So good." Zhen lifts his head from where he's sleeping and looks at me. "I said chicken and you decide to look. Thanks, Zhen." He lowers his head again, not interested.

"Did you go to culinary school?" Dad asks.

"It's a prestige culinary school called YouTube," Dylan jokes. Dad cracks a smile.

"Dylan, I think everything's ready. You can take it out of the oven, and place it on the table," Mom instructs.

"Yes, chef!" He obediently does what Mom's asked of him.

Once done, he takes off the oven mitts, and sits beside me. Mom and Dad sit in their regular spot at the heads of the table, and Tina and Preston sit opposite us. "What do your parents do, Dylan?" Dad asks.

"Mom took off when I was young, so I don't have anything to do with her. And Dad's retired now, but he used to be an aircraft mechanic." Dad's eyes light up. He moves in his seat, positioning himself so he can ask more questions.

"Why'd your mom take off?" Preston asks getting in before Dad.

Dylan shakes his head. "She never said, at least to me, and if she told my father, he kept it to himself. I'm sure she had her reasons. Ones I'm not keen on finding out."

"Dylan, would you like some roast vegetables?" Mom asks.

"Thank you." He scoops some onto my plate, then his own.

"Why don't you want to know?" Preston persists. "Do you know where she lives? I'd be hunting her down and demanding she tell me why she abandoned me."

Every word he speaks, makes me angrier and angrier. "Why don't we go out for dinner one night, with Mark?" I say, trying to defuse and distract Preston.

"Yeah, I'd love to meet a colleague," Dad says excitedly. "Someone who gets what I'm going through."

"What about your parents, Preston? What do they do?" Mom asks.

Preston sits back in his chair, puffing his chest out proudly. "My parents are both lawyers."

"Impressive," I say.

"They're quite important," Preston replies.

"I work for a law firm. Where do they work?" Dylan asks.

"You're a lawyer?" Preston asks while sitting straighter, suddenly guarded.

"No, I'm a security analyst for a law firm. Where did you say your parents work?"

"You probably wouldn't know them. It's a small firm."

Did he contradict himself? I'm sure he did. "I know a lot of the firms around. I probably even know who your parents are. What are their names?"

"They don't practice in the area," Preston replies cryptically.

"Yeah, I've met them. They're really nice. They live on the other side of town, about fifteen minutes from here. You should see their house, it's so big," Tina says.

I catch the unyielding hard stare Preston's giving Dylan. Why did Preston avoid the question?

"You live at home?" I ask.

"For now," Preston replies. He shifts in his seat, uncomfortable. "I'm looking at moving out soon. Hopefully I can convince this one to come with me."

Warning.

Warning.

Red flag.

Abandon ship.

"You're moving out?" I ask Tina. "I think it's best if we discuss that first."

"Molly, leave it alone," Mom snaps at me.

What did I do? Although I want to fight Mom on this, I also know now's not the time or place to have this discussion.

"I haven't decided yet," Tina says, and glances toward Preston.

"This is beautiful," Dylan says as he eats his dinner. "I love these vegetables, Mrs. Dawson."

"It's Paris," she counters. "And thank you."

Subtly I look over to Preston. His jaw is locked tight, and his eyes are focused on his plate. His shoulders are back in an upright, rigid posture. I drop my hand, and place it on Dylan's leg. Dylan looks over to me, while Mom, Dad and Tina talk about some off-beat subject.

Dylan narrows his eyes slightly, then moves his hand to cover mine.

Zhen's wet nose sniffs at my leg. He leans his head on my lap.

Something's definitely off. I know it is. I can't allow Tina to get involved with someone who avoids an easy question about his parents. There's no reason to lie. Dylan was open and honest about his mom. Tina and I are adopted, and we have no shame in telling people if we need to.

Preston's hiding something.

The rest of dinner goes by with Preston trying to avoid any personal questions, but making it look like he's not trying to avoid them.

The whole table is tense, and uncomfortable.

"How about we clean considering you cooked?" Dylan says to Mom.

She smiles at him. "A perfect idea! That works for me."

"I'll wash and you wipe?" Dylan offers.

"I have a better idea. You rinse, and I'll stack. I like the dishwasher stacked a certain way. It irritates me when it's not done right," I say.

"I'm okay with that."

"Here, I'll help." Tina starts bringing dishes over and places them in the kitchen sink. Preston remains seated, still obviously seething at Dylan calling him out. Is he ashamed? Is that why he danced around the question?

"I have to go. Thank you for dinner," Preston says as he stands.

"Oh, you're welcome," Mom replies.

"Nice meeting you, Preston," Dad says.

"Have a good night." He gives my parents a curt nod, and heads out. His entire exit is short, and abrupt.

"Good night," I call.

"Bye," Dylan shouts.

The front door closes and we know he's gone.

Tina stands in the kitchen, looking between us, and the front door. "Thanks a lot," she bitterly spits. "Preston, wait." She runs out after him, leaving us all quite shocked by her hasty departure.

"What just happened?" I ask.

Dad looks to Dylan, then me. He doesn't want to say anything in front of Dylan. Dylan notices how my parents are looking at each other, having a silent conversation.

"I have to go too. I've got some work I need to get done tonight." He dries his hands on a kitchen towel, then approaches Mom. "Thank you so much for dinner. Truly delicious."

"You're welcome. Any time you want to use my kitchen, you're more than welcome."

"Thank you, Paris." He leans down and gives Mom a kiss on the cheek. Then he heads over to Dad. Dad stands, and begins to walk Dylan out. "Thank you for inviting me into your home, sir. It was a pleasure meeting you. And I'll talk to Dad about a dinner. I'm sure you both have a lot to talk about." He extends his hand, and Dad shakes it happily.

"Looking forward to it. Drive safe, Dylan."

"Thank you, sir. I will." We both walk out together. The moment the door shuts, Dylan lets out a large breath. "I'm going to sound like an insecure high schooler. But I hope your parents like me."

"They do. I can tell." I exhale deeply. "Was Preston avoiding your question about his parents?"

"Yeah, he was. It went downhill really fast after that."

"I have to say, I'm more convinced he's not a good guy." I can feel it in my bones.

"Oh, he's not."

I look at Dylan. "What makes you so sure?" my question is asked too forcefully. "Sorry." I hold a hand up stopping him from responding. "I didn't mean to sound nasty."

"I know." He adds in a small smile. "It's experience. Look, if it makes you feel more comfortable, I can ask around, see what I can find out."

I feel like his offer, although it's made with good intentions, is wrong. But I can't help wanting to make sure Preston is indeed good enough for my sister. "I don't want to say yes. I'd be devastated if Tina did that to you. I would hope that she, and my parents trusted my judgement."

"I don't have to ask around. But there's something that's definitely not right. He was cagey and elusive when I asked him about his parents. Maybe there's nothing there, and he doesn't want us knowing how successful they are." He shrugs.

It doesn't make sense. Why would he be embarrassed by his parents? "No, you really shouldn't." I'm trying to convince myself more than Dylan. "It's an invasion of Tina's privacy."

"It is. And it's something you have to live with if I do it. At the same time, you'll have to live with yourself if I don't and there's something really wrong with him."

I lean against his car, and run my hands through my hair. I don't know what to do. I'd hate Tina if she did something like this to me. And I'm positive, it would take me a long time to forgive her. It would cause a rift in our relationship, and it would never really be the same again. "I don't know what to do," I say as I rub my temples.

"You have to go with your heart, Molly." Dylan moves in front of me, cradling me in a tight embrace. Resting my head on his chest, I listen to the rhythmic sound of his heartbeat. "There's no right or wrong decision. Whatever you decide has consequences."

"And that's what I'm telling myself." I exhale, frustrated at myself, and angry at Tina for putting me in this position to start with. "Can I think about it?"

"Absolutely. There's no pressure from me. The offer is there, and when you're ready with whatever decision is most comfortable for you, just let me know." He kisses the top of my head. "But Molly, I really do have to go," he says.

"I know. Thank you for coming on such short notice."

He leans down, lacing his hands in my hair. His lips brush against mine. "You're welcome. I'll see you tomorrow night, right?"

"Of course."

He kisses me, making my tummy flip, and my heart beat quickly.

Dylan gets in the car, and leaves.

I really, *really* like him.

Heading inside, Mom and Dad are sitting in the dining room. Zhen's still asleep by the back door, and Zorro is laying at Dad's feet.

"Is it me, or are there red flags with Preston?" I ask.

"Yeah, there are some huge red flags. Something doesn't sit quite right with me about him," Mom says. Dad nods.

"Tina's with him, and I'm scared."

"We'll talk to her when she gets home," Dad says.

"Um, I'm not sure what to do," I say, pulling out a chair and sitting opposite my parents.

"With what?" Dad asks. He picks his coffee cup up, and sips.

"Dylan offered to do some investigation on his parents. I don't want to say yes, but a part of me knows by Preston's reaction, he's hiding something."

"He is. He certainly became uncomfortable when Dylan started asking questions. I can tell you, Preston wasn't happy with those questions," Mom says.

"Should I let Dylan dig around? If I'm being honest, I wouldn't forgive you or Tina if either of you did it to me."

"It's not about invading her privacy. It's about keeping her safe. And if she's with someone who's either not going to do everything in his power to make sure she's safe, or, if he's going to use her for something, then we need to know," Dad says. "Either way, Tina will be hurt. If we do nothing, and he tries to extort money or sex out of her, she'll be hurt. If we poke around and find nothing, then she'll be hurt we didn't trust her."

I feel physically sick. "I don't know what to do."

"I think it's a good idea if you take him up on his offer. *We'd* like you to do it," Mom says.

I nod my head.

My parents are right. Either way, this sucks.

CHAPTER 13

"It's time."

"No, I don't want to go."

"You can hear the music, can't you?" the boy in the white t-shirt asks.

"I can't hear it. I'm not going."

"Take the bunny, Neve. You have to do this. We go over this every time." He's frustrated with me. "This is why we're here. We need to protect her. We each have a role to play."

Startled, I wake covered in sweat. "What was that?" I ask.

Zhen stands and comes to lay right beside me, his head lying on my lap.

Blinking, I try adjusting my sight in the dark.

I try to sleep, but every time I close my eyes, I see images of the stupid white rabbit. I sit up, push the covers off me and head downstairs to get a glass of water. Turning the faucet on, I pour water into my glass, and take a huge gulp.

I hear the front door open. Placing my glass on the counter, I walk to the foyer to see who's sneaking out, or sneaking in. I suspect I know which and who.

"Tina," I say as she tries to close the door as quietly as possible.

"Shit!" She jumps when I call her name. "Are you waiting up for me?" she attacks me verbally, like I'm doing something wrong.

"No, I was getting a drink of water. Had a dream, or nightmare… I'm not sure."

She looks me up and down, and steps forward. "Are you okay?"

I shrug. "I can't remember all of it. Except for this stupid white rabbit." I'm getting so disheartened, because I don't know why I keep seeing it.

"Like Alice in Wonderland?"

I chuckle. "I wish, but no. A stuffed rabbit. Anyway, where were you?"

"Ugh, stop trying to control me," she grunts at me through a tight jaw.

"Hey. Stop this shit, Tina. I'm not trying to control you. I don't know what's gotten into you, but you're so different."

She walks past me, about to ascend the staircase. I grab her upper arm to stop her leaving. "Ahh," she cries out in pain.

"What the hell?" I pull her back, and lift her shirt sleeve. There's a large bruise on her arm. "How did this happen? Did Preston hurt you?"

"What? Don't be stupid, Molly. I walked into a door knob." She stares me straight in the eyes, and I can see she's lying to my face.

"You walked into a door knob? Is that the bullshit story you're sticking to?"

"It's the truth," her voice elevates.

"I've never seen a door knob that high. Unless you were pushed into it. And do me a favor, yell as loud as you want, because it'll wake Mom and Dad."

We both look up the staircase to see if they've woken. She holds her breath, and I secretly will them to wake. "I swear, it's not what it looks like."

"Yeah? How do you think it appears to me?"

"You think Preston hits me. He doesn't. He loves me, so much. He told me he's never felt like this about anyone."

"I'm sure," I say sarcastically. "Which is why you've got a bruise, because he loves you, right?"

She steps closer to me. Her jaw is tense and there's a wild fire burning in her eyes. "It was just a stupid accident. I was being dumb, asking him questions about his parents, he got mad and shoved me aside. See? I was stupid. He said he was sorry. That's all it is."

"That's all it is? You can't be so blinded by him that you don't see this is a form of domestic violence."

"He said he was sorry," she says again through a clenched jaw. "Drop it, okay?"

"I can't let this go, Tina. He's dangerous. He's already making us fight over him. Is he really worth hurting all of us?"

She steps back, and clutches at the balustrade. Her grip around it tightens. "You'd make me choose? He'd never make me choose between you and him." She shakes her head and takes one step up the staircase. "And you call *him* the monster." Turning, she walks up the stairs.

"I never said he was a monster, Tina. Those are your words." She pauses for a second, then runs up the stairs.

Standing at the bottom of the stairs looking up, I know asking Dylan to look into his past and his parents is the best decision I've ever made. Tina may end up hating me, but I'm going to do everything in my power to ensure she doesn't become another statistic to domestic violence.

Pressing the buzzer to Dylan's apartment, a huge yawn escapes me. "Hey, I'll be down in a second. Let yourself in." The door unlocks and I walk into the foyer. I press the button for the elevator, and wait.

The elevator descends, and the doors open. It's empty, Dylan must be waiting for it. I head up to his floor, and when the doors open, Dylan's standing, waiting for it. "Hey," I say when I see him.

"I was going to come get you."

"I know my way."

"I hope you're hungry." He scoops me up, and twirls me around. Burying his head in my hair, he sniffs. "You smell like vanilla."

"It's my shampoo."

He puts me down, and links our fingers together as we walk to his apartment. "It reminds me of ice cream. Damn, now I want ice cream."

"Pizza first," I say.

"After dinner, I think we head downtown and get ice cream."

"If you want. I'm not really an ice cream fan." He stops walking, and I hear him gasp. "What?' I ask as I turn to see if he's alright.

"You're not an ice cream fan? Are you kidding? Who in their right mind isn't an ice cream fan? I'm not sure I can do this…" he jokes.

I lift my shoulders. "I've never really been an ice cream lover."

"Are you more a cheese and crackers girl?"

"I'm a lover of all foods. Just not a huge fan of ice cream."

"Nope." He shakes his head in disbelief. "Nope, not good enough. Ice cream is the nectar of the Gods." He opens the door and his father is sitting in the living room watching TV. "She's not a fan of ice cream, Dad. I'm not sure about this."

"Hello, Molly." His dad stands and makes his way over to me. "Nice to see you again. Although this time, it's official." He leans in and gives me a small kiss on the cheek.

"Mr. Walker, it's nice to see you too."

"Please, it's Mark. Now what's this nonsense of you not liking ice cream? Who doesn't like ice cream? I thought the entire population of the world…actually the universe likes ice cream."

I slowly lift my shoulders and grin. "Sorry, I'm not a big fan," I say. "It's okay, but I don't love it."

"Son, this one will have to be converted. We can't have a member of the family not liking ice cream."

"You know it, Dad," Dylan says from the kitchen. "I bet she's never had ice cream that's used as a dip for popcorn, either."

"How can you call this living? I can't deal with all this crazy talk," Mark says. He turns to me, stares me straight in the eyes and says, "Tell me you've tried ice cream and popcorn?" He slightly lowers his chin, bursting with anticipation.

"I'm afraid not. Ice cream and popcorn? These are flavor combinations I can't quite wrap my head around."

"And you're not a pineapple on pizza gal either, right?" Mark asks.

"Oh no, I like pineapple on pizza. I also like grapes in my salad. And peanut butter and banana together."

"There may be hope for her," Mark calls to Dylan.

Dylan chuckles from the kitchen. "Pizzas are nearly done, just another few moments. Molly, do you want to help with setting the table?"

"Now I have a question for you both to see if I actually do belong here."

"Oh." Mark puffs his chest out. "Please, ask away.'

"Forks and knives, or hands for pizza?"

Dylan and Mark look at each other. "You're right, this will confirm if you're a little bit crazy, or a lot crazy. What's your answer?" Mark asks.

"Hang on, I asked the question. I don't know, you two may be in a league of your own here." I point to Mark, then Dylan. Dylan's smiling as he takes one of the pizzas out of the oven.

"No cutlery. Hands only," Mark answers.

"Okay, then I'm not in a house with crazy people. You'll do," I tease.

Mark hugs me while laughing. "You're alright, Molly."

"Dinner's done. Let me cut these up and we're ready to go."

Dylan brings the pizzas over to the table. "How many people are you feeding?" I ask when he places a third on the table. Sure, they're much smaller than normal pizzas, but still that's a lot of food.

"I take leftovers to work," Dylan says.

"And I take leftovers home too," Mark adds. "I heard you enjoyed the curry my son made you."

"It was delicious. I'm looking forward to more meals I've never had before."

"Make her something Greek," Mark says to Dylan.

Dylan's eyes light up. "Oh yeah. Yum. Stuffed tomatoes and lemon and herb potatoes."

My mouth salivates. "Oh my God. Yes, make those," I beg not even knowing what they are, but dying to try them. They sound delicious.

Dylan sits beside me, and Mark opposite us. Dylan rests his hand on my thigh. I like it when he does that. "I wanted to ask, what happened with Tina?"

My shoulders slump as I sigh. "It's not good. She came home early this morning, snuck in actually. I was downstairs getting some water, and I heard her. She was defensive, and short with me. I found a bruise on her arm."

"Oh," Mark sighs. "That's not a good sign."

"I'm worried for her," I say. "I haven't told Mom and Dad yet, because I don't know what to say. I don't want to push her further away, but I'm terrified of what might happen. She said it was an accident, but I'm not stupid. I know this is a sign of violence."

"You have to tell your parents. That's a given," Dylan says. "And I've started looking into Preston and his parents. It's a bit challenging, but I know someone who's going to help out with that."

"Are you asking Gemma?" Mark asks Dylan.

"Gemma? Your cousin?" I look to Dylan. He nods. "Why would you be asking Gemma to help?"

"You don't know?" Mark asks.

"I have no idea what you're talking about. I met her; she seems lovely. I really like her."

"Gemma's a private investigator," Dylan says. "And a damn good one too."

"She is?" I'm shocked. I had no idea, I suppose that's what makes a good investigator, being unassuming.

"Yeah, I've already talked to her, and she's on board. She's working on another job, but she'll find a way to fit us in."

"She's very good, she can find out things most people think are dead and buried. She has a nose for it," Mark says. "If there's anything to find, you can be sure she'll find it."

I feel uneasy. I shouldn't involve them. "What's wrong? Don't you like the pizza?" Dylan asks looking at the piece on my plate that I haven't touched yet.

"It's not that." I turn my head, averting my gaze.

"Hey, what's wrong?"

"Excuse me, kids. Nature calls at the worst of times." Mark stands and walks away from the table. But I know he's just going to the bathroom so Dylan and I can talk.

"Why are you upset?" Dylan turns in his chair to face me. I mimic his move.

"I shouldn't involve you. It's really not your problem. I feel so bad."

"I see," he says. "Tell me this. Do you love Tina?"

"So much."

"If you could see into the future and see she's involved in a car accident, would you warn her?"

"Warn her? I'd confiscate her car keys to make sure she doesn't go."

"Humans are creatures of habit. A lot don't learn from their pasts, and they keep making the same mistakes over and over again. All I'm doing, is seeing if Preston's past errors are worth knowing about."

I hate feeling so conflicted about this. "I have to listen to my heart, and not my head."

"You have to listen to both. But you also have to make the right choice for you and your sister's relationship."

"I just couldn't live with myself if he keeps hurting her, and I could've stopped it. I'd rather her not talk to me for the rest of our lives, than experience the absolute worst outcome. I need to know he's not some kind of control freak who'll end up seriously hurting her."

Dylan cloaks me in one of his generous hugs. He gives the best embraces. Not too tight, not constricting, but also not weak and unsupportive. I love being in his arms.

"I think you better get your dad. He's probably staying away so we can talk."

"Yeah, he does that. He doesn't like to get involved in things that aren't his business." Standing, he walks over to the bathroom and knocks on the door. "Need help in there, old man? Maybe you've fallen into the toilet and we need to call a plumber to get you out?"

From the other side, his dad calls out, "You're never too old for an ass-whupping, boy."

I chuckle, and start eating a slice of the pizza. Dylan comes back, grabs a piece, folds it and shoves half of it into his mouth. "Good, huh?" he asks.

Mark joins us at the table. "Dylan's pizzas are the best.

"Hmm," I grumble. "It's alright, I've had better," I tease.

"Better? I don't think so," Dylan scolds me, his voice breaking on a high pitch.

"Oh no she didn't," Mark murmurs as he looks down at his plate.

"Oh yes she did!" Dylan playfully snaps. "Next time I'll get you a store-bought pizza while Dad and I enjoy my own home-cooked one."

"I'm surprised there'll be a next time," Mark says under his breath. He's remaining on the quieter side so he doesn't get in trouble with either Dylan or me.

I'm laughing quietly. The pizza is really good. It's nothing like a store-bought pizza. The crust is light with a slight crunch. The sauce on it is homemade, because there's still chunks of tomatoes that haven't cooked all the way down. "I suppose it's okay," I say adding fuel to the fire.

"Suppose?" Dylan shrieks.

"Alright, alright. I admit…" I cover my mouth with my hand and add, "It'sreallygoodbuti'mnotadmittingit." But the only sound they can hear is a cross between a mumble and a slur of incoherent words.

"What was that? I couldn't understand you," Dylan asks.

I shove pizza into my mouth, chew and point to my mouth. "Can't talk," I say through a mouth full of food.

"Yeah, thought so," Dylan says, cracking a smile.

"She keeps you on your toes, doesn't she?" Mark chuckles. Dylan nods, and I can't help but return the huge smile. "I definitely like you, Molly. I hope my son's bad cooking doesn't scare you away."

"Hey!" Dylan objects.

I finish chewing, then say, "It's not the worst I've ever had. But, you know, he could improve."

Dylan stands dramatically. "That's it. Neither of you are invited back." He heads into the kitchen to get another bottle of soda.

"You sure about that?" Mark teases.

Dylan returns, opens the bottle and tops up my glass. "I'll have to rethink you having a key to my place, Dad. Give it to Molly, so she can come over any time she wants."

My brows fly up in surprise. What? He's joking, right?

Mark leans to the side, dips his hand in his pocket, and takes out his keys. "There, take them." He crams more pizza in his mouth.

I sit very still, not sure how to react here. I don't want his keys, we're not ready for this yet. "Maybe I'll get you out of my hair," Dylan says.

"You'll be bald soon, so it doesn't really matter," his dad counters.

Their sparring is quite amusing. They're so comfortable with each other, and I love this. "No feeding you anymore."

Mark flicks his hand defiantly at Dylan then jams the keys back in his pocket. "I'm not giving you the keys back. Instead I've decided to make sure I'm here every night waiting for you to cook."

"You're a pain in my ass," Dylan retaliates.

Mark chuckles, and gives Dylan a thumbs up. These two antagonize each other for fun. And in the interim, they amuse me.

Sitting back, I sip on my drink. I like being here, it's easy.

CHAPTER 14

"Tina's been really distant," Mom says as we sit having our morning coffee. "She's barely home."

"Dylan's cousin is checking out Preston's family."

"In a way, I hope he finds nothing, but I also want him to find something too, so we can get her away from that Preston." Mom sips on her coffee. She clasps her mug in her hands, and looks distantly out to the rolling greenery of our yard.

"Dylan's cousin is a *she,* not a *he.* I'm torn at what I'm hoping she finds. I have a bad feeling about it. I don't want her to find anything, but she may. Ugh. Mom, why does this feel so wrong?"

"Because Tina's judgement is off at the moment. We have to be her ears, and her brain, because her judgement is being hijacked by her heart, and by someone who knows how to play her."

"I need a hug," I say to Mom. Standing, I walk over to her and embrace her. Mom's hugs will always beat everyone else's, including Dylan's. She's soft and squishy, and she has the best, subtle smell of fresh-baked cupcakes. I don't know what it is, but it's comforting.

My phone rings, and I instantly regret having to let go of Mom to answer it. Dylan's name flashes up on the screen. "Hi, beautiful," he says when I answer.

He makes me smile. "Hi."

"I'm on my way over to your house."

"Aren't you at work?"

"I am, but I need to come over. Are your parents home?"

My stomach tightens, and a ball of steel drops in my stomach. He's found something, and he's coming to tell us. "Is everything okay? Dad's at work, but Mom's still here."

"Can you ask her to stay please? Gemma did some digging and found something. I need to show you, and talk to you about it."

I look over at Mom, and nod. "He's found something," I say to Mom while still holding the phone to my ear. "Mom and I are here. How long will you be?"

"I'm about fifteen minutes away. I'll see you soon."

Hanging up, I place my phone on the counter. "Dylan will be here in about fifteen minutes."

Mom looks down at her mis-matched pajamas, and stands. "I'll go get changed." She leaves the kitchen, and I'm left alone with my wild thoughts. Zhen trots over to me, and rubs his body up against my leg. "I know, boy," I say to him as I scratch his stomach.

Nervously, I pace the kitchen, waiting for Dylan to arrive. With every sound my heart skips a beat as I stop and wait for the knock on the door.

"I've called your father," Mom says when she enters the kitchen, dressed in whatever her hands touched first. She doesn't look like the graceful, fully put-together woman she usually is. She's wearing sweats, and a t-shirt. Not her usual elegant style. "He's on his way home from work."

We're expecting the worst. Something sinister lies beneath the surface. It's bubbling away steadily, waiting to erupt.

I hear a car, and know it's Dylan. Mom and I look to the door, and wait. There's a knock. "Okay, it might not be bad," I say to Mom.

"You're right. Perhaps we've misjudged the boy, and..." she can't finish the sentence.

"If we have, we'll own up to it, and apologize for the intrusion into his personal life."

"We will," Mom says but her head is shaking.

I open the door. Zhen greets Dylan first. Dylan's features are flat, and solemn. He has not come bearing good news. "Paris." He gives Mom a curt head nod. "Sweetheart," he says as he embraces me. He's holding a tablet in his hand, and it brushes against me. It instantly feels like it's made of hot iron, and weighs a thousand pounds, and all he's doing is pressing the heat against my back while he hugs me. "I'm going to cut right to it. Can we sit?"

"In the dining room, Dylan," Mom says as she walks ahead of him and takes a seat.

Dylan sits beside Mom, and indicates I should sit on the other side of him. "I'm not sure what Molly has told you, but my cousin, Gemma is a private investigator. She did a little digging and found some things on Preston and his family." He taps the screen of the tablet, waking it. "I'll give you a run down. First, Preston is an only child. His parents are lawyers, but their reputation isn't as prestigious as Preston made out. Both his parents deal with the dubious kind of clients," Dylan says grimacing.

I'm trying to read between the lines, but I'm not sure what he means. "As in… who?"

"As in people who contend they're innocent, regardless of what they've done."

"Aha," Mom says, looking down at an image of Preston's parents. His mom is in a pant-suit sipping a coffee, and his dad is walking beside her, dressed in nice slacks and a white button-down shirt.

"Now, Gemma found some information on Preston."

"What information?" I eagerly ask.

"Two women have had restraining orders against him. Gemma tried to talk to them, but neither wanted to say anything against him. One is now living overseas in England, the other is on the opposite side of the country."

I gulp, feeling sick to the stomach. "Why did they have a

restraining order against him?" I'm not sure I'm prepared for the Dylan's answer.

"He's abusive." He flicks to an image of one of the restraining orders.

"Abuse comes in many forms, what are we dealing with here?" Mom asks.

"Physical and mental. He degrades and hurts women."

"Fuck," Mom sighs as she covers her mouth in horror.

"Well, we have to get her away from him," I say, trying to come up with a plan.

"Gemma also found some images of one of the women." He flicks to a picture, and I can't believe what I'm seeing. Vomit rises from my stomach. The various shades of blue and purple indicate fresh bruises, the enormous fat lip, the broken bone beneath the eyes. I can't unsee the level of hatred he must have for this woman, whose face is virtually unrecognizable. "His parents are very good at getting him nothing more than a slap on the wrist." I feel sick.

"I can't deal with this," I say as I look away from the horror of reality. "This is real. It's not a damn movie, it's real. And it's my sister. Mom, we have to do something," I plead.

"We will." Mom looks distracted. I want to yell and scream, and lock Tina in her room until she comes to her senses. "Is there anything else?" Mom asks in a calm, almost subdued voice.

"Gemma's going to keep digging. She's going to try and ask the two women if she can hear their side of why they got a restraining order, but they're not cooperating and for now, I don't have anything else." He takes a breath, powers down the tablet, and rubs his hand on my back. "I'm sorry to be the bearer of such awful news."

"Please, Dylan, the fact you did this for us is incredibly generous. But I insist we pay your cousin."

Dylan shakes his head. "She was happy to help."

"Mom, we have to do something."

"We will, we will. We just need to have a clear head, so your father and I can figure out how to talk to Tina about this. We don't want to drive her away." Mom stands and gives Dylan a small smile. Her eyes are red, and she's on the brink of a meltdown. "Please excuse me, I need to call your father." She doesn't wait for an answer, she walks out, and heads up to her room.

"I'm so sorry," Dylan says as he hugs me tight to his body.

"I have so many feelings conflicting with each other. I don't know how to feel. I'm confused. What do I do, Dylan?"

He lets out a deep breath. "I'm not sure. You need to talk to your parents, and come up with something to keep Tina safe."

"He's a predator," I whisper.

"He's a monster," Dylan replies.

Dylan keeps me close to him for a long time. My frantic brain settles, and I try to think of something I can say to Tina so she will see the danger for herself. I'm frightened I'll lose her to him, terrified she'll choose him over us. She can't, not with what we know. I play with the pendant she gave me on our birthday, twirling it around my fingers, praying I can try and figure out a way to break her out of this toxic relationship.

"Molly?"

"Hm?"

"I have to go back to work. I'm sorry. I'd stay if I could." His grip on me tightens. I know he'd stay.

"It's okay. I have to get ready to teach."

He hesitantly lets me go, and steps back. His hands run gently up and down my arms. "I'm only a phone call away. If you need anything, call me."

"I will." I gather as much strength as I can as I smile. But my mind defeats me, playing that horrific image of his poor victim over and over again. "You're at work early today."

Dylan rolls his eyes as he lets out a frustrated groan. "I've got a problem I'm trying to solve. It's taking up too much time and energy, but it has to get done."

"Can I help? I'd welcome a distraction."

"I can't. It's confidential."

"I get it. You work for lawyers, and I can only imagine the things you see and have to deal with."

"I have to go away for work again, but not until next week. It's a quick trip, just overnight. Maybe, if you'd like, you can come with me?" he asks sheepishly.

"But you have to work."

"I do. But the job shouldn't take longer than four or five hours. It's in Washington DC. Maybe you would like to go to one of the Smithsonian museums?"

"I've been wanting to go to the National Museum of American History. Maybe I'll… actually, let me see what happens here. I might not be able to."

"Of course. There's no pressure at all." He leans down, and gives me a kiss on the lips. "I have to go."

"I wish you didn't."

"Trust me, I'd rather be with you than heading back to work. I'm hoping to have this sorted soon. However, in my line of work, when one problem ends, another begins. Part of the job."

"It's okay. I understand."

We walk to the front door, where I open it and watch as he leaves. But he stops, stands rooted to the spot for a moment before he spins and returns to me. Without a word, he laces his hands in my messy hair and leans down until our lips meet. With gentle hands, he tenderly trickles his fingertips down my neck, then back up to my hair. Pulling away, we lean our foreheads together. "I couldn't leave without showing you how much you mean to me."

"I don't want you to go," I whisper.

"Molly, you change the air I breathe." He kisses my forehead. "But I have to go." He quickly turns, and leaves, this time, not stopping until he gets to his car. He doesn't even look back. Probably because he knows if he does, he won't leave.

Tina didn't come home for dinner, and this worries me. She's been missing out on a lot of dinners, and a lot of family time.

The atmosphere was strained at the table. Mom and Dad both lost in the knowledge of what Preston is capable of.

I'm consumed with fear, absolutely terrified that we're going to lose her to *him*, to the cycle of domestic abuse. Break her down, use her, beat her, then break her down some more.

Mom and Dad are watching TV, but I know they're waiting for Tina to arrive home so we can talk to her. I'm in my room, trying to meditate so I can calm down enough to talk to her without losing my mind.

Zhen's lying beside me. His head near me, his eyes closed as he sleeps.

I can't clear my mind. I'm obsessing over Tina. I have to make sure she's safe from *him*.

I hear the front door open, and I jump up, and run as fast as I can down the stairs, nearly falling when I reach the bottom. "You're home," I say to Tina as I run into her, hugging her tightly.

"Yeah, why wouldn't I be." She backs away from me.

"Oh my God!" I say as I step backward. "What's happened?"

"What? Nothing." Her hair flops over her face. I can see the concealer. The tell-tale signs of his fist is obvious.

"He's hit you." It's not a question.

"Tina!" Both Mom and Dad come into the foyer.

"I'm going to bed, I'm tired," Tina says, ducking her head down so our parents don't see the bruise.

"No, you're not. We need to talk," Dad says in a deep, assertive voice.

"We'll talk tomorrow." Tina tries to get away, but I grab onto her hand, pulling her back.

"Back off!" she snaps at me and tries to pull her hand out of mine.

"We know he hits you. And it's not the first time he's done it," Mom says. Tina stops. Her chin falling to her chest. "If you don't walk away now, he'll keep hurting you."

"He loves me. He doesn't mean to. I'm the one who says something stupid," Tina defends him.

"This isn't normal," I say. "He put a woman in the hospital."

"Oh, right, and that was his fault? Well, he told me what happened with her. She attacked him. She came at him with a baseball bat, because she was a junkie. Probably still is. Did you find that out too?" she spits angrily.

"I had him investigated," I say to her.

Tina slowly turns her head. Her eyes are wide and filled with anger. "You had him investigated? Are you shitting me right now? I expected this from them," she maliciously spews toward our parents. "But you. You're supposed to be my best friend. You're nothing but a traitor. All you've wanted to do from the start is tear us apart."

"Tina, can't you see? You and I were good, and we've been nothing but distant roomies. He's doing this, filling your head with shit so he can separate you from us. Once he does that, he can do anything he wants."

"He loves me!" she screams at me. "He. Loves. Me!" she yells louder.

"We love you, Tina," Dad says as he steps forward to approach her.

"Don't you dare touch me."

Dad backs away from Tina, his hands up yielding to her hysteria. "Tina, you have to break it off with him, before this becomes dangerous."

"Fuck off! You all don't know what you're talking about. He loves me, and I love him."

"He's messing with your brain. He's a predator. He's no good," I say.

"Shut up! You've betrayed me. I don't ever want to talk to you again." She takes off up the stairs, all of us follow her. "Stay away," she shouts over her shoulder at all three of us.

"Tina, we love you, and want to make sure you're safe," Dad says, charging ahead of us.

Tina gets to the top of stairs, and before she goes into her room turns to face us. "I hate each and every one of you! Get out of my life!" she screams and runs into her room, slamming the door.

"She's angry and hurt. She doesn't mean it," Dad says.

I can't help but burst into tears. My best friend just told me she hates me.

"Tina!" I bash on her door, demanding she let me in.

"Go away," she yells back.

"Tina, honey, we need to talk," Mom says. We're all trying.

Tina doesn't respond. "Tina!" I say again.

Suddenly the door swings open, and Tina's there with a bag on her shoulder, carrying a pair of shoes in her hands. "You can all go to hell," she shouts. "I'm moving out." She flails her hand out aggressively, pushing us out of her way. "Don't bother trying to call me, because I won't answer."

"Tina, please don't go. We can talk about this," I beg.

She swings around, enraged. Her jaw is tight, and her lips are pursed shut. "He said you'd all try to split us up. I told him he was crazy, but obviously not. Because you all have come up with some imaginary bullshit. But the worst thing, is *you* betrayed me. I'll never forgive you for that, Molly. You're dead to me."

"Tina, I forbid you to leave," Dad says.

Tina laughs bitterly. "Forbid me? You forbid me? You're not even my real dad."

Dad stumbles backward a step, and his hand flies up to his chest. Mom gasps, and bursts into tears.

"Tina, don't do this," I plead. "It's not too late. Please. He's not a good guy. His parents aren't good people."

"Don't tell me, you've investigated them too."

"What do we have to do to prove to you, Preston is trouble? He's not a good person. He doesn't have your best interest at heart," Mom says.

"And you do? Like him." She flicks her head to Dad. "You're not even my mother. You have no say in what I do. I'm old enough to leave, and guess what, I'm out of this hell hole." She flees down the stairs eager to go to Preston.

Mom chases after her, refusing to give up. I have tears streaming down my cheeks, but I refuse to let her go like this. Dad is hot on our heels, running like his life depends on it. "We won't give up on you, Tina. We'll fight with everything we have to get you back," he shouts to her retreating back.

She sticks up her middle finger, and runs out the front door to her car. She throws everything in the back, gets in, and takes off so fast she nearly hits the gate before it fully opens.

Mom, Dad, and I stand at the door. Mom and I are crying so hard our chests are heaving. Dad's face says it all. He's heartbroken. Tears well in his eyes. He grabs onto Mom and me, and brings us in for a tight embrace. I hear his muffled cries as he holds us.

It takes many moments of us embracing, before Mom breaks away to head back inside. Once there, we sit at the dining table. "What are we going to do?" I ask.

"I'm going to the police," Dad says.

"I'm coming with you," Mom says. "Stay here, Molly in case she comes back. We'll go to the police department. See what our options are."

"Okay." I watch as Mom and Dad, holding hands, leave the house. It's dark and a ridiculous hour of the night. But we can't let her leave without fighting for her. I pick my phone up, and dial her number. It rings out. I dial again. It rings out. I dial for a third time, and it goes straight to voicemail.

I hate this feeling of being powerless to help. But most of all, I hate knowing Tina is on her way to Preston's, where he'll probably beat her. No one deserves that.

I dial Dylan's number. I know it's late, but I have to hear his voice. "Sweetheart, everything okay?" he asks in a sleepy voice.

I burst into tears. "She's left. She's gone to him."

"Oh shit. I'm sorry. I'm coming over."

"No, don't. I'm sorry, I shouldn't have bothered you," I say through the heavy tears.

"I'll be there in a few minutes. Where are your parents?"

"They've gone to the police to see what they can do." Zhen pushes his nose into my free hand to let me know he's close.

"Ugh," he grumbles. "I don't think they can do anything. She's gone freely."

"He's going to hurt her, Dylan. I can't let that happen."

"I know." I hear the ding of the elevator. "I'll be there soon."

"Okay, thank you," I say before I hang up. Zhen's by my side. He's staying so close to me, aware I'm upset. "What are we going to do, boy?" I ask Zhen as I sit on the floor and hug him. I stay there, hugging Zhen until I hear Dylan's car come up the driveway. He knocks, and I yell, "It's open."

He walks in, and sees me sitting on the floor, a trembling mess, hugging Zhen. "Come here," he says and scoops me up. Zhen follows as Dylan takes me into the living room, and places me on his lap. He cradles me tight, gently running his hand down my back.

"I'm scared," I admit.

"I know you are."

"I don't know what to do."

"Let me take care of you, Molly. Let me help." His offer isn't hollow. I know Dylan wants to be here, and wants to be a huge part of my life. I love how passionate he is when he's around me. It's like I'm the only thing that matters to him.

"I feel like a part of me is gone."

"You and Tina have always had such an intense bond, it's natural to feel empty. Now we wait for your parents to return, and strategize how to deal with this. Okay?" He tilts my chin up with his finger, and kisses me softly.

"Okay," I say.

He wipes away my tears with his thumbs and kisses my cheeks before bringing me in close to his body. I lay my head on his shoulder, and try not to think about what *could* be happening.

Before I know it, my eyes are drifting closed, and I fall into an uneasy sleep.

"Molly." I feel a kiss before I even open my eyes. "Wake up, sweetheart. Your parents are back."

I startle awake, and jump off Dylan's lap. "I'm sorry," I automatically say, not entirely sure what I'm sorry for. "What happened?" I ask Mom and Dad.

Mom sits in the arm chair, and Dad sits on the arm of it. "I'm afraid it's not good news," Mom starts. "The police are going to go and talk to her, make sure she wasn't extorted or threatened into going, but she's of legal age. They said she has a right to exercise her free will. When we told the police officer about his past, they said until something happens, they can't do anything. If he broke the restraining order, then they could step in."

"Did you ask if you could put a restraining order on him on Tina's behalf?" I ask.

"If she was a minor, we could. But we can't," Dad replies.

My stomach knots as I pace back and forth. "So that's it? We can't do anything? We just have to wait until he puts her in the hospital before we do something?" I yell, too wound up and upset to be able to talk in a reasonable manner.

"We'll get her back, Molly. We have to," Mom says.

"Do you think she meant what she said?" I ask.

"I think she was angry, upset, and most likely manipulated. And I also think, once she calms down, she'll see that we only did what we did because we care," Dad says.

"Unless *that thing* gets in her head," Mom says.

"I'll ask Gemma to dig up as much as we can about him," Dylan says.

Mom and Dad both give him a small smile. But none of this matters if he ends up hurting Tina.

"I think I'm going to go for a shower, and go to bed. I'm not sure if I'll be able to sleep or not, but my head's a mess," I say.

"I've got work, so I should head off," Dylan says.

"Mom, can Dylan stay, please?" I beg. I haven't even asked Dylan if he can stay, but I need him close.

"No, that's not a good idea," Dylan replies. I look to him, hurt he'd want to dismiss me so quickly.

"Good night. Thank you for your help, Dylan." Dad shakes Dylan's hand before heading up to bed.

"Thank you for being here for Molly." Mom gives Dylan a kiss on the cheek and follows Dad.

"You don't want to stay?" I ask.

Dylan links our fingers together and leads us out to the foyer. "Tonight isn't the time or place for me to stay. Your family is going through a lot, and to have me staying, especially considering you didn't clear it with your parents first isn't right. I know you're emotional, and I'd love to stay so I can protect and comfort you, but this isn't how it should be done."

He's right. Springing something like this on my parents isn't the most appropriate thing right now. "I'm sorry I dragged you into this."

"It means a lot to me to know that when you need me, you'll call me."

"Thank you." I reach up and give him a kiss.

"Good night." He kisses my nose, opens the front door, and walks to his car.

I watch as he drives away. My heart is completely shattered by tonight's events with Tina. But also full, because Dylan was so wonderful and supportive.

I think I'm falling for him.

CHAPTER 15

Clutching my boarding pass in my hand, I nervously look toward Dylan.

"Are you okay?" he asks. I nod, and smile weakly. "You have flown before, right?"

"Yeah, to go on vacation with my family." I think about Tina and where she is. Sadness overtakes my nervousness about flying, and I feel like someone's ripped my heart out of my chest, stomped on it, and left it to rot.

"This way to the Delta Sky Club," Dylan says as he guides me along the wide corridor.

We get into the Sky Club, and I instantly relax against one of the beautiful leather chairs. I look out the window, watching as planes taxi on the runway. "This is relaxing," I say as I watch.

"What is?"

"Watching the planes fly in. Then watching them go out, and wait their turn to take off and go. It's almost like a well-rehearsed ballet. It's calming."

"Tell me what's happening with Tina."

I feel my eyes water, but I hold it together. "She hasn't spoken to any of us. But we keep persisting. It's been eight days since she left, and I feel like a part of me is missing. I wish she'd come back."

"As long as he..."

My phone rings, and I look down at the screen. "It's Tina," I say. "I have to take it."

"Go ahead."

"Hello?" I answer the phone, too excited to hear from her. *Please, tell me he hasn't hurt you.*

"If you people don't back off, I'm getting a restraining order against you and your parents," she says in an eerily flat voice.

"Tina, we can talk about this. We just want you safe. Please, come home."

"I'm warning you, Molly. This is your only chance. Back off or you'll regret it." She hangs up.

I look at my phone, and see the call's been dropped. I instantly call her back, and it goes to voicemail. "Shit," I groan.

"What happened?" Dylan asks.

"Hang on." I hold a finger up, and call Mom. She picks up immediately. "Mom."

"I thought you'd be on the plane by now."

"Not yet. But Tina just called me."

"Did she? Is she okay? Does she need anything?" Mom sounds frantic.

"Mom, she threatened us."

"What? Wh-wh-what do you mean?"

"She said we have to back off or she'll get a restraining order against all of us."

Dylan's face drops. It's obvious he's hurting for me. For how Tina is treating us.

"Molly, I'm so sorry she called and said that to you. Look, your Dad, and I have it under control. You have a nice night with Dylan, and we'll see you tomorrow, okay?"

"Okay, Mom. I love you."

"I love you too."

Hanging up, I stare at my phone. I can feel Dylan's eyes boring onto me. "I'm sorry, sweetheart," he says. "This is a terrible time for you." He takes a deep breath. "But I promise to try and make today as fun as possible. When we land, I've got to go to the office, but I should be finished by about four. I have dinner planned for us."

"You do?" I ask. I'm happily surprised. Dylan has a way of making me feel something other than the sadness I feel for Tina.

"I do."

"Oh." Now I'm worried. "Do I need to go and buy anything to wear?"

"No. Like I said, I've organized it." He smiles cheekily. "I should be back at the hotel by no later than four-thirty, then we'll head out for dinner about six. Oh, I need you at the hotel by three-thirty."

"What? Why? I thought I was going to the Smithsonian."

"You are." He looks at his watch. The light reflects off the solid silver band. The black face and silver hands catch my attention. I can't help but stare at the beautiful watch. "We'll be landing by seven-thirty, and by the time we get the car and get to the hotel, it'll be shortly before nine. Plenty of time for you to explore the Smithsonian."

"Do you know how big that place is? Although I've never been, I know plenty of people who have. And one day isn't enough."

"How about I promise to bring you back. And we can do all the Smithsonian museums next time we're in Washington."

"Hmm." I narrow my eyes at him. "Pinky promise, and I'll make sure I'm back at the hotel by three-thirty."

"Pinky promise it is." He holds his pinky out.

"You know, you can't break a pinky promise."

"I have no intention of foolishly violating something so sacred," he teases. He's managed to get my mind off of Tina and her threats. We link pinkies together, and shake. "It's time to board. I'm sorry, but I'm going to have to ignore you on the plane. I've still got a lot of work I need to get done."

"Ignore away. I've got my Kindle fully stocked with books."

They announce our plane's boarding.

Standing, we head toward the gate. Absentmindedly I find I'm twirling Tina's pendant between my finger. Although I'm worried about Tina, in this moment, I'm really happy with how Dylan and I are working out.

Opening the door to our hotel room, I walk in and collapse on the bed. The Smithsonian was interesting, but huge. I knew it was big, but I can't believe how large it is. I can't wait to return to see it at a more leisurely pace, and with Dylan.

I look at the alarm clock beside the bed, and sigh. I'm back with five minutes to spare. I promised Dylan I'd be back by three-thirty, and I am. My eyelids feel heavy. I think I could easily sleep right here, fully clothed and with my shoes still on, although the view of the Capitol building makes me want to stay awake to admire it.

There's a knock on the door, and I don't really want to answer it. But I do. In front of me is a lady in a hotel uniform. "Hello?"

"Hi. Miss Molly?" she asks.

"Ah, yeah." I look beside her, and see she has a large suitcase folded flat.

"I'm Mandy. Mr. Dylan has asked that I come to give you a massage."

Oh. "A massage?" This is exciting.

"Yes, ma'am. A full-body massage. May I enter and set up, please?" She's courteous and softly spoken.

"Sure." Stepping aside, I let her in.

"How are you liking your stay here in Washington?" she asks as she makes quick work of assembling a massage table.

"I was at one of the Smithsonian museums. It's huge."

"Which one did you visit?" She places a white sheet on the table.

"American History."

"Oh, that's my favorite. I love the room they have dedicated to the Star-Spangled Banner. The dim lighting, no flash photography, it's breathtaking." She's really engaging.

"The story behind it was amazing. I love seeing it, and noticing just how fragile it is."

"Miss Molly, would you care to go into your bathroom and strip down to just your panties please. I have a robe here for you."

"Do you want me to take a quick shower first? I've been walking around all day, and I'm sweaty."

"I can come back in a few moments if you're more comfortable having a shower first."

"Do you mind?"

"Not at all." She smiles. "Ten minutes?"

"Perfect, thank you."

She leaves the room, and I quickly multitask by stripping and calling Dylan. He answers immediately. "I'm sorry, I can't talk long, Molly. Everything okay?" he says hastily.

"I just want to say thank you. Mandy just arrived for my massage, but I sent her away for ten minutes while I grab a shower. I'm juggling calling you to say thank you, and stripping for a shower."

Dylan catches a deep breath. "You're welcome," he says, his voice breaking on *welcome.* He makes me smile. He clears his throat before he says, "I have to go, if I want to make it back by four-thirty. I might be running a bit late as it is."

"Okay. I'll see you when you get back."

"Bye." He hangs up, and I'm staring at my phone like a damn goof. He makes me so happy.

Jumping in the shower, I make it in record time. I dry myself off and pull on a pair of panties and the robe. True to Mandy's word, there's a knock on the door exactly ten minutes after she left. I answer the door to find her there, still smiling. "Are you ready?" she asks.

"You have no idea how ready I am."

"Take your robe off, please, and get up on the table lying on your tummy." Don't have to tell me twice. "Do you have any skin irritations? Anything I should know about?"

"No, nothing at all."

"I have a gentle oil I like to use. It's scented very lightly with vanilla. Is it okay if I use this, or would you prefer a lotion for sensitive skin?"

"The oil is fine."

"Great."

She starts working on my shoulders and I think, this must be what heaven feels like. Instantly, my eyes close and I fall in love with the slow, rhythmic movement of her hands on me. She's strong, yet gentle. "I think I want to marry you," I try to say, but it sounds like a slur.

"Is that a marriage proposition? I'll let my partner know I'm moving," she says and laughs.

"Your partner can come with us." Crap, did I just offer to have a threesome with her? "Oh, I didn't mean it like that."

She laughs again. "It's okay, I get daily proposals."

"Damn it, I'm not the only one?" She works down my back, and gets right into my waist. "Oh yeah," I groan when she applies the precise amount of pressure my body is craving.

I feel myself drifting into a very relaxed state, wishing it would never end.

On the brink of slumber, I feel her work my entire body. Every inch of skin touched by her magic hands. A few times I swallow the saliva pooling in my mouth. That would've been embarrassing, drooling on her table. But I'm sure that's why she lays a sheet down first.

"Turn over for me please."

Huh? What? She can't be nearly done already. "No, keep going. Never leave," I shamelessly beg as I turn. She places a towel over my breasts, keeping them covered. Working on my head, she massages my scalp. "Oh my God." This is a thousand times better than getting my hair washed at the hairdressers. Holy crap. She is so good.

She lets out another small chuckle and continues de-stressing me.

I tune out, completely melting into the best massage I've ever had in my life.

I wake myself with a small snore, and realize Mandy's already down to my legs. "Did I fall asleep?" I ask.

"You sure did. Only for about twenty minutes."

"I'm so sorry."

"Don't be. I take it as a personal victory if my clients fall asleep while I'm massaging them."

"I hate to say it, but if you're going to massage my feet, I'm afraid I'll probably end up falling asleep again."

"Lucky that's my next spot."

She works her way down my legs, and onto my feet. I'm higher than heaven. I never want her to leave. She finishes one foot and moves to the other, when the door opens. I don't care who's here, I'm loving every moment of this, enjoying it way too much to even look up to see who's walked in.

"You look relaxed," Dylan says as he stands at my head, and looks down at me.

"You have no idea," my voice is tranquil. "I'm so lazy. I don't want to move." Suddenly a quick panic frightens me, and I feel my body to make sure I'm not exposed in front of Dylan. I think it would be uncomfortable for him to see me naked. I feel my body, and realize I have a towel covering my body from my chest to my thigh.

"I'm going to go down to the bar and have a drink while you're getting your massage."

"I should only be another ten minutes," Mandy says.

"Take your time. I'll be back in about twenty." Dylan leaves, and I'm suddenly feeling guilty that I don't want Mandy to leave.

Before I know it, Mandy's finished. "How did that feel?"

"I'm marrying you," I say without thinking.

"Maybe next time. But for now, I'll have to decline," she says while smiling.

"That oil you used. Wow. It's so nice. And it's not overpowering at all."

"Thank you. Here, let me help you up." She takes my arm, and assists. "You'll feel tired, and you should probably rest. Tomorrow you may even feel a little stiff and sore. That's all perfectly normal." I get off the foldable bed, and get a bottle of water from the mini-fridge in the room. Opening it, I guzzle it. "You'll also be thirsty."

"I'm feeling that."

Mandy folds up her table and cleans up. She starts heading to the door. "Have a good night," she says.

"Oh wait."

I go to my purse to give her a tip, but she waves it away. "Mr. Dylan already took care of everything. Enjoy your stay here in Washington." She smiles, opens the door and leaves.

I lay on the bed, and curl into a ball. I pray I don't have to move for the rest of the evening. The door opens and Dylan returns. He comes over, sits on the bed beside me, and gently strokes my hair. "You look comfortable."

"Do we have to leave? Can we stay here forever?"

"As much as I love the thought of staying here with you, that's not going to work. But if you want, you can have a short nap before we head out for dinner."

I close my eyes, wanting to whine that I don't want to leave. But Dylan has been so generous and kind, I decide I'm not going to ruin anything he's planned for us. "It's okay. If I fall asleep now, I doubt I'll wake up until tomorrow morning."

"I'm going to go for a shower, so how about you stay in bed until I'm done? We can have dinner whenever you want."

I look over at the clock. Holy crap. How is it possible that it's nearly six? "Can we have dinner in about an hour?"

"Whenever you want."

"Do I have to dress in something nice?"

"You can dress in whatever you feel most comfortable in."

"Hmm," I happily hum. "Smell here, I smell like vanilla." I hold my wrist out to Dylan.

He takes my hand, smelling my wrist, then slowly pushes the sleeve of the robe up, peppering a trail of feather light kisses up my arm, and to my neck. My eyes roll back as I close them, and really let myself go in the moment. Dylan's lips caress my blazing skin. I give myself over to him. He nuzzles into my neck, and lowers his body onto mine. His frame covers mine completely. I can feel him so close.

Our breathing increases, our mouths collide, and our bodies entwine.

"Shit," he says, as he pulls away from me. "I'm, um, going for a shower," he says then clears his throat.

Yeah, right. Well, what?

I hear the shower start, and I look to the door. Did I do something wrong?

I sit up in bed, and get changed into jeans and a t-shirt. I take my light cardigan and hang it on the back of the chair. Now I'm worried, afraid I did something I shouldn't have done.

I hear the shower stop, and soon, the door opens. Dylan comes out, in nothing but a towel hanging low on his hips.

"Oh, come on," I grumble.

"What?" Water droplets cover his body. His chest is ripped and he has a damned six-pack.

"Are you kidding me?" I point to his body. "You come out here, soaking wet with just a towel, and what? You think I'm not going to ogle you like some kind of porn star? Seriously, how is this fair? Especially considering you just rejected me too. You can't do this." I wave my hand up and down his perfect, lean, and quite muscular body. "And while we're on the subject, why do you have such a nice body? I haven't heard you once say you go to the gym. And if you tell me you don't work out, then I'm going to throw you out the damned window. Because this isn't fair."

He's laughing at me. "There's a gym up on the tenth floor of my building. And no, I have to work to look like this. And the reason I rejected you was because it was moving way too quick and we haven't talked about how fast you want that to happen. So…"

"Damn you," I grumble. "I hate how…" I choke on the words I want to say, "…stupid you are."

"Stupid?" He laughs.

"I'm going to go out to the balcony and sulk while you get dressed. I can't deal with this at the moment." I make a circular motion with my hand indicating his smoking hot body. "Just, get dressed." I can hear him laughing as I walk out to the balcony, and sit in one of the deck chairs provided.

I hate how perfect he is. Well, not really. I love it.

Looking out, it's still daylight, but the sun is sinking, and soon we'll be plunged into darkness lit only by the half-moon that is already rising and the lights of the Capitol.

I fall into a fit of worry for Tina. She's been on my mind ever since I met that dick, Preston. I'm so scared for her. And now that I know what he's capable of, I'm even more frightened for her safety.

"There you are," Dylan says, interrupting me from my heavy thoughts.

"Hey." I look up at him, smiling. "This is a look I'm okay with." I let my gaze fall up and down his lean body dressed in sweats and a t-shirt.

"What were you thinking about when I walked out? You looked like you were lost in thought." He sits on the chair beside me.

"I was. I was thinking about Tina. If I'm being truthful, I was thinking how terrified I am for her safety with Preston. That photo you showed us of the woman he put in hospital…" I shake my head, unable to verbalize what I'm feeling. "If he can hurt a person like that, what else is he capable of?" I let my head fall into my hands, as I try to come to grips with everything. "What can I do to help?"

"You said that your parents are going to his house, and demanding to see Tina to make sure she's okay, right?"

"Yeah." I nod. "Every day."

"The fact she called you to warn you off, well it's kind of a good thing."

"How?"

"It means she not in the hospital."

My stomach churns. I lift my head, and notice the last of the sunlight twinkling on his watch. I need to get my head away from Tina and the dire situation she's in. "Tell me about your watch," I say as I grab his wrist, and run my fingers over the black face. "Oh, it's a Rolex."

"It's a Submariner." He laughs at something he hasn't told me. "Most guys like fast cars, or motorbikes, boats even. I've always admired a nice watch."

"Okay. Nothing strange about that. Although, I've never known anyone to have a watch fetish. My Mom bought Dad a watch for their twenty-year anniversary. An Omega watch. It has a tan leather strap, and a white face. Anyway, Dad flipped over it because Mom spent like five thousand dollars on it. It wasn't about the money. Dad is happy to spend that kind of money on Mom, or me and Tina. Dad's just really humble. Doesn't like too many fancy things."

"That's sweet of Paris to do that for Thomas."

"So tell me what the story is with yours."

He looks down at his watch, and smiles again. "Through college, I worked some crappy jobs, but I saved everything I could, because I wanted a Rolex. There's all different types of Rolexs, but I really wanted this one. Anyway, I saved, and saved, and when I landed my first big-paying job, I managed to buy this. I had already saved two thousand dollars from working in college, and then when I got an unexpected bonus , it was enough to buy one of my favorite watches."

"Your favorite? Does this mean you have others?"

"I do. But now, I'm saving to buy a Submariner Date."

I stare at him because I have no idea what he's talking about. "Speak Greek again, I love it," I tease.

"It's another Rolex model. Man, it's so sexy. The band is gold, and the face is a cobalt blue. It's heavy, and just wow… it's stunning. I fell in love with it the moment I saw it." He shivers with excitement. I smile. When he talks about watches, his eyes come to life. He's immersed in happy thoughts. Suddenly, his smile fades, and he sighs. "Sadly, I'm only about half-way to saving for it."

I so want to know how much this watch costs. I know I shouldn't, but come on. Anyone would want to know the price. "Is it more than the five thousand my Mom paid for the Omega?"

He can shut me down and tell me it's none of my business, or he'll tell me. "Considerably. This one here was about eight thousand. The one I'm saving for, is about thirty-five thousand."

My head tilts, and my mouth falls open. "For a watch?" I ask, the pitch of my voice going too high.

"It's an investment. People buy cars for that amount of money, and the car depreciates, I buy watches, and they appreciate. Especially if they're kept in mint condition."

I nod my head. I get it. "You have a valid point, Dylan. Who knew watches could be worth that much?"

"Ha! Thirty-five thousand isn't even expensive."

"There's only one thing I can say. And that's wow."

He looks at his watch, then turns his head toward the balcony door. "Dinner will be ready soon."

"Okay," I say, standing. It's an effort to stand fluidly, especially after that awesome massage.

"Where are you going?" he asks.

"Um, I don't know now." I look around, feeling awkward. "I'll just sit again." What's happening?

"Just wait, okay?" Dylan stands, and heads inside.

I look out over to the Capitol Building which is lit up with bright lights. It's not completely dark yet, but the sun is setting rapidly.

Dylan comes out to the balcony with numerous paper bags. "What's this?" I ask.

"Dinner. I thought we could sit out here and enjoy the evening. The weather's beautiful, the company is breathtaking, and I know the food is to die for."

"Oh, really. Where's tonight's cuisine from?" I sit forward, and lick my lips.

He drags over a low table. "Well, tonight we're going to Russia. I discovered this tiny hole-in-the-wall restaurants on one of the streets near the Lincoln Theatre when I came to Washington last year. It was pure accident that I found it. I tried some of their dishes, and well, loved them. So I had them make up an order of everything I loved, so we could share it." He starts taking all these containers out of the paper bags.

"Russia? That's a bit controversial, isn't it?"

"It's just about the food," he says, grinning.

"How much did you order?" I ask as he takes out five rather large containers. One being round in shape and filled with a rich purple liquid. "What's this?" I pick it up, take the lid off and smell it. There's a beautiful earthy aroma to it with a tinge of sweetness.

"That's beet soup. It's called borscht."

"Beets?" I screw my nose up, repulsed. "I don't like beets, so I won't try it."

"Nope, sorry. You have to try everything. If you don't like it after you try it, that's fine. But you can't decide you don't like it without trying it."

I softly growl at him. I hate when he's right. I might love it. "Fine, I'll try it."

"Good. There's a cold version of borscht, and a warm version. So a summer one and winter one. They're each made differently." He picks up a spoon, dips it into the soup and brings it up for me to try. I go to take the spoon. "No, I'd like to feed you."

"It's very runny, what if I miss my mouth?"

"Then you'll have a stain down the front of your t-shirt. Now, open." He pushes the spoon toward my mouth. Closing my eyes, I decide to fully submerge myself in the tasting of this soup. I savor the richness and the earthiness. It's like nothing I've ever eaten before. I open my mouth again, wanting more. "It's delicious, isn't it?" I don't answer, I simply wait for more.

But I don't get any more soup. Instead I get something else. Opening my eyes, I look to see where he's scooping from. "Yum. What's this?"

"These are called pelmeni. They're like a dumpling filled with beef and pork and served with sour cream and butter."

"These are so good. What else do we have?" I ask excited to keep trying whatever he's ordered.

"Try this." He cuts what looks like a crepe. "These are called bliny, and can be sweet or savory. This one is filled with cheese."

The entire thing melts in my mouth, and I can't decide which I love more. "I'm in food heaven."

"Now try this one. It's called kasha. It can be a main meal, or breakfast, or even a comfort food when someone's sick." He takes the spoon, scoops up something that looks like oats. "This is a combination of grains, and depending what you add to it, depends when you can eat it. Add fruits and jams and you can have it for breakfast. Or like this one, onions, and mushrooms, and you can have it for dinner."

"Everything is delicious. I'm not sure which of these dishes is my favorite. I think I need to try them all again."

This time he hands me the spoon, and a fork. "I really love the bliny. Russian food is really convenient. It's a food culture where one or two ingredients are changed, and you can have the same dish for either breakfast, or dinner."

"You've got such great knowledge of food. And watches." I look down at his wrist.

"When I love something, I find out everything I can about it."

Heat rises to my cheeks. I wonder if he loves me. "I get it," I say.

We continue to eat, enjoying each other's company, watching the night take over.

CHAPTER 16

With dinner finished, we clean up the trash and leave the few leftovers on the low table.

Dylan moves me to sit on his lap. His hands are traveling all over my body, his lips touch every part of my exposed skin.

I turn, straddling his lap. I know Dylan's turned on; I can feel him. But I'm crazy turned on too. "Dylan," I whisper.

"Mmm." He kisses my neck, and my eyes roll back because I'm loving everything he's doing.

"Can we go to bed?" He stops kissing me. I swallow, waiting for him to say something.

"Only if you're sure you want this. There's no rush for sex, Molly, none at all."

I place my hands on his cheeks, and lower my mouth to his. Kissing him, I show him how much I want this. "I'm sure," I whisper.

He stands, grabbing onto my butt, picks me up, and walks us into our hotel room. He lowers me to the bed, and takes his shirt off.

Everything about him is beautiful. He kneels in front of me, and I open my legs so he fits snug between them. He takes the hem of my t-shirt in his hands, and lifts it over my head.

He stops once my upper body is exposed, with only my bra on. "Are you okay?" he asks. He's attentive and caring.

"Perfect. Don't stop."

He hesitates for a few seconds, then leans forward and begins kissing my neck again. With a slight lick, he trails his tongue to the top of my breast. Unclipping my bra with one hand, he flicks my bra off.

My heart begins to beat quickly, and my stomach churns with anxiety.

This is my first time. I've never had sex with anyone before. I've never wanted to, until now.

His hands tenderly explore my body. I fall back on the bed, and Dylan hovers over me. "You're beautiful," he says.

My heart pounds stronger with each passing second.

I close my eyes, and try to push everything else out of my mind. I try to focus on what Dylan is doing.

My hands tremble as I reach for Dylan.

"Hey, I can stop," he says.

I open my eyes, to find him staring down at me. "I'm okay, just keep going," I encourage Dylan.

"Molly, if you're not ready, I'm not going to keep going."

"Please." I grab onto him, and drag him toward me. "I'm ready." He hesitates for a second, but continues to kiss my neck. Slower, more reluctantly. "I'm okay."

"I know, I'm just taking my time. I'm enjoying you."

Closing my eyes, I feel every brush of his lips, every tender stroke of his hand.

My body sweats, and I try to stop the trembling.

My breathing changes. It becomes short and labored. I can't breathe. I can't breathe. My chest feels like I have a ton of bricks sitting atop it. And I'm trembling so hard I can't make it stop. "Stop!" I yell, but my voice comes out tiny and hoarse. It feels like hands are closing tight around my throat. "I can't. I'm sorry; I can't."

Dylan jumps up off the bed and backs away from me.

"I'm sorry," he says as he stands up against the wall. "I'm sorry." Panic shrouds him.

"I'm sorry, I can't." I leap off the bed, and run to the bathroom, where I slam the door shut, and fall in front of the toilet. I heave into the bowl, bringing my dinner up.

"Molly, are you okay?" Dylan asks from the other side of the door.

"I'm sorry," I say then burst into tears. My hands are still trembling, and my entire body is shaking from fear. I'm so embarrassed. I'm not even sure why I reacted this way. It takes me a long time to find the courage to open the door to the bathroom.

Dylan's sitting on the bed, his head in his hands, as his elbows balancing on his knees. "Molly," he says when he hears the door open. "I'm sorry. Is it something I did?"

I shake my head, unable to speak. I burst into tears again. I'm such a mess.

"It's okay that you're not ready. I can wait."

"I'm so sorry."

He walks toward me slowly and takes me into his arms, hugging me tight to his now-clothed chest. "You don't have to be sorry. It's okay. Look, why don't you put your pajamas on, and we can just lie down. I promise you, nothing will happen until you're a thousand per cent sure you want to."

"I want to, really I do. But I freaked out. I'm not sure why."

"It's okay, really it is."

I grab my pajamas, and head into the bathroom to change. I feel bad for not being able to have sex with Dylan. I don't think it would be nice of me to strip in front of him. That's teasing him with something I obviously can't give him.

I brush my teeth again, and head out to find Dylan in bed already. "Come here," he says as he pats the bed.

I crawl into bed, into his open arms and lay my head on his chest. I address the giant gray elephant in the room. "I'm not sure why I reacted like that. And please don't say it's okay; it's not."

"I know this is your first time, Molly. And it can't be easy for you."

Running my fingers over his chest, I think back to when Tina lost her virginity. "When Tina told me she had sex for the first time, I had no interest in knowing anything about it. But she wanted to tell me, so I let her. I remember thinking, how uninteresting sex sounded. And how I couldn't see why all the girls in school were busting their asses to have sex with whomever they could. Don't get me wrong, I'm not trying to shame them, I just didn't get it."

"You don't have to explain that to me."

"Here's the thing, Dylan. I never wanted to have sex with anyone. But I met you, and all these feelings started to develop, and having sex with you was—is—something I'm actually looking forward to. I have no idea why I just freaked out like that. You didn't do anything wrong. It's all me."

"I don't know what to say to you."

"I'm embarrassed by my mini panic attack. That's what it felt like. My chest became tight, I was shaking and sweating, and I ran to the bathroom to vomit. I can't explain it. It's not you, Dylan because I love you. It's..." I stop myself. Shit, did I just say the L word to Dylan? If so, did he hear it? Crap, what have I done?

His embrace tightens around me. "You love me?" he asks in the sweetest of voices. It's almost like he doesn't believe me.

I close my eyes and take a deep breath. I might as well admit it. "I love you," I say as I tilt my head up to look at him.

He smiles at me, and leans down to kiss me. "I feel the same way about you, too. I've loved you since the day you sassed me at the mall. You're exactly what my heart craves."

"But I flaked out, and I'm obviously not ready for sex."

"When you're ready, I'll be waiting."

"I hate how perfect you are. I feel inadequate. Like you deserve better."

"You're my better, Molly. You're my everything."

I lean on one elbow, and hover over him for a kiss.

Laying on his body, I place my head on his chest and close my eyes. We may not have had sex, but now he knows exactly how I feel, and I know precisely how he feels about me.

I move to roll off Dylan so I don't squish him, but he tightens his grip on me. "Stay. I like this."

"Okay," I whisper, and place a kiss over his heart.

I have his heart, and he has mine. I'm so lucky to have him, nothing can ruin this for me.

CHAPTER 17

"How was it?" Mom asks as we prepare dinner.

I look around, making sure Dylan's not anywhere near. I know he's in the family room with Dad. I muster a weak smile. "Yeah, it was good."

"Did you two have sex?" Mom doesn't mix her words.

I look down at the pepper I'm chopping and I can feel my cheeks redden. This is a very personal question. "No, we didn't."

"What? Why?" she sounds shocked.

"I don't know what happened. We were getting quite intimate, and I freaked out." I stop chopping the pepper, and walk away from Mom. Sitting at the dining table, I keep looking down at the floor. Zhen, gets up from where he was lying and follows me to sit between my legs.

"What do you mean by freaked out?" She comes and sits beside me.

I make some awkward hand gestures, like I'm trying to explain what happened. My voice gets stuck in my throat, and all I can do is shake my head while tears well in my eyes.

"It's okay if you're not ready yet. There's no timeline or schedule for this kind of stuff, Molly. We're all different."

"I feel like I'm defective. Something up here isn't working." I tap my head. "I have no idea why I freaked out."

"You're putting too much pressure on yourself, Molly. How did Dylan react? Because from what I know of him, I highly doubt he would've demanded you to keep going."

"He didn't. He was perfect. Honestly, Mom, I don't know how I got so lucky with him."

"Your father and I had our reservations about him."

"What?"

She puts up a hand to stop me from saying anything more. "Let me finish, before you get defensive." She takes a breath. "We were concerned about the age difference. And we thought he may want things from life that you don't. But you're like an old soul. And once we met him, interacted with him a few times, and got a chance to see him with you, we knew you are in good hands with him."

"Oh," I say, letting out a long sigh.

"We can't say the same about Preston though."

"Have you heard anything from Tina today?" I ask. Mom shakes her head. Her eyes fill with sadness, and I see she's choking back the emotions. "Me either. I've sent her text messages, and tried calling her, but she's not answering."

"We went to his parents' house this morning, trying to see her to make sure she's okay, but… nothing." Mom wipes at a tear as it rolls down her cheek. "She's disabled *find my iPhone* on her phone, we don't even know if they're still at his parents' house. Her car's not there. We don't know. The police called yesterday afternoon to say they went to see if she's okay, and she told them she didn't want anything to do with us. There's nothing they can do. She's of legal age."

"Sorry, Mom, but this is absolute bullshit. He's an abuser. He beats women, how can they do nothing when they know what he's capable of."

"Because no one has pressed charges against him."

"Why can't we?" I stand and begin to pace. Zhen follows me as I walk back and forth. "We have to do *something* before it's too late."

"I know."

"Actually." I stop and turn to face Mom. "I once saw a documentary about a group that kidnaps people who have been brainwashed and they de-condition them. Maybe we can do something like that?" I ask, eager to get my sister back. I miss her so much.

"I know exactly what you're talking about, because we're going to do this. We have someone going to their house tomorrow to get her away from him, and put her in a safe house where we and they can help her."

"Wait. How? When?" I'm speechless.

"We met with someone this morning, and told them about our situation. They have to go in fast, because time is not our friend. And every moment she's with him, is a moment he could be hurting her. We need to be really quick with this. We'll do whatever's in our power to get her away from him."

I let out a huge sigh of relief. "I can finally breathe. I'm happy she'll be out of there tomorrow." I find a ray of hope in these plans, but I won't truly rest until I know she's safe.

"We'll do whatever we have to do, to make sure you and your sister are safe. We love you both with everything we have." Mom cries, and it breaks my heart to see her like this. I wipe at my own tears.

"I love you, Mom." I walk over to her, and throw my arms around her. "This has got to be so hard on you."

"I never wanted you to go through anything like this. But this is what family does. We're there for each other regardless of how tough the times are."

"Oh shit," Dad says. Mom and I pull away, and look over to Dad. "You told her?" Mom nods. "We were going to tell you at dinner."

"I'm so grateful that you thought of something like this," I say to Dad.

"We're going to fight back. That bastard thinks he's tougher than us, but he has no idea what we're capable of," Dad says.

Dad's determination and passion are in his voice. His eyes say he'll kill Preston if he tries to do anything to stop us. "No one tears our family apart," Mom adds.

Dylan walks into the kitchen, and steps back assessing what's happening. "Um, sorry." He looks between us. "Am I interrupting something?"

"Only the best news I've heard in a while," I reply enthusiastically as I walk over to him and hug him.

"What's happening? Can I help?" he asks. I give him a quick run-down of what's going to happen tomorrow. "You're right, that is fantastic news. What time are they going in?"

"They're sending us an email with details of that. From the meeting we had this morning, it'll be just after his parents leave for work. They'll go in, take her, and get her to a safe house," Mom replies.

"Is there anything I can do?" Dylan offers.

"No. Now it's a waiting game," Dad says. "But we appreciate that you want to help."

"We've got to finish dinner," I say as I stand and head back into the kitchen.

"What are we having?" Dad asks.

"Stir fry tonight," Mom replies.

"I can help," Dylan proposes.

"Do you want to get the bowls? It shouldn't take too long."

"Sure."

I feel so much better and lighter knowing I'm going to have Tina back soon. My heart has been breaking and my soul has been wracked with anguish and fear. There's a new lightness in the house. It feels like joy is creeping back in. Mom and Dad are both smiling for the first time I've seen since Tina left home. They look as relieved as I feel.

"Tell me about the Smithsonian," Dad asks as we sit at the table to eat our dinner.

"It's huge. I didn't get a chance to fully appreciate it all. But Dylan has promised to take me back, and visit it with me."

"Which one did you go to?"

"American History, but I want to go back and also see Air and Space Museum and the Art Museum."

"Both of them?" Dylan asks.

"Hey, you promised to take me back. I didn't say which one I wanted to see. So suck it up, buttercup." I tease as I lean into him.

"Buttercup? Really? Do I look like a buttercup?" he says in a flat, playful tone.

I roll my eyes. "Whatever." Mom laughs. "Oh my God. Last night, Dylan bought Russian food for us. This beet soup I had, um, what's it called again?"

"Borscht," Dylan says.

"We have to have it one night. It's so good. He's opening my palette to a whole range of different foods."

"I heard about your homemade pizzas," Dad says. "You know we have a wood-fired pizza oven out in the garden."

Dylan gasps. "You do?" he asks, all excited as he cranes his neck to see, even though it's dark.

"We do. We never use it, but we have it."

"You'll just have to come over and make pizzas for us all," I say.

"I will. I'd love to have a pizza oven, but my apartment doesn't allow it. Besides, there's nowhere for me to put it."

"Do you own your apartment?" Mom asks.

"Not all of it. The bank owns about two-thirds."

"You own property, at your age?" my Dad asks. "I'm impressed."

"Actually, I own two apartments. Well kind of. I have another apartment in the same building. I lease it out."

"You do?" I ask.

Dylan nods. "They both came up at the same time. The one I'm living in I was renting, so it made sense for me to buy it. The other one is one floor down. It's a one bedroom not like mine. I bought that one too. It was already rented, and the tenant was happy to stay on."

"The more time you spend with us, the more I like you," Dad says.

"Um, thank you?" Dylan replies. "This is really nice." He eats another forkful of stir fry.

"When are we…" I'm interrupted by a knock on the front door. "I'll get it," I say.

"No, no. You stay and eat, I'll get it," Mom says as she stands and heads to the door.

"When are we going back to Washington?"

"NOOOO!" I hear Mom wailing from the foyer. We all jump out of our seats and run to see what's happening.

I see them and my heart stops.

My body erupts into goosebumps.

I feel my throat tighten, and I can hardly breathe.

I freeze, terrified of the words they're saying.

Two female police officers are standing at the door. Their caps under their arms.

Mom's on the floor, hysterically crying.

I hear the word. That one word. *"…killed."*

I collapse to the floor in a boneless heap.

"We're sorry for your loss."

She's dead. Tina is dead.

I can't cry, I can't do anything. My body is numb, my mind is blank. I stare at nothing.

"Molly, Molly…" I look at the man kneeling beside me. I turn to him, and blink. "Molly." He grabs me and embraces me.

Screaming, I back away from the man. Why's he trying to touch me?

"Molly," he says again.

I look up to him. "Why are you calling me Molly? My name's Neve."

CHAPTER 18

"Neve, it's time," I say as I hand her the bunny.

Neve looks around, and shakes her head. "I can't hear the music," she says. "I'm not going anywhere.

"She needs our help. She's shutting down."

"But I can't hear the music."

"It doesn't matter. She needs us, Neve. It's what we do."

Neve stands from where she's sitting at her desk, coloring in one of her books. She snatches the bunny from my hand and cuddles it. "I don't understand. If I can't hear the song, then why am I going?"

"Because she needs us," I say again, this time with more frustration.

She looks around, and a small smile draws her lips up. "It's not *him*. She doesn't need us for him. It's something else."

I try to listen to what Neve can hear. "What do you mean it's not him?" I ask, stepping closer to her.

"It's not *him*."

"But M needs us." I look around, confused by what's happening.

"She does, so I'm going. But it's not because of him." Neve holds my hand, taking me by complete surprise. "I'll take care of her," she says and smiles. Neve disappears, and I sit on her bed, anxiously waiting for her to return.

"Why are you in Neve's room?" Kate asks.

"She was needed," I reply.

Kate looks around Neve's room and crinkles her forehead. "Is he back?"

"No, not him. Something else."

Kate stands still for a moment, listening. "He's been gone for such a long time, I didn't think she'd ever need us again."

"Right now, she needs Neve. And we're going to be here for her whenever she needs us."

Kate shakes her head and huffs. "That girl can't keep doing this."

"Who? Neve?"

"No, M. She's broken. This'll send her over the edge. This will destroy her," she pauses and looks to the corner of the room. "She's been through so much, she won't be able to deal with this too."

"That's why we're here. We have to be here for her. It's our job to protect her."

"And it's your job to protect us." She squeezes my upper arm. "You've been here for us since I can remember, AJ. You've always looked out for us."

"This is going to sound terrible, Kate. But I've only ever wanted to look after M."

"I know." She takes another deep breath. "We *all* know."

CHAPTER 19

OLLY

Mom, Dad, and Dylan are standing on the other side of the room. Two police officers are in the foyer, with my parents. All five of them are staring at me.

I blink a few times. Yawning, I notice how exhausted I'm feeling. My mind is foggy, and it's taking me a few moments to work out what's happening.

And then I remember. "Tina," I say as I jump up off the floor and run toward the door.

"Molly?" Mom asks stepping forward and blocking my path.

"What?" I stare at Mom like she's lost her mind. "Where's Tina?" I ask the police.

Both are really young, and look as confused as my parents and Dylan. "Are you okay?" one of the police officers asks.

"I'm fine." I rub at my eyes, trying to ease the brain fog happening inside my head.

Stay strong, M. We're here for you.

I look around, trying to figure out where that voice came from. My hands tremble, and my breathing rapidly escalates. "Who said that?" I ask.

They all look at each other. Their worried looks speaks volumes. No one said anything.

I knock the side of my head, trying to dislodge the voice.

You have to calm down.

"Who are you?" I shout. I back myself into a corner and press my hands over my ears, trying to get away from this voice.

You know who we are.

"No, I don't. Where are you?"

"Requesting ambulance at…"

Calm down.

"How can I calm down when I don't know what's going on?" I burst into tears. Dylan steps closer, but I hold my hand up to him. "Don't," I plead. "Just don't."

One of the police officer's steps forward. "Molly, my name is Sarah. Is it okay if I come to you?" I watch as she slowly approaches me. I shake my head, I don't know what's happening. "It's okay. We're here to help."

"Where's Tina?" I crumble to the floor, knowing where she is. Maybe I got it wrong, maybe she's not d-d… I can't think it.

"Molly," Mom says. My gaze snaps up to her. She's broken. Her shoulders are slumped downward, and her cheeks are tear-streaked. "He…" Mom takes a breath. Dad grabs her, as she bursts into tears again.

The other police officer steps toward me, and with difficulty says, "We're sorry to tell you this, but your sister Tina has been killed." My entire body trembles. My brain can't quite comprehend what's going on. "But we're concerned about you."

I stare at the police officer, tilting my head to the side.

I can take over.

"No, I don't want you to," I reply.

"Who are you talking to?" Dad asks.

I look to Dad, unsure why he's asking me such a stupid question.

They can't hear me, only you can.

Distressed, I look to my parents and Dylan. "What's happening?" I grab at my hair, trying to tug. "The walls are closing in." My head's spinning, I can't focus, I can't think.

M, you have to listen to me. You need to calm down or I'm going to send Neve back in to help you.

"Who's Neve?" Everyone's looking at me like I've lost my mind. "Am I crazy?" I ask them. But no one answers. No one else knows what's happening in my head.

M! Listen to me. Calm down.

"I don't know who you are." A barrage of tears erupts.

Yes, you do. I'm AJ.

"AJ?" I don't understand. I run my hand through my hair, confused. I know that name. "Why would I know you?"

You know who I am. You know who we are.

"We?"

"Molly, who are you talking to?" one of the police officers asks.

I back up until I can feel the wall behind me, and slide down. "What happened to Tina?" I ask again, in case this is some kind of nightmare.

The police officer steps closer, and kneels in front of me. Dylan takes hesitant steps closer, and finally sits beside me. "Molly," Dylan says while carefully reaching for my hand. "Tina was killed."

"I know," I say. But nothing makes sense. Nothing logical is happening. "Why?"

The police officer looks over her shoulder to my parents, then back to me. "We've called for an ambulance to come. I think it's best if you go to the hospital."

"Why? What's wrong with me?"

"The stress of your sister being murdered could've triggered something."

"Murdered?" I ask. "Who…why…how?" I can't even…wait, what's happening?

Let me take over, I can help.

"No, you can't."

"No who can't?" Dylan asks. "Who are you talking to, sweetheart?"

I close my eyes, and place my palm to my head. "He's trying to tell me he can help."

"Who can help?" Mom asks.

"AJ. But I don't know how."

"Who's AJ?" Mom asks.

I look up to her, unsure on how to answer her question. "I don't know," I whisper. "I don't know," I repeat in a softer voice.

"Sometimes with trauma, the brain can shut down to protect itself," the other police officer says. "It's why we've called an ambulance. Molly needs to go to the hospital to make sure she's okay."

"Okay," Dad replies as he holds on to Mom.

"I'm coming with you," Dylan says as he hugs me tight to his body.

"We all will," Mom says.

"No! I just need to know what happened to Tina," I beg someone to tell me.

"Preston killed Tina," Dad says while he struggles to hold back his emotions. "That bastard strangled her." His breathing deepens. Mom's tears return, heavier than before.

I feel dead.

What?

I look over to the police, and stare at them. "Tell me he's not going to get away with this."

"He's been arrested."

Calm down, M.

A lump sits in my throat, making it hard for me to swallow. My brain is foggy, and I have a voice telling me to calm down. "I'm calm," I whisper.

"We know," Dylan replies.

"Please, just...don't." I shake my head, desperately trying to make some kind of sense of everything. It's like I'm standing in a room with a thousand people trying to talk to me at once. I don't know where to look, or who to listen to. It's too much.

Let me help you, M. Let me take over so you can rest for a moment.

I spring to my feet, frustrated with myself. "I don't need to rest, I need to figure out what's happening." I hit my head with the palm of my hand, trying to dislodge the voice.

"Who are you talking to?" Mom asks again.

"Him." I make a fist with my hand and hit the side of my head again.

"This is a highly emotional time, and we need to all take a deep breath," the police officer says. She steps toward me. "Molly, the ambulance will be here soon, and we can get you to the hospital. Just to make sure you're okay."

I look up at her, and shake my head. "You just told me my sister was murdered by a man whose parents always find loopholes and manage to get him off. I have this AJ guy in my head telling me to calm down. My family is falling apart, and you want to make sure I'm okay? What part of any of this do you think is okay? Because in my head, I'm falling apart. Actually, we all are." I refer to my parents.

"We won't fall apart, Molly. We'll stay strong, through everything," Dad says, and finally lets go of all his tears, holding Mom close.

Dylan stands, and heads to the door. There's a lot of talking, most of which I can't focus on. The voice inside my head is loudest.

We'll get through this. Let me help you.

"How? Can you bring Tina back?"

No, but I can protect you. It's my job. It's always been my job.

"How can you protect me?"

I can look after you. Take your pain away.

"No one can take my pain away."

I can help, if you let me.

"There's nothing you can do."

"Hi, Molly." A man kneels in front of me. "My name's Adam, and I'm a paramedic. How are you?"

"Is this a trick question?" I ask.

He gives me a sympathetic smile, and nods. "I'm so sorry to hear about your sister. But right now, everyone is concerned about you."

"Because I'm having a conversation with someone in my head?"

"That can be brought on by extreme trauma. And you've experienced it here tonight with the sudden loss of your sister. It's a perfectly normal reaction, but we all think it'll be a good idea to take you to the hospital, just to make sure you're okay."

"I'm not crazy." Or am I?

No, you're not.

"You have to stop talking to me. I can't deal with you."

"Who are you talking to?" the paramedic asks.

I slowly shut my eyes, and huddle into myself. I can't do this. Not at anymore.

Yes, you can. Please, I'm begging you, let me help.

"Stop it!" I yell at the voice inside my head calling himself AJ. "Just stop. Give me room to breathe for one minute."

"Molly," Dylan says. I look over at him and fear flutters in my stomach. The puzzled look on his face makes my heart shudder. "Please, go with them," he pleads.

I look around the room, and see my father's ashen gaze. The color has been sucked from my mother's cheeks. And panic flares in Dylan's eyes.

"I'll go," I say as I stand and walk out with the paramedic officer. We hit the steamy evening, and I notice how unusually suffocating the air is. Although the evening's warm I'm trembling, unable to regulate my body temperature. My body is going through the motions, taking one step after another while my world is rapidly collapsing.

You need to rest.

I blink several times as the paramedic helps get me in the ambulance. My stomach growls with hunger, although I don't feel hungry. I stare out the window, unsure of what's happening.

"I feel lost."

The paramedic looks over to me and smiles. "We'll get you to the hospital soon. Your parents and your boyfriend are following us."

I look around, blank. Are we in transit? Are we moving?

Please M, let me take over. I can help protect you.

"No one can protect me," I say with an emotionless voice.

"Sorry?" the paramedic replies.

I can't help but stare at him. "I'm not talking to you," I say. Closing my eyes, I lay my head back, and try to figure out what's happening.

Hopefully, soon, I'll wake up and find out this whole thing is nothing but a cruel and senseless nightmare.

CHAPTER 20

"Hello, Molly. My name is Nick Powers, and I'm a psychologist here at the hospital. Do you mind if I sit with you?"

I look over to him, and nod my head.

"I know some fairly traumatic things have happened to you."

"My sister was murdered by a violent repeat offender." I clutch at the tissue I'm holding. Looking around the room, I notice we're alone. There's a big screen TV playing something, which I haven't been paying attention to. My parents and Dylan were all here since I was admitted last night, but I've sent them all home.

The talking in my head is loud, and having the voices in there has made it harder for me to concentrate.

My parents also have a funeral to plan.

The funeral of my best friend.

I've got you.

"No, you don't," I say.

"No I don't what?" Nick asks.

"I wasn't talking to you."

Nick scribbles something on his notepad. "Who were you talking to?"

"You think I'm crazy, right?" I shake my head, and roll my eyes. The pain in my head is a constant reminder how AJ is here, waiting for me to talk to him.

"Not at all. I think sometimes in our lives, things happen to us, and we try to cope the best way we can. Tell me about the relationship between you and your sister."

I rub my fingers across my temple, trying to massage the tightness. I take several deep breaths. "It became strained. But it was never like that before."

"Tell me about how it was. How did you see Tina?"

I smile. "She's…energetic, and outspoken. She tells you exactly what she thinks. She has no filter, at all. She's bubbly, and really likeable. She gets on with virtually everyone. She's the exact opposite of me."

"You don't get on with people?"

"It's not that I don't get on with people, I prefer the company of my dog, Zhen. And I have a really small circle of friends." My brows crinkle as I think about it. "Actually, I don't really have friends. I never really thought about that before."

"Why do you think that is?"

I shrug. "I don't know. Dogs are more loyal then people maybe."

"Tell me about your childhood. Your parents told me you were adopted."

"I had a great childhood. Mom and Dad are really supportive, and they just adore Tina and me. Both Tina and I are really lucky they're the parents we got. You hear so many horror stories, but Tina and I we're just so…" I inhale deeply. "Fortunate."

Nick smiles. "I like the love you have for your parents. Not in a weird way." He chuckles. "At what age were you adopted?"

"I was seven."

"Do you remember that?"

I stare past him, shaking my head. "I don't even remember the day I came to live with them." I try to recall that time, but I can't.

"What's your earliest memory?"

"Specific memory?" He nods. "I don't know. It's hard, it's like my brain has blocked things out, although I know they happened. For example, I know I was adopted, I've seen the adoption papers. But I don't recall the day I came home. I know… I know…" A memory flashes in my mind. I feel my face tighten as I struggle to recall it in its entirety. "I think I remember sitting on the bed, crying." Closing my eyes, I try to focus.

"Why were you crying?"

The memory is fragile. I can't make a whole memory, only the fragments are there. "I was sad." Opening my eyes, I fixate on a small spider walking across the floor. My heart lurches, as my stomach cramps with fear. "I was scared." Panic infiltrates my body. "I didn't like the dark."

"What would happen in the dark?"

"No, it wasn't the dark. There was something else."

The spider dashes across the floor, I watch as it scurries away.

"What was it?"

Let me tell him about it.

"What can you tell him?" I ask.

"Who are you talking to, Molly?" Nick sits forward, and stares at me.

I can tell him about the memory, I can tell him about the truth.

"What truth? What are you talking about?"

I can tell him what happened to you.

"You need to tell me first," I say becoming increasingly frustrated.

You know what happened.

"How do I know?" I jump to my feet, and begin to pace, back and forth. Trying to figure all this out. "I don't remember."

Then let me explain it to both of you.

"I want to know. But how do I let you take over?"

"Molly, who are you talking to?" Nick asks again.

Sit down, M. If you allow me, I can help.

I move to sit.

Are you ready?

"I think so."

It's not going to hurt, but you'll find it exhausting.

Staring at Nick, I nod my head.

A wave of fogginess clouds my head. I begin to rub at my eyes, and I can feel myself being sucked away from being me. I have no control over myself. My body is not my own. It's shared with a person who lives inside of me.

"Let's get this straight from the start. I don't trust you, and I don't know you. But I'm doing this for M, because she needs the help."

"Your voice is different." The guy sitting in front of me looks like a dweeb. "Who are you?" he asks as he scribbles furiously on his stupid note pad.

"I'm AJ. I protect M. I always have, and I always will. What's your name?" I ask as I cast a careful look over him.

"I'm Nick, and I'm a psychologist here at the hospital."

"Yeah. Hmmm. You're not impressing me." I arch a brow and cross my arms in front of my chest.

"Um."

"Ugh," I grunt as I roll my eyes. "I thought you'd be able to help M, instead of a damned loser. If you can't help her, I'm sorry. We're not talking to you."

"We?"

"Yes, *we*." M, I'm sorry but you can't talk to this dick. He hasn't got a clue what he's doing.

I don't have a clue either. Please, tell him something.

"Go." I flick my hand at him. "Go find me someone else I can talk to. You're useless." I roll my eyes at him, and sit back in the chair.

"Who are you?" Nick asks without budging from his seat.

"I'm not explaining it twice. Go, and find someone who can help us. You're useless." He continues sitting, scribbling his stupid notes.

"Molly, you need to talk to me."

"You're a damn idiot. She's not here. I am. And I'm telling you to go and get someone who can actually help." M, I know you can hear me, but I need you to trust me, and go to sleep.

I wait for a moment, and know she's no longer here. Satisfied, I leap up out of the chair, and walk over to this Nick guy. He's too busy writing to notice I've moved. When he looks up, he startles back. "Why don't you take a seat so we can talk, AJ, is it?"

I don't want M living in torment any longer than she has been. I try to comply with Nick. Although I'm certain he's not the one who can help. I pace a few times, trying to deal with my inner turmoil before I decide to sit, again. "M needs help."

"And who's M to you?"

I drag my hand across my forehead trying to ease the tension I feel quickly mounting. "Look, Kate, Neve, and I live inside M."

"Different personalities."

"We're different people, not just different personalities."

"Why do you live inside Molly?"

Frustrated, I let out a huge sigh. I can't deal with this level of stupidity. "Do you have any weights anywhere?" I look around, hoping I see a set of dumbbells.

"Weights?"

"Ugh," I grunt. "Yes, weights. Dumbbells, kettlebells, a bar, anything?"

"Why do you want weights?" He crosses his legs and sits back in his chair.

Looking at him, I squint and tilt my head. "You're kidding right?"

"What am I kidding about?"

"Do you honestly think you get muscles like this…" I flex my arms to show off the bulging muscles from years of training. "Without doing weights? How about this?" I stand and lift my shirt, showing off my ripped stomach. "You frustrate me, and I need to work this frustration out. You're not listening, and I'm seriously only moments away from telling you to go fuck yourself."

"I'm trying to find out what's happening here."

"I'm not letting M back until you go and get someone else who can help her. You're too busy sitting there scribbling your stupid damn notes. My job is to protect M, and I'm going to protect her even from pricks like you." I sit back down, and cross my arms in front of my chest.

"I think it's..."

"No." I shake my head. "I'm done with you."

"If I can..."

"No," I say again, more forcefully. "I'm done with you," I say slower, in case he didn't get it the first time.

Nick takes several deep breaths, clicks the top of his pen, and finally stands to leave. "Alright, then."

Good riddance. He's as useless as tits on a damn bull. He can't offer us anything of value. And my job, is to make sure M is always protected.

Nick leaves the room, and I stay seated, looking around. The room is large, and I suppose it's comfortable. The walls are lined with posters for several different medications. Some have help numbers on them if you're feeling sad and shit. It really doesn't interest me, I just need to find some weights.

Standing, I pace back and forth. "Come on," I say to no one.

To pass time, I read each and every poster. Twice.

And I look over to the manky bookshelf housing some old and irrelevant books. I pick one up, and flick through it, noticing the dog-eared pages. "Who does that?" I'm not a reader at all, but even I know you don't bend the corners of pages.

I huff, and keep looking around. I suppose I can leave, I haven't tried the door, but I need to get M proper help. She's buried so much over her life, that I'm actually frightened for her.

Keeping an eye on the clock, my frustration is escalating into anger. I don't want to be angry, I want this to be resolved.

Pushing two chairs together, I lay across them and wait.

And wait.

And damn well wait.

It's been hours since Nick left. What the hell are they doing out there?

Sitting up, I tap my foot on the ground, trying to let this annoyance out. Finally, I'm pushed to my breaking point. Standing, I walk over to the door, and just as I reach for the handle, the door opens and a woman approaches me.

She's short, and has a nearly shaved head. She's wearing square, black glasses that sit perfectly on her slightly bent nose. She's older, yet, quite attractive for someone her age.

"Hi," she greets me with a genuine smile. "AJ, right?" She holds her hand out to me.

"Yeah, who are you?" I take her hand and shake. She has soft skin and warm hands.

"My name's Amelia Morgan. I'm a psychotherapist, and I'm here to listen."

I take a step back, assessing this old chick. Now, that's interesting. She said she's here to listen, not here to help. I back away from her, and head toward the opposite end of the room.

"Is it okay if I sit with you for a while?" she asks.

"You know what I thought was interesting?"

"What?"

"You said you're here to listen. Aren't shrinks supposed to say they're here to help?"

She smiles, and lets out a small chuckle. "I'm not your average shrink."

"Yeah?" I step toward her, feeling kinda okay she's here. At least that other dick isn't.

"Yeah," she responds. "I spoke with Nick, and he told me how you didn't want to talk to him."

"I was just thinking how much of a dick he is."

"I suppose he can be," she replies. Yeah, I like her. "But you didn't answer. Can I come in?"

"Yeah, you can." She comes into the room armed only with a

small silver tape-recorder. "Old school." I pointedly look to the recorder.

"Yeah, I'm a classic sort of gal."

"Classic as in a Corvette?"

She laughs again. "I haven't been a Corvette for many years, let's go with classic as in a Mustang. A Mustang not quite finished with its rebuild."

I can't help but let out a full laugh. She's funny. I like her. I think she might be able to help M. "What experience have you got with people like us?"

"Well, first, I need to know what you mean by 'people like us.' From what Nick told me, you live inside Molly."

"I do."

"I'm going to sit, and record what we're talking about. Is that okay with you?" I nod. I feel at ease with Amelia. "I'd like to ask some questions."

"Okay," I reply and sit opposite her.

"I know your name is AJ. What do you like to do?"

"Lift weights. I love me some weights. It's why I look so good." I stare down at my body, hoping she's impressed by the hours I put in for my body to look so good.

"Can you describe yourself for me?"

"In what way? My looks?"

"Yeah, tell me anything you want me to know about you. Let's start with your looks."

"Now that's a subject I can talk about for hours. Obviously, I'm hot. I know my muscles make people stare at me, and I love getting the attention. Short blond hair, brown eyes, and like I said, damn good looking."

"I can't deny that," Amelia says. "Who are you to Molly."

Ah, the serious questions. It was bound to happen. "I'm Molly's protector."

"What do you protect her from?"

I think carefully, being cautious with my choice of words. "Dangers." I crack my knuckles then wring my hands together.

"Are you nervous."

Again, I think before I say anything. "I am."

"Why?"

"Because this isn't just my story to tell."

Amelia's brows rise, as she nods her head. "Whose story is it?"

"Not only mine."

"That's pretty vague. Who else can help me with the best way to help Molly?"

"You want to know how many of us there are?"

"Absolutely. I think it's important to understand each of you before I can understand Molly. And I don't think this is something that we can do only after an hour or two. I think this is long term."

"You think we're crazy."

Amelia smiles and sits back in her chair. "I think there's crazy in all of us. Normal is just a word, a subjective word. My normal and your normal aren't the same. Does it make your normal wrong? Nope, it makes us human. It makes us different. How boring would the world be if all our normals were the same?"

"You don't think we're crazy?"

"I think you're a part of Molly for a reason. And I'd love to find out that reason. Does Molly know why you exist?"

I stare down at my sneaker covered feet. Slowly, I shake my head. "She's pushed it all so far down, we're buried. But little glimpses are coming through, and I have to protect her."

"What do you have to protect her from?"

"From..." I don't know exactly how to answer this. "From suffering."

"Is she suffering with her family?"

"She loves her family so much. But now that Tina's dead, I don't know if M can cope. I need to keep her safe." I feel lost in my head. I have this huge responsibility to shield M from everything bad, and I feel like I'm failing.

"AJ?"

"Sorry what?" I look up at Amelia.

"Where did you go?" I gaze at Amelia. "Just then. Where did you go?"

"It's all my fault. I feel like I'm not doing enough to protect M."

"AJ, you've done a wonderful job of protecting Molly. But now, you can let me help you both."

"Both? You mean all four of us."

"I haven't had the pleasure of meeting anyone but you. Do you think I might be able to?"

I lift my gaze to look into the eyes of Amelia Morgan. She really does want to help. She's not judgmental or dismissive. I like her. "I'll have to talk with the others, make sure they're okay to talk to you."

"I think that's a reasonable request. I'd like to get to know all of you. Do you think I could talk with Molly?"

I'm debating if I can trust her to M. M's incredibly special, and I don't want her hurt. "I'm not ready for you to meet her yet."

"Okay. That's fair. Tell me what your role is among the four of you."

"I told you already, I'm the protector."

"I know. And I respect the fact you are. Because that's an especially important job. How do you protect her?"

A shiver runs up my spine. Having to tell another person what I have to do, makes me sick to the stomach. "It's my job to get Neve to take over when..." I pause, struggling with my words. Trying to find the correct wording makes me look like some kind of sicko, someone who doesn't care. But I do, I care so much for M. "... when it's time."

"Time for what?" Amelia asks in a gentle tone.

"When I hear the door closing, I get the bunny out of the box in my cupboard, and take it to Neve. I loathe the moment I have to do that. Absolutely abhor it with every fiber of my body. It makes me sick."

"Okay," she says while looking at me. "Then why do it?"

"Don't you see?" I jump to my feet, and walk over to the furthest wall. "I don't have a choice. If I don't do it, then M would have to deal with it by herself. She's not strong enough; she can't."

"Deal with it? As in it's happening now?"

"No, not now. Not since she was adopted. Before that." My frustration is mounting, and it's nibbling away at me. I'm angry at myself because I seem to making everything worse. "She wasn't able to cope. And she can't cope now. I have to do this to make sure she's safe. M is..." My arms tremble with irritation. Turning, I make a fist and punch the damn wall. My hand goes through the wall, and as I pull back, I notice there's a cut above my knuckle. It's bleeding, but not a lot. Just enough for a few drops to fall to the ground.

"AJ, show me your hand," Amelia says as she jumps up off her chair, and runs toward me. She grips my hand in hers, and looks at the wound. "Now, that was stupid, wasn't it?" she scolds me.

I'm not sure how to take that remark. I start laughing. "You just reprimanded me like you're my mother."

"Well, if you want to behave like a child then I'll treat you like one," she says with a smile. "Let me get a nurse to come in and look at you. I'll be back in a moment. And by the way, I think you'll need a stitch."

I flick my other hand at her. "I've suffered worse."

Amelia shakes her head, then walks out of the room. I stand looking at my knuckle, and blame myself for being a hot-headed jerk.

Holding my throbbing hand up, I wait for someone to come back into the room.

Amelia comes in holding a small first aid kit. "The nurse was going to come in, but I thought you'd be more comfortable with me." She juts her chin, indicating for me to sit. "Do you know where we are?"

"Of course, in the hospital. You'd think that would've been one of the first questions to ask."

She smiles as she takes a cleaning solution out of the kit. "You're a smart-ass," she sasses.

"Only to people I like," I counter.

"Good. You like me."

"And to people who irritate me," I quickly add.

She smiles again, even bigger this time. "Definitely a smart-ass." She cleans the small wound, and we get a better view of it. It's more like a scratch than anything else. "It's not as bad as I thought."

"I was just thinking the same thing." I look at my rough hands, and notice how small the wound is on my knuckle. "That'll bruise by tomorrow."

"Yeah, it will." She finishes cleaning, then quickly dresses it. "How are you feeling?" Amelia sits back in her seat, and places her finger to her chin.

"You look like a therapist when you do that with your finger."

"Do I? Funny thing is, I actually am."

I roll my eyes. "I know," I say. I cradle my hand, but try to keep it elevated so it doesn't throb so much when the blood runs to it.

"How are you feeling? We were talking about you and how you help Molly."

"I feel like I don't do enough for her. I've always tried to protect her, but I'm failing." I run my hand through my short hair.

"AJ, I think what you've done for Molly, is exceptional. You've kept her safe, and you've guarded her from things she couldn't deal with. Honestly, I think you saved her when she needed you the most."

I look up at Amelia. "You think I saved her?"

"I do. And, I think it's important for me to get to know all of you, including Molly."

A huge knot forms in my stomach. My throat becomes parched, and I try to swallow to moisten it, but I can't. I'm worried. So damn worried.

"What's wrong? You've gone white," Amelia says as she sits forward, leaning her elbows on her knees.

"I'm terrified of what *can* happen to M. I feel it, in here." I make a fist with my good hand, and lean it against my stomach. "I've protected her for so long, I don't know if I'm ready for you to do this."

"Doesn't she deserve to heal? Don't *you* deserve to heal?" It's never been about me. Ever. I blink at Amelia, trying to focus on her words. "Your hardened eyes carry a mixture of shock, and sadness."

"I've never really thought about myself. Everything I've ever done has all been for M."

"I know. And I respect you for everything you've done. But I'm here because I want to help, and I think I can."

I stare blankly for a few seconds. "I think you can too."

She gives me a half-crooked smile. "Yeah." She nods her head. "I think it's time I meet everyone else. But not today. Today we've had enough, and you should be exhausted."

One cue, a huge yawn overtakes me. She's right. How did she know I'm tired? I didn't even know until she mentioned it. "When will you come back?"

"I'm going to talk with Molly's parents first, because it's important we're all on the same page. We want what's best for all of you."

"What if they think we're crazy?"

"Would you like to talk to Molly's parents? They know I'm here."

"M's parents are here?"

"Yep, and Dylan." Her boyfriend is here too? I shake my head. "When you're ready to meet them, you can. Baby steps first. We'll start with Molly's parents, when you're ready."

I nod my head. I can do that. I like her Mom and Dad; I always have. "I'm tired, do you mind if I go back to my room to get some sleep?"

"I'll take you," she offers.

"I can take myself." I stand to leave, but hesitate. "You best go first. I'm not ready to face M's parents yet."

"I'll see you soon. Right, AJ?" I nod my head. "Nice meeting you." She gives me her hand, and I shake it.

Yeah, I like her. And I think she's right, she'll be able to help us.

CHAPTER 21

I stretch in the bed and open my eyes. Looking around, I'm temporarily displaced. Where am I?

"Mom?" I call as I notice her asleep on the chair.

"Sweetheart," she says as she leaps to her feet. "Molly?"

"What? Yeah. Wait." I look down at my hand and notice the bandage. "What happened to my hand?" I try to flex it, but the ache is too bad and I wince in pain. I search Mom's averted eyes, and I'm taken back by her silence. Suddenly, I remember. I remember everything. My heart beats like crazy as I try to make sense of the memories flooding me.

"I don't understand," I say as I desperately search for answers.

"Doctor Morgan is on her way to see you," Mom says.

"Tina? Please tell me that was a nightmare."

Mom's eyes fill with tears, she lowers her chin and shakes her head. I see tears drip to the top of her shoe. "Preston's been arrested," she replies while choking on the words.

I lift my trembling hands to my face. The ache of my hand is unbearable, but it's nowhere near as bad as the misery in my heart.

The door opens, and a short woman walks in. "Hi. How are you today?" she asks me.

Wiping the tears away, I nod once. "My hand hurts and I don't know why. Who are you?"

"My name is Amelia Morgan. Maybe I can help with that. Do you mind if I sit and speak with you?" I shake my head. "Would you like your Mom to stay?"

"Don't go, Mom," I beg.

"I won't," Mom says offering me a slight smile.

Amelia drags a chair over to sit beside me on the bed. "I'll properly introduce myself. My name is Amelia Morgan, and I'm a psychotherapist. I specialize in dissociative identity disorder. Or, as it's more commonly known, DID."

My head whirls. What and huh? "Dis… huh?"

Amelia smiles. "Dissociative identity disorder."

"I don't know what you're talking about. What is that? Is it bad? I don't…" I shrug, trying to form a coherent sentence.

"No, it's not that bad."

"Am I like, crazy?"

"No, not at all." She takes a recorder out of her bag, and holds it up to me. "I'm not a fan of taking notes. I find it distracts me. Do you mind if I record our conversation?"

"I'm okay with it," I say in a weary, softer tone. "I think."

"Paris, would you mind?" Amelia asks.

"Not at all." Mom turns to me, and says, "It's okay, Molly. She's here to help all of us."

I trust Mom with my life. "Okay then."

Amelia starts recording our conversation. "Can I have a look at your hand?"

I hold it out to her. "I don't know what I did. I can't remember."

"I was here yesterday, and I spoke with AJ."

"AJ?" I turn my head, and furrow my brows together. AJ. I know that name. Closing my eyes, I try to place where I know AJ from. "Wait. You spoke with AJ?" The fogginess is lifting, and I'm regaining clarity.

"I did," Amelia confirms.

Opening my eyes, I'm unsure of what to think. "I thought he was a figment of my imagination. He's not real. He's like an imaginary friend. I think."

"He is real. And he lives inside of you." She pointedly looks down at my hand. "Do you remember how this happened?"

I try to flex my hand again. The ache is still there, like a new wound. "I don't."

"AJ was frustrated with himself, and punched a wall."

I blink rapidly for what feels like hours. I'm trying to come to terms with what she's saying. My hands tremble, and my breathing elevates. "I don't understand. How can this other person live inside me? What's wrong with me?" Hysteria seems to be taking over all of me. I hit the side of my head with my fist. "Get it out, get it out of me."

"Molly, calm down. There's nothing wrong."

"Sweetheart." Mom flies to her feet, and comes over to me, embracing me. "Shh, it's okay. Everything will be okay."

"Molly," Amelia's voice is strong, and authoritative. I peep out from under-Mom's arm. "You need to focus on me, okay?"

I take several deep breaths, trying to calm my inner tsunami of mixed emotions. The overwhelming fear of being crazy is the strongest one.

"I'm focusing," I say as I close my eyes and calm my breathing.

"Okay. That's good. Breathing techniques can really help."

"I do yoga, so I can do that."

"Perfect." Mom steps away, and I can hear the squeak of the plastic chair as she returns to her seat. "Open your eyes for me, Molly." Amelia is standing in front of me. "What do you know about AJ?"

I turn my chin to look away, unsure of how to answer the question. "I don't know anything."

"Do you remember the first time you met him?"

I strain my memory bank, but everything is fuzzy. "I don't know," I say again.

"Molly, there's no right or wrong answers. And I'm here to help the best way I can."

Instead of me struggling with memories I can't focus on, I change direction. "You said you're a psychologist?"

"No, not a psychologist. I'm a psychotherapist and I specialize in dissociative identity disorder."

"What exactly is that?"

"Have you ever heard of multiple personality disorder?" I nod. "Dissociative identity disorder used to be known as multiple personality disorder."

"So I'm like, schizophrenic? I have a split personality or something?" What the actual fuck!

"No, you're not schizophrenic at all. Schizophrenia is something altogether different. What I think, and I have to have more sessions with you to be sure, is that you have DID. The difference is, DID is brought on by trauma in the younger, formative years."

"Trauma?" Mom asks the question I'm thinking.

"What kind of trauma?" I ask.

"When the mind is faced with an overwhelming, life-threatening situation, it can create what we call alters, or other personalities, to deal with that particular trauma. It's a survival mechanism we have when we have to deal with certain events before we're emotionally mature enough to do so."

"But what could've brought this on?" Mom asks.

"In Molly's case, I don't know yet. AJ was as open as he could be, but he did indicate I had to ask one of the other alters."

"Wait? I have more than one? This isn't normal," I screech. "It's not normal!"

"Tina's death." Mom brings her shaky hand to her mouth. "Molly said her name wasn't Molly, it was Neve. Could it have started then?"

"I did?" It's all so vague. I'm struggling with all of this.

"I can't know for sure, but I highly doubt it. I need to speak to the other alters first before I can confirm anything."

Amelia can't tell me why I've developed these voices in my

head. "Will they go away?" Maybe they'll leave me, and never come back. If I try hard enough. Ignore them if they try to talk to me, then maybe they'll leave.

"In my experience, alters are here to stay. Locking an alter out can do more damage than learning to embrace them, and live with them."

"You're talking about voices in my head. How the fuck am I supposed to live with this?"

"Molly, please," Mom begs. "I know this is a lot, but you have to hear her out. We all do."

"I'm being told I'm fucking psychotic. How the hell do I know if one of these assholes in my head won't turn nuts and go on a killing spree? Get them out! Get them out now! I don't care what you have to do. Shock therapy. Drugs. Take part of my brain out. Just...Get. Them. Out!" A frenzied madness takes over. I'm screaming and yelling, while crying and trying to hit my head my non-injured hand. "Why? Why me? Why can't you leave?"

In my panicked state, I feel a prick on my arm, unsure on who or what just happened. All I'm aware of is that my is mind becoming quiet, and my eyes droop shut. Order and peace quickly replace the out-of-control delirium.

"What's happ..."

"Shh, it's okay," Mom whispers. Her cheeks are wet from tears; her eyes red from crying.

I'll take care of you.

"Who are you?" I slur as I lose the fight I had in me.

I'm AJ, and I'll always care for you.

Closing my eyes, I'm forced into a place where my mind is tranquil.

CHAPTER
22

All I've done is cry. Amelia cleared me to go home, and I've been here since yesterday. Thankfully Mom's called Sky at work to tell her what happened with Tina, and Sky has given me as much time off work as I need. Dylan has been here with me. Well, by with me, I mean he's down stairs while I'm in my room. I don't want to see him.

I can't deal with anything.

I can barely think about the funeral in two days. I'm a damn mess.

Amelia is coming for home visits too.

I'm in zombie-robot mode. All I want to do is lock everyone out, and not talk to anyone.

My best friend is gone. Tina was always what I could only hope to be. She was happy, and energetic, and fucking sane.

Unlike me.

M, it's time we talk.

"How can I talk to you when I can't even see you? I made you up, and now I want you to go."

I'm sorry. That's not how this works. I think it's time you talk to Neve.

"No, I don't want to talk to any of you."

You need to know why we're here.

"You think I don't know?"

Do you? Do you really know? Because there's a part of your life you buried.

"Buried? Is that what Amelia was talking about? Trauma and stuff?"

Zhen moves on the bed, laying on his back, and gives my nose a lick before he closes his eyes again and falls asleep immediately.

Yep. M, you need to talk to her. She wants to talk to you, fill in some of the blanks. She'll be able to explain why we're here.

I sit up in bed, disturbing Zhen's sleep. He lazily jumps off the bed, and sluggishly walks over to my bedroom door. He sits, thumping his tail. He needs to go to the bathroom. Pushing back the covers, I get up, and open the door for Zhen so he can go out the doggie door to the back yard. Happily, he trots off down the stairs.

Taking a deep breath, I turn to go back to bed. But Tina's door makes me stop. It's closed, and for a split second, I wait for her to come happily bouncing out of her room, busting with excitement, and eager to tell me about what she's doing.

I hold my breath, anticipating. Praying.

I slowly walk over to her room, and place my palm on her door. Leaning my forehead against it, I hold in the tears. "She's never coming back, is she?" I ask in a whisper.

No. The voice is soft, almost childlike.

"Who are you?"

I'm Neve.

"Great, another one." I roll my eyes.

Please, don't say that.

I have to give her the opportunity to talk to me and tell me about why she's here. "I'm sorry. This is all too much for me. I'm not sure I can deal with..."

Me? Us?

"I don't know how..." I can't complete a sentence. I'm struggling with everything.

Let me explain why.

I take several deep breaths, open Tina's door and go to her closet. I sit at the bottom, surrounded by all her clothes. I breathe in; Tina's smell clings to her clothes. Fresh summer breeze straight after a light rainfall. It's the subtle perfume she wore every day.

Curling into myself, I lean my head on my drawn-up knees. "Okay, why."

I was the first.

"You were the first what?"

I came to you first.

"Why?"

Because of what he used to do to you.

"Who? My biological father?"

No, not him. Your father was careless, nothing more. He couldn't cope with you. He tried, but he lost his way after your biological mother left. No, definitely not him.

"I don't remember anything before I came to live here. Wait, you mean Dad?"

No, not him either.

"I don't understand what you're talking about. Or who it is you're referring to."

No, you wouldn't. Because I saved you. I took all the abuse. Every time he came into your room, every time he looked at you, I'd come forward and let you sleep while I took on what he did.

My breathing intensifies. I don't know... I...

The foster family you went to live with after your biological father surrendered you.

"I was given away?" I say slowly. "I thought the authorities took me."

They did. But authorities want to keep families together, so they asked him what he wanted. He said he couldn't care for you, and told them not to return you.

"How..." I gulp. "How do you know this? They would never have told us this." Would they?

They told the foster parents. They were talking one night, we overheard them.

My father didn't want me. I take several moments, trying to come to terms with that. But something so huge can't be dealt with in only a moment. "Tell me about the man who hurt me." I think about that for a moment before adding, "Who hurt us."

He was a foster boy. Sixteen when you went to live with them. You were nearly three. He started to touch you soon after you arrived. He warned you if you told anyone, he'd kill you.

I notice my breathing is short and shallow, though fast. My mouth is open and dry. I can't comprehend anything. "How long did he..." I can't bring myself to say the words.

Until he aged out and was told to leave the foster home.

"Months?"

Nearly two years. It started as touching, then it became more. He would play a song so no one would hear you crying. Neve's voice becomes small. *So no one would hear our cries.*

I feel sick. I haven't eaten more than a few mouthfuls of food, and I want to bring it all up. "You took all of that burden?" I ask.

I did. For you.

"You should've left me. You allowed him to hurt you?"

We didn't know, M. None of us knew. We were all scared of him. I took the hurt, because I love you. Because I need to protect you.

"Neve, I don't think I can hear you tell me any more. I'm sorry."

Will you let me talk with Amelia?

"I think we all have to talk to her."

M, please, go tell your family. We desperately want you to heal.

I stand from my sister's closet, and head out. Standing at the top of the stairs, I'm overwhelmed with everything. I was sexually abused as a child. I look down to the foyer, and suddenly the thought of ending it all becomes appealing. Inching closer to the railing, I grip it with the hand not in the bandage. I can push myself over, and hopefully end it all here. I'm struggling though. A part of me doesn't want to die, but another part just wants silence, peace. A peace I'm not sure I can find while I'm alive.

With tears streaming down my face, I lift my leg and hook it over the railing.

Woof.

Zhen's bark is loud, and frightens me. He's standing beneath, looking up at me, dancing and barking.

Woof.

"What is it, Zhen?" Mom asks, coming out to see what he's barking at. She looks up, and sees me ready to jump. Ready to end this absolute shit show of a fucked-up life. "Dylan!" she yells.

Dylan runs out, and sees me. Without any hesitation, he runs up the stairs three at a time, grabs me around the waist, and pulls me down to the floor. "You can't do this. I love you," he pleads into my hair as he holds me.

"You can't love me. I'm damaged." I burst into tears as I grip onto his shirt.

"We'll get through this, Molly. Whatever it is, we'll get through this together." He lays kiss after kiss on my forehead while stroking my hair.

"Sweetheart, why would you do that?" Dad asks coming up the stairs, Mom right beside him. They're both sobbing.

I stare at them, unable to tell them. I'm hurting so much. I can barely breathe. It's going to ruin them. I can't talk. I close my eyes, and lower my head, weeping.

Everything about me is a lie. They got a dud of a daughter. "I wish you could give me back," I wail. "I don't deserve you."

"That's bullshit. We're the lucky ones," Mom says. "We've always been so fortunate to have you, and your sister. We couldn't have asked for anyone better. We got two girls who are *our* girls. It doesn't matter to us if your father and I didn't create you. What matters is you belong with us. We love you so much." Mom steps toward me, Dylan steps back and Mom takes over with a hug. Dad joins in.

"Family is not about blood, Molly. Family is the people we choose to have a bond with. And we choose you," Dad whispers. "Please, don't leave us."

I have to tell them. I can't let this go on. I have to find strength. What are they going to think? What are they going to say?

We're here for you. We'll always be here.

"I know," I whisper.

"What do you know?" Dad asks.

I shake my head. Pursing my mouth shut, I nibble on my lips as I try to find courage. "I need to tell you all something." I look to Dylan first. He's the one who's going to leave when he finds out. Why would he want to stick around? I'm defective. I can't function properly. I have these other people in my head, I was sexually abused as a child, my sister has been brutally murdered, and I'm never going to be a whole person again.

"What is it?" Dylan asks. Mom and Dad hold hands as they all stare at me.

"I um…" I'm furiously attempting to hold back the tears pooling behind my cracked dam walls. "When I was young, nearly three, I went into foster care before I was adopted here."

"Okay," Dad says, not knowing where I'm going with this.

"There was a boy who lived in the house. Another foster child."

"Okay," Dylan says even slower and lower than Dad. "Why are you telling us this?" His shoulders straighten and he pushes out his chest. His jaw tightens, and his eyes narrow. Dylan suspects my next words.

"He…" I look away, a lump sitting like a hot coal in my throat. I can't meet any of their eyes. I just can't. "He… um." No, I can't say it. Closing my eyes, I shake my head. Unable to tell them the truth. It's obscene, and horrible, and unspeakable.

"What is it?" Mom asks. Her soft hand gently stroking my hair. "You can tell us anything, Molly."

"I, um, I'm um. He um…he ahh. He um." Shit, just say it. Tell them. Find your courage, Molly.

We're here for you.

I run my hand over my forehead, rubbing the tension that's building. "He used to do things to me."

"Like what?" Dad's voice is rigid, hard with anger.

"What?" Mom's breathless expression is filled with pain.

"He started soon after I arrived into the foster home. Touching at first, then it progressed to more." No one says anything, and I'm too afraid to look at anyone. I'm so scared. I'm also embarrassed.

Why didn't I speak up when he started doing that?

Why didn't I tell my foster parents?

Why didn't I kick him in the penis, and hurt him?

Why didn't I do something?

This isn't our fault, M. This is all him. He did this to us, he hurt us. He manipulated us. He's a monster. You were only a baby.

"I'm sorry," I say, bursting into tears. The miserable feeling of impotence strangles my soul. Crushing it. I have nothing left in me. I have no courage. I have no fight. I have no spirit.

Collapsing to the floor, I pray for sanctuary.

Please God, show me some kindness. Show my parents some humanity, and take me. I can't keep hurting them. They've suffered enough. It's not fair for them to have to endure any more pain.

"No, no. You have nothing to be sorry for," Dylan says as he scoops me up in his embrace. "We'll get through this. I promise, we'll get through this." With gentle hands, he smooths my hair down while placing loving kisses on my head.

My parents don't say anything. I can't bring myself to look at them, I don't want to see the shame in their eyes.

I hear heavy footsteps leaving.

I'm so ashamed of myself.

I've driven one of my parents to leave. They must be so repulsed by me.

"Who is he, and where can I find him?" Dad says in a cold, steely voice.

Opening my eyes, I see Dad standing near the top of stairs, with his gun in his hand. He's deadly serious. He's going to hurt *him.*

"Dad, you can't." I jump to my feet, and run over to him. "You can't."

"The only reason Preston is still alive is because the police got to him first. I'm not making the same mistake with *that* lowlife pedophile. I'm going to kill him." Dad's jaw is so tight, he's barely opening his mouth to speak.

"Thomas, we need to calm down, and think about what we're going to do," Mom says.

"I'm going to find him, and I'm going to kill him. There, I thought about it."

"Mr. Dawson, we need to get the police involved."

"What? No, no police," I protest. "I'm not going to the police. And you're not going to find him and kill him. It's done, it's in the past. We forget all about it, and move on."

"Move on?" Dad seethes.

"Molly, until we all deal with this, there's no moving on," Mom says as she steps in front of Dad and moves toward me.

"Well I'm not going to the police. What am I going to say? Someone who lives in my head told me I was… you know, when I was three? Do you even know how crazy that sounds? You can't think, that anyone will believe me. I have no proof."

"If you don't go to the police, then I'll find him, and kill him. End of story," Dad says as he walks back to his room.

"Mom?" I plead. "Please, make him see sense."

She shakes her head. "This *is* your father seeing sense. We need to involve the authorities."

"No!" I shout. "They'll put me in a psych hospital and say I'm making everything up. I don't want this. They'll dope me up on medication trying to prove I'm crazy. I'm not crazy!"

"No one is putting you anywhere," Dylan says.

The air is thick with such sadness and anger. Not toward me, but toward the unbearable and unspeakable situation.

"We all need to calm down," Mom says. "Everyone, downstairs so we can talk about this and figure it out." Mom leaves ahead of Dylan and me, Dad passes us as he follows Mom.

Dylan and I stay upstairs for a moment. He hugs me tighter than he has ever before. "We're breaking up," I say, trying to spare him from a lifetime of crazy.

"What?" He slightly pushes on my shoulders so he can look at me. "No, we're not."

"There is too much happening. I've got voices talking to me. I don't know if I'll ever be able to function in any type of relationship, sexual or otherwise. I'm a damn mess. We're breaking up." It's not an option for him to say no.

"Well, I'm glad you acknowledge you hear voices, and as far as sex goes, I've never pressured you before, so why do you think I'd change now? And no, we're not breaking up."

"Yes, we have to," my tone is unwavering.

"No, we don't." He's as determined as I am.

"We can't work, Dylan. We can't be together."

"And you think you can decide for me? Right?"

"You'll end up being miserable."

"Ah, I see. So you're being humane and sparing me? Making sure my feelings don't get hurt?"

Finally, he gets it. "Exactly."

"Bullshit. You just want to hide away, and hope to God no one ever sees you. You want to hide from the world. Well, too bad, Molly. Because we're not breaking up, and I'm not going anywhere. Tell me you don't care for me."

"Of course, I do, which is why we have to break up."

"That's the reason why we *won't* break up."

Girl, he loves us, he ain't going nowhere.

That voice sounded different. It's not Neve's, or AJ's. "Who are you?"

I'm Kate.

"Kate?"

"Who's Kate?" Dylan asks.

I hold a finger up to Dylan. "Are you new?"

She giggles. *No, silly. I've been here since AJ.*

"Can you do me a favor please?"

Sure, anything I can do to help.

"Can we talk later? I need to get through everything Neve told me about."

I can come back.

"Before you go. It's just the three of you, right?"

You really are silly. Nope, it's the four of us. Including you.

"It's a lot to handle, but okay. I'll see you soon?" Even saying that aloud sounds stupid.

Bye.

I look at Dylan, and he's staring at me like I've grown three heads. "I know, it's a lot."

"It's amazing. And I'm looking forward to meeting all of you."

Is he serious? "You don't think I'm crazy?"

He shakes his head. "I think you're incredibly smart. And I think if you have these voices inside you, there's a reason why. I also think we all need to be on the same page, and figure out exactly what's happening. And we need to go to the police about what happened to you. In order to have a future, we need to confront the past."

He links our hands together, and leads me down the staircase toward the back of the house where the kitchen and dining room is. Sitting at the table, Mom and Dad are already drinking cups of coffee.

Dylan walks over to the fridge, pours me a glass of cold water, and gets ingredients out to make a sandwich.

I look at all the paperwork on the table, and my heart lurches as I see Tina's name across it. It's paperwork from the funeral home.

My parents are talking between themselves, and I'm staring at a photo of Tina from when we went on vacation. She's wearing a large, oversized straw hat, and is holding up a mocktail, smiling at the camera in her bikini. The sun reflects off the crystal-clear blue pool behind her.

I pick the photo up, and run my thumb over Tina's happy face. "Remember how she snuck a bottle of whiskey, drunk it all and was throwing up for two days after that?" I say with a smile.

"She had vomit in her hair," Mom says and rolls her eyes.

Dad chuckles.

"She was so drunk. She sat at the bottom of the shower, trying to sober up so you wouldn't find out. She made me promise not to tell you," I say.

"Because obviously, we wouldn't have known." Mom laughs.

"She tried to blame it on food poisoning," I say.

"Yes. That stench of drinking hard alcohol for hours wasn't conspicuous or anything," Dad chuckles. "We knew what she was doing. And we let her do it."

"Why?" I ask.

"Because she drank herself into oblivion. And we knew she'd feel so sick for days and we were hoping it would teach her a lesson."

"It did. She hates whiskey now," I say. The smile on my face quickly disappears as I correct myself. "She hated whiskey."

The mood quickly swings to somber, my heart feeling the sharp pang of loss. I hate not having her here. Not talking to her. Tina would've told me how lucky I am that I have these other personalities living inside. She would've seen the light side of it, and made me feel something other than shame and embarrassment.

I have to push on, for my parents.

For Dylan.

But especially for Tina.

Her life was horrifically ripped away from us, and I have to preserve the good.

I take several deep breaths trying to calm my nerves.

"You need to eat," Dylan says as he places a sandwich in front of me.

I nod. I do. I feel like I've barely had anything to eat or drink for a long time.

"You're all right. I need to go to the police. But first, I have to talk to Amelia."

"She's coming first thing tomorrow. She'll be here at seven, before she goes to work," Mom says.

"Good. We all need to talk to her." I tap my temple. "Neve especially."

Mom, Dad, and Dylan all look to each other, unsure on how to respond. This is unchartered territory for all of us. Hell, if it wasn't happening to me, I'd say I was crazy too.

I pick the sandwich up, and nibble.

I must move forward.

CHAPTER 23

MOLLY

I feel better this morning. Calmer. Although tomorrow is Tina's funeral, and I know that's going to trigger strong emotions inside of me. I'm hoping Amelia can be there for me. I'm not sure how much strength I'll have seeing my sister in her coffin. I think I'm going to crumble.

I've had a shower, and a light breakfast, and now we're waiting for Amelia.

Dylan said he'd like to be here too, but he's spent too much time here, and I'm afraid he's on dangerous ground at work. I don't want him losing his job because of me. Although he assures me, with his skillset, he'd be headhunted before they even had a chance to say, 'you've been fired.' But I don't want the guilt of that hanging over me too. So he agreed to go to work today, and take a day for the funeral tomorrow.

"How are you?" Mom asks as she walks into the kitchen and sees Zhen and me sitting at the dining table, looking outside.

"Tired, but not as bad as yesterday. Where's Dad?"

"He had some things to do at work. He'll be back soon. He wanted to be here when Amelia arrives."

"I'm nervous," I say.

"Why?"

"Everything happening in here, it's not normal." I tap on my head, then lower my hand in search of Zhen.

"Normal is such a difficult word, Molly. I don't want to say, 'no, it's not normal,' because in reality, this is how your life is going to be. We all have to accept it. Especially you, because you're the one who has to live with it."

"I tried to break up with Dylan. It's the kindest thing I can do for him."

"Because you can't see a future with him?"

"It's not that." I let out a long sigh. "How can he be with someone like me?"

"Like you? You're not an alien, honey. You have alters. There's nothing to be ashamed of, or embarrassed about." She makes her coffee, and comes to sit opposite me. Zhen moves his butt closer to me.

"How do I explain this to people?"

"You don't owe anything to anyone. If you want to tell them, tell them. If you don't, then don't. The only people who matter are the ones you care about. Who cares what others think? You've never really been one who's hung up on others' opinions."

"But this is different. This is potentially life-changing."

"It *is* life-changing. But only to you, and to Dylan. I don't give a damn if you have ten alters, or none. You're my daughter, and I'll love you forever."

"But..."

"Molly, it's like this. What if I told you I'm bisexual? What would you say?"

"I'd say, I hope Dad knows."

"And?"

I shrug. "That's it."

She picks her coffee up and takes a sip. "Would you be happy, or upset or disappointed with me?"

"No. It's not my business. I'd still love you; you're my Mom."

She looks at me pointedly. "Exactly. This is no different. I love you, regardless of who I'm talking with."

"But there are four of us."

"Four times the love." Mom smiles.

"You make it sound easy."

Mom coughs, and waves her finger at me. "Hell no. This is anything *but* easy. But I still love you, and always will."

Mom makes me smile. "What did I miss?" Dad asks as he comes into the kitchen. Zorro is right behind him, wagging his tail, and looking for Dad's attention.

"Nothing, yet. Amelia hasn't arrived," I say.

"Good. Just give me a few moments to go get changed." Dad turns to leave and Zorro follows.

"I've been doing some research on DID, and it really blows my mind," Mom says. "It's complex, with so many layers. For most people who have alters and DID, it usually develops from early childhood trauma."

"Yeah?"

"I'm not a psychologist, or psychotherapist, like Amelia is. It's what I've read on the Internet. I've watched a few YouTube videos too. It's fascinating."

Dad returns, this time with Amelia. "Hello," Amelia says as she enters. Zhen stands, makes his way over to her, and sniffs her. "Aren't you a beautiful dog." She squats down, in her expensive, well-cut pant suit, and pets Zhen. Zhen wags his tail, then gives her a quick lick on the cheek before returning to me.

"Zhen likes you," I say.

"Zhen. I love the name."

"Please, sit. Would you like a coffee?" Mom offers.

Amelia stands, and makes her way over to me. She sits opposite me, and takes her little recorder out of her bag. "I'd love a coffee. Black." She holds up the recorder. "Do you mind?" she asks.

"It's fine," I reply.

She brushes Zhen's hair off her pants, but really, she doesn't appear to be fazed by the fact she has dog hair on her. Mom brings over a coffee, and places in front of her. "Thank you." She gives Mom a genuine smile. "Molly?" She looks to me for confirmation. I nod. "How are you today?"

I want to talk to her please. AJ's voice is the loudest.

I have things I need to say. Neve's soft tone, and calmness makes me pay more attention than AJ's.

"Molly?" Amelia brings my attention back to her.

"They're loud. AJ and Neve both know you're here, and want to talk to you."

"Would you mind if I spoke with them?" Amelia asks.

"I don't know how to answer that."

Let me go first, AJ. You've already spoken with her. She needs to know why we're here.

It goes quiet for a few seconds. Then AJ replies. *Okay, you're right. Do you want the bunny?*

"Molly?" I indicate for Amelia to wait a moment.

I don't need the bunny.

Okay. But I'd like to talk to her too.

"You can both talk to her. But just Neve for now. Okay?" I ask.

Yeah.

Yep.

I look at Amelia. "Neve wants to talk."

"I'll be here when she's ready." She picks her coffee up, and takes a small sip.

Molly, can you close your eyes please?

My eyelids become unusually heavy. They feel dry and scratchy. I rub at them several times. The more I do it, the more I fall into a blackness.

Neve

Opening my eyes, I examine the room. Cautiously, I shrink away from Molly's parents, and Amelia. Amelia especially. I don't trust her, but I know I need to talk to her.

"Hello, Neve," she says with a gentle smile.

I cast my eyes down, not wanting to look at her. "Do you have colored pencils and some paper?" I ask.

"I don't. But I can make sure I have some for you next time we speak. Would that be okay?"

I nod my head, and hug my arms around my body.

"I have some paper, and some plain pencils. Would you like them…Neve?" M's Mom asks.

"Yes, please."

I hear the scraping of the chair, then footsteps as she leaves. I try to sneak a little look at M's Dad. He catches me peeking at him, and offers me a smile. "Hello," he says in a gentle voice. He reaches out to touch me and I cower away from him. He quickly retracts his hand.

"Hello," I say in a small voice.

"My name's Thomas, and I'm really happy to meet you."

I nod my head. I don't want to talk to him. He seems nice, but I don't trust him yet. I know he's never hurt M, but I'm still careful.

"Neve, would you like to talk to me?" Amelia asks.

I cast a side glance at Thomas, a little bit afraid of him. It's like he's reading my thoughts. "Would you like me to leave?" he asks. I slowly nod. "Okay. I'll go." He stands and walks out of the room.

M's Mom returns caring a stack of blank paper, and some pencils. A big smile comes to me. "Yay!" I say as I clap my hands together.

"I could only find some pencils. I'm sorry I don't have more. But I'll get you some for next time." She sits next to Amelia.

"I like to read too." I pick one of the pencils up, and start to draw on the paper.

"What do you like to read? I'll get you some books."

"I want to read the Harry Potter books. And the Percy Jackson ones. I like things that are about magic."

"I love Harry Potter, so I'll make sure I get them for you," M's Mom says.

"Thank you, Mrs. Dawson."

"You can call me Paris." I meet her eyes for a second, and smile.

"Neve, can you tell me about yourself?" Amelia asks.

"My name's Neve. And I help M when she needs me."

"How old are you?"

"I'm eleven."

"You said you help Molly when she needs you. How do you help her?"

"I take her pain away and make her go to sleep." I keep drawing, not looking at Paris or Amelia. "Why are you here?" I ask.

"Me?" Paris asks.

"Not you. But her." I point to Amelia.

"I'm here to help Molly. I work with people who are like you and her."

"How can you help us?"

"I'd like to help all of you get along. You all have to live together, just like a very close family. And sometimes, in a very close family, there could be fighting, and nasty things said. I'm here to talk to you all, so we can find a way for all of you to be happy together. But before I can do that, I have to understand everything about you."

"I have to take the pain," I admit openly.

"How do you do that?"

"When *he* used to come into the room, I'd make sure M was asleep. I'd send her to a place where she couldn't feel what he was doing. I took all that for her. I never want M to feel what I felt."

"How do you know when he'd come into the room?"

"First it was the song. He'd play a song, and I knew what was going to happen. I couldn't let M go through that. The first few times, she cried, and I knew I had to do something. She was very young. Younger than me. I knew I had to protect her."

"Can you tell me what song it was?"

My shoulders tense, and I shake my head so much it feels like my brain is jiggling around. "No, I don't want to remember."

"That's okay. How long would you stay to help Molly?"

"I'd stay until it was over. I love M, and I never wanted her to remember what *he* used to do. I took everything away from her. *His* smell, *his* words, *his* sounds." A tear rolls down my cheek, and fractures my heart. "I don't want to talk about *him* anymore."

"We don't need to talk about him. How about AJ, do you like him?"

"I like AJ, but he blames himself."

"Why does he blame himself?"

"He feels bad, because after AJ came to live with us, he decided he was the protector. The one who kept us all safe. He would come into my room with the bunny when it was time to go to *him.* He hated having to tell me that. I hated having to hear it. But I don't blame him. Kate helps AJ not hate himself."

"What would you like to happen, Neve?"

I look up from my drawing, and focus on Amelia. "I think this is the first time anyone's every asked me what I want." M's Mom gasps as she struggles to hold back tears. "It's okay, Paris. I understand." I stand, walk over to her, and hug her.

She hesitantly lifts her arms, and hugs me back.

"I don't like anyone touching me, but I like your hugs. You're cuddly," I say as I tighten my arms around her. "Is it okay if I hug you?"

"You can hug me any time you want, my sweet girl."

I sit down, and give her a little smile. I like M's Mom. She's so nice. Just then I notice the doggy staring at me. "Hello," I say to the doggy.

"That's Zhen, he's Molly's dog," M's Mom offers.

"Hello, Zhen." I slide off the chair, and sit on the floor. Zhen is hesitant, not sure of who I am. "Come here, boy." I pat the place in front of my little legs. Zhen stands, with a slight wag to his tail, he paces over.

"Neve, can you describe to me what you look like?" Amelia asks.

"I don't like my hair." I pick up a strand and look at it. "It's dull. See?" I hold it up to Amelia. "I don't like mirrors either. I'm not very pretty so I don't like to look at myself. My legs are little, but I'll get taller one day." Zhen cuddles into me, and I hug him so tight. "I don't really like people. But I like you." I look up to M's Mom. "And I like Zhen." I give him kisses on the back of his neck. "I think I like you," I say to Amelia.

"I really like you, Neve," M's Mom says.

"I'm tired, can I go to sleep now?" I ask.

"You can. Do you mind if we have Molly back?"

"I can ask her. Night." I'm exhausted, I need to go to sleep.

MOLLY

Opening my eyes, I try to blink a few times. I feel so tired.

"What happened?" I ask Mom and Amelia, but turn, looking for Dad.

"We spoke with Neve," Mom replies.

I listen to the voices, and they're quiet.

"How are you feeling?" Amelia asks.

"Tired. I um…" I close my eyes to try and concentrate, but I hear nothing. "They're quiet." I notice I'm on the floor, and Zhen's panting in front of me. Standing, I brush off my butt, and sit in the chair again.

Mom stands, walks over to the fridge, and pours some cold water into a glass. She brings it over to me. "Here, have some water." She pushes the glasses closer to me.

"I feel tired." Picking up the water, I take a sip. "Why?"

"You're just learning about your alters. You'll find certain triggers may bring them out. Maybe they want to be out," Amelia says.

"Neve asked your father to leave," Mom says.

"Is that why Dad's not here?"

"I'm here," Dad says. "I was sitting outside in the foyer. I was listening to everything that happened." He walks in, and sits beside me. "I don't know what to think." He appears confused. But I doubt he's anywhere near as puzzled as I am.

I chuckle to myself.

"What's funny?" Amelia asks.

"Up until recently I thought I was a relatively normal person. Now I find out, I have these…alters, living inside of me. And probably have had them for many years."

"You're still you," she says.

"With these other personalities living inside me?"

"Yes, that's correct." She nods her head. "And the four of you have to learn how to live together. You no longer own this body. It belongs to the four of you. Don't try to lock your alters out."

This is heavy. I run my hand through my hair, trying to come to terms with this.

"Talk to me, Molly," Amelia says.

I let out a deep sigh. "I feel like it's all my fault."

"What?"

"I'm responsible for them." I tap my temple.

"Do you want to know what I know about DID?"

"I want to know why I am the way I am."

"Because you suffered horrific childhood trauma. And your brain went into fight or flight mode, but with repeated and long-term trauma, fight or flight fails. Which is where our brains do whatever they can to survive. And what yours did was dissociate. It said, *I'm going to turn off, and surrender.* Which is where Neve, AJ and Kate live."

"I could've fought him."

"No, you couldn't. I'll tell you why. As young children, we love unconditionally. Our brains aren't capable of seeing any family member as evil. It goes against our fundamental belief that our families are there to give us love, attention, food, and safety. So when trauma is forced on us from someone we trust, we start internalizing it. Questioning ourselves. *Was it something I did? Could I have stopped this? Is it my fault this happened?* The answer is no, to all those questions. Obviously, as a three-year-old, you couldn't do anything to stop what a sixteen-year-old boy did to you. None of this is your fault. And nothing you could've said or done would've made him stop. Nothing. This is not your fault."

A shiver rips through my body. And I feel sick to my stomach. I want to believe what Amelia is saying, but the guilt has become far too big for me to try and come to terms with it.

It's not your fault. AJ says.

It's not your fault. Neve repeats.

It's not your fault. Kate recites.

"You're all echoes of me," I say to my alters

We are all echoes of you.

CHAPTER 24

We're here with you, M. Let me take over.

"No, AJ. I have to face this."

Dylan takes my hand in his. I haven't been able to talk to him yet about everything I've found out. I will, but for right now I have to be here, in the present, for Tina.

"Are you okay?" Dylan whispers on the way to the funeral. Mom and Dad are in the car in front of us. I peek at the chauffeur, and notice he's not paying any attention to us at all.

"It's hard. AJ, Neve, and Kate all want to help. But *I* have to do this." Dylan nods his head like he understands. "I know we have to talk about it, and I want to. But not today."

"It's okay. I've been doing my own research, and I want to be here. For all of you."

I tighten my fingers around his. "Thank you."

The car slows, and I look out the window. We're approaching the chapel where the service will take place. My parents' car stops first. The driver gets out and opens the door for them. Mom slides out first, then Dad.

The car slowly pulls away, and then it's our turn.

Outside the chapel there are so many people. Everyone dressed in dark, somber colors. All the faces blend into one. I can barely open my eyes let alone see who's here for Tina.

A huge lump sits in my throat.

"Miss Molly?" the chauffeur asks.

I haven't even noticed that he has the door open for me. I slide out of the car, voiceless…internally dying from the sadness. I should say thank you to the driver. My brain can't contain any emotion other than heart-shattering grief.

Let me help you. AJ whispers.

"*I* have to do this," I whisper in reply. For everyone who doesn't know about my *condition,* I simply look like I'm encouraging myself to move forward.

But right now, I don't care what anyone thinks.

My parents are right here, waiting for me. My father is crumbling. Tears are falling down his face and his chin is trembling. He's struggling with having to bury his daughter. My mother is an emotional wreck. Smashed, with her own inner demons eating her alive.

I wedge myself between my parents, and hug them with everything I have. I can feel them both trembling with the sobs. I struggle to keep from crying.

It feels like time is moving at sonic speed.

"Mr. and Mrs. Dawson. Molly," Dylan's strong voice cracks.

We turn to look at him, and see the hearse approaching.

Quivers tear through my body as I reach to take Dylan's hand in mine. Mom and Dad gravitate toward each other, holding one another tight.

Dylan wraps his arm around my shoulder, and pulls me into his body.

I can't take my eyes off the hearse. It slows, and finally stops a mere few feet from us. People begin to enter the chapel, leaving only our family standing outside.

"How can she be in there?" I ask.

"I'm sorry," Dylan whispers.

The driver is a woman, dressed in white. The passenger is also a woman dressed in white. Both are simply elegant, regal. They look so loving and serene.

They walk around to the back of the hearse, and open the door. They slide something out, and I nearly vomit. It's my sister's coffin. "Wow," I whisper. It's not a traditional coffin, it's a woven wicker casket, light in color, with a beautiful spray of bold flowers. "I'm sorry I couldn't help you with this," I say to my parents.

Both of them shake their heads, unable to speak.

My tears dry, as I stare at the graceful basket holding my sister.

My Dad, Dylan, Gabriella, Willow, and the two women from the funeral home all take a handle. They carry Tina's coffin into the chapel, and place it on the bier in the front of the sanctuary.

I follow with Mom, and we sit in the front row.

Dad walks over and sits between Mom and me, Dylan on my other side. Gabriella and Willow sit next to Dylan.

One of the women in white stands at the podium and greets us all. She asks for me to come forward and give my eulogy.

Standing, I make my way to the front.

Taking the paper out of my pocket, my hands tremble as I lay it flat on the podium.

We're here for you. AJ whispers to me.

"Hello," I start with a shaky voice. I'm not sure how long I will be able to talk for before I crack and burst into tears.

Dylan stands, buttons up his suit jacket, and comes to stand beside me. He places his arm around me, leans in and gives me a kiss on the forehead. "You've got this," he whispers encouragingly.

Yeah, I do.

For Tina.

"Tina and I were adopted by our parents at a young age. Tina's life didn't start off all happy and rosy. She was surrendered because her mother couldn't care for her and her father was nowhere to be found. Tina was six when our parents adopted her. I first met her when we were seven, one year later.

"Tina and I were both fortunate to grow up in a loving, stable home. We have two incredibly generous and loving parents who have given us everything we could've wanted, and more."

I look to Mom and Dad, and smile. They have to know they're the best parents in the world.

"Tina and I became close from a very early age. The first night I came to live with them, she snuck into my room, crawled under my bed covers, and hugged me. She told me she'd never had a sister before, and now that she had one, she was never going to let me go."

I hold in my tears, and let out a deep sigh. I look away, trying to focus on anything but the words on the page. I catch myself, obliviously playing with the pendant she gave me on our birthday.

"Tina and I grew up with love in our hearts, and stability in our home. Tina was the very essence of beauty, grace, happiness, and love. She always had a smile on her face, and was ready to take on the world."

I swallow back the lump. Dylan hugs me tighter for a few seconds, before slightly releasing his grip.

"We have all surrendered to the loss of our beautiful Tina since that dreadful moment when the monster took her from us. He ripped away a woman whose potential was only beginning to bloom. We will never know what greatness she might have achieved."

I look down to the paper, gathering the remainder of my strength.

"I'll never see Tina again. I won't be able to share all my joys with her, or my failures, or my life. I won't be able to share in hers. I won't hold her hand and eat a tray of brownies when her heart is broken. I won't be able to scream in joy when she tells me she's met the man she wants to spend the rest of her life with. I won't be able to stand beside as her greatest supporter when she says 'I do.' I'll never hold my niece or nephew. I'll never talk with her again."

I swallow back the lump sitting in my throat.

"All because she was viciously ripped away from us. From me, my parents, her friends, and the world."

I take a deep breath and let it out slowly, barely holding on. "I thank you, Tina. You gave me the best memories I could ever ask for. And for that reason, I pledge to you that I will honor and love you until my very last breath.

"I give thanks to being able to find Tina and my family when in my life I had nothing. Tina…" I turn to face her casket and my voice breaks. "You will never be forgotten." I bow my head, collect every emotion, every thought, every memory and return to my seat.

I can't hold on to my emotions any more.

I let them go.

And with the devastating torrent running through my body, I collapse into Dylan's arms.

We're so proud of you.

We all are.

"Please, for now. Let me grieve," I whisper.

AJ's voice is the loudest. Neve and Kate step back. *We're here when you need us.*

I know… I know.

CHAPTER 25

I scratch my nail down a bump on my jeans, trying to flick whatever it is off.

Zhen's laying across my left foot, deep in sleep. He lets out a small whine, then tries to run. It makes me smile. I wonder what he's dreaming about?

"Hey," Dylan says as he comes into the family room and sits beside me.

"Hey," I reply as I avoid contact with his gaze. We haven't spoken about my… um, I'm not sure what to call them. Amelia has called them alters. So have my parents.

"We need to talk about what's happening," he says.

The tension in the room is thick, nearly suffocating.

I nod slowly, "I suppose we do."

"I think the longer we leave it, the harder it'll be to get a handle on where we're heading."

Huh. I figure, now he knows everything, *we* won't be heading anywhere together. "I get it." I suck in the air to fill my lungs, trying to contain all my emotions. But since the funeral yesterday, I've been paralyzed emotionally. I feel like I'm stuck between the plane of dead, and the living. "This is all too much for any person to handle. It's too much for me, so I can only imagine what you're thinking, and how you're feeling." I turn to look at him. "I get it," I say again but in a softer voice.

"I don't think you do."

"There's no shame in wanting to leave, Dylan. Hell, I don't know how I'd react if this was happening to you."

"You wouldn't leave," he says with certainty. "Just like, I'm not going to."

I crinkle my brows questioningly at him. "Why not?" I sigh, somewhat frustrated at him *and* with myself.

"Because I've been spending my time researching, talking with Amelia, and other psychotherapists. And I'm learning about DID and what it means for you, for me, and for us." He waits for me to respond, but I don't. I don't know what to say. "If AJ, Neve, and Kate want to meet me, then I'd really like to meet them too. And I understand that none of them are in a rush to want to do that. But I'd like them to know that I have no intentions to go anywhere, and when they're comfortable, I want them to give me an opportunity to meet them."

I shake my head, and hold in my tears. He can't really want this. "How can you willingly go into this not knowing who'll want to come out from one hour to the next?"

"Because I love you."

"You have to stop saying that."

"But I do."

"Stop!" I snap. "Stop telling me you love me. Stop *showing* me you love me. Just...stop loving me. Please. I don't know how I'm going to survive when you finally realize this is all too much. I have too much baggage. I'm so damaged I'm not sure if I can function."

"Pfft." He stands and flicks his hand at me dismissively. "Just admit it. You want out."

"No, I don't. But I know I'm a freak and a mess."

He paces in front of me, and stops long enough to shake his head and roll his eyes. "Bullshit. You're trying to find a way for us *not* to work. You're a damn coward, Molly."

"Me!" I shriek. "I'm not a coward."

"Again, bullshit."

"I'm fucked up in the head, Dylan. Fucked. Up." I stand and come toe to toe with him.

"Yeah? So what? You're not the only person in the world like this. There are thousands, maybe even millions who have DID. Do they not deserve love? Are you saying you don't deserve to be loved?"

"No, that's not what I'm saying. I'm just so confused!" I nearly yell the last word. I have no idea why I'm holding back.

"You're afraid," he says with confidence.

"Of course, I'm afraid. I'm scared to death. I'm absolutely terrified."

"Why?"

"Because eventually this'll all be too hard for you and you'll leave." I want to cry, to burst into tears and let them fall.

Dylan shakes his head, and steps back from me. He runs his hands through his hair, and shakes his head, again. He looks away from me, his inner turmoil killing him. His tight jaw, and hard shoulders are obvious signs of stress. Finally, after what feels like hours, though it's been only seconds, he faces me and says, "You can allow yourself to be vulnerable, Molly. You can allow yourself to love me back. If I wanted to run, I would've done that already. But I don't. I never want to be anywhere without you."

He floors me. When I think I'm getting through to him to leave, he does the exact opposite of what I'm expecting. He convinces *me* to hang in and fight for myself, just like he's fighting for me.

"You have to stop battling this imaginary rift you think is happening between us. We are too important together for us to end."

"I can't…"

"It ends with us passing away in our sleep together. Holding hands."

"You're too intense," I whisper.

"Says the chick with three other personalities," he snaps.

I stand, staring at him. My mouth gaping open, my eyes wide open in surprise. "Did you just say that out loud?"

He doesn't respond immediately, but that gives me enough time to catch my breath. "Yes, I did. I'm not going to pussy-foot around the fact that my love has other personalities. And you shouldn't either. I'm getting it out in the open."

"You can't say shit like that."

"Why? Isn't it true?"

"Well, yeah, it's true."

"Or is this because you want to fight?"

What? "I don't want to fight. I hate confrontation."

"You hate confrontation? Really?" he asks sarcastically. "Says the woman who stood up to a man abusing his dog."

"That was different."

"No, it's not. You stand up for what you believe. And I think you believe you're less than."

"Less than what?"

"Exactly. I ask you the same question. Less than what? Less than others? Less than what you're supposed to be? Less than what you think I deserve? You have to stop hating yourself."

"I hate when you do that," I say as I pace the room. Dylan smirks, he knows exactly what he's doing. "You twist words and somehow make me see how we *do* belong together. I want to be left alone, so I can't hurt you."

"This isn't about self-preservation? You want to protect me?"

"It's about all of the above. I want to protect myself, and I want to protect you. Because one day, someone better, prettier, smarter and with only one personality is going to turn your head. And I won't be able to survive that as well as this." I grip the front of my head, like I'm having a severe headache while closing my eyes.

"And do you know what I want?"

"What?" I open my eyes and look over to see him leaning against the wall, his hands behind his back.

"I want you."

Dylan's words are powerful, raw, and real. And I hold my breath, waiting for the *but.* He stands, as far away from me as he can be in the room, waiting. He's quiet, not responding. He's waiting for me. I want to argue, to scream for him to run as fast and far as he can. I want to cry. I want to tell these voices to leave and never return. I want to be normal. I want to love him. I want… I want…

So much.

"You're fighting with yourself," he says.

"I am," I reply.

"Stop talking yourself out of us. We work, and we'll find a way to work together. All of us."

Mom walks in, carrying a clear bag. My eyes are drawn to the colored pencils.

Oh, pencils. Neve claps her hands together happily.

Suddenly, I become weak in the legs, and stumble backward.

"Molly," Dylan says as he runs toward me to catch me before I fall.

My head clouds, and I start rubbing my eyes.

"What's happening?" Dylan asks.

I close my eyes.

EVE

Looking at the man, I back away from him until I find the wall. I slide down it, and curl into myself. "Please, no more," I beg.

He looks at me with a blank expression. "I won't hurt you," he says as he stands further away from me.

"Paris," I call for M's mom. "Paris!" I say even louder.

"Molly, are you okay?" the man asks.

"My name's Neve." I look up at him, and recognize him from the first time. He won't hurt me. But I don't trust him, not yet. "I know you."

He smiles at me. He takes a step closer, and my eyes widen with his step. He notices, and steps back. "Paris," he calls M's mom. He looks around the room, then sinks to the floor where he's standing. He crosses his legs in front of him and places his hands in his lap. "My name's Dylan. I'm really happy to meet you, Neve." M's mom walks in and sees me and Dylan sitting on the floor. She's just about to ask why, when Dylan says, "Neve's with us." He offers her a smile.

"Oh, hi Neve. I got those colored pencils you wanted, and some books to color in. I also bought the first two Harry Potter books. Would you like me to get them?"

"Can I have the pencils and the books to color in, please?"

"I'll go get them." I look between her and Dylan, silently asking if he's going to try to hurt me. "He's a good person, Neve," she answers my unasked question.

I nod, but I'm still cautious. People can say whatever they want. Their words mean nothing if their actions don't back them up. People think that because I'm a kid, I'm dumb. But I'm not like other kids. I've lived a life full of lies, horror and betrayal. I'm not trusting anyone, other than M, AJ, and Kate. And Paris.

"Neve, here you go," M's mom says as she approaches me carefully.

I look at Dylan, and he appears worried. "Are you okay?" I ask as I reach for the pencils.

"I'm okay, sweetheart," Paris says.

"Not you, Paris. Dylan, Are you okay? You seem worried. Did I do something wrong? Do you want me to do something for you?"

"What? God no. I don't want you to do anything for me… Neve," he stutters when he says my name. "I never want you to do anything for me."

"*He* used to make me do things to him. Is that what you want?"

"No!" Dylan nearly shouts at me. I cower backward, afraid. "I'm sorry," he says immediately. "I just want to be friends, that's it. I'll never ask you to do anything like *he* used to."

I take one of the pencils out of the packet, and start coloring in. "*He'd* yell at me if I told him it hurt. *He'd* scare me. He'd tell me he'd hurt everyone if I didn't do what he wanted. He'd tell me no one would believe me. *He* said I'd be taken away, and no one would know where I went. *He* told me he'd kill me."

"Dear Lord," Paris gasps.

"I'll never do anything like that to you, Neve."

I keep coloring, while chewing on the inside of my cheek. "Do you want to color with me?"

"Me?" Dylan asks. I nod my head without lifting my eyes to look at him. "I'd love to."

"Don't touch me," I warn.

"I won't." Although I'm not looking at him, I can hear him sliding across the floor. I know he's here, opposite me. He's far enough away he can't reach out to touch me. I take two colors, and slide them over to him. "Thank you."

"You're welcome," I say as I slide the coloring book over so we both have a page each. I lay flat on my stomach, and hook my ankles together.

"You like coloring, and Harry Potter. Harry Potter is cool. I actually think without Hermione, Harry wouldn't have made it as far as he did."

"Do you like the movies, or the books?"

"The books rock. But the movies were pretty good too."

I smile. "There's a Harry Potter studio in England. I want to go one day."

"Yeah? I'd love to go there too."

"Have you ever had Butter Beer?" I ask.

"No, but I want to try it. I wish I had Harry's invisibility cloak too."

"Me too!" I say happily.

We continue to color in quietly for a little while. I like how he hasn't tried anything on me. But it doesn't mean he won't. I just have to be really careful around him. He used to pretend he was nice when we were with our foster parents, then at night, it would all be different. "I didn't like to be left alone with him," I say out loud.

"Yeah?"

"Every time our foster parents would go anywhere, *he'd* start to touch me."

"Is that right?" Dylan asks, his voice tight.

"*He* never hit me where they'd see the marks." I look up right at the moment where Dylan stops coloring, rolls his eyes, and does a funny move with his mouth. "Are you sad?"

He hesitates with his reply. "I'm upset," he finally says.

"I'm sorry," I automatically respond. I used to say sorry to *him* all the time, and hope he wouldn't hurt me.

"You don't have to say sorry to me, Neve."

"Do you want to do what he did to me?"

"Never."

"I didn't like it." I hear someone crying, and look up. M's mom is sniffling into a tissue. "Did I hurt your feelings?"

She shakes her head slowly. "Sweet girl, you have the most beautiful and pure heart. There's no way you could ever hurt my feelings."

Neve, I need to come back.

I nod my head.

Everything becomes fuzzy, and I feel so tired. It's time for M to come back.

CHAPTER 26

I have so many questions for Amelia. My mind hasn't stopped. Kate and AJ both are talking all the time, and it's driving me crazy. Neve's quiet, not interacting at all.

Zhen places his head on my lap, and waits for me to scratch behind his ear. His eyes droop when I start scratching. "You okay, boy?" I ask, half expecting him to respond in some kind of way.

Dylan's at work today, but he wants to be here when Amelia arrives, so I asked Amelia if she can come a bit later. I've been on edge all day, wandering around the house looking for things to do. But nothing's caught my attention.

Mom and Dad are both at work. They're working half days for now.

I find myself sitting outside Tina's door, just staring at it.

I start crying, feeling overwhelmed by so much. "I want to be angry at you," I say to Tina's door. "I want to tell you how mad I am that you chose him over us. Over me." I wipe at my cheeks. "I loved you so much, and you went to him. Look at what he did to you." I suck in a deep breath. "I'm so mad. I'm mad at you, I'm mad at him, but mostly, I'm mad with myself. I knew what he was doing, and I didn't do enough to get you away from him." I close my eyes, and lower my head in shame. "Why didn't I do more?" I lift my hands and begin tearing at my hair, punishing myself for not being able to get her away from him. I lower my hands, and look up at her door. I jump to my feet, and walk toward her door. "Fuck you! Fuck you!" I scream at the door. "Fuck you!" I bash at her door. Yelling and crying, broken hearted that she's never going to come back. "Fuck you! You should've lived. You should've lived!" I keep screaming. "I hate you so much. You had everything going for you, you should've lived." I beat the door so hard my hand goes through the door. Pulling it back, I keep pounding on the door. "It should've been me! It should've been me." My beating on the door slows. My arms protest; my hand hurts. Leaning my forehead against her door, I cry and lift my other hand to place it on the door. "You could've lived, and I should've died."

"Molly," I hear Dylan's deep voice. He's standing behind me, not touching me.

Closing my eyes, I slide down the door, and lay heaped on the floor across the threshold.

Silently, Dylan's strong arms scoop me up, take me into my room and he lays me on my bed. He walks into my bathroom, and turns the shower on. He returns to me, helps me up, takes my clothes off then leads me to the shower. The steam in the bathroom has already fogged up my mirror. The tears in my eyes make it all too fuzzy to see. Like a zombie, I stand at the shower, waiting for him to lead.

I turn to see him stripping off. He takes my hand in his, and guides me into the shower. He turns us so the water is running over me. Dylan holds me in his arms, my body trembling against his.

Although we're both naked, standing body to body, this isn't sexual. It's so much more. But it's still an intimate connection. Tilting my head, I look up to him. "I'm lost," I say as the water keeps cascading down my body.

"I know," he replies.

"I don't know what to do."

He leans down, and places a kiss to my forehead. "You have to learn how to forgive yourself so you can move forward."

I purse my lips together, afraid of what might come out of my mouth. I tighten my hold on Dylan, and lean my head against his chest. We stand under the water until our bodies feel more like entwined souls. His lean frame wraps around mine, protectively blanketing me. I feel safe in his arms. Somehow, I know Dylan won't ever hurt me. He'd do everything in his power to keep harm away from me.

"Dylan," I whisper, my lips touching his chest.

"Yeah," he replies in a low, pained voice. I know what my body is doing to him, but now isn't the time to seal our connection.

"I think I love you," the words cascade from my mouth easier than I thought they would.

"I know. You've said it before, but I thought maybe you weren't really ready to say those words then. But I know, deep down, that you do." He kisses the top of my head. He's already confessed the same words to me. "I love you."

"Those words frightened me when you first spoke them. Now, I'm not afraid."

"Don't ever be afraid of my feelings for you."

I half-chuckle. "It wasn't your feelings I was afraid of." I feel his chest pull in a sharp breath. Stepping back, I look up at him and give him a small smile. "Amelia will be here soon." I lower my gaze, open the shower door, and step out. Grabbing a towel, I wrap it around my body, and leave the bathroom.

Dylan stays in the shower for a while longer, and by the time he's out, I'm already dressed in jeans and a t-shirt and sitting on my bed. He comes into my room, with a towel hanging around his hips. I look down at my toes, then up to him. "Are you alright?" he asks.

"I'm sorry," I reply in a small voice. "I'm embarrassed." I lower my head again.

Dylan walks over to me, and kneels between my legs. He places his hands on my thighs, and gently rubs the top of them. "This will hands-down be the most difficult part of your life. You can get through this, Molly. We're all here for you."

"I know, but I can't help feeling ashamed. And angry."

"Angry at what?"

"At myself mostly. I should've tried harder to save her."

"I'm not going to pretend to have all the answers, because I don't. But what happened to Tina was *not* your fault."

I look up, finally meeting Dylan's eyes. His bare chest is distracting, but it's his beautiful, deep eyes that captivate me. "The logical part of my brain agrees with you. But I can't say the same for the emotional part."

He nods his head. "When is Amelia coming?"

I lean over and lift my phone, looking at the time. "She'll be here soon. Mom and Dad will back soon, too."

"I better get changed, before they see me like this. They may think we..." He looks at me, and gives me a strained smile. "I don't want them to think I took advantage of their daughter."

"They like you too much to think that."

He pushes up off his knees, grabs his clothes that I've folded and placed on the bottom of my bed, and heads back into the bathroom.

"How are you today, Molly?" Amelia asks.

Dylan's sitting beside me on the sofa, holding my hand. Mom and Dad are opposite us, and Amelia is sitting on one of the armchairs. I look over to my parents, and I know I have to tell them I had a mini breakdown. "Does putting my hand through my sister's bedroom door tell you anything?"

"You what?" Mom asks.

Dylan squeezes my hand tight, reassuring me. "I put a hole in her door."

"What happened?" Amelia asks. She picks up her bottled water, unscrews the lid, and has a sip. "Tell me about it."

"I don't know what to tell you. I lost myself. I was angry, and I beat her door."

"You were angry, or you *are* angry?"

I half shrug. "Does it matter? It can't change what's happened."

"What are you angry about?" Amelia asks.

"Everything. Tina shouldn't have been the one to die. If there really is a God, then God chose wrong. *He* or *she,* should've put me in harm's way, let me take what happened. Tina didn't deserve what happened to her."

"And you think you deserve to die?" Amelia's asking all the questions with a calm, non-judgmental tone.

"Let's face it. I'm the one who's forever going to have multiple personalities living inside. She was the normal one of us. She could've been so much more than I'll ever be. She had potential. I have nothing to offer." I hear Dylan let out a sigh.

"Do you believe your life is worth less than Tina's?"

I crinkle my brows together, thinking about Amelia's question. "I think she would've added more value to the world than I ever could." Mom gasps, and when I turn to face her, she's looking away so I can't see her, but I know she's crying. "Please, Mom," I beg. "Don't cry, I'm trying to be honest."

Mom nods, but doesn't say anything, instead offering a strained, fake smile with her eyes shimmering with tears.

"Why do you think she could add more value than you?"

"I'm..." What am I? "I'm not whole."

Amelia looks to me, her eyes roaming over my body. "You don't look like you're missing any parts."

"I'm damaged in ways I never knew I was." I chew on my bottom lip, thinking about all of me. "Why didn't I know about *them* before Tina's death?"

"You probably did. But you buried them once *he* left the foster home. And then you were adopted into a loving family who welcomed you and loved you. As humans, we bury what we haven't learnt to accept. Or what we're afraid of."

"I don't know how to move forward."

"We need to find a way for you to forgive."

"Forgive? I can never forgive him for what he did." Tears begin to well up in my eyes. "I may not remember, but Neve does. And I can't, hand on my heart," I place my hand to my chest, "ever forgive him for hurting us. I will never, ever forgive him."

"I'm not asking you to. But I'm asking you to forgive yourself."

I burst into tears. "I can't. I should've stopped him. I should've yelled, and tried to get away from him." Dylan carefully moves closer, as he slings his arm over my shoulders and draws me in for a tight embrace. "I should've done something, said something. I shouldn't have allowed him to do that to us," I say through the sobs.

"You were only a baby. A small child who looked to him for protection."

"I should've done something. I should've killed him." I don't even know who I'm talking about now. I'm torn, my insides are fighting with so many emotions. "I should've killed them both."

"This is survivor's guilt, Molly."

"I don't care what it is. Help me make it go away."

"Molly, the only way we can move forward, is if you face your past. Every ugly, horror-filled aspect of it."

I nod my head. "I can't live a life where I'm drowning in guilt and shame. But I don't know how to breathe anymore."

"Let us breathe for you," Dad says.

"We all need help, Molly. Your Dad, me, and you. We're all barely drifting through each day. But we have to keep fighting, for you and for Tina," Mom says.

"I feel like I need to do something." I shrug, not sure what that something is. "But I don't know what."

"What do you want to achieve?" Amelia asks.

"I need to do something that'll make a difference."

"A difference to you?"

"What happened to me has already happened, but maybe I can help someone else. Maybe I can give a voice to someone who's going through it now, and is too frightened to speak up."

Amelia nods. "First, you need to acknowledge what happened, Molly. Not to Neve, not to AJ and not to Kate, but to you." She points at me.

"I acknowledge it," I say.

"No, you need to be able to say it."

I let go of Dylan's hand, and stand. Zhen gets up from where he's lying and follows me as I pace back and forth. "I'm not sure I can say the words aloud. Because once they're out, there's no hiding from them."

The strongest you'll ever be, is the day you tell everyone what he did to us. Neve's voice is soft, but firm.

"You want me to say the words?" I ask Neve.

I want you to heal, and this is the first step to healing.

"Who's with you?" Amelia asks.

For a moment, I forget they can't hear Neve. *I can tell them if you want.*

"No," I say. "I have to do it, or I'll never be able to move on."

"Who are you talking to?" Amelia asks again.

Tell them.

"Neve. I'm talking with Neve. She's here with me." I look past Amelia, focusing on a small dust bunny in the corner of the room. "She's encouraging me."

"Encouraging you to do what?" Dylan stands, and walks over to me.

I lift my gaze, and stare at him. The weight of the world is on my shoulders. My chest feels like it's caving in. "I…" I suck in a deep breath. "I um." I let out an audible loud sigh. "Whoa." I click my tongue, struggling to say what I have to say.

We're all here for you.

"We're here for you, Molly," Amelia says.

I let out a humorless chuckle while shaking my head. Neve, Amelia, Mom, Dad, Dylan, Kate, and AJ, they are all here for me. In a weird way, I know Tina is, too. I just need to find the courage and say the words.

"I…ah. I was, um." A giant knot tightens in my stomach, my gut twists with apprehension.

It's okay to say the words that have been haunting all of us.

"You're so strong, I don't know how you survived," I reply to Neve.

We had to survive to keep you safe. You survived because you had to.

I lower my gaze again, tears filling my eyes. "Neve just said, they survived for me, to keep me safe, and I survived because I had to." A few tears leak out of my eyes, and I quickly wipe them away.

Don't wipe our tears. Let them fall. Let them show the world how strong we are.

Neve's right. We are strong. Together, and separately. I turn so I'm facing my parents, Dylan, and Amelia. "He's a pedophile, and he sexually assaulted me." My body is hyperaware of every sound, every movement in the room. My arms cover in goosebumps as a bolt of ice runs the length of my spine. "He assaulted us," I correct.

Mom is the first on her feet, pushing past Dylan as she wraps her arms around me. She extends her arms, including Dylan then Dad. I can hear her sobbing.

Dad's breathless whimpers break my heart. "I'm sorry I couldn't protect you," he says through his own sobbing. "I'm sorry, Molly. I'm so sorry."

The air in the room is overpowered by strain, though suddenly, I feel free. "It makes sense now," I say while I look into the corner of the room.

"What does?" Amelia asks.

"The bunny." I turn to Mom and take a breath. "Remember how I asked you about the rabbit?" Mom nods. "That bunny was a warning, wasn't it?" I ask Neve.

It used to be something I found comfort in, then it became something I hated, because I knew what was about to happen.

"It was a warning." Stepping back, I stare at the people I love. "I have to do something. I can't let him get away with what he did." I get an overwhelming feeling of strength.

"What do you want to do?" Amelia asks.

We all sit down again, Zhen by my feet. "It's funny, because I didn't want to admit what he did. I was dreading saying the words, but once they left my lips, I feel different. Stronger than I ever have. Powerful even."

"Be prepared. There will be a part of you that will regret it. Even want to hide from it," Amelia says.

No, not us. We'll face this, head on.

Neve may be the youngest out of all of us, but I think she's the toughest. "Thank you, Neve," I mumble.

We need for him to be held accountable. Kate's now the loudest.

He needs to pay. AJ echoes.

I walk over to my parents, and wedge my way between them. "I'm sorry for what has to be done. I don't want to drag you through this, not with everything else that's happened with Tina."

"What are you talking about?" Mom asks, perplexed.

"I think I want to go to the police."

Mom's reaction isn't what I was expecting. She smiles, and nods. "Make that cunt pay," Mom says in a tone so dark, and serious that it actually frightens me. I've never heard her say the C word in all my life. "Both of them have to answer for their crimes."

Yes, they do.

CHAPTER 27

We're waiting outside the office of Eveline Bradford, the district attorney who is prosecuting Preston. Mom nervously wrings her hands together. Dad's sitting beside Mom, with his hand on her thigh. Dylan and I are holding hands in the quaint, small waiting room.

We've all been fairly quiet the whole morning.

We knew today would be hard, but we had no idea how traumatic it actually is.

"Mr. and Mrs. Dawson?" a young man asks as he steps forward.

We all stand, and follow him. "Eveline will be with you in a moment. Please, take a seat." He shows us into a glass-enclosed conference room. There's a long wooden table in the center, with twelve high-backed chairs around it. There's an opened laptop facing away from us, and a pitcher of water with glasses stacked in front of it. The room is cool, cold enough to cause my arms to cover in goosebumps. I shiver as I sit.

"Are you cold?" Dylan asks.

"I'll be fine," I say. He takes his jacket off, and slings it over my shoulders, covering my thin cardigan. "You'll get cold." I shrug the jacket off.

"No, I won't. I'll be fine. Have it." He places it over my shoulders again.

"Thank you," I say.

Within seconds an older woman walks in and introduces herself. "Eveline Bradford," she says as she extends her hand to Mom first. She's got silvery blonde hair, pulled back in a severe chignon. She's wearing thick, black-rimmed glasses, and a black pant suit with a white shirt. She has the hard look of an uncompromising victor who'll do whatever it takes to annihilate those who dare stand before her.

She is the most no-nonsense person I've ever met. She even intimidates me.

The introductions among us are pertinent and to the point.

Eveline doesn't waste time. "Preston's changed his plea from guilty to not guilty."

"What?" we all yell in unison.

"He's pleading not guilty due to reason of insanity." Eveline looks down at her laptop, and types something quickly.

"Insanity? He's a monster. A controlling asshole who manipulated my sister!"

"I know. Which is why now, we go to a preliminary hearing."

"What's that?" I ask.

"We go to court, and have to provide sufficient evidence that he is, in fact, guilty. It's like a mini-trial. It's up to me to show that we have substantial proof that he's guilty, and not insane—like he's claiming."

"How do you do that?" Dad asks.

"With evidence. And with testimony. Testimony from all of you."

"My cousin is a private investigator, and she found evidence that he's done this before," Dylan offers.

Eveline lifts her chin to look at Dylan. She types something on her computer again, then sits back in the chair. The young guy who showed us in, comes back into the room. "Speak to Dylan, get his cousin's name and phone number. Put her on retainer for this case. Get whatever information she has. Tell her we'll need her for more," Eveline spouts quickly to the young guy.

"Can you come with me please?" he asks Dylan.

This is all happening so fast. Eveline is undeniably a powerful woman who knows how to get things done. "How do you do it?" I ask, not realizing I've actually spoken aloud.

"Do what?" she asks without hesitation.

"How can you see cases like this, and remain detached?"

Eveline slides her glasses down her nose with her finger, and looks over them at me. "Because I have to make sure I have a good case, or these bastards walk free," she responds in a deadpan, even voice. "And in this particular case, I've come up against his parents before. His mother is a pit bull, she'll do everything she can to prove her son didn't intentionally harm Tina."

I look to my parents. Both are staring at Eveline. I know what's going through their minds, because it's going through mine. What if he gets away with it again?

I'll kill him. I'll kill them both. Kate's voice is as deadly as Eveline's.

"You can't. We have to let the system do its job," I say to Kate.

"Pardon?" Eveline asks.

Mom places her hand on my thigh, and I quickly realize I'm replying out loud instead of in my head. "I'm sorry," I say instantly.

Crap, Eveline's staring at me. She narrows her eyes, and clicks her tongue. "Who were you talking to?"

"Um, no…nothing." I wave my hand at her.

Tell her.

"No! Shh."

Eveline sits back in her seat, and crosses her arms in front of her chest. "Who are you talking to?"

Closing my eyes, I lean my elbow on the arm of the chair. I run my hand over my face, and through my hair. She's not going to let this go. I have to tell her.

Good, tell her.

"Kate, please," I whisper under my breath.

"Who's Kate?" Eveline persists in asking.

I feel sick, like I'm going to vomit. Other than my parents,

Amelia, and Dylan, I have not told anyone about my other... *personalities.* My stomach twists and turns, and my breathing becomes short and rapid. "I'm sorry, I shouldn't have said anything," I try my hardest to avoid answering Eveline. I sneak a look at her, and everything is telling me, she'll wait all day for me to give her an answer. She lifts her brows at me, waiting. "I...um." I duck my face, unable to look in her stern eyes. Tapping my head, I take a deep breath before saying, "I have three people who live inside me."

I wait for her to say something. I refuse to look at anyone.

"Molly has dissociative identity disorder," Mom says.

"You were sexually abused as a child?" Eveline asks, although her tone is more a statement than a question.

"What? No, why would you say that?" I fling defensively at her.

"Molly," Dad says as gives me a small pleading look.

She nods her head, and interlocks her hands. "You were sexually abused as a child. Who by?"

I struggle to hold in my tears. I look up, trying to contain them. *Tell her.*

"Do you know how hard this is?" I say as I finally meet her hardened eyes. "Talking about this isn't something I was prepared to do today. I thought we were here for Tina."

"We are here for Tina. But now, we're here for you too. Tell me who it was. Have they been arrested? When did this happen?" The barrage of questions is overwhelming. I can hear Kate, AJ, and Neve all coming closer to the surface. Soon, they'll want to talk to Eveline, and I have to take control if I want them to step back.

"It happened when I was in my foster home. He was a foster kid too. Neve dealt with him the most."

"Neve is who?" She starts typing on the computer, not looking at me but listening.

"Neve is one of my alters. She's young, and the one who took the abuse."

Eveline nods her head. "Who else is there?"

"AJ, and Kate. Kate's always been pretty quiet, but she's quite vocal today."

"And AJ?"

Let me tell her. AJ whispers.

"No, I'll tell her." I look back to Eveline who's watching me closely. "AJ is my protector. He'd go to Neve when it was time."

"And the foster kid, what happened to him?"

I shrug. "He aged out and left. But I want to find him."

"Right." She sits back again, staring at me. "Recently there was a case in Australia where the female had been horribly sexually abused for many years by her father. She developed over two thousand personalities because of the magnitude of the trauma. She tried to get help for many years, and she couldn't. Until, she met a police officer who not only believed her, but started the proceedings to have her father arrested."

"Why are you telling us this?" Mom asks slowly.

I'm not sure where Eveline is going either.

"Are you seeking any professional help?"

I nod. "I'm seeing a psychotherapist. I'm learning a lot about them, and about me." I shrug. "I buried them, for many years. They all came to the surface the night the police came to our house and told us what happened to Tina." The last of the sentence is barely whispered.

"If it's okay with all of you, I want to speak with the therapist. I mean, all of you." She pointedly looks to me.

Maybe she can help us. Neve says.

AJ replies, *I like her. She's tough and doesn't bullshit around.*

My answer is yes. Let her talk to Amelia.

"It's not your decision, it's mine," I snap at Neve, AJ, and Kate.

"What's happening?" Eveline asks.

"They want you to talk to Amelia. But it's my decision, not theirs."

"Look," Eveline starts. "I want to talk to Amelia, who I assume is your therapist, is that right?" I nod. "Let me talk to her. If nothing further happens, then that's where we'll leave it."

I shrug. "What's the purpose of all this though? What difference will it make?"

"The difference is, I want to get some background on you, Kate, Neve and AJ. And I think, we can make sure this guy, if he's still alive, is brought to justice."

I furrow my brows. "You believe me?"

"I just sat here and watched you have a conversation with people we can't see or hear." She points to herself, then Mom and Dad. "Do I believe you? There's no question about it."

"Sweetheart, let her help," Dad urges me.

"If you're okay with Eveline talking to Amelia, then your father and I are okay with it." Mom grasps my hand, and squeezes.

The door opens, and I turn to see Dylan walking in. He quickly looks around the room, and protectively comes to sit beside me. "What happened?" he asks.

"Eveline knows." I tap my head. Dylan gives me a small nod of acknowledgment. "She wants to talk to Amelia."

"Why?" Dylan questions.

"Because I'm the best district attorney in this state. And I want to make sure that both Preston and the foster brother are dealt with."

Dylan's lip slightly twitches. "My cousin will do whatever's necessary to find him."

Eveline smirks. "Good." Something seems to have happened. There's a shift in the room. "Now back to Preston and the preliminary hearing. It's like a mini-trial, I'll admit evidence, and call witnesses. If the judge concludes there's probable cause, then we'll go to trial, where there'll be a jury. His mother will try to say he was insane. It's my job to prove he knew right from wrong, knew what he was doing was wrong, and I have enough evidence to prove it."

"What happens if the judge thinks he's innocent?" Dad asks.

"The judge can dismiss the charges."

"What?" I scream. "He can be let off? He killed my sister. Wrapped his hands around her neck and strangled her. He killed my fucking sister!" I yell louder. Slamming my hands on the table, I stand and begin to pace.

Kate's in my head. She quickly talking, but I'm pushing her out. *Calm down, M.*

"Shut up, Kate. Just shut up!"

M, you need to calm down. I'll send Kate in to give you a chance to settle down. AJ says.

"Don't you dare tell me what you're going to do. You have no right. He killed my sister. And he might get away with it." I hit the side of my head.

Kate, go in.

On my way.

"No!"

I feel weak in the legs, and sit. Everything becomes foggy and clouded. I'm tired, so damn tired.

KATE

Opening my eyes, I look around the room. Yawning, I stretch my arms. A huge smile tugs at my lips.

"Hi!" I say as I look around at everyone. I feel tired, but I should be okay in a moment or two. "Oh yeah, you're pretty cute," I say to M's boyfriend.

"Are you Kate?" he asks.

I hold my hand out so he can kiss the top of it. "I sure am, cutie. I like you." I wink at him. He takes my hand and slowly brings it to his lips. "Oh, soft lips. I like that."

"Kate, is it?"

I drag my eyes away from Mr. Eye Candy for a moment. "Oh, you're that lawyer we're all arguing over. Hell yeah, you can talk to Amelia. She's totes cool. I like her. You're a hard-ass, right? You're not going to let that Preston guy get away with killing M's sister, are you?"

"I'm going to do everything I can to make sure he sees the inside of a prison cell for a long time. What can you tell me about this foster brother of Molly's?"

"Neve's the one to talk to about him. Mind you, we all know what he used to do to her. Neve had it the worst though. She had to be ready for whenever he played the song." I feel my happiness quickly dwindling. I hate talking about him. I'm the happy one, God damn it. I don't like being sad.

"What song did he used to play?"

A shiver runs up my spine just thinking about those dark, horror-filled days. "I don't want to talk about him. But I do want you to find him, and make him suffer the way he made Neve suffer." Instantly I cheer up, happy at the thought of him going to prison, and knowing pedophiles are welcomed in a different kind of way there. "Hopefully, someone has some barbed wire ready for him." I smile cheekily and clap my hands together. I look over to M's parents. They're staring at me. "Do I have something on my face?" I wipe at my nose.

"Not at all. You're just so… different," M's mom says.

"I know. I'm the cool one. I'm the one who cheers everybody up." I jump up, and sit on her lap. "I love your hair. You should wear it down. Maybe put some makeup on. Not too much. Just some lipstick. Oh my God! You'd rock knee-high boots. You have such nice legs."

"I'm really not into boots," she replies.

"But you'd rock them. High-heeled black boots."

We have to talk, Kate. You can't take over whenever you want.

I roll my eyes. "Fine, you can have your body back. Before I go, we all give you permission to talk with Amelia, and to go after that bastard. And while I'm here, get the death penalty for that prick, Preston."

"We don't have the death penalty in this state," Eveline says.

"What a shame. Bullet, brain. Easy solution. For both of them."

Kate!

MOLLY

The cloud lifts and I find myself sitting on Mom's lap. I vaguely recall Kate saying something about boots to Mom.

"I'm sorry," I apologize to everyone. I get up off Mom's lap, and sit in my seat again. Rubbing my hand over my eyes, I try and drag myself out of the heavily clouded head space I'm in. It takes several moments of quiet before I start feeling like myself. I rub at the back of my neck, trying to calm my worry. What are they all thinking? Especially Eveline. I'm worried she thinks I'm crazy. I can't bear to bring my gaze to hers. I shift in my chair, impatiently waiting for something to happen.

"Molly?" Eveline asks.

"Yeah, I'm really sorry." I feel sweat beading on the back of my neck. Jesus, what does she think? "I, um, couldn't help that."

"You're a remarkable woman, Molly," Eveline says.

I lower my chin, struggling with Eveline's obvious acceptance of what just happened. I wet my lips, taking extra care not to say or do anything else weird.

"Molly?" I slowly bring my eyes up to meet Eveline's. "You are extraordinary."

"I don't feel like I am," I reply in a slower tone. My mouth becomes parched, and I reach for the water.

"I'll get it," Dylan says as he stands and pours some water into a glass then hands it to me.

"Thank you." I smile. There's a part of me that really doesn't like all this attention. I've never liked people staring at me, or me being in the center of anything. I'm fine with melting into the wall, and watching rather than being watched.

"Molly, perhaps Dylan can take you out for a coffee? I'd like to speak to your parents alone. Are you okay with that?"

"Is it about me?" I ask nervously.

"Some of it will be. But some will be about your sister."

Standing, I lean into Dylan and wrap my arm around his waist.

I feel like he's my strength. I trust him, and know he'll never hurt me. "What do you think?" I ask, unsure on what I should be saying.

"I think Eveline is right. You're exceptional, but you need us. And for now, I think you should let your parents talk with Eveline while I buy you a coffee."

"I suppose it's not like they don't know I'm crazy," I say trying to lighten the mood.

"You're not crazy, Molly. You're vulnerable, and it's our duty to protect you," Dylan says. "Because we all love you."

I look between my parents, Eveline, then Dylan. "Okay," I say in a small voice, "Take me for a coffee." I have unconditional trust in my parents, and I know, they'd never do or say anything to hurt me.

CHAPTER 28

"How are you feeling, Molly?" Amelia asks.

Curling up on the sofa, I look out the window and see the trees moving with the wind. I hug my legs as I considering how I'm feeling. "I'm kind of relieved. Preston's going to trial for what he did to Tina."

"Kind of? I thought you'd be happier."

"I am. I'm struggling with a few other things, that's all." I look down, away from Amelia. I can feel her eyes boring into me. She's going to ask me what's bothering me.

"What are you struggling with? Is it one of the alters?"

I move on the sofa, readjusting my position. I'm delaying telling Amelia what I'm thinking and feeling. My stomach pulsates, and my hands sweat. "Not really, but kind of."

"Kind of, again, huh? Tell me, what are you thinking?"

"I've been thinking about Dylan."

"Go ahead." She extends her legs, and crosses them at the ankles.

"I'm conflicted," is the only words I offer.

"Over what?"

Why does this feel like I'm struggling to find the right words? Actually, to find any words? My thoughts are torturous. I shouldn't be thinking about this, I should be more focused on Preston's trial.

"I'm going to make a speculation here, Molly. But I'm getting the feeling you're burdened by whatever it is you want to talk to me about. You know, wanting to feel happy isn't a bad thing. You're probably questioning yourself, and beating yourself up, maybe even wanting to punish yourself for things that are out of your control."

It's like she can read my mind. I roll my eyes, frustrated with myself. "I want to get closer to Dylan, but I don't know if I can. We tried once, and I freaked out."

"Is Dylan putting pressure on you?"

"Oh my God, no. Not at all. He's so understanding. But I feel guilty for a range of reasons." I stand and pace before Amelia, darting a look over to her every few seconds. "I want to take it to the next level. But I feel like I shouldn't. I feel like I should focus on them," I tap my head, "and Tina's trial. Like I should put them all before me."

"There's nothing wrong with you taking care of you. The only tricky part will be talking to the others. First Dylan. You both have to be on the same page when it comes to intimacy. But I suspect you'll need to talk to Neve, AJ, and Kate. I have a feeling Neve will struggle with this the most."

"Why Neve?" I ask.

"Neve's been conditioned to take over when an act like that occurs, something that will hurt you."

"But this is different. It's not forced like it used to be when I was little."

"But remember, Neve is only a young child herself, and she doesn't know the difference. All she knows, is when you were about to be hurt, it was her job to take you away from the horror, and for her to step in. You're going to have to talk to Neve before you and Dylan make that connection."

"Should I talk to Neve with Dylan here?" I really don't know what to do.

"I think you should speak with Dylan first, and ask him what he wants. From what I've seen of him, I think he'll support you any way he can."

I let out a chuckle. "Do you have any idea how hard this is? Every decision I make is a decision for four people, not just one. I have to consider what AJ, Kate, and Neve want whenever I make any type of choice or arrangement."

"Molly, you have something that's not common. Thankfully there's a wide community of other people who have DID. Have you considered reaching out to them and making contact with others?"

"What do I say? *Hey, I have DID. Want to compare notes?*" I laugh at how stupid that sounds. How ridiculous. "Do you realize how much of a loser that makes me sound like?"

"What are you saying, that other people who have DID are losers?"

"No, that's not what I meant."

"What about if by you reaching out, you unknowingly give somebody else the courage to do the same?"

"What do you mean? Like someone else is afraid and doesn't want to tell?"

"That's precisely what I'm saying."

"Well, that's dumb. Why wouldn't someone try to reach out for help?" Amelia tilts her head, and her eyes widen. "Oh, yeah, I get it." She used my words against me. Smart.

"It's certainly necessary you speak with all the others. And Dylan, but also reach out and ask the DID community how they manage having a healthy sexual relationship with their significant others. Because sex is also about intimacy too. It's not all based on the act of sexual intercourse all the time. For Neve and you, you'll have to find the balance of when Neve comes forward, and when you do."

I shiver in disgust. "I don't ever want Neve to be there for that. She's only a child."

"I think you'll find Dylan won't want that either. But have the conversation with him first. You both need clear boundaries and plans. What if Neve does come forward when you're being intimate with Dylan? Both you and Dylan need to have a plan at how to handle that if it does happen. But the plan needs to be discussed with Neve, too. It's only fair for her to have input. And she needs to know that you *want* intimacy with Dylan."

"I don't want her exposed to that. We need to talk about her staying away when Dylan and I… you know."

"Neve is her own person. She may be young, but you should give her the option of what she wants to do. And before you think it, I'm not condoning her joining you and Dylan when you're intimate. I'm saying she needs to feel like she's being heard."

"I think for Neve, it'll be traumatic, and I'm really worried for her."

"Talk to her. And next time I'm here, if you're both okay with it, I can talk to her too. Perhaps, involve Dylan too."

"This is never going to be easy, is it?" I ask sighing heavily.

"Easy? Life isn't easy. Instead, this is a long, tedious journey and no one has a road map. Don't expect each of your alters to automatically fall in love with Dylan just because you have. They all need to develop a relationship with him, just like you did."

"What if this is too much for him, and he wants to leave?" I keep beating myself up over this.

"Relationships break up all the time. But a relationship based on trust, and in this case, strength, has less of an opportunity to crumble. You're stronger than you think, Molly. The biggest thing I think you have to remember is to be patient with your alters. Remember that for the most part, they're reactionary. These last two months have been a learning curve for everyone. You can't expect for everything to be smooth and easy. It never is."

"I feel like I have no control over myself."

Amelia laughs. "Does anyone have control over themselves? Life is a series of events. Some good, some not. But other than waking up every morning if you're lucky, you have no say in anything."

I screw my nose up. "That's quite pessimistic, isn't it? So negative."

She laughs again. "I'm a realist, Molly. I like knowing that each day, I have no idea what challenges will present themselves. We have to arm ourselves with knowledge, because knowledge is the ultimate power. If you choose to remain unschooled, then others will always find a way to take advantage of you. Equip yourself with power. Become an ultimate weapon. Because once you learn to understand AJ, Kate, and Neve, your life will become a lot less stressful, and a lot more enjoyable."

"You make it seem easy."

"Never easy." She holds a finger up at me. "Just not impossible."

I sit back down, and look out the window again. The tree is still moving in the wind, but somehow it doesn't look as menacing as it did before. "I'll talk with Dylan, and listen to what he wants to do. I keep giving him the option to leave, but he doesn't want to take it."

"Why would he? He loves you. You're a beautiful young lady, both inside and out."

"Because this is hard."

"Yet, not impossible," she reminds me.

It's my turn to smile. "Nothing's impossible," I say. "I once read something on social media that says it's only impossible until it's not. I thought it was stupid when I first read it. But now, I understand it better."

"How are you feeling about finding the person who did this to you?"

"Hard question," I answer candidly. "I'm not really sure. I know Kate wants him dead. I'm concerned for Neve though. I'm not sure how she's going to cope."

"But she has you, Kate, and AJ to help her through."

"Truth be told, I'm not even sure how *I'm* going to cope. I know this is something that has to happen. Because honestly, I'd feel worse about myself if I found out he had children of his own and he was…" I close my eyes, still finding it difficult to say the words. I take a several deep breaths. "…touching them. Especially if I could've done something to stop him. The guilt would eat me alive." I open my tear-filled eyes to look at Amelia. "But in a way, I never want to see him again."

"Your emotions are all normal. You'll go through so many, and sometimes all in the space of moments. There's something you have to tell yourself, and AJ, Neve, and Kate need to listen."

"What?"

"It wasn't your fault."

"What if…"

"Nope. Stop right there. There's no other version of that statement. It was *not* your fault."

"But…"

"No." She shuts me down again. "It was not your fault."

My hand flutters to my mouth, I nervously run my fingertips across my lips. My muscles all tense, and I'm overwhelmed by with reluctance to believe the words Amelia is desperately trying to get me to understand. I avoid her eyes, putting off responding

"It was not your fault," she says again.

I blink several times, keeping the tears at bay. I lift my hand, stopping Amelia from repeating herself. A shudder rips through my shoulders, making them tremble. "I need to get out of here," I say as I stand.

"There's nowhere you can go that'll give you peace until you allow yourself to heal, and forgive yourself. You'll always be at war." I hate how she's right. She repeats the words. Slowly. "It. Was. Not. Your. Fault."

Zhen finds his way over to me, and pushes his nose into my leg. I lower my hand, and stroke his head. "It's hard for me to come to terms with that."

"Yep."

"That's it? Just 'yep'? I was expecting something a little more profound."

"Molly, I think we've had a hard session today. But I'm going to assign you some homework."

"Homework?"

"Yes. Homework. Once you've had your shower, I want you to stand in front of the mirror, naked, and repeat these words. 'It was not my fault.'"

"Why naked?"

"Because you have to see that you own your body. And no one has the right to touch it, not without your approval. No matter what you're wearing, or not wearing, no person has the right to put their hands on you. It was not your fault."

My mind replays her words over and over. I feel dirty knowing he did things to me when I was so young. I shouldn't feel like that. It wasn't my fault. "It wasn't my fault," I say aloud, almost shocked that I thought and said the words.

"Now, I'm not going to be here on Friday because I'll be out of state for a family event. But I'll see you Monday." Amelia stands, picks her bag up and her little recorder. "You have homework. If you need me, you can call me at any time."

"Okay, thank you." I offer her a small smile.

I walk Amelia out and close the front door behind her. Zhen's tail lightly smacks up against my leg.

Mom and Dad will be home soon, and I think it's best if I start on my homework before they get home, while I still have my courage.

Zhen follows me upstairs, and I strip off in my room before heading into my bathroom. I usually avoid the mirror knowing it will cause me a lot of anguish when I have to face it.

I turn on the shower faucet and get the water to the temperature I want. Stepping in, I let the water fall over my body. I close my eyes, lightly rocking from side to side, dreading what I have to do next. I can feel the tension in my stomach tightening with every breath I take. I don't want to do this. What good can come of it? I don't need to do this, I really don't. What was Amelia thinking? How can looking at myself and repeating those stupid words actually help? How ridiculous.

Yet, there's a part of me that knows Amelia is right. But there's another part of me that's arguing, and doesn't want to do this.

I can feel Neve close by. She's starting to force her way forward. But I don't want to talk to her, not yet. I'm sure Neve can feel my trepidation, my edginess for what I have to do and she's ready to take over.

God, I hate this.

I take the soap and lather myself up, absentmindedly washing my body time and time again. I stare at the water running down the glass, and try my hardest to keep Neve back. I need to do this, but I don't want to.

I soap my body up again. I know I'm delaying this, but I can't bring myself to do what Amelia's asked. I keep dragging this shower out, resisting the inevitable.

"The first time's the hardest," I say to myself, as the water begins to cool.

Closing my eyes, I reach for the faucet and turn the water off. Opening the door, I stretch for my towel, and pray something significant will happen so I don't have to complete my homework.

"You can do this," I say to myself.

Yes, I can.

I dry myself off, then head to the full-length mirror in my bedroom. Standing before it, I look at the sad girl reflected in the glass. Her wet, dark brown hair is plastered flat to her head. Her nearly-black eyes appear soulless. Her body is thin, almost sickly skinny. It's no wonder though, with everything she's gone through. The girl in front of me has so much hidden behind her eyes. Her forehead is crinkled, and her lips are drawn tightly together. Water leaks from her eyes as she stares back at me.

"I have words for you," I say.

My stomach stirs with uncertainty.

The girl gives me a small, doubtful nod. "It's okay," she replies.

I hesitate at the words I'm to speak.

"It's okay," she encourages again. "Say them."

I want to say anything other than the words I desperately *need* to say. I open my mouth, wanting to speak, but my throat seizes and my voice refuses to work. The girl does something I wasn't expecting. She smiles. Her face changes from harshness to softness. She's waiting for me to say the words. She's giving me unconditional permission.

I drop my towel, and look at the girl in the mirror. I stare at her. She stares at me.

"It wasn't my fault," I finally say. The words thunder out of me like lightning bolts.

"No, it wasn't," she replies.

"It wasn't my fault," I say once again.

"No, it wasn't," she says in a softer voice.

I straighten my shoulders, and lift my chin. The girl in the mirror mimics my stance. "It was not my fault," I repeat. I maintain eye contact with the girl. She seems to have gained in power. "It was not my fault." She pushes her chest out, and gives me a bigger smile. Her face is strong, *powerful.* "It was not my fault."

My arms cover in small goosebumps.

My body stands taller.

It was not my fault.

It was his. *I was only a child.*

CHAPTER 29

I head into the kitchen to help Dad with dinner. A gentle aroma of cooked onions flows through the house.

"Hey, sweetheart." Dad smiles. "You okay?"

"I think I'm okay." I pick the knife up, and start chopping the carrots he has sitting on the counter. "What's for dinner?"

"Pot roast and dark gravy. How's it going with Amelia?"

"Good. Yesterday she gave me some homework to do."

"Yeah, like what?" He stirs the pot on the stove top.

"She had me stand in front of the mirror naked, and tell myself it wasn't my fault."

Dad looks at me sideways. "How did that go?"

"It was hard. Really hard, actually."

"Yeah? You okay? Why didn't you tell us you were going to do that? Did anyone make themselves heard when you did that?"

I chuckle at Dad. "No, it was just me. The others stayed away."

"Huh," Dad huffs. "So, you're okay?"

"Yeah, I'm doing okay, Dad. How are you and Mom? I know so much has happened, and I really haven't asked how you both are."

"We're concerned for you."

"Why?"

He walks over to me, takes me by my shoulders and gently turns me around. "Molly, you have three other personalities inside of you because of trauma you suffered when you were very young. This isn't easy for anyone to digest. Your mother and I are grown adults, and we can barely comprehend what's happening with you. We want to support you as much as we can, but we don't know if we're screwing up, or doing a half-way decent job."

I lean over and give him a kiss on the cheek. "You didn't bury your head in the sand, Dad. You and Mom have found and are paying for an amazing therapist for me. You support me..." I chuckle. "You support all of me, every personality, every person who comes out. I can't ask for anything more."

Dad's eyes fill with tears. "We need to make sure we're here for you. No matter what happens." He wipes his face, before turning away from me so I can't see. "It's the onions," he quickly adds.

"You're here for me. In case I haven't shown it, thank you. I can't imagine how people with DID could go through life without love and support."

"Thankfully, you'll never have to know."

"I'm home!" we hear Mom say as the front door closes.

She walks into the kitchen, and I notice how frail Mom's looking. The pant suit she's wearing is way too baggy on her, and she has dark circles under her eyes. I walk over to her, and without saying a single word, I hug her tight I feel her body completely relax into mine after only a few seconds. Her chest shakes, and I know she's crying. I hug her tighter. "I love you," I say as I slowly pull away from her.

She wipes the tears from her cheeks, and offers me the sweetest smile. "You have no idea how much I needed that."

We're interrupted by a knock on the front door.

I walk out, open the door to see Dylan with his cousin Gemma. "Hey," I say as I open the door further to let them in. I instantly notice Gemma's face. Her right eye is heavily bruised, and her lip is split.

Dylan steps aside to let Gemma in, then he follows and gives me a kiss on the lips.

"Sorry to come over unannounced," Dylan says.

"You don't have to tell me you're coming. Gemma, nice to see you again." I lean in to give her a hug. "Are you okay? What happened?" I'm worried for her.

"Hey, Molly. It's good to see you too. This is nothing. Some guy underestimated me." She shrugs. "Downside of the job. But that guy's now in the hospital." She grins.

"She's a black belt. Used to beat the crap out of me when we were kids."

"Also protected him when the other kids picked on him," Gemma adds.

"Kids used to pick on you?" I ask Dylan.

"Hi, Dylan. You staying for dinner?" Dad asks as he comes into the foyer, wiping his hands on a tea towel. "Hi." Dad extends his hand to Gemma.

"Dad, this is Gemma, Dylan's cousin. Gemma, this is my Dad, Thomas. And this is my Mom, Paris." I introduce them all.

"Hi." Mom gives Gemma a quick hug.

"I'd like to say I'm here for a social reason, but I'm not," Gemma says slightly elevating her tablet.

I look at Dylan who gives me a sympathetic smile.

Shit, what have they found?

"Does anyone want a coffee, or a drink?" Dad offers as he leads us into the kitchen, so we can sit at the dining table.

"Just some water please," Gemma replies.

"I'll have a coffee, but I can make it," Dylan says as he heads into the kitchen and goes about making a coffee. He brings Gemma and me each a glass of water, before bringing his coffee over.

The nervous tension in the room is making my heart beat quicker than normal. My breath is short, and I can barely pick my glass up without it spilling over the rim because I'm shaking.

I break the strained, dark mood in the room. "You've found him, haven't you?"

Good, we'll make that bastard pay for what he did to us. AJ is angry, and he's ready to come out fighting.

"I have," Gemma confirms.

Let me at the bastard. I'll fucking kill him. AJ's wrath is growing with every breath I take.

"AJ, please. This is hard enough."

I need him dead.

"Just, stop. Please." I hold up my hand in a ceasing motion.

"Are you okay?" Dylan asks as he places his hand on my thigh for support.

Lifting my hand, I rub the back of my neck, but nod. "It's just AJ. Please, go on."

Gemma wets her lips, before taking a deep breath. "Okay," she pauses, then flicks her tablet to life. "I've found him," she confirms.

I take in a long, deep breath. I stand and I head to the back door, and look out to the darkening sky at the horizon. "There's a part of me that doesn't want to know." I let out a long sigh. "And there's a part of me that wants to know, so I can drive over there, and kill him."

"The choice is yours, Molly. I don't have to tell you. I can take this information straight to Eveline without involving you," Gemma offers.

"Do we need to know, AJ?"

Of course, we do. We need closure, M. You need to see him brought to justice.

"What about Neve? How do you think she's going to react?"

I want him to suffer, like he made me suffer. Neve's voice is small, but powerful.

"I don't know if I can do this."

We're here for you. Kate says.

Yes, we're all in this together. AJ adds.

"What if no one believes us?" I ask.

It's not up to us to make people believe. It's up to us to protect you. And it's up to you to protect anyone else he may be doing this to. AJ's words send a chill up my spine. He's so damn strong, I don't know how he does it.

"They might call me crazy."

Do you really care what others think of you? Kate asks.

We don't care what others think of us. We know what we are, and what we mean to each other. We're a family. And just like any family, sometimes we're dysfunctional, and sometimes we're not. But most importantly, we will always have each other's back. Neve may be the youngest, but she's so damned smart.

"Are we sure?" I ask them.

We're sure. They respond in unison.

Turning, I face my parents, Gemma, and Dylan. All four are staring at me. "We all need to know, because we all need to heal."

"Okay." Gemma nods. She taps on the screen again, enters a password and takes a deep breath before turning the tablet around so we all can see.

The person in the photo is crossing the road. He's wearing a blue overall uniform. He looks much older than I thought he would be. I do the math in my head. If I was three, and he was sixteen then that makes him thirty-one. "He looks so old," I say. I'm not even sure if it's him.

It's him. Neve whispers in a tiny, petrified voice. *It's him.*

I don't want to go against Neve or doubt her, but this man looks like he's in his early forties. "Are you sure?" I ask Gemma.

Gemma nods. "I double checked. Triple checked, actually, to make sure it's him."

"But this guy looks so old."

"His name is Mack Hewitt, and he's thirty-one."

"Mack Hewitt?" Oh my God. I cover my mouth with my hand. Turning away from everyone, a brutal memory surfaces. "No," my voice trembles, rejecting the flashback. "It can't be." My chest aches, it feels like someone's sitting on it, constricting my breathing. "I can't." I step back, trying to put more distance between me and everyone else.

"Molly." Dylan steps forward, and reaches for me.

"No," I whisper, as I grasp at my hair. "He used to say, 'I'm as powerful as a Mack truck.' He'd say it when he'd…" my voice trails off. I don't need to say anymore.

My entire body feels like it's shutting down. My mind can't think straight. It's him.

Now let's go get the bastard and castrate him. AJ jumps up and down. He's ready for a fight.

This is about all of us, AJ, not just you. Kate steps in to calm him. *We need to consider what we all want to do.*

Chop his dick off. Dirty fucker.

No, AJ, we all have to agree. Kate reminds him.

"Neve, what do you want to do?" I ask.

Neve's timid, sitting back and listening. She's terrified, I can tell just by how she's curled into herself and barely talking.

"Neve?"

We need to go to the police.

"Are you sure you want to do that?"

It's the only way. If we hurt him, we'll feel guilty for hurting him. We're not him. We're better than him.

"We are." I gather every ounce of strength I have, and go to sit at the table. "We're going to go to the police," I say.

"There's more to this," Gemma adds.

"This can't be good," Mom murmurs.

"He works as a janitor. In an elementary school. And he lives about forty minutes from here."

"He's nearby? And he works in a kids' school?" I shake my head, unable to fully comprehend the barrage of information. "Please tell me he doesn't have kids of his own?" I beg.

"He doesn't. But here's something I found out. He's not married, but he wears a wedding ring, so parents won't suspect him. He does it to throw everyone off his scent. I've been interacting with him on a social media site young kids use. He thinks I'm a ten-year-old girl."

"Can't you get in trouble for doing that?" Dad asks.

Gemma smiles proudly. "I'm working with a phenomenal district attorney. She's got my back."

"It's decided. We go to the police. He needs to be stopped."

"We'll be right there with you, Molly," Mom says as she reaches across the table and places her hand over mine, giving me a gentle squeeze.

Tonight's been overwhelming. My body aches from all the traumatizing recollections I've faced. "I'm going to go to bed," I say abruptly. I can't sit here and talk about *him,* or what Gemma's doing to gather information. I just can't. I hardly make eye contact with anyone, before I take off up the stairs and disappear into my room. Zhen follows and when I get in bed, he lays beside me.

My mind is racing. They're all talking, but I'm trying to zone out and ignore them. AJ's anger is making my heart race. He's furious. He wants to hurt *him.*

"Molly," I hear Dylan's voice from the door.

"Yeah?"

"Is it okay if I come in?"

I try and muffle the voices. The angry, the sad, the calm. "Yeah."

Dylan walks into the room, toes off his shoes, and climbs into bed beside me. He swaddles me in his arms, holding me against his chest. My head is to his chest, and I can hear the rhythmic, steady pace of his heart beating.

I try to be strong, for all of us.

But being wrapped in Dylan's arms makes me feel safe.

"Am I doing the right thing?" I clear my throat, and swallow back the lump.

"I don't think there are any other options."

"I don't know what to do," my voice is small.

"I can't tell you what to do, Molly. All I can say is, if you do nothing, one day you're going to hate yourself for enabling him to hurt others. But if you do something, then you'll forever be proud of acting on your strength."

I bring my thumb up to my mouth, and flick my nail against my teeth several times. I try and play every possible scenario in my head. He's right—if I do nothing, I'll hate myself. But if I go to the police, I might not be believed.

The only good thing that'll come from this is that this monster will not be able to hurt anyone else.

I have to do it. I have to.

Yes, M, you do.

CHAPTER 30

The palms of my hands are sweating.

Standing in front of an unassuming building, I look up to see its sheer size. Still it's inconspicuous because it looks exactly like all the other buildings surrounding it.

The sun breaks from behind the brick building, casting the entrance into shadow.

Funny, that. Because I've been living in the shadows all my life. Now is the time for me to come out of the shadows, and speak my truth. Speak *our* truth.

There's a line of cars in front of the building, all marked with the same lettering.

My heart beats quickly as a shock of finality runs through my veins.

This is where part of me will die and another part of me will live.

We're here for you.

All my life I've been worried about what people think of me. But I can't continue on in a life where I'm only breathing. I need to learn to live.

I take several deep breaths, ready to cross the street and take the leap I've been longing for.

"You can do this," I say to myself. The sun is moving higher, the shadow becoming smaller.

Yes, you can.

I look to my left, and to my right, checking for oncoming cars.

I keep walking, crossing the street. I know if I stop for even a second, I'll talk myself out of going.

You can do it.

I walk until I come to the automated doors that slowly slide open.

Hopefully, they'll believe you.

I head to the counter, where a woman who's wearing a uniform, her dark hair pulled back in a severe ponytail, is working on a computer. She looks up, but remains seated. "Can I help you?" she says in a curt voice.

My hands tremble, so I knit them together to stop the emotion bursting to come forward.

"I um," my voice quivers with uncertainty.

"Are you okay?" Hearing something in my voice, she stands and comes closer to the counter. She looks behind me, searching for a hint as to why I'm so edgy.

"I um need to talk to police unit who deals with sexual abuse."

The lady furrows her brows together, and straightens. She asks a question I wasn't expecting. "Are you okay?"

I look at her, surprised. "I'm okay," I reply, skeptically. "But I need to talk to someone about what happened to me as a child."

Realization dawns on her. She thought I was recently sexually abused. "Okay." She offers me a small smile. "Wait just a moment." She walks away, and picks up the phone.

I step back from the counter. My stomach quivers with nerves, as I fidget with the hem of my t-shirt. My parents and Dylan wanted to come with me, but I didn't want them here, so I snuck out of the house early and came to the police station. I just need to do this by myself. By *our*selves.

My skin prickles with nerves. I'm unsure of what I'm doing. I was so confident up until a moment ago. Now, I'm petrified.

I turn, and begin walking out and back to where my car's parked.

I can't do this.

Stop! You have to do this.

"No, AJ, I can't. They won't believe me. They'll think I'm making this up. It's been too long, and I can't do it." I keep walking, refusing to stop.

"Molly!" I hear Dylan calling. I look to my left, and I see him jogging down the street. "You didn't wait for us." He looks behind him, and my parents are only a few steps behind.

"I thought I could do this, Dylan. But I can't. I can't tell them about AJ, Kate, and Neve. They're going to think I've lost my mind."

He steps in and places his hands on my shoulders. "You have no idea what they're going to say or do. But you have to tell them."

My cheeks burn with embarrassment, as I step back away from Dylan. I try to speak, but my chin is trembling with fear. "I don't think I can," I finally manage to whisper.

"You have to," Mom says. "You have to stop him from hurting anyone else. You tried to save Tina and you couldn't. But you can save another little girl from what was done to you."

"And we'll all be right here with you," Dad adds.

I look to the three of them, searching for something, but the heaviness in my throat makes it nearly impossible to breathe.

"It's okay," Dylan says as he steps closer, and embraces me in his arms. "You have to unburden yourself of this colossal weight you've been carrying. It's too much for one person, Molly, to go through life and not have some kind of reprieve from this. You're the only person who has the power to make a difference."

I feel like shrinking away and hiding forever. But what good can come from that? Not a God damned thing.

"You have the power," Mom echoes.

Mom's hand is warm as she places it on my back and rubs gentle circles. Dad hugs me, while I'm hugging Dylan. I know what I have to do, it's just finding the strength to do it.

We'll all be there, and we're all going to be ready to step in if you need us.

"Thank you, Neve," I say in a small voice. "I have to do this, don't I?"

"No, you don't," Dad answers before Neve can. We all separate from the hug. "You really don't." He steps closer, and slings his arm over my shoulder. "Let's go home, and forget about it. Pretend this didn't happen."

"Pretend what didn't happen?" I ask.

"Everything. We'll go home, and in a little while everything will go back to normal, like it was before Tina passed away. We'll all learn how to live without her, and hopefully Kate, AJ, and Neve just drift into the background and never return. Come on, sweetheart. Let's go."

"Thomas, you can't be serious?" Mom snaps at Dad.

"She doesn't want to do this. We can't force her. Maybe this is for the best."

For the best?

"Are you kidding? She'll never know peace because of what that monster did to her." Mom's emotions are making her angry at Dad.

"It doesn't matter. The only thing that matters is Molly. And if she says she can't do it, then she can't do it. There's nothing more to it. We don't need to waste our time, or hers, arguing here."

Waste our time?

Neve's remaining quiet, but AJ is trying to come through. He's so angry.

I can't believe your dad, M. Why is he so cold?

"He's not cold, AJ. He's trying to protect me."

Dad links our hands together, and pulls me in the direction of my car. Every part of me wants to stop. My feet, my head, my alters. "Wait!" I say.

"No, you've made your mind up."

"Dad, I have to do this. I can't *not* do anything about him. They have to know."

Dad smiles at me. "See."

"See what?"

"Didn't like that feeling of hopelessness, did you? That's how you'll feel for the rest of your life if you don't find your strength right this moment."

Oh.

"Yeah," I echo Neve's tiny sigh. "I understand."

"Yeah?" Dad says. "What do you understand?"

"I know I have a choice. And one decision is right, and the other decision is right for me. I have to choose which decision I'm going to act upon. And I know what I have to do."

"No one is going to judge you if you choose to walk away from this," Dylan says.

"I know. But I'm going to judge myself. Neve, AJ, and Kate will all have been for nothing. They need to have a voice. Just like every child who's being or has been groomed and abused. I need to fight for everyone who can't."

Mom beams with pride.

"Then let's head back inside, and do this," Dylan states.

I nod. "Yeah, let's do this."

The first thing I notice is the lady who I spoke with earlier. She's talking to a really tall, older man, whose build is solid. They both look over to us, and the guy walks toward us.

"Hi," he greets me. "I'm David Baxter, part of the sex crimes unit. Amy was telling me you came in to speak to someone from sex crimes. Can I help you?"

I look around, taken aback by the fact we're out in the foyer and anybody can walk past. "Actually…" I don't finish the sentence. I can't do this out here. I shake my head.

David looks to all of us. "How about I make you a cup of the worst coffee in the area?" He made me smile. "It's really terrible. But I'm happy to make five cups, one for each of us."

"I'd love a cup," Dylan replies first and squeezes my hand. "Molly?"

"Molly? I'm David." He holds his hand out for me to take.

"I'd like a coffee," I say as I take his hand and shake it.

"Great, let's go up to my office."

We all follow him to the elevator, where we take it up to the fourth floor. Walking through the door, the office space is fairly bare, only a handful of police officers in at this time of the morning. "There aren't many of you," I say trying to distract myself.

"It's still fairly early, but there are always people here." He leads us into his office. It's bigger than I thought it would be, and actually fairly neat too. There's a large bookcase on the side containing a heap of police manuals, law books, and files. There are some weird knick-knacks from different destinations. But the thing I notice most is a bunch of framed certificates on the wall. But the one that sticks out, is a hand-written letter. I step toward it and notice immediately the juvenile writing. It says,

thank you for making it safe for me to sleep at night.

It has two Xs below the name: Susan.

"That came from the first case I worked on in sex crimes."

"How's Susan now?" I ask.

"Susan is going to graduate high school next year, and is on track to become a police officer. She wants to come work for me," he says with a huge smile, and pride in his eyes. He offers us all a chair, and waits until we're seated. "Now, what's happening with you, Molly?"

And so it begins.

I take a deep breath, then clear my throat. Biting on the inside of my cheek, I'm finding ways to hesitate. I draw in a longer breath, holding for a second while I worry over his response. "I um…"

Tell him, he'll understand.

"Please, AJ, not now."

"Who's AJ? Is that you?" David pointedly looks toward Dylan.

"Ah, no. This is a bit more complicated. I'm Dylan Walker, Molly's boyfriend." Dylan half stands and leans over the table to shake David's hand.

"I'm Paris, and this is my husband Thomas." They both shake David's hand.

He quickly sits again, and jots some notes down on his note pad. "Okay, now that we all know each other, who's AJ?"

"Can I back track a bit before I tell you about them, please?" I ask.

"Them? Okay, please start where you need to."

"I'm adopted, and they're my adoptive parents. But I call them Mom and Dad. This is Dylan, and he's my boyfriend."

"Okay. When were you adopted?"

"I was seven. I'm eighteen now."

"Eleven years ago."

I nod. "Before that my biological father surrendered me and I was put into foster care."

"Do you know when you were taken out?"

Again, I nod. "Just before my third birthday. I lived with the same foster family until I was adopted at seven."

"And what do you remember about them?"

"Oh man, I wasn't expecting that question."

"Were they good people?"

"I think so. I don't recall much from that time."

"Okay." He places his pen on the notepad, and sits back. "What do you recall?"

Tell him, or I'm going to have to.

"Shh," I whisper under my breath. David looks to me, and to Dylan, then to my parents. Wringing my hands together, I fidget under the table, not wanting David to see how nervous I am. My fingers tingle with ice, as my heart beats crazily. My body shakes as I try to form some kind of sentence to tell David. I have to tell him something.

This is it, for all of us, M. You have to tell him.

Neve's pleading little voice brings tears to my eyes. I close my eyes, hoping to disappear. "There was a boy who came to live with us shortly after I was fostered. He used to…" I pause. My heart is now hammering in my chest. The words are stuck in my throat. Panic cripples me, rendering me powerless.

Only you can do this.

"I'm trying," I say to Neve.

I know. Don't give him the power anymore. He's weak, a monster, a damn coward.

"This is the hardest thing I've ever had to do."

It's the hardest thing we'll ever have to do. But if you don't do it now, we'll never be free.

What a word. Free.

I feel like I'm going to throw up.

I click my tongue several times, trying everything to delay saying the words. "He used to do things to me."

And just like that, my skin tingles and I breathe the easiest I've ever done before.

"What did he do?"

Opening my eyes, I'm amazed by how much pressure has been lifted. "At first he'd touch me. But it progressed to…more."

"I'm proud of you, Sweetheart," Dad says.

"I'm so proud." Dylan's hand squeezes my thigh.

"Do you remember much of what happened?" David asks.

"I don't."

No, but I do. Let me talk to him.

"I'm not sure, Neve."

"Who's Neve?" David looks to me, questioning.

"I thought telling you about him was going to be hard." I shake my head as I purse my lips together. "Neve is one of my alters." My shoulders droop as I wait for the disbelief.

David's face doesn't falter. Not for a single second. He doesn't make the face I was expecting. The widening of the eyes, the O mouth, the shaking of the head. None of it. "How many alters do you have?"

"Wait, you believe me?" I ask.

"Early childhood trauma has a huge range of effects. Some people turn to drugs, suicide, they may even go on to be offenders themselves. Dissociative identity disorder isn't as common, but it's not unheard of either."

"You know what I have?" I asked, surprised.

"I've done a lot of research, and talked with a lot of therapists about DID. I know what it is, and guess what, Molly?" I shrug. "I believe you. But here's where it gets tricky. I need as much information as I can get in order to go after this guy."

"My cousin is a PI, and she tracked him down," Dylan offers.

David half smiles. "Did she? Wow, I'm impressed."

"She helping the DA now."

"Eveline?" David asks. Dylan nods. "Good. Eveline is one of the best DA's I've ever met. She has an amazing team that works with her. And Eveline is a good person to have on your side. I'll talk to her about you."

"We've already spoken with Eveline," Mom interrupts.

"You have?" David lifts his brows. "In what way have you spoken with Eveline?"

"Our daughter, our other daughter, Tina," Dad starts. "She was murdered."

David places his pen down, and lifts his head to look at us. "I'm sorry for your loss. What happened with Tina? How is Eveline involved and not one of her team?"

I look around to my parent's blank faces. "No one really knows why she's handling it herself and not one of her team. But while we were there talking about Tina, and the guy she was involved with who killed her, one of my alters came forward."

"Okay, let me back-pedal for a moment. Your sister, Tina was killed by her partner?"

"Yeah," Dad answers.

"Domestic violence. Okay." He rubs his fingers across his forehead. "And you spoke with Eveline?"

"Yeah. Maybe it has something to do with his parents," Mom says.

"The person who killed your daughter, what's his name?"

"Preston Mills," Mom replies.

David's mouth falls open, then he quickly closes it. "And that's why Eveline is involved."

"Why?" I ask.

"Because if she isn't, his parents will do everything in their power to get him off with a slap on the wrist." He rubs his hand across the back of his neck. "Now, what can you tell me about the person who abused you?"

"I can't tell you much. I don't remember much, just some small things. But Neve can talk to you."

"Neve is one of your alters?"

"Yeah. I need to ask her if she'll talk to you." *I'm here and I want to talk to him.* "Okay," I reply to Neve. "She wants to talk."

"Do you need anything before Neve comes forward?"

"Neve likes to draw," Mom says.

"I'll leave the room," Dad says as he stands. I know Neve doesn't like men. She struggles with being around them. She's okay with Dylan, and obviously okay with AJ.

"Neve, the police officer wants to talk you."

I'm here. Your dad doesn't have to go.

"Will you talk to him about Mack? Dad, Neve said you can stay." Dad sits again.

I'll tell him everything he wants to know.

"Are you sure?" She's quiet for some time. I'm nervous now she's disappeared and doesn't want to talk to David.

"What's happening?" Dylan asks.

"Neve's gone quiet. She's not talking. I don't know what's going on."

I'm here. AJ will be with me.

"She's here." I point to my head. "She has AJ here too, in case she'll need him."

"Are you sure you can do this?" Dylan asks.

"We have to," I reply on behalf of all of us.

David nods. "I'll be back in a moment." He stands and leaves the room.

"You don't have to do this," Mom says.

I smile at her and exhale deeply. "Yeah, I do. It's the only way we know David will have enough information to get this guy. I've spent countless hours agonizing over this. I've changed my mind so many times. We just have to do it."

"For everything you've been through, I think you're the strongest person I know," Dylan says. He leans over and gives me a small kiss on the cheek.

"Your mother and I are so proud of you."

"Okay, I have some paper, and some pencils. I'm sorry, this is the best I could get at this time of the morning." David places some blank paper, and half a dozen coloring pencils on the table. "I'm going to record this too." He places a video recorder on the table, and clicks the record button.

Neve's already bursting to come through. She saw the pencils. My mind clouds, as a deep darkness is desperately tugging me toward it.

NEVE

It takes me a little while before I can focus.

"M's mom!" I squeal with excitement. I eye the pencils on the table and I can feel my face erupting with a huge smile. "I love coloring."

The man sitting opposite me is the man M wants me to talk to. "Hi," he says in a soft voice.

"Dylan, will you draw with me?"

"I sure will," he says as he slides a piece of paper over to me and keeps one for himself. "What color would you like?"

"Hmmm." I look at the pencils. "Green please." Dylan slips the green pencil over to me. "Thank you." I notice M's dad sitting next to Paris. "Hi." I sheepishly smile at him. He gives me a little wave.

"Hi, Neve. My name's David. I'm a police officer."

"I know." I draw a picture of a tree on my paper.

"Can you tell me about yourself?"

"I'm only talking to you because M said we need to so you can arrest Mack. Are you going to put him in jail?"

"I'm going to do whatever I can to make sure he's put in jail."

"That's not really an answer, is it?"

David chuckles. "I'll do everything I can to make sure he doesn't hurt anyone ever again, Neve."

"I would beg for him to stop, and he'd laugh at me. He'd tell me I liked what he used to do to me, and no one would believe a stupid cunt like me." Dylan flinches catching my attention. "I'm sorry, Dylan. Did I say something wrong?"

"No, not at all." He smiles at me. But I can see his eyes have tears in them.

"He used to say, he's as powerful as a Mack truck when he'd finish touching me. He used to play music so no one knew what he was doing."

"Did you ever tell anyone?"

I shake my head. "He told me he'd kill me, and our foster parents. Once, he took the cat and beat its head in with a rock. He was laughing when he did it. I was crying. He told me he'd do to me what he did to the cat if I ever told. Our foster parents found the cat and had no idea who'd do something so horrible. I was sad too, because I knew he did it, and I knew what he'd do to me."

"You're a very brave girl, Neve. It takes a lot of strength to talk to a complete stranger."

"If M trusts you, then I trust you. Don't betray us."

"I won't. I promise. I'll even work with Eveline so we can make sure Mack doesn't get away with what he did to you."

I smile. "Good. My hope for him is to get the same treatment he gave to us."

You're doing a good job, Neve. I'm here for you if you need me.

"I know AJ."

"Tell me about AJ."

"AJ protects M. He hates doing what he has to do, but we all understand the roles we have. Now, we have to work together to make sure Mack goes to jail."

"Neve, do you remember the first time it started?"

I look up at him. "I remember everything. The way he smelt of cigarettes, because he used to get cigarettes from one of the boys who lived down the street. I remember the smell of beer when he'd sneak one out of the fridge, and bring it into my room to drink it. I remember the sounds he'd make. The way his hair would fall in his eyes. I remember him asking me if I wanted to play a game with his friends, but I knew by the way he licked his lips what that meant, and I would never go with him when he wanted me to play with his friends. They were scarier than Mack. I remember everything. I can never forget. But I remember, so M never has to."

I hear someone crying, and I look over to M's mom. M's dad looks sadder than Paris.

"I'm sorry for making you sad," I say.

"Oh no!" She leans over, and covers me in a huge cuddle. "You're an amazing person, Neve. Do you hear me? You're such a beautiful, and amazing young lady."

"Thank you." I'm not sure why she said that. Actually, I'm not even sure why I didn't react when she hugged me. All I know is it felt nice. "I'll tell you whatever you need to know."

"Good. Let's get this guy, Neve," David says.

Yes, let's.

CHAPTER 31

I knock on Dylan's door, waiting for him to answer. The amazing aroma wafts through, making my stomach growl with hunger. Dylan opens the door, he looks frazzled. He doesn't say anything before he runs back to the kitchen and leaves me to come in without even a kiss.

"You okay? Do you need help?" I ask as I walk in, close the door then place my bag and cardigan on his sofa.

"I burnt the pasta," he calls from the kitchen.

"You burnt the pasta? How does pasta become burnt?" I head into the kitchen to see what he's doing.

"Ugh. Like this." With the tongs he's holding, he tries to pick up some pasta. It's mushy and collapses as he tries to show me. "I forgot about it." He moves the pot over to the sink, and tips it down the drain, then turns on the garbage disposal. "What a waste."

"I'm pretty sure we could've eaten it."

"It was mush." His mouth flattens into a thin, disapproving line. "Worse than mush. But it's okay. I've got more." He turns to face his pantry, and takes another box of pasta out of the cupboard. "I won't burn this one." He fills the pot with water, and puts it back on the range. "I'll watch it like a hawk."

I walk over to him, and give him a hug. He holds me close, and kisses my forehead. "I've missed you." Closing my eyes, I lean into him. He smells nice. Freshly showered, mixed with hint of spice. God, he smells so good.

"What a day." He sighs. "What a week," he quickly adds.

"Tell me about it. David called me, and said Gemma went in to see him. I'm kinda nervous about everything."

"What are you nervous about?"

I pull away from Dylan, and lean against the counter. "I'm nervous that Gemma's made a mistake."

"A mistake? Gemma doesn't make mistakes. She's incredibly thorough with her investigations."

"I'm not doubting Gemma, that's not what I mean. I'm worried Mack's somehow deceived her, or really isn't this monster pedophile who committed unspeakable acts on me. I'm nervous that when it comes to charging him with those crimes, his attorney will do everything possible to debunk me and make me look like I'm crazy." I can feel myself getting worked up. I keep dragging my hands through my hair, and avoiding Dylan's eyes.

"You're uncertain about everything. There's a lot happening in your life, Molly. But, remember, you have your parents and me here to support you. Not to mention Amelia, and David. We're all here for you, and for AJ, and Kate, and Neve."

"I need a hug," I say as I step close again. Dylan smiles, and holds me again. "I feel like I haven't had a single moment to myself to breathe. I'd love a day where I don't have to think about anything, and I'm not terrified of what people will think once they find out about my…" I pause, and half smile. "…my extended family." I chuckle.

"Extended family? I like that!" I feel Dylan snicker.

I let go of Dylan, and start setting the table for dinner. "I have to say, I'm really worried Preston is going to get away with what he did to Tina."

"There's no way, not with his past. Not with what Gemma found out about him."

"I have a feeling if his parents find out about my extended family, they'll use that somehow to get Preston off of the charges."

Dylan nods, lifting his brows in agreeance. "They're shady, and don't have a good bone in their body. And, I think you're right. They would exploit you in order to get Preston out of the trouble he's in. But your situation doesn't have any bearing on what he did to Tina."

My stomach knots with fear, and I worry my lower lip between my teeth. "This feels like it's too much for me to handle."

"One day at a time. It's the only thing we can do." He pours some of the packet of pasta into the rapidly boiling water. "How are Zhen and Zorro?"

I smile. "I love them so much. Zhen's by my side all the time. It's like he knows something's going on."

"I'm amazed you didn't bring him tonight."

I perk up. "Would you mind? Can I bring him next time?"

"If you want. I'm happy to have him here. Here's a good dog."

"I think he thinks he's a human." Heat warms my chest when I think about Zhen. He makes me smile; he's such a good dog. Dylan's watching me, smiling. "What?"

"You. You're so cute."

I beam happily. I love the way Dylan makes me feel like I'm the only woman on this planet. "I am?"

"Yeah, you are. So, I want to ask, how has your extended family been?" He grabs the tongs and brings out a piece of pasta, popping it into his mouth. "Nearly," he mutters to himself.

"They've all been quiet since we got back from the police station. Very quiet, actually." I crinkle my forehead, definitely surprised by their silence.

"I thought maybe they'd have a lot to say. Not even Neve?" I shake my head. "Quiet is good, right?" he asks, but he doesn't sound convinced.

"Yeah," I say in a higher than usual pitch. But the fact Dylan's asking about them, means he really does care. And maybe he's not as freaked out about them as I thought he'd be. He's been by my side this whole time, ready to help in any way he can.

Sorry, M, I have to do it.

"AJ, what are you doing?"

I'm sorry.

I can feel myself being dragged under. My head fogs over, and I'm losing all control over myself. Seriously, AJ?

AJ

I steady myself against the chair as the cloud lifts from my head.

So, this is Dylan, the guy M's totally in love with. Huh. Well, he better be ready for some hard questions.

I pace back and forth, puffing my chest out as I stare at him.

"Do you want cheese?" he asks.

"Why the fuck would I want cheese?" I snap at him.

Dylan looks up from what he's doing, his eyes search over my body. "Are you okay?" He steps closer to me.

"Back off, buddy. Before I put you on your ass."

He looks confused. "AJ?" he asks.

"Were you expecting someone else? M's gone to sleep for a bit. You and I need to have a talk. Sit." I pull the chair out and wait for him to sit.

"Wait, let me finish this, and we can talk. I'm not burning the pasta again." He quickly does something in the kitchen. What an odd guy. "Okay, I'm here." He sits in the chair I've pulled out for him. Grabbing one of the others, I turn the chair and swing my leg over, straddling it. "I'm Dylan," he says as he holds his hand out for me.

"I know who you are. M's totally in love with you. Do you know why I'm here?" I don't take his hand to shake it. For all I know, he's another sick perve who just wants to screw with M, and Neve, and maybe even Kate and me.

"I've wanted to meet you. I'd like for us to get to know one another."

I scoff. "Do you like her?"

"No," he replies with a stoic face. I stare at him as my hands curl into fists. "I love her," he adds.

"Why?" I get up and move to stand in front of him, and cross my arms in front of my chest. "I'm protective of her. I don't want some dick to do to her what that other asshole did."

"I don't want Molly to get hurt either. And, I'd never do anything to be the perpetrator of that. She means too much to me."

"Words. All I'm hearing is words." I make a duck bill with my hand, and open it and close it. "Why should I believe you? You're much older than she is. Why don't you find yourself someone closer to your age? Or can't you get anyone?" I mock.

Dylan rolls his eyes. "Because I don't want anyone else. Molly is…" he stops talking to think about what he wants to say. "Molly's more."

"More? How so?"

"She's more than I ever imagined. She makes me want to be more, for her."

"Buddy, I've got no idea what the hell you're trying to say. You're talking like a love-sick hormonal teenage boy. Just spit it out, this ain't no romance novel. No need to say shit for the hell of saying shit. I don't work that way."

Dylan laughs. "I love her. She's important to me. I want to protect her, and cherish her, and make her feel like she's the most important person in the world." Huh, right. I wasn't expecting that much from him. "Is that straight forward enough for you?"

I scoff and click my tongue to the roof of my mouth. "She's someone special."

"She certainly is." He sighs deeply. "Considering it's not just her I'm in a relationship with, I think it's important we get along too. I know you don't know me, so I intend to prove to you that I'm not going to hurt her. Or you. Or Kate. And especially not Neve."

"Especially not Neve?" I question.

"Because Neve is just a child. And she's suffered enough at the hands of a monster."

"What about sex?" I ask the hard question.

Dylan looks away as he smashes his lips together. "That's something I need to talk to Molly about first."

"You can talk to me."

"I don't feel comfortable having this conversation with you before I have it with Molly."

"Why? Are you going to just keep going regardless of what she wants?"

Dylan stands abruptly, and comes right up to my face. "Don't you dare say that about me. You have no idea what kind of person I am." He pokes me in the shoulder. "I would never hurt anyone, let alone Molly! Don't you dare." He backs away, and places both his hands on his hips. "I'm not that type of person. I never have been."

I think I've pushed him too far. But I had to know. I had to know *him.* Dylan's restless, moving from foot to foot while taking deep breaths. "Look, man," I say as I approach him. "I had to know the kind of guy you are."

"This was some kind of test? Are you serious?" He closes his eyes, and pinches the bridge of his nose.

"It wasn't a test. I'm responsible for the lives of three other people. So I have to make sure the guy she's fallen in love with is a good guy, and not a monster who's going to hurt her. Don't get me wrong, I'll fucking kill you if you lay a hand on her, but from what I've seen, you're okay."

"AJ, you don't have to be responsible for her anymore. I've got this. Actually, I've got all of you."

I shake my head. "They will always be my responsibility."

Dylan steps forward, and claps a hand to my shoulder. "You've done a really good job of looking after them for as long as you have. You can take a rest, AJ. Let me help. Please."

His plea is somewhat surprising, but definitely heartfelt. He's not a monster, he's not a bad guy, not like *him.*

We can trust him. Neve's softness is what draws me to her.

"I've got a feeling we can too, Neve."

Dylan's brows crinkle.

I think he'll look after us. Let him help, AJ. You've had to be strong for so long, let him help.

"Neve likes you."

Dylan smiles. "I like Neve too. I like you all, but I love Molly. I love her with all my heart."

I know.

Although I believe Dylan, I still have reservations. "I'm going to be keeping an eye on you. And don't for one moment think I won't come forward to protect her."

"I know." Dylan holds his hand out, waiting for me to shake it. I look down, hesitant about showing him my acceptance so early on. I won't be fooled. Not ever again. But I take it, and vow to myself, Kate, Neve, and M that I'll watch over them forever.

I push myself back, and force M to come forward.

MOLLY

The fogginess is slowly lifting. I'm sitting on Dylan's lap when I become fully aware of what's happening. "I'm sorry," I say then clear my throat. I can feel my ears tingling with a sure sign of embarrassment. "I can't believe AJ did that." Standing, I walk away from Dylan, my pulse now pounding with anger.

"Molly. Stop." Dylan stands, and approaches me.

"I'm so damn angry at AJ. He just forced his way through and took over. What the hell is his problem?"

"Stop!" Dylan says again.

"How can you be so calm, he just…" I feel like punching the wall.

"Look. I don't think he's going to do that again. Just, please, listen to me." Dylan walks over to the kitchen, and takes a pitcher of water out of the fridge, pours me a glass and brings it to his table. "AJ was concerned about me."

"You?"

"Yeah, and I get it. He had to make sure my intentions aren't villainous."

"Villainous?" What a weird word.

"He's concerned about all of you. He's Kate's, Neve's, and your protector. He's spent his life protecting you, making sure he steps in when you can't deal with what's happened. It's normal he wants to protect you from another threat."

"What did he say?" I ask as I slump in the chair, pick the water up and drink it all in one go.

"He wanted to check me out, make sure I wasn't going to hurt you. We met, we talked, things got a little heated for a few moments, but I think we came to an understanding."

I focus on anyone talking at the moment, but they're all quiet. No one is saying anything. "They're quiet," I say as I point up toward my head.

"Let's have dinner, and enjoy our night."

"I need a rest from everything." I really do. "A few days without them in my head, without the worry of Mack and Preston. I just need a vacation."

"Yeah, you do."

Dylan moves around the kitchen like a professional. He prepares our bowls of pasta and sauce, then brings them over to the table. I'm not really hungry, not now. But I'll definitely eat. "Thank you," I say.

"Life as we know it won't ever be the same, Molly. But I want you to know, whatever challenges you have are challenges *we* have, and we deal with them together."

I shake my head, tears threatening to spill. "You're too good for me, Dylan."

"No, Molly. We're perfect for each other."

Yeah, I'm totally in love with Dylan. But I'm going to have to talk to AJ, Neve, and Kate, and establish some rules and guidelines.

CHAPTER 32

"Dylan's on his way over, is that okay?" I ask Mom as we cook in the kitchen together.

"I know," Mom replies with a smile.

I look over to her, she's got a huge cheeky smile. "What are you up to?"

"Me? Nothing." She shrugs, but I know she's hiding something. Though the smile tells me, it's got to be good.

Dad's in the den, doing something for Eveline.

The doorbell rings, and Zhen walks out first to see who's at the door. He's wagging his tail when I get there, so I know it's definitely Dylan. Opening the door, I find Dylan standing in front of me, looking rather sexy in jeans, and a tight, light green t-shirt. "Hello," I say as I lean in for a kiss.

He snakes his hand around my waist, pulls me in tight and dips me. His lips are soft, and gentle. "Hello, beautiful," he says when he straightens us and pulls away from the kiss.

My cheeks flush, as I forget about everything for a moment, and think dirty thoughts about Dylan and me together. My head is swimming from that kiss. I swallow back the lump sitting in my throat, and walk away from Dylan, gathering myself.

"Mom and I are cooking," I say as I quickly head into the kitchen.

"Hey, boy." I turn to see Dylan petting Zhen, and scratching him behind the ears. Zhen sees me leaving, and quickly catches up to me, with Dylan following a few steps behind. "Hi Paris." Dylan walks over to Mom, and gives her a quick kiss on the cheek.

"How are you, Dylan?"

"Yeah, I'm good now." He winks at Mom.

Mom's cheeky smile growing even larger. "What have you two done?" I know they're up to something.

"I don't know what you're talking about, darling," Mom replies, but looks away, letting her hair fall over her face so I can't see her expression.

"Ah, Dylan. I didn't hear you come in." Dad looks around the kitchen, like he's searching for something. "Where's Molly's bag?"

"Thomas!" Mom scolds Dad.

"What?"

"For God's sake. He hasn't told her yet!" Mom reprimands Dad. "I swear to…ugh. You can't keep a damn secret, can you?"

"Oh, shit," Dad mumbles in a low voice. "You didn't tell her yet?" He asks Dylan. Dylan shakes his head, but smiles. "Okay. Um, let's pretend I'm still in the den, and I've got Tourette syndrome, and I'm just saying whatever comes to mind."

"Why do I need my bag? Where are we going?" I ask Dylan. "Dad said we're going somewhere, so where?"

"Well, we're going upstate for a few days. Just two nights, leaving after dinner. A friend of mine has a farm, and he has a guest house, so we're going there."

"We are?"

"We are."

"Mom, you're okay with this?"

"We're both okay with this," Dad says. "With everything going on, a few days away is exactly what the three of you need."

"Three?" I ask.

"Zhen's coming too," Dylan says.

My heart fills with more love for Dylan. He couldn't be any more wonderful even if he tried. "Am I packed then?" I look to Mom for the answer.

"Yeah, I've packed a bag for you. Come." She gestures for me to follow, while Dad and Dylan stay in the kitchen. "Keep an eye on dinner," she instructs over her shoulder.

"Okay," Dylan replies.

That makes me giggle. "Mom, why didn't you tell me?" We head upstairs.

"Dylan asked me two days ago, and I told him I'd talk to your father about it. We like Dylan. He's very much a family person. You can tell a lot about a person by how they treat the people who are important in your life. We like how he treats us, and we like how he treats Zhen. So when he asked, I didn't have a problem with him taking you on a mini vacation. God only knows, you need it."

"You do realize we'll probably have sex, right?"

"You're eighteen, Molly. And you've lived a thousand lifetimes in your eighteen years. Your father and I could only hope for someone as wonderful as Dylan to be the person you want to be with." We both sit on Mom's bed, and she hugs me close to her. "We like him, Molly. We like him a lot. And we trust him."

"I trust him too. I know he won't do anything to jeopardize that. He's told me he loves me."

"We know." Mom smiles.

"I love him too."

"Do you?"

"I've never felt like this before. He's come out of nowhere, and he's completely won me over. He's trying to be friends with my alters, and he's taking it as slow as I need."

"Then go, and have fun. I've packed your bag, and I've put in a packet of condoms too."

"Mom!" I cringe.

"Be safe. And if you need anything, you can always call. Or, if you want, ask Dylan to bring you home. Try and put everything that's happening on hold, just for a few days and focus on what's between the two of you. You deserve this."

I let out a deep breath, and nod. "Okay, we'll go. Thanks, Mom."

Mom goes to her walk-in closet, and brings out an overnight bag. It's packed to the brim. "I've got Zhen's food packed down stairs." I stand, walk over to her, and hug her. "Come on."

Mom takes the bag, and places it by the front door. Dad and Dylan are in the kitchen, talking. I try to sneak in so I can eavesdrop on what they're saying, but both stop when I walk in. Mom quickly follows.

I look around the kitchen to see what they've been doing, and notice they've made a salad. "Yum," I say as I pick a piece of tomato and pop it into my mouth.

"Dinner's ready," Mom announces, as she takes a chicken out of the oven and places it on the table.

"Wow, this really is in the middle of nowhere." It's nearly dark when we reach our destination.

"There's no cell reception out here either. There's a landline in the cottage, but other than that, it's fairly isolated."

"I can't wait to see what it's like in the morning." Getting out of the car, Zhen jumps out, and runs to pee. Dylan takes his bag, and my bag out of the trunk, and uses the headlights to illuminate our path up to the cottage. "It's cute, from what I can see." The night is still, with nothing more than a rather loud hum of frogs breaking the peace.

"Wait until the morning. The sunrise is simply electric."

"So, who's this friend of yours?" I ask as we walk up the three wide steps to the porch.

"He's a guy I went to school with. He was a dork in high school, and we kinda hit it off."

"You were a dork?"

"Well, I wasn't exactly popular."

"Huh?" I question. He looks around the porch, and lifts a small plant revealing a key. "So what kind of guy were you in high school?"

"A nerd."

I burst into laughter. Dylan opens the door, and Zhen pushes ahead of us, sniffing everything in his path. "So you weren't a dork, but you were a nerd. How does that work?"

"I was into everything computers. Loved them. I fell in love with the security aspect of computers, which led me to do what I do."

"And your friend?"

"Yeah, he loved computers too, but the coding side of it. He created an app, made himself a ton of money from it, and moved out here."

"Cool. What's his name?"

"Tommie Higbee. Maybe you've heard of the app, it's SafeT4Women."

"Really? Isn't that the female-only ride sharing app, the one where a text goes out to a designated friend to let them know where you're going and who's taking you? He created that?"

"Yeah. He actually created it in the last year of high school. It did so well that a company bought it, and he's gone on to become an app developer. He just needs internet access and his home."

"And there's no cell reception out here? Really?" I question as I tilt my head to the side.

Dylan smiles. "Damn it, you caught me. There is reception. Actually, it's really good. I just wanted you to not worry about anything."

"You could've said that. I'm happy to keep my phone off for the next few days."

"We both will. Here. We can put them in the drawer in the kitchen." He turns his phone off and drops it into the last drawer of the kitchen. I place mine in there too. It quickly becomes awkward between us. Tension building at a fast rate. "Are you hungry?" he offers.

"Nah, I'm good." I wipe my sweaty hands down the side of my pants, hoping he doesn't notice my nervousness. "I might take a shower if that's okay?"

"Yeah, sure. Look, I'm just going to say it. Don't think I've brought you up here for anything to happen. We'll take everything slow, Molly. There's no reason to be nervous, I just want you to relax, and let me take care of you." He walks toward me, and hugs me, placing a soft kiss to my forehead. Closing my eyes, I take a calming breath.

"Thank you," I say as I open my eyes. He leans down and places his finger under my chin, lifting my face so I can look at him. With sweet gentleness, he presses his lips against mine. Kissing me, first with tenderness, and care. But I escalate the kiss, wanting more of him. Needing more of him. I slide my hands under his shirt, feeling his taut stomach beneath his clothes. I scrape my nails across his skin, and he grumbles against my lips.

"Dear lord," he mutters as he picks me up. I wrap my legs around his hips, while he moves us to the sofa. He sits, and I'm straddled across his hips. He rakes his fingers through my hair, and pulls me closer to his body. I can feel his excitement. It's turning me on, making me crazy for him. I slide his shirt up, over his head, and sit back looking at this beautiful man. "What are you thinking?" he asks as he leans forward to take my mouth with his again.

"How much I want you right now." Jesus, where did that confidence come from?

"We don't have to rush."

"I want to rush. I want this, with you." I hover over his mouth, teasing him with a promise of what's to come.

Suddenly, I feel tired. Exhausted.

EVE

"Is this where we have sex now? Can we color after?" I take my shirt off, dropping it to the ground.

"Whoa. Wait, Neve?" Dylan asks.

"Yeah. What do you want to do to me? Just sex? More?"

He lifts me off him, and places me next to him on the sofa then stands, grabs his t-shirt and puts it on. "Neve. Um, what are you doing here?"

"We're going to have sex, right?" I twirl my hair around my fingers. "But can we color after, please?"

"Shit," Dylan mumbles under his breath. He runs his hands through his hair, clutching at the strands. Shaking his head, he remains quiet.

"We don't have to color if you don't want," I say in a small voice, trying to hide my disappointment.

"Neve, you and I have to have a talk. Can I sit down beside you please?"

I nod my head. He picks my top up, and hands it to me. "Thank you," I say.

"Neve, I like you." He sits beside me, but I notice how he's left room between us. "But I don't like you the way I like Molly."

"Okay."

He looks around the room, and exhales a couple of times. I bite my lip, waiting for him to tell me what he wants to do to me. "Neve, I don't want to have sex with you."

"Did I do something wrong?"

"God, no! But you're a child. And I don't want to have sex with you, or any other child. I love Molly, and I want to be with her, not you."

"You don't want me?" I feel my bottom lip quivering as I try my hardest to hold in the tears.

"Not that way, Neve. Not like how I want Molly. I want to color with you, and play games with you, but I don't ever want to have sex with you. I want you to be a kid, and sex is not for kids."

"But…"

"No, sweetheart, you're like Molly's little sister. And little sisters should never be in the bedroom when adults are having sex. I'm sorry you were exposed to that, and I'm really sorry you had to go through that, but I am not *him,* and I don't want you to do those things with me."

"But you still want to color with me?"

"Of course. I want to go to the amusement park with you, and I want to watch movies with you, and do all kind of fun things. But this level of intimacy isn't something I want you to ever have to experience again. Do you understand?"

I look away from him and chew on my lip again. "You want to be my friend?"

"Absolutely. But I can never have sex with you."

"Because I'm a kid? And kids should never have sex?"

"Yes. And because I know you're here now because you want to protect Molly. But could you maybe try to not protect her when we're kissing and cuddling?"

"But you want to have sex. I don't understand."

"I do, but never with you. Because…"

"I'm a kid," I say. "Will you still like me even if we don't have sex?"

"I can't help but like you, Neve. You're a very special young lady, who only wants to take care of Molly. But I want to take care of her too, and I want this time to be with Molly. When we're kissing, and cuddling, and when we're ready to have sex, I don't want you in the bed with us. It isn't a place for kids."

"I think I understand. But, if you want me in there, will you tell M?"

"I can promise you I'll *never* want you in the bed with me. It's not a place for you. I want you to feel safe knowing I'll never ask you to do anything like that."

I look around the room, and smile. "Okay."

"Do you still want to color?"

I shake my head. "You know what's funny?"

"What's funny, Neve?"

"I don't want to have sex with you either."

Dylan chuckles. "First, you're way too young to even think about having sex. And second, good. I'm glad."

"Can I have a hug, Dylan?" He doesn't hesitate, he moves in and hugs me close to him. His hands are high up on my back, and his lower body is angled away from me. "Dylan?"

"Yeah?"

"Can I go back to my room now? I've got pencils and a new coloring book Kate brought me."

"Yeah, I think that's a great idea. And, Neve? Remember, you keep coloring when Molly and I are together in the bedroom."

"I promise, I'll stay away." I close my eyes, and force my way back to my room.

MOLLY

It takes me a few seconds to realize I'm back. "Was it AJ again?" I ask.

"Neve."

"Neve?" My gut tightens as I worry about why she had to come out. I replay what was happening in my head, and I feel sick to my stomach when I recall what we were doing. "I'm sorry," I whisper.

"Don't be. Neve and I spoke."

"About?" My throat narrows and I feel vomit quickly rising.

"I told Neve that I don't want her here when you and I are being intimate. She didn't understand at first, she thought she'd done something wrong to make me not like her. But I explained to her how sex isn't for kids. And if or when you and I do have sex, then I want her to stay in her room and keep coloring."

"You said that to her?" I lower my gaze, embarrassed because of what's happened. "Dylan..."

"Don't you dare tell me that you and I aren't going to work. Don't hide behind Neve, or AJ, or Kate. AJ, Neve, and I have come to an understanding. You're a family, a family who has to learn where *I* fit in. I'm patient, and I'm willing to work with all members of the family for them to be comfortable with me."

"But..."

"Look." Dylan sighs. He sits closer and takes my hands in his.

"There's no manual for this. There's no rule book. There's no GPS. Nothing. What we have to do is work together. All five of us."

I pull my hand away, and rub at my temple. "You're so gentle, and… and… willing to accept anything that's going to come my way. It's not too late."

He scoffs as he shrugs. "It might not be too late for you. But me, I'm a goner. You're the most incredible person I've ever met. And I don't care how long I have to wait. I will. An eternity? Pffft." He flicks his hand at me. "I'll wait five eternities."

"You know what's scary?"

"What?"

"The depth of your love for me."

He scratches at his chin for a moment, thinking. "It shouldn't be scary. It should be comforting. Because I'll always be there to catch you. I'm your safety net, and you're mine." He chuckles again. "In time, all four of you will be my safety net, so I'm winning more in this relationship thing more than you."

I stare at him, my mouth open. "Did you just make a joke about my alters?"

"I made a joke about all of you." He winks, as he falls back against the sofa, dragging me on top of him. Straddling his legs, I lean down and kiss him.

This kiss isn't as fevered as the first.

But that's okay, for tonight.

CHAPTER 33

"Hey, wake up," Dylan says as he peppers kisses down my cheek, to the top of my neck.

"Do I have to?" I moan as I turn over in bed.

"Yeah, I've made you a hot chocolate. I want you to see the sunrise, come on."

Painfully aware of my morning breath, I flick my hand at him. "I need the bathroom. I'll be out in a moment."

"Don't take too long." He kisses me on the cheek again, before pushing off the bed and leaving. I hear Zhen's toenails scrape against the floor as he follows Dylan. "Come on, boy. Want some breakfast?"

I know Zhen's favorite word, other than ball, is breakfast and dinner. I can imagine he's wagging his tail, waiting for Dylan to feed him.

Last night ended up disastrous. We didn't have sex. Dylan couldn't go through with it. He was shaken by the fact Neve forced her way through. He needs time, and I'm okay with that. I won't push for him to do anything he's not comfortable with, just like he's patient with me.

Throwing the covers back, I head into the bathroom to take care of my morning business.

I can hear Dylan talking to Zhen from the front porch, asking him how he liked sleeping on the sofa. I can't help but giggle. "You know, I think you should sleep on the sofa tonight too. Try not to come into the room."

I quickly brush my teeth, and fix my hair so I don't have bed-head, then leave the bathroom so I can find Dylan and Zhen.

Dylan's sitting on a bench seat out on the porch. Zhen's at his feet, sitting with his head on Dylan's lap, his tail swishing on the porch floor as it wags.

"I think you've definitely found a best friend there." I indicate to Zhen.

"I gave him food. I think that's the only reason he likes me." He scratches Zhen's head. Zhen's eyes begin to close. "Here, take a seat. Let me grab you your hot chocolate." He stands and rushes into the cottage, then comes back within seconds, carrying two mugs. "I've fed Zhen. He seemed to like what I gave him."

"That's because he's not a food snob, and likes everything we put in his bowl. He isn't a fussy dog."

Dylan sits beside me, and slings his arm over my shoulder. We sit and look over the vast grounds. The sun is rising, and the light is only just breaking over the land. "It's so peaceful here," Dylan says, and kisses the side of my head.

"It's so quiet. All night long all I could hear were the frogs." I look around, and see a large house in the distance. "Wow, is that Tommy's house over there?"

"Yeah."

"It's huge. Mind you, this cottage is pretty big too. Especially considering it's a cottage."

"Yeah, he bought the land and built the houses on here. He offers this for whoever needs a few days away. His parents travel often, and they come to stay here for the holidays. He's a good guy. We'll go over later for lunch, if that's okay with you."

I instantly become apprehensive. My stomach churns as I mentally start creating tension about what could happen. "I don't know," I say slowly.

"It's okay, Molly. I told him about you, and your incredible life. He's eager to meet you."

"You don't think he'll think I'm some kind of freak?"

"Ahhh, freak? No. Weird?" He playfully grimaces. "Maybe."

I smack his chest in fun. Dylan always eases my anxiety. Just knowing he's here for me, makes having alters a lot easier. "Okay, I'll meet him. I'm sure he's a nice guy."

"Yeah, he is. But you can't tell him I said that."

I stand, and maneuver myself so I'm sitting on Dylan's lap. Zhen walks away, and goes to lay down at the top of the steps with a heavy sigh. "I love you," I say again. I find myself not really saying these words often to Dylan. I don't know why. I do love him. But for some reason, they're difficult words to say.

"What's wrong?" he asks.

"I don't know why I can't tell you I love you more often. I feel like something's holding me back."

"I don't know either. But it doesn't matter how often you tell me. I know you do, and that's all that matters to me."

"No, I should be able to say it more than once every now and then. I don't know why I struggle to say it."

"Maybe as we grow as a couple and you feel safer with me, you'll be able to open up to me more."

"Do you think I'm cold toward you?"

"No, not cold. But reserved. In saying that though, it's understandable. You have to learn how to trust me."

"I do trust you."

"I know you do, but I haven't been in your life as long as your parents, or Tina. They've proven to you that you can trust them, and love easily flows between you all. Your guard is still up with me, but I'm breaking down those barriers, and one day you'll easily tell me you love me often. I'm patient."

"Yes, you are."

"Uncharted lands for all of us. You, me, Kate, AJ, and Neve. But we'll get there, in time."

"I do love you."

"I know." He kisses my nose, then my lips. I deepen the kiss, wanting to take this to the next level, desperately wanting to be able to take control of myself, and my internal family. I grind against him, feeling exactly what I'm doing to him. "Molly," he whispers as I kiss down his throat. Gently sucking the skin between my teeth.

"I want this, please tell me you do too."

"Of course, I do. But..."

"Please, let me take the lead here. If anything changes, we can stop. Please."

"Molly." He breathes out, sighing deeply. Pinching his nose, he closes his eyes. "I'm not sure."

"I know; I understand. It's unfair for me to push you to do this when you don't know if you can."

"Oh, don't get me wrong. I *definitely* can. I'm just trying to be cautious, for all of us."

"Look at me, Dylan." He opens his eyes, and stares into mine. "I promise, if I think someone else is going to come forward, I'll stop before that happens."

"But you don't always know they're going to come through, do you?"

"No, I don't. But I trust you to stop. Like you did last night."

He runs his hands up and down my back, settling them on my hips. "We can try," he says.

"That's all I'm asking for."

He stands, picking me up with him, and takes me into the bedroom.

I wring my hands together as we stand at Tommy's door, waiting for him to open it. "You'll love him," Dylan says. "Oh, and by the way, he has no filter."

"What do you mean?" I ask, my trembling increasing. Zhen nuzzles into my leg, and gives me a quick lick on the top of my foot.

The door opens, and a really tall, red-haired guy opens the door.

He has the full mountain man beard going on, with short hair, and blue eyes that could rival the cleanest of oceans. He's wearing a plaid shirt, and jeans. "Dylan, man." He steps forward, and gives Dylan a half hug, then this macho shake of their hands. "Oh my God. You're gorgeous. And you, buddy, are batting way above your average," he says to Dylan about me. "You're a cute looking dog. He's not going to make a mess inside, is he?"

"Um, hi. No, Zhen won't make a mess. He's a good dog. I'm Molly," I introduce myself as I hold my hand out.

"You're the one who has a bunch of weird-ass personalities living inside them, right?" Yep, Dylan was right, no filter. He steps forward, grabs me around the waist and picks me up in a huge bear hug.

What is going on? Kate asks, and pastes a huge smile on my face. *This looks like fun.*

"Not now, Kate," I whisper reasserting control as Tommy places me to my feet.

"Shit, sorry. Did I do that?" Tommy asks. "Come in, come in." He steps aside, and leads us into his huge house, I'd describe more like a mansion. From the outside it's massive, from the inside it's even bigger.

"Wow, this place is huge!" I say as I look around.

"Ah, yeah. Personal space and all."

"Dude, I told you. You can't be your normal self around Molly," Dylan reprimands Tommy.

I feel bad that Tommy can't be Tommy in his own home. "Oh no, please, be your normal self. It's Kate. She likes having fun. Thank you for letting us stay in your cottage."

"I designed it for my parents to come and stay for the holidays. But Dylan has a standing invitation whenever Mom and Dad aren't here. Who wants a drink?"

"Ah, I'm not old enough to drink."

"I meant a soda, or water or something? Anyway, come on through. Lunch is nearly ready." He takes us through his home, and I notice a room enclosed in glass walls that has a bank of laptops and computers all lined up. There's got to be at least fifteen in the room. Tommy notices me looking at it. "That's where I work from. Wanna look?"

"Sure."

He leads us into the room, and I automatically notice how cool it is in here. "It's quite cold in here."

"Better environment for all the computers. And for me. I work better when it's cold."

"There are so many. Why do you need so many computers?"

Tommie shrugs. "I don't know. I just like them."

"He's a dork, that's why," Dylan adds.

"Whatever, man." Tommy rolls his eyes. "Anyway, up the stairs are the bedrooms. Down that hall is a guest suite. Down the opposite hall is a bathroom, laundry, and the access to a cellar. All the boring shit."

I smile at Tommy. He's really easy to like. I see how Dylan and Tommy can be friends. "Dylan told me you were a dork in school."

"Yeah? Did he tell you about prom?"

"Prom? No, what happened?" I ask as we follow Tommy into his huge kitchen.

"No, man. Don't do it," Dylan begs.

"Oh come on. You gotta tell her about prom."

"Don't." I turn to look at Dylan who's burying his face in his hands.

"Now I have to know. Please, go ahead." I eagerly wait for this story. Tommy opens the back sliding doors, and we sit under the pergola on the back deck at the massive outdoor set of table and chairs. Zhen runs off to discover what's happening in the garden.

"Do you still talk to her? What was her name? J-something, wasn't it?" Tommie asks.

"Janet," Dylan grumbles. "And no, she didn't look me in the eyes after prom. She never spoke to me again. You know that."

Tommy is laughing, and Dylan is cringing. "Come on, don't make me wait. I *need* to know," I plead.

"Are you going to tell it, or am I?" Tommy asks.

"Ugh. What are you cooking?" Dylan stands, and heads inside. "I don't want to hear this again."

"I'm not cooking. The chef has come to make me food for the week. And to make our lunch. I have no idea where he is or what he's making. Probably gone on a break, the lazy bastard."

"I heard that," a guy calls from the kitchen. "Hey, I'm Scott," he announces as he comes out back where Tommy and I are sitting. He's an older guy, maybe in his fifties, with short gray hair, and a porn star moustache. "He's an ass. Don't believe a single thing he says."

"Get inside before I fire you," Tommy threatens playfully.

Scott turns and walks inside, but not before flipping Tommy the bird over his shoulder. "Whatever, man. If you fire me, you'll starve. By the way, now's a good time to talk about a pay raise. I think ten percent is good."

"How about you get your ass into the kitchen?" I have to laugh, are these two lovers or boss and employee? Either way, they're amusing me. "So, our stud Dylan in there decided to ask a girl to prom."

"I've never been a stud," Dylan yells from inside.

"I thought you wanted Tommy to tell the story. Which means you have to be quiet and let him tell it," I call to him.

"Great, now my girlfriend and my best friend are conspiring against me," he mumbles loud enough for us to hear him.

"As I was saying, stud-muffin in there asked a girl to prom. Now, picture this. We were so uncool. Mr. Sexy in there, finally grew into his head. Yes, I know." He holds his hand up. "It's impossible to actually think of us as uncool, but we were. So, Dylan asks the girl, the girl says to him, 'Let me think about it.'"

"Ouch, that's terrible," I say as my hand flies up to my chest. "How horrible."

"Yeah, well, it gets worse. About four days before prom, she comes up to him and says, 'I suppose I can go with you if you want.'"

"Oh, now that's nasty. Please tell me he told her no?"

"Yeah…nah, he didn't. He was so happy to be going with her. He'd been crushing hard on her for the whole school year."

"No, I wasn't!"

Tommy nods his head, leans in and whispers, "Yeah, he was."

Scott comes out, holding a pitcher of what looks like soda, and four glasses. It appears, Scott will be joining us for lunch. I don't mind; he seems like a cool guy. "Here." He places the pitcher down, and pours me a glass before disappearing back into the kitchen.

"What about me?" Tommy calls after him.

"You've got two hands, and a perfectly good heartbeat. Do it yourself."

Tommy rolls his eyes. "He's such a damn diva. Anyway, as I was saying. Mr. Hot Pants gets so excited that Janet said yes, that he goes all out. Buys her a corsage, hires a muscle car, books a dinner at a beautiful, expensive restaurant."

"I sense a *but* coming along. Did she back out?"

"Oh no. But I think Dylan would've wanted her to."

"You can stop now. Look at the beautiful garden, Molly. Shall we take a walk, and leave this loser here?" Dylan asks as he emerges outside, and gives me a light kiss on the lips. "Come on, let's go." He playfully takes my hand in his and gently pulls me up.

"No, it's okay. I can look at the garden later. Tommy and I are getting to know each other."

"Ugh," Dylan scoffs. "Fine." He sits beside me, and pours himself a drink. "I may as well sit here, and correct the lies he's going to tell you about me."

"Lies? More like hilariously funny truths."

"Shut up."

"He had this beautiful date prepared for himself and Janet. Everything was organized, perfect. She was going to love saying 'yes' to our man, and hopefully, he would've scored because he was so attentive toward her and because of everything he'd done for her."

I'm already shaking my head, knowing something funny is coming. "Go on."

"Please don't," Dylan pleads one last time.

Tommy flicks his hand at Dylan. "They go to dinner at this expensive restaurant. She's not really enjoying herself."

"Yes, she was. She was warming up to me."

"You and your pimply face."

"You gotta stop making me worse than I was."

"Buddy, should I break out the year book to show her?" Tommy begins to stand.

"NO!" Dylan yells. "I was pimply, and dweeby and I wasn't very confident."

I'm looking between them, and Tommy nods his head before sitting again. "They get to prom. She's walking two steps ahead of Dylan, he's trying to chase her and she's all but ignoring him. They get inside, and found their table, which was with me and my date."

"You took my cousin Gemma, because you couldn't get a date," Dylan mocks Tommy.

"Yep, that's right. Actually, how is Gemma? I haven't seen her in years. Anyway, tell me about her later. So, we're all sitting there, Janet keeps looking around the room probably trying to find her friends, and Dylan over here, starts sweating."

"Sweating, why?" I ask.

"Seems he ate something that was spoiled."

My hand flies up to my gaping mouth. Oh no, the poor guy. "No, don't tell me you were sick?"

"Worse," Dylan confirms with a straight face.

"Worse? Did you vomit on her?"

"That would've been the best-case scenario," Tommy says, laughing between the words.

"What happened?"

"I'm not sure I can hang around for this," Dylan stands, then sits again. "Just tell her. Rip the band-aid off quickly."

"He shit himself." My mouth falls wide open, but I'm trying my hardest not to laugh too. "Yep. It was bad. He had explosive diarrhea. But then, while he had the shits, he vomited too. All happened so fast. He ran out of there with a trail of shit behind him. Janet copped some chunks of vomit on her dress. I never knew I had such a strong vomit reflex when I see someone else being sick. Seems a lot of us at the table have that reflex. Worst prom ever."

"Oh no." I place my hand on Dylan's thigh. "I shouldn't be laughing, really I shouldn't. But how did you go back to school after that?"

"Let's just say, it took me a few days to get over the food poisoning, and the rest of the school year was spent hiding in the library or the bathrooms. No one ever let me live it down, including this bastard over here."

"I'm sure you've got something embarrassing to tell about Tommy."

"I do." Dylan stands, puffs out his chest and lifts his chin. "But I choose to be the better man and not humiliate him."

"That's because my most embarrassing story is of the first time I had sex with a chick, and I came before I got my dick in her. That was embarrassing." He shakes his head at himself. I'm left staring at him. I can't believe he admitted that to me. "Sorry. TMI?" He shrugs.

"Lunch. Stop grossing the girl out. She's never going to let Dylan bring her back. And you'll end up an old fart living here on your own with a thousand cats and no visitors!" Scott snaps at Tommy.

"I'll still have you," Tommy lovingly replies.

"'Til I leave your skinny ass." He turns to me, smiling. "Sorry, I should be nicer. But he hurts my head."

"It's okay. I'm enjoying the banter between you all. And truthfully, I love knowing Dylan shit himself and was totally embarrassed."

Dylan leans over and whispers in my ear, "I'd be quiet if I were you, because I'm not doing to you tonight what I did this morning." My cheeks instantly burn, and my eyes widen. God, I hope no one heard that.

"Oh yeah? What did you do to her?" Tommy asks. *Great.*

"Wouldn't you like to know, you freak."

"So it was R- rated then?"

"More like X," I quickly reply.

"Oh, girl. As long as you enjoyed yourself, and didn't let this dork take and not give, it's all good," Tommy says, hazing Dylan some more.

"He gave. Twice," I say under my breath.

"I'm a sick, perverted bastard. Don't say any more, 'cause if you do, I'm going to want to know details. You know, so I can add it to the spank bank for later. So, how's that cousin of yours? She still a private investigator?"

Spank bank? Oh my God! Tommy is great.

Yeah, I like him. Can I meet him?

"No, you can't, Kate."

"Wait, is Kate one of the people living in your head?" Tommy asks.

"Um, yeah." I feel myself going back into my shell, more reserved. Dylan takes my hand in his while Scott brings out some platters of food.

"Don't be embarrassed. It's okay, you can tell me anything."

"Kate lives with me," I say as I add in a humorless chuckle.

"That's cool. Who are the others?" Tommy reaches across and begins to fill his plate from the various dishes Scott has placed on the table. "Unless you don't want to tell me. Which, you will in time, so you may as well tell me now."

I really like him. He makes me laugh.

"Me too," I answer Kate. "Well, Kate's talking to me now. She wants to meet you, she says you seem like lots of fun. Kate likes having fun."

"Well, hi Kate."

Tell him I said hi.

"She says hi."

"And who else lives with you?" He bites into his food, chewing it while he watches me.

"Tommy," Dylan warns with a slight head shake.

"It's okay," I reply. "Um, well, there's AJ, he protects us. All of us. And there's Neve. Neve's young, and she um…" What do I say about Neve. "She likes to color. And she likes Harry Potter."

"And AJ is male?"

"Yeah. He's really protective."

"Wow. This is super intriguing, but I won't ask any more

questions. But I will say, I'll listen to anything you want to tell me. I've never met anyone with multiple personalities."

"It's not called multiple personalities. It's DID, which stands for dissociative identity disorder," Dylan explains.

"I must admit, I did a bit of research online when Dylan told me about you, and I watched some YouTube uploads. Really interesting. I take my hat off to you, Molly. You're a strong person to be able to get through that every day."

"It's not about strength, it's about learning to live together with three other people. Just like any family. Sometimes they come through without giving me a second's warning, but we'll work it out. We have to if we all want to live together."

"I think it would be strange, but then again, I'm strange, so maybe strange times two equals a normal." He begins to laugh.

"Yeah, you're weird. Probably weirder than me." Dylan chuckles. "Thank you for lunch, though." I drag a platter over to me, and move some of the food onto my plate. "So, do you have a girlfriend?" I ask Tommy.

"He has me," Scott replies.

"Oh, you're gay. That's cool. My bosses at the gym where I work are married and gay."

"We're not gay," Tommy says.

"Oh, I thought." I point between him and Scott, now not fully understanding the dynamic between them. "I thought from what Scott said, you two were gay."

"He couldn't handle this." Scott flippantly waves his hand at his body.

"We're brothers," Tommy adds.

"Brothers? I thought he was your chef."

"He is. And my brother. Same Dad, different Mom. You know, our father had an affair with my mother, and they had me. He's older, I'm better looking," Tommy says.

"You're better looking? If you need to tell yourself that to get through the day, then you do that," Scott says. "But yes, he's employed me to be his chef. Because he's an antisocial bastard who doesn't like people, so he chooses to not go out anywhere, and he can't cook. So I come in to do a massive cook once a week, and whenever else he needs me."

"Aww, you're sweet. Are you married?" I ask.

"Nope. I'm not the marrying kind."

That's a weird thing to say. "Why aren't you the marrying kind?" I ask.

"I used to be a junkie. Tommy paid to get me clean, and since, I keep to myself and try not to socialize with many people. Especially the people who I used to hang out with. My habit nearly killed me, and Tommy saved me."

"So you're a good guy," I say to Tommy.

"He's always been a good guy," Dylan replies. "If he likes you, he'll have your back."

"Shut up the both of you," Tommy says to Dylan and Scott. "You're making me look soft in front of this gorgeous young lady. Hey, you know, I'm better hung then that shithead over there." Tommy sidles up close to me.

"You have the smallest dick anyone has ever seen. By seen, I mean, you need a magnifying glass to see it," Scott teases.

"Do you look at your brother's penis often?" I mock.

"Oh, she's got you there." Dylan slings his arm around me, and gives me a kiss.

Zhen comes back from discovering the garden, and sits at my feet. "He's so well trained," Tommy says. "I'd love a dog, but I don't know." He shrugs.

There's a deep bell sound coming from inside. "I wonder who that can be?" Scott says as he stands and walks out to the door.

"I'm not expecting anyone." We all turn to see Gemma following Scott. "Gemma?" Tommy asks as he stands. "I... ah, whoa." He fixes his hair, then rubs his palms down his jeans. Oh my, is Tommy nervous?

"Hi Tommy. It's been a long time. But, I'm actually here for them." She looks over Tommy's shoulder toward Dylan and me, but I notice her cheeks turning pink when she sees Tommy.

"How did you find us?" Dylan asks.

"Really? You're asking me how I found you?" her voice raising in pitch. "You both need to get back home."

"Why didn't you just call?" Dylan asks.

Gemma's cheeks flush with a quick tinge of red. "First your phones are turned off, and second I thought I'd enjoy coming out for a drive."

"A three-hour drive? Okay, then," Dylan says.

He doesn't see it, but I do. Tommy and Gemma like each other. Probably have for years, and neither of them have said anything. "When do we have to head back?" I ask.

"Now," Gemma replies. "David needs you."

My fists clench at my side, as my body trembles. I find my breathing has escalated too. "What's happening?" I ask. A sudden shot of ice forces its way up my spine, and into my blood.

"They've got him."

And with only those three words, my life is forever altered.

CHAPTER 34

The ride back home is quiet. Dylan occasionally speaks, but my mind is working so fast. Kate, AJ, and Neve are all talking at the same time. Neve's frightened of what's about to happen.

I'm scared.

"I'm scared too," I say to her.

We'll get through this, I'll protect you. AJ's strong and protective.

"Are you okay?" Dylan asks as we approach the police station.

"I'm um..." Tears are welling in my eyes. "I'm terrified. Absolutely terrified. I feel like my stomach is twisting and churning. My hands won't stop sweating, and Neve's not coping very well. Kate's trying to talk to her, and we're all trying to calm her. But this is scary." My throat constricts, and I start coughing, unable to get air into my lungs.

"Hey." Dylan pulls the car over, unclicks both our seatbelts and pulls me protectively into his arms. "It'll be okay. We'll get through this. Your parents are at the police station. Amelia is on her way there. Gemma's in the car behind us. We've got this. We're all here for you, AJ, Kate, and Neve. No matter what happens."

I sob into his chest, knowing I have to face this. I know everyone is here for us, but it doesn't stop me from worrying. It takes me a few moments to compose myself. Every step has been taken to ensure we don't fail at this. "Okay, we can go," I say after a few moments of crying. I need to pull myself together.

We continue on our way. It takes another fifteen minutes before we arrive at the police station. Fifteen minutes of all four of us being in turmoil.

Dylan parks, and we get out of the car and walk toward the police station holding hands. My heart is beating so fast, I can feel it thumping in my ears. A car drives past and honks its horn. I jump at the sound.

"You're shaking," Dylan says.

I nod my head, and squeeze my eyes tight. My breathing is quick and shallow as I feel us shuffling closer and closer to the building. I can see Mom and Dad waiting on the sidewalk.

"Sweetheart," Mom says as she throws her arms around me. I desperately hold onto her, not wanting to let her go. My feet are trying to run away, but AJ, Kate, and Neve are yelling at me to get in there as quick as possible.

"I don't know if I can do this," I whisper to Mom.

Yes, you can. AJ's tone is firm. *We have to do this.*

There's no other choice. Kate adds.

"I know," I answer them both, but I'm so worried about Neve.

I'll be strong for you, M. Neve says in her small voice.

"No, no more, Neve. I don't want you to be strong for me. I want you to be just a kid, and stop worrying about me. Please."

There's a tight tingling in my chest, and I feel like I'm going to throw up. But I have to be strong, for all of us. "We're here, for you. For all of you," Dad says.

Dread shrouds every part of me, but I know I have to face this. Closing my eyes, I take deep, controlled breaths. "Okay, I'm ready," I say as I move forward toward the police station.

David's striding back and forth in front of the counter, obviously waiting for us. The moment he sees me, he walks straight over and gives everyone a quick head nod, before he turns to ask, "Are you okay?" I nod, silently. "We need to get upstairs." I nod again.

The moment he's in his office, he sits down, and looks at me.

"Tell me you've got him?" I'm not sure if I'm ready for the answer. I feel myself crumpling back into the chair. I press my lips tight, trying to stop my quivering chin. Maybe this isn't a good idea. Maybe we should walk away now, while we still have the chance.

"We've got him," David says.

I sit staring at David. I'm unsure on what to do or how to react. I bring my hand to my mouth, holding back a frenzied wail trying to escape. What do I say?

"Molly, are you okay?" Dylan asks as he calmly takes my hand in his.

"I'm..." No. Yes. I don't know.

Let me help.

"No, AJ. I need you all to stay still, let me process this." I look around the room, seeing everyone who loves me and supports me here. For me. For us.

I feel myself withdrawing, trying to retreat away from everyone. But I'm painfully aware I can't do that, not now. I have to be strong and present.

"Molly?" Mom says, her voice shaking.

I look over to Mom, and smile softly, silently telling her I'll be okay. "Tell me he..." I close my eyes, not wanting to saying what I'm going to. "...hasn't hurt anyone else."

"What I can tell you is that Mack Hewitt has been arrested. He's been a janitor at an elementary school."

"We already knew that from Gemma," Dylan says.

"And when we arrested him, we seized all his computers. He'd hardwired cameras in the girls' bathrooms at the elementary school."

"Oh God," I say, feeling like I'm about to vomit.

"He also had thousands of images on his computer. Out of those, a lot of them were pictures of him offending."

My stomach twists, and vomit quickly makes its way up my throat.

Does he have any pictures of me?

"Oh shit, Neve." I burst into tears. "Does he have anything from when he..." I place my hand to my chest, unable to say the words.

The room is quiet, filled with tension and sorrow. I can feel the pain everyone is surrounded with. Neve's crying. She's not coping with the silence. I can barely breathe. I start to claw at my throat, trying to move pull away the clothing that's suffocating me. "I can't breathe," I yell.

"Molly." Amelia steps into the room.

I'm helping her!

"No AJ. Stop."

"Molly. Look at me," Amelia crouches in front of me, grasping my attention with her strong voice. "It wasn't your fault."

My skin tingles when she says the words. A chill covers me, and my stomach suddenly calms.

"Say the words. 'It wasn't my fault.'"

"It wasn't my fault," I say in a voiceless whisper.

"Molly. 'It wasn't my fault.'" She nods her head.

Those words have such an impact on me. They give me strength. Courage. *Freedom.*

"It wasn't my fault," I say with intensity. "I shouldn't be made to feel like I did something wrong. I refuse to let him to rob me of my freedom."

Yes! We've got it.

"Yeah, we do, Neve." I can feel Neve smiling proudly. "Did you find images of us?" I ask David.

"Yes. We found a lot of images of you, and many other children. Um, Molly. We need you to confirm the images are in fact of you. I'm sorry to have to ask you to do this."

"I… what?" I quickly begin to regress. Curling into myself.

She's going into panic. AJ says as I feel him coming forward.

We need to help her, AJ. Kate pleads.

Neve, M needs you, right now.

I'm not sure I can. Neve replies.

"I just need you to confirm one image. We have enough to charge him, but without identity of the other children, this will become a difficult case."

"One picture?" I ask.

David looks down, he opens his laptop, and types something into it. "It's the clearest picture of the girl's face. I'm sorry, but it's likely to be traumatic."

"I don't know what I looked like when I was young."

I do. Neve says. *Let me help.*

I'll take over. You can't go through this again, Neve. And M's not going to be able to help. AJ's presence is growing.

"Just wait," I yell to everyone as I hold my hand up in a halt.

"You don't have to do this, I'm sure David can find another way," Mom says.

"She doesn't have to do this, does she?" Dylan asks David.

"She doesn't have to. But without a positive ID, we don't have much of a case."

"Has he been charged yet?" I ask.

"He's been charged, and the judge considered him dangerous to the community, so he denied him bail. Which means now it's up to Eveline and her team to ensure that when it goes to trial, she has a convincing enough case to keep him in jail."

"So if I confirm that image, it'll help with the evidence?" I ask. I'll call Eveline, and beg her to put me on the stand. "Neve can help, won't you, Neve?"

If this means he goes to prison, then yes.

"She said yes," I say with a half-smile. Because even Neve sounds more confident and self-assured.

David nods his head.

"But me looking at the image, and confirming it… that means?"

"It means our case is one-thousand-percent watertight."

I'm ready. Neve whispers in a terrified voice.

I stand and walk around the office. "AJ, Kate, Neve. You've protected me all my life. You've been there to take my pain away. But it's time, I—Molly face this. I have to look at the picture, and I beg all of you, to not come forward. Please stay where you are."

But…

"No, AJ. I have to face this. You've all dealt with it, now I have to, too."

"I'm so proud of you," Dylan says.

I straighten my shoulders, and feel empowered. "He needs to be accountable for what he's done. To me, and to the others. Show me the picture."

"Are you sure you want to do this, Molly?" Amelia asks.

"You'll all be here, right?" I turn to everyone in the room, and one by one, they nod their heads.

We're here. AJ says on behalf of my internal family.

"Show me."

David looks down at his laptop, and exhales quite loudly. "Okay." He swings the computer around, and I'm faced with an image of the saddest little girl I've ever seen. Her light brown hair is splayed across the pillow, and her dark eyes are filled with so much hurt and sadness, I almost don't recognize her. My eyes drift all over the unhappy little girl.

"I'm not sure. She doesn't look like me." But then I see it. The sheets on the bed. The pink and yellow flowers on the sheets. Like an out of focus memory fiercely trying to correct itself. "I remember sitting on the bed. Reading." The fogginess is clouding what I can see, but I remember the flowers. I nod my head. "That picture is of me," I confirm. "Those sheets. I know them."

David swings the laptop around, and closes it. "Thank you, Molly. I know how hard that had to be."

"I'm proud of you," Dylan whispers.

"What about my foster parents? I don't even remember them."

"We tracked them down, and they had no idea this was happening. They're exemplary foster parents. They've looked after hundreds of kids over the years, and they were devastated when we were asking about Mack."

He was very good at hiding what he really was.

"Neve said he was very good at hiding what he really was. He must be, to be able to do this for so many years."

"He hasn't admitted to any of the abuse. Instead, he says he has no idea how the images got on his computer. He couldn't explain the images of himself though. He tried to say they must've been Photoshopped, and done by someone who hates him."

"He's literally been caught, and he still won't admit to it," Dad says as he shakes his head in disgust. "What an animal."

"It doesn't matter, Dad. Because he's got no idea what's coming for him. I don't care what happens to me, we'll all be standing in court, and giving our testimony. I can't let him get away with this. The other kids…what's happened to them?"

"Well…," David starts.

"How many are there? Have you made contact? Can I help? Can I do anything to help with them?"

David holds his hand up. He walks around to the front of his desk, and leans against it. "We don't know exactly how many there are. But Eveline's working on her case against him. I can't tell you how many there are, because we simply don't know. But there are a lot. From what we found, easily thirty children, so far."

That sick feeling is back. Thirty is such a large number. Just one is enormous. "What can I do to help? I have a great network of support, I have my parents, Amelia, Dylan, Neve, Kate, and AJ. I have to be able to do something to help them."

"You can't. Not now. But Eveline and I spoke in length about you, and your family, and I know she needs you up on the stand to testify against him."

"Just tell me when."

What can we do to help those kids? Kate surprises me.

"I don't know," I reply.

Talking to myself has become normal, and now, no one really questions it. Amelia, my parents, and David all talk. I've zoned out because I'm thinking about what I can do to try and help not only these kids who've been abused by Mack, but others too.

What about Zhen?

"Tommy's going to bring him down tomorrow," I say to Kate.

No, not where is he. But what about Zhen?

"I don't understand, what about Zhen? Is he okay?" A new panic rises.

Kate chuckles. *He's fine. But I mean, can Zhen help? He helped you.*

Huh. Zhen. Right. There are studies that show pets can be an important part of therapy for children.

"There's nothing more for you to do here today. But, I'd like for you to stay close by, so you're accessible to either Eveline or myself," David instructs as he pushes off from where he was leaning against his desk.

"Any chance he could accidently hang himself in custody?" Dad asks.

"Dad! No. He has to answer for his crimes. I want him to get the same treatment he showed us."

Yeah! Neve says.

You girls are vengeful. Wow, glad I'm not on your wrong side.

AJ makes me smile. He's surprisingly relaxed. I thought he'd be more intense than he is right now. *I'm not stressed out, because I have the strongest group of women around me, and I know you've got this.*

"Yeah, we do," I say.

Standing, I shake David's hand, and one by one, we file out of his office.

"You okay?" Dylan asks.

"I need a bubble bath and a glass of wine and to chill the fuck down," I say as I look to him.

I see Mom do a quick double take. "Well, I wasn't expecting that from you, Molly. Wait, it is Molly…right?"

I smile. "Yeah, it's me. But I do need to unwind. And don't worry. I know wine is for after I turn twenty-one."

Mom places her arm around my waist, leans in and gives me a kiss on the cheek. "Maybe we can make an exception this one time. Let's get home, and get some food."

"Molly," Amelia calls me. I turn to face her. Amelia takes three fast steps to catch up to us. "I'll be coming by your house tomorrow to debrief."

"Okay."

"You did well today."

"Thank you."

There's still a cloud of uncertainty swirling around. I have so many questions, and I suppose in time they'll all be answered. But for now, I have to find comfort in knowing Mack Hewitt has been denied bail, and is sitting in a holding cell somewhere. He won't be hurting anyone else tonight.

Perhaps he's frightened.

Perhaps he's being taunted by the other inmates.

Perhaps he's being subjected to the same atrocities he put me through.

Perhaps he'll be torn to shreds, abused, and beaten.

I can't help but feel content to know he's in the best place for a monster.

A cage.

CHAPTER 35

Dad walks into the kitchen. His face is pale and he's shaking his head. "What is it, Dad?"

He slides back the chair, and collapses into it. "Thomas?" Mom questions while she sits beside me. "You look like you've seen a ghost. What is it?"

"Eveline just called." He takes his phone out of his pocket, and places it on the dining table.

"What happened?" I ask. Mom and I rally around Dad. Something big has happened. Or it wouldn't affect him to this point. "Dad," I urge as I grab his hand.

He stares at me for a moment, shaking his head with his mouth open. "Preston," he whispers.

"What about that filthy piece of shit?" Mom says, her tone changing to anger.

"He's dead."

"What?" I ask.

"What?" Mom echoes.

"He's dead. He killed himself while he was out on bail. Took a lethal overdose and killed himself. Wrote us a letter."

"I don't want to read it," I say without missing a beat. Standing,

I go to the back door, Zhen lifts his head to look at me, then places it on the ground again. "He destroyed our family, tore us apart. He took the life of my sister, I don't want to hear about how sorry he is, and how much he regrets wrapping his fingers around her throat and choking her until she could no longer breathe."

"We need to heal," Mom says softly.

"And he's taken that away from us too. What a coward. A damn chicken for not accepting responsibility. I want to spit on him, and hurt him, and kill him myself!" I yell, bursting into tears.

"We need to find another way to heal, Molly. Or this will consume us. And then what kind of legacy would we live for Tina? She wouldn't want us to live a life of hate."

"We don't know what Tina would want, because he killed her," I bite out.

"Would you want Tina to live her life filled with anger, hate, and misery?" Dad asks.

I turn away from them, and stare outside. I hear Zhen stand, and come to nudge me with his wet nose. Zorro's toenails click on the floor as he enters the kitchen. Zorro always goes to Dad, but this time, he comes to stand on the other side of me, and licks my foot. "I wouldn't want it to consume her. But I don't know if I can let this go."

"We're not asking you to let it go. We're asking you to heal," Mom says. "These circumstances are not ordinary, Molly. None of it. But we lost our daughter, just like you lost your sister, your best friend. Tina wouldn't want us to be eaten up by hate for the rest of our lives. For whatever reason, Preston took his own life. I know I wanted to look him in the eyes and tell him what a bastard he was for what he did, but I won't have that opportunity. Now I have to decide if I want to spend the rest of my life hating so much that I can't *live* the rest of my life."

She's right, M. We have to focus on the future, we can't forever look at our past. I thought AJ would be the one willing to break through and smash someone, or something. But his voice of reason makes me stop to really think.

"I can't forgive him," I say.

"We're not asking you to," Dad replies. "That pathetic animal took my daughter's life. I cannot and will not ever forgive him. I was waiting for him to have his day in court so I could watch as he agonized while Eveline tore him limb from limb. I wanted to see him suffer. In pain. And hopefully beg and plead, just the way I imagine Tina begged for him to stop hurting her. I wanted that so badly, you have no idea. But the universe had other plans for him, plans none of us can understand. I'll hate him until my very last breath, and I'll never forgive him either. But I refuse to allow him to take away my ability to love. Because without you, and your mother, my life is worth nothing. We're not asking you to forgive, we're asking you to move forward, no matter how tiny the first step is." His eyebrows pinch together, and he hangs his head low. Dad's in soul-altering pain. I know he is, because so am I. We all are.

I chew on my nail as I turn to look out the glass door to the back yard again. I'm thankful Amelia is on her way over, because I need to talk to her about so many things. "I want to hurt him," I say in a small voice.

"So do I," Mom replies.

"We all wanted to hurt him," Dad adds. "I wish he died from my hands, not his own."

The mood in the room is agonizingly raw. The three of us are all barely hanging on. "I'm devastated he ended his life. He didn't deserve anything that easy."

"No, he didn't," Dad says. "But it's done and there's nothing more we can do about it. Now we need to focus on you, and making that piece of shit Mack answer for his sick crimes."

The doorbell rings, and Zhen and Zorro both run toward the door.

I head out, knowing it'll be Amelia. When I answer the door, she steps in, and immediately sees the hurt I'm feeling. "Molly?" she asks cautiously. I nod. "What happened?"

"Preston killed himself."

She grimaces, and shakes her head. "Are your parents here?"

"Yeah, we are," Dad says as he and Mom walk into the foyer holding hands.

"Today may benefit everyone, if you'd like to join us," Amelia offers.

Mom and Dad are already walking in, before Amelia really has the chance to finish her sentence. We all sit in our regular seats, Amelia takes her water bottle out of her bag, takes a sip, then places it beside her on the floor.

Zhen and Zorro both walk in. Zhen lies at my feet, and Zorro goes to Dad.

"Will Dylan be joining us?" Amelia asks.

"No, he's got work he needs to catch up on. He'll be here later tonight, maybe. If he gets his work finished."

"So...," Amelia starts. "Molly, how do you feel?"

"I can't forgive him."

"No one is asking you to. Forgiveness isn't something that's easily given. But you have to be comfortable with whatever decision you make in reference to how you feel about him."

"I'm comfortable knowing I hate him. And I'm comfortable knowing I hope he suffered and hurt for at least a moment before he died. And I'm comfortable hoping that moment felt like an eternity before he took his last breath."

"Those words are strong. And maybe over time, and with some techniques I'll show you, you can find some peace."

I want to tell her that I'm already at peace, but reality is, I'm not. I've been in a world of chaos for what feels like forever. My life will never be like as easy as it was the night Tina and I had dinner with our parents for our eighteenth birthday. That night seems like decades ago, when in fact, only months have passed.

I sit silently, and listen to my parents telling Amelia how they feel. I'm lost in my thoughts, not adding to the conversation. I can feel AJ surfacing, worried for me. He's near, circling, waiting for me to stumble so he can step in and protect.

"Molly, are you okay?" Amelia asks. I nod, and offer her a weak smile. "No, you're not. What's happening?"

"I can feel that AJ's antsy. He wants to come through."

I purse my lips together, and flick my gaze to the side. It takes me a few moments to say what I've been feeling for a while. "I want to be able to live with AJ, Kate, and Neve, without them forcing their way out. We need to figure out a way that works for all of us. I don't want AJ forcing himself out because he needs to protect me. I don't want Neve coming through when Dylan and I are intimate." I look over to my parents, and Dad winces. "Kate seems to be a bit more mellow and not as intense as AJ in particular."

"Perhaps AJ is intense because his life has always been like that. He's had to protect you, and Neve, and Kate. You all need to find a balance, between not only the four of you, but also with Dylan, and your parents. You all need to work together. After all, you're all a family."

"When Dylan comes over, do you want us all to have a discussion?" Mom offers. "Or…?" She shrugs.

"I think I need to sort this out with them first." I tap my temple. "When we come to an arrangement of who comes forward when, we can have this discussion with you too."

"I um…" Mom huffs. "Don't take this the wrong way, Molly. But they've spent their lives protecting you. Now it's our job as your parents to protect all four of you. They've done a wonderful job, fighting for you when you were too young to do it for yourself. They guarded, and made sure you were safe when safety wasn't given to you. Your father and I, we want all of you to know, we understand. You must be so tired, and we're here for all of you. If Kate, or AJ, or Neve, want to talk to us, we're here. We'll listen, and we'll protect all of you."

I wipe the tears falling from my eyes.

"You don't have to be strong anymore. We'll be your strength for as long you need us," Dad says.

We'll always need you.

My hand clutches at my chest. "AJ just said, we'll always need you."

Dad smiles triumphantly. "Good, because this is our family."

I sit back in my chair, somewhat satisfied. "We have to talk," I say.

"Sorry, what?" Mom asks.

"Not you, sorry. I meant them." I tap my temple again.

Is everything okay? Kate asks.

"We all need to be together, so we can set some ground rules."

What kind of ground rules? AJ sounds apprehensive.

"I don't think now is the best time," I respond.

"Are you talking with AJ, Neve, and Kate now?" Amelia asks.

"Kate and AJ are here, but Neve isn't." I focus on them, trying to listen, and feel for Neve. "Neve?" I call.

I'm here. Comes a tiny voice.

"We need to talk."

Did I do something wrong?

"No, nothing like that." I look to Amelia and smile. "Neve asked if she's done something wrong."

"If they're all with you, you need to tell them how you feel," Amelia suggests.

What's going on? Don't you like us anymore?

"No, nothing like that, Neve. You're all so important to me. But I think we need to all work together now."

How? Kate asks.

"This is a part of my healing, and I think it needs to be a part of yours too. What we went through with *him* was nothing short of a nightmare. But now, it's our time to mend from within. We have to find a way for all of us to be free of him, but to still work together."

What are you thinking? Neve asks.

"Maybe we can have a schedule. Something like a roster. Maybe certain days you can be free for a few hours, Neve. Other days, AJ and Kate can."

I want to go to the movies. I feel Kate excitedly jumping up and down. *And I want popcorn. Lots and lots of popcorn.*

I smile. "Do you want to go to the movies on your own? Or would you prefer someone go with you? My parents? Dylan?"

Oh my God! You're giving me a choice?

"What's happening?" Dad asks. "You're offering us to do something, and we don't have an issue with that, but we'd like to know what you're signing us up for."

"Kate wants to go to the movies and eat lots of popcorn."

Lots and lots of popcorn.

I chuckle. "Sorry, Kate corrected me, she said lots and *lots* of popcorn." I emphasize the second 'lots.'

"I can take her to the movies," Mom offers.

I want to watch shoot 'em up, gory movies.

"Well, I wasn't expecting that from you, Kate. I think that'll be Dad's department, not Mom's."

"Hey!" Mom grumbles and frowns.

She can take me to a chick flick, but yeah, I'll go with your Dad.

"Kate wants to watch gory, shoot 'em up movies. So I think, Dad, you're up for that one. But she also said she wants chick flicks, so Mom, that's you."

I just want to draw. I like drawing with Dylan. Do you think he'll draw with me?

"I think he'll love it. How about I ask him when we see him tonight, or tomorrow? Do you want to do anything else?"

I can hear Neve 'hmmming.' If I think of something else, can I tell you?

"Of course, you can. AJ, what about you?"

I like Dylan, and I'd like to hang out with him sometimes. Maybe we can go to the gym.

"I'm glad you like him. I can ask him that too."

How about if we all agree to not force our way out without M's permission? AJ questions.

"I'd really appreciate that happening. I'm sure they'll be times you can't help it, but if we can all agree to try and give me an opportunity to either say yes or no first, would be helpful to me. It means in time I'll be able to maintain a kind of normal life."

Okay. They all agree together.

But don't think for one moment, we'll ever stop protecting you. AJ adds.

I take a deep breath and look around the room. "And I'll never stop protecting you, either."

My world will never be the same again.

And I'm okay with that.

EPILOGUE

The last five years have been nothing short of a whirlwind. I've become a pillar in the DID community, with people reaching out to me from all over the world. It started at Mack's trial. For the first time in American history, the judge allowed my alters to give evidence. It was Neve's strength and words that ultimately saw Mack's sentence go from life imprisonment with parole, to life imprisonment with no parole.

The media got a whiff of the woman giving evidence who had what they called multiple personalities. I had to step forward and school them, but in fact, that's Kate's department. She loves coming out and dealing with all the hype and media, and that works so well for me, because I'm definitely not the type who likes to be the center of attention. Kate thrives on it.

For me though, I'm a homebody. I prefer the company of Dylan and my dogs to anyone else—other than my family, of course.

Sitting in the family room, I'm waiting for Dylan to return from work. He shouldn't be too long, he's on a short day today because he's taking me somewhere special for our one-year wedding anniversary.

Zelda and Zeus sit beside me, waiting for me to take them out to play fetch. Zhen lays on his bed, looks over to me, and puts his head down again. I stand and walk over to him, crouching down. "Hey, boy. You okay?" He wags his tail and gives me a lick. "Yeah,

I know. You're tired." A tear escapes, because I know Zhen won't be with me for too much longer. He's really old, but he's been the best dog anyone could ask for. When Dylan and I bought our Labradors, Zelda and Zeus, Zhen took to them and protected them while I trained them. "You want to come outside and play?" I ask Zhen. He stands and slowly makes his way out to the backyard. Zelda and Zeus playfully run into each other, and wrestle.

Zhen goes to the back deck of our home, and lays on his outdoor bed.

I watch as he watches us, then slowly closes his eyes. I know any day now, he won't reopen them, and that'll tear me apart. Zhen has been so important in my survival, and although I now have Zelda and Zeus, I know no other dog will ever be able to come close to how amazing he's been. He's always been there, never being a diva or wanting all the attention on him, he's just been *there.*

"Hey, sweetheart," Dylan calls as he comes out to the back deck. Zhen lifts his head, wags his tail then lowers his head ahead. "Hey, Zhen. You okay, boy?" Dylan feels it too.

I throw the ball for Zelda and Zeus a few times before I return up to the deck to sit with Dylan and Zhen. Dylan leans over and gives me a kiss. "How was your day?" I ask.

Dylan rolls his eyes, and shrugs. "Some clients are so damn stupid. But, other than that, it's our wedding anniversary. And I can't wait for tonight." He grabs me and pulls me onto his lap, and begins to kiss down my neck, making my eyes roll back and my body totally relax into him. "How was your day?"

"Hmmm," I mumble enjoying his kisses. I sigh, and look down to Zhen and smile. "I'm so grateful he's still here with us, but I know it's any day now."

"He's been so loyal, and faithful. I just hope he says goodbye before he goes." I notice Dylan's eyes tearing up. He's always loved Zhen, from the moment he met him. And Zhen has always loved Dylan too.

I feel my phone vibrating in my pocket, and I move so I can get it. I look at the screen and see David's name. "David," I say to Dylan. "Hey," I answer the call.

"I know it's your wedding anniversary, but I need you."

"Today?" I want to say no, but I understand the importance too.

"Yeah, like now."

"You have to go to work?" Dylan asks in a low voice. I catch a tinge of disappointment in his voice. I nod, and grimace.

"I'm sorry," I whisper.

"It's okay." Dylan smiles.

I stand and walk back into the house. "We'll be right there," I sigh. "Give me fifteen."

"Thank you. And tell Dylan I'm sorry."

I smile. "Yeah, I already have." I hang up and whistle. Zelda and Zeus both run up to me and sit at my feet. "Come here, girl." I reach for Zelda's harness from the hook near the back door, and harness her in. "You look after Dad, and Zhen, okay?" I give Zeus a scratch behind the ears before he runs out the back again. "Door," I say to Zelda, who goes and sits by the front door, waiting for me. As I walk out, Zhen and Dylan are both walking in. Zhen slowly, Dylan in front. "I'm off to work. I'm sorry."

"It's okay." Dylan holds his hand up to stop me from apologizing. "We'll reschedule."

"But I feel bad."

"Don't. This is how it all works. I understand. Anyway, we still have our party on Saturday. And everyone will be there. It's fine." He gives me a kiss and a soft pat on the butt.

"Thank you. I love you," I say as I clip Zelda's leash onto her harness.

"Love you too. Come on, boys. Let's see what there is for dinner," Dylan says to both Zhen and Zeus.

Zelda and I head out to my car. I open the back door for her. I clip her in, and she lays on the back seat, ready for the quick ride down to the station.

Getting into the car, I back out of the driveway. "AJ, Kate, Neve, are you here?"

I wait a few moments before I feel them all stirring. *We're here.* AJ answers for all of them.

"David called. He needs me, I'm not sure if I'm going to need you, but can you stay close?"

We've got your back, don't stress it. Kate replies.

"Neve, you okay?"

I'm tired, but I'm okay.

I pull into my spot under the building, take Zelda out and walk up to the elevator. I swipe my ID tag, and press the button for the floor I work from when David calls.

The door opens, and I head toward David's office. "Thank you for coming. I'm so sorry that I had to call you."

I shake my head and dismissively flick my hand to him. "It's important, so it's fine. We understand."

"Okay. Here." I sit down in his seat, and flick the computer to life. "Shit," I say as I shake my head.

"Yeah, female, six years old. Amelia is in there with her now, but Juliette isn't responding to her."

"Amelia's in there? Great. We'll help Juliette." I lower my hand to pet Zelda. She's working now, and understands what she has to do. "Anything else I should know? Anything not noted yet?" I quickly review the records. My stomach churns, and I can feel AJ inching closer.

We're here. We can help.

"I know. But for now, stay where you are, let's see how Juliette is."

"No other notes. She's really withdrawn. Won't do anything but hug her blanket and keep her eyes down."

"Okay." Standing, Zelda and I head to the room I know she'll be in. I look in through the window, and Amelia is speaking softly with Juliette, but Juliette is sitting in the corner, her legs up and her arms are wrapped around her knees while she clutches the blanket. I stand watching for a moment, trying to assess how I'm going to handle it.

Amelia is trying, but Juliette isn't responding at all. It's like she's switched off.

She's me.

"I know, Neve. This is how you were."

Maybe I can help.

"You might be able to. Let's go in, and see what we can do. Can you hang around for a moment?"

I'll wait. I know what she's going through though.

"Zelda, work," I instruct. Zelda's posture changes, she becomes more rigid and knows what she has to do.

I knock on the door before walking in with Zelda. Amelia sees me, and smiles. It's a silent greeting. We're not here to be social, we're here to help a little girl who's come from trauma and abuse.

I head over to the opposite corner from where Juliette is sitting, and sit on the floor. Zelda sits beside me, wagging her tail when she sees Juliette huddled in the corner. "Hi Juliette. My name's Molly, and this is Zelda." Zelda wags her tail more. Juliette lifts her eyes, then quickly lowers them again.

Amelia and I have been working together for a while now, and I know what her cues are. Her brows raise, and her lips quickly turn up giving me the confirmation I need.

"Would it be okay if Zelda comes and sniffs you? She loves people."

I keep petting Zelda, waiting for some kind of permission from Juliette. Zelda yawns, and lays down.

It takes a long time before I get what I'm looking for. In a tiny voice, I hear Juliette say, "I love puppies."

This is the confirmation I need to start the conversation we require. "Is it okay if Zelda and I come over to you?" Here is where I'm giving Juliette all the power in the world to say yes or no. We'll work with her and try to reestablish how important it is that she has a voice. Juliette doesn't say anything, but she gives us a small nod. I stand to my feet, and move closer to Juliette. When she flinches, I know I've come as close as she's comfortable with. "Zelda, would you like to say hello to our new friend, Juliette?" Zelda wags her tail. I give Zelda a sign to tell her she can go over to Juliette.

Zelda lowers her head, and with a wagging tail, she slowly walks toward Juliette. I watch carefully, because once we had a young boy who freaked out and started screaming, and tried to punch Zeus in the head. But most children have a positive reaction to my dogs.

Juliette gives Zelda a small side glance, before I notice a glimpse of a smile on her face. Zelda licks her face. Juliette quickly hides her face in the blanket, then peeks from around it to see if Zelda is still there. Zelda licks her again. This time on the mouth. This earns us the tiniest of giggles. But it's our way in.

"Amelia, you like dogs too, don't you?"

"I love them so much. They're amazing aren't they, Molly? I love how no matter how sad you are, they're always there to make you feel happy."

"Do you know what Zelda does when she knows you're sad?" I say to Amelia, but for Juliette's benefit.

"What does she do?"

"Zelda tends to give kisses either on the lips, or in your ear. I've had her tongue in my ear many times when I'm sad."

"You get sad too?" Juliette asks, her voice so tiny I nearly have to strain to hear her. This is a normal part of the process.

"I get sad sometimes. And when I'm sad, Zelda comes and nuzzles with me. Like she's doing with you now. How about you, Juliette? Are you sad? Is that why Zelda is giving you kisses?" Juliette rolls her shoulders, and clutches her blanket tighter. She squeezes her eyes shut and tightens her lips. "You know, it's okay if you're sad, because we all get sad sometimes."

She opens her eyes, and gives me the smallest of nods. "I get really sad when he touches me."

"When who touches you, Juliette?" Amelia asks. This is her gateway, her opportunity to win Juliette's trust and work with her. This is also my time to be here, let Zelda give her love to Juliette and help Amelia work.

I did my part. I brought in my service dog to help when a child feels like they have no one to trust.

You got this. Neve says.

Yeah, I do.

I smile to myself. It's taken me a long time to be comfortable with myself and my alters.

But it took me no time at all to realize, we all have a role to play.

The End

Thank you for reading

ECHOES
OF YOU

I hope you enjoy this bonus chapter.

Bonus Chapter

YLAN

I pace nervously back and forth outside Thomas and Paris's home. Molly's back home training our new puppies, Zelda and Zeus. She loves those dogs so much. I know having therapy dogs can be incredibly useful, and I know Molly needs to feel like something good has come from her years of abuse.

The front door opens before I work up the nerve to knock, and I come face-to-face with Paris. She's wearing oversized sunglasses, and has her bag dangling from the crook of her elbow. "Dylan," she says surprised to see me.

"Uh, hi," I reply hesitantly.

Her forehead rumples in question. "Are you here to see Thomas? Are you two going somewhere? He didn't tell me." She looks behind her, before quickly turning back. "Are you okay? You look like you're going to be sick. Is Molly okay?" Paris's face flushes. "Is she okay? Are the others okay?" Her anxiety is ratcheting up as I watch.

"No, everyone's fine," I manage to say in a shaky voice. "But I am here to speak to you and Thomas. Are you leaving?"

"I was. But it's okay; it can wait. What do you need? Are you in trouble? Do you need money?"

Oh my God. "No, no, we don't need money. Molly and I are doing fine."

"Well, come in. You have me worried. Darling?" she calls loudly.

"I thought you were going?" Thomas calls from the den.

"Dylan's here, he needs to talk to us."

"Give me a minute."

"Coffee, Dylan?" Paris asks as we head toward the back.

"Um, no, I'm okay. Actually, maybe something stronger," I mumble under my breath.

"Oh sweetheart." Paris gives me a sympathetic smile. "It can't be that bad."

"Dylan," Thomas announces as he walks into the kitchen. He extends his hand so I can shake it, and the moment he sees my face, he steps back. "Are you sick? You're sweating and look a little green. Are you okay?"

"Man, you two aren't going to make this easy, are you?" I chuckle and wipe at the sweat beading across my forehead.

"Dylan, if you're in some kind of trouble, we're here to help. No matter what. Do you need money?" Thomas asks.

"Why do you both think this is money related? It's not," I snap. I regret saying the words. "I'm sorry. I'm wound up."

"We're just worried. What is it? If it's not money, and it's not Molly, AJ, Kate, or Neve, what is it?" Paris asks.

I take a deep breath, and try to swallow the gigantic knot sitting in my throat. "I wanted to ask you...if you would be okay with..." I'm using a lot of hand gestures, trying to slow down what I'm here to ask while pumping up the courage to ask it.

"For the sake of my age, get on with it. I'm not getting any younger here, Dylan," Thomas encourages playfully.

Here goes. I take a deep breath and in one continuous word I say, "IwanttoaskyouforyourblessingtomarryMolly."

Paris looks to Thomas. Slowly, a huge smile brightens her face. "What?" Thomas asks. "I'm a bit hard of hearing. What is it you want?" He cups his ear, and turns his head to hear me better.

"He's asking us for our blessing to marry Molly," Paris happily shrieks, excitedly clasping her hands in front of her chest.

Thomas turns to stare at me. "You want to marry Molly?" Shit, he looks angry. "*My* Molly?"

"Well, she's grown up now, so she kinda doesn't belong to anyone. And yes, I want to marry her."

"Huh," Thomas grumbles. He takes a step toward me, his jaw tight. I don't know what he's thinking. I thought he'd be happy, not angry. Shit, did I ask too early? Should I backtrack and say anything else? Like don't worry about it? Man, my gut twists with agony.

"Thomas, I adore her. This is the most right thing I could ever do in my life. And I'm hoping this is the most right thing she could do too." I know I'm not adequately explaining the depth of my feelings I have for his daughter, but at the moment, I'm just hoping he doesn't hit me.

"Huh." Thomas clicks his tongue to the roof of his mouth. He turns and looks at Paris, then shakes his head. "About damned time."

"Huh?" Now it's my turn to be baffled. "Is that a no or a yes? I'm confused." My knees are feeling weak. I slide out a chair, and sit in it, waiting for them to say something.

"It's about time, son. Paris and I were talking about this only the other night. Molly and you are the best thing to happen to us too. We'd love for you to be our son-in-law." I stand as Thomas walks forward to shake my hand.

I let out a huge breath, and smile. "Wow! I was so nervous. I had no idea what you'd say."

Paris approaches and gives me a hug and a kiss. "How are you going to do this?"

"Actually, you're the first ones I'm asking. I still have to ask AJ, Kate, and Neve. I'm a little scared, to tell you the truth."

"Why? You all get on, don't you?" Paris asks like she suspects I'm holding something back.

"Of course. They've worked out a great way for all of them to have their time out. But it doesn't make it any less nerve wracking. I'm mostly worried for Neve. She might not understand."

Paris gives me a hug. "That little girl loves you, Dylan. If I can give you any advice, that would be to go slow with Neve. Talk to her. I'm sure she'll be happy for you both."

I nod, still not convinced. Thankfully, I have Thomas's and Paris's blessing. That's one third of the family on board. Now for the rest.

I know what I'm going to do isn't something Molly likes. As a matter of fact, she hates it. Forcing one of her alters out is the one thing she absolutely despises. Not that Molly hates her alters. No, she loves them like she loved Tina.

I've bought a new vampire book that Neve's been wanting to read. I have no interest in anything vampire related, but Neve loves them. And if she loves them, well, I'll try to love them too.

I've hidden the book on the chair beside me, and I'm going to try to force Neve to come out just before dinner. God, I hate doing this. I once accidently brought Kate forward because she's totally obsessed with popcorn. I popped some one night and forgot to ask Molly if that was okay. Kate was like a stick of dynamite when she came through, she wouldn't calm down. She's always so bubbly. Molly was furious at me, but she quickly forgave me when she saw I was beating myself up over it more than she ever could.

"Hey," I call nervously as Molly and the dogs all walk into the dining room. "Dinner's almost ready."

"Yum, it smells fantastic. What is it?"

"Jambalaya." I stir the pot, and the aroma wafts up.

"Is that what I can smell? Yum. Tell me you added chicken *and* shrimp."

"Yep."

She groans happily. "I'll go wash up and come help you."

I feel sick to my stomach. "Okay," I say trying to remain as normal as I can.

Molly runs to the bathroom, while Zelda, Zeus, and Zhen all sit in the kitchen, wagging their tails. I chuckle and crouch down to pet them. "Don't tell Molly, but I'm asking her to marry me tonight." Zhen licks me on the cheek as if he understands what I'm saying. The other two start wrestling together. *Siblings.*

"Okay, what can I do?"

"Um, there's um something on the chair, if you can move it for me please."

"Sure," she happily chirps and goes to where I've placed the book for Neve. I watch carefully, and I instantly regret the decision to force Neve out without talking to Molly first. I'm such an idiot.

I know the moment Neve comes through. Neve blinks really fast, and her entire stance changes. She becomes introverted, and shy. She twirls her hair around her finger. I give her a moment, making sure she's okay.

"Neve?" I ask when I think she's out.

"Hi, Dylan." She runs over to me and gives me a quick kiss. "Did you get this for me?"

"I did." I swallow.

"Yay! Can we read it together? Oh, and can we draw too?"

"Actually, Neve, I feel really bad, but I actually need to talk to you, first."

"Okay." She takes the book, and goes into the living room and sits on the floor cross-legged. She opens the book, and starts reading it.

"Neve," I say again, getting her attention.

"Yeah?" She doesn't look up from her book. This frustrates me, because she's just like a child. It's hard sometimes to not feel guilty when I'm frustrated with Neve, because I have to keep remembering that she's only a child. And a child's attention span is not like an adult's. I sit on the floor in front of her, and close the book. "Oh, sorry," she says as she smiles. "What do you want to talk to me about? You can't take me to the zoo this weekend, right?" Her lower lip quivers with sadness. "It's okay, I understand."

"No! Of course, I'm still taking you. I'm really looking forward to it. Are you?" She nods her head, and a huge smile replaces the sadness. "But I have something important to ask you, and Kate, and AJ. Can you see if you can contact the other two so I can talk to all of you please?"

"Yeah." She twirls her hair around her finger, and looks off to the distance.

"But not Molly."

"Okay." She stares around the room, and giggles. "AJ said this better be good, because he was working out." Neve lifts her hand to cover her cute little laugh. She's so sweet.

Gee, my hands are sweating and shaking. This is harder than asking Thomas and Paris.

"AJ said hurry up."

"Is Kate here?"

She focuses on something behind me, and nod her head. "Yep," she chirps.

"Okay, well. Tonight, I'm going to ask Molly to marry me. And I want to ask the three of you if you're okay with that?"

Neve tilts her head to the side. "So you'll be like my brother? Or like my daddy?" she asks. Molly's forehead wrinkles in confusion.

"I'll be just me," I reply. This is confusing enough as it is for me, I can't imagine how this'll be for Neve.

"AJ said yeah, sure, you're part of our family anyway. He asked if he can go back to his weights?"

"Thank you, AJ. And sure."

"But I don't understand. What will I have to call you?" Neve asks.

"Neve, nothing is going to change between you and I. Or between you and Molly. I just want to be a permanent part of your family. You don't have to do anything different than what you're already doing. I want to be here, with all of you forever."

Neve looks down at her feet, and nervously plays with her toes. "Does that mean you'll never leave?"

"I'd never leave anyway. Because I love you all."

Neve throws her arms around me, and gives me a kiss on the cheek. "I love you too, Dylan. And yes, it's okay if you ask M to marry you. I hope she says yes."

She keeps hugging me tight. "Can you ask Kate if it's okay?"

As she's hugging me, she goes silent. It doesn't take long for her to tell me, "Kate said, it's taken you long enough."

"Does that mean Kate's okay with me asking Molly?"

"It means, and these are her words, why the hell didn't you do this earlier? Hurry up, and do it." Neve giggles again. She lets go of the hug, and sits opposite me again. Suddenly, a sad look crosses her face. "I can't read this now, can I?"

"I'm sorry I tricked you, Neve. But if it's okay with you, can I have Molly back? And remember, we're still going to the zoo on Saturday. And, I promise, you can eat anything you want, and I won't tell Molly."

A smile creeps across her lips again, and she nods. "I hope she says yes," she says before closing her eyes for a moment.

Man, I'm in for a huge explosion when Molly comes back. I hope she can forgive me when she understands why I had to do that.

I scoot back, and wait. She blinks a few times, and rubs at her temple. She looks around the room, and notices me staring at her. She picks up the book, and crinkles her forehead. "What happened?" she asks. I remain silent, because I know she's going to piece it together quickly. "Why did you do that?" She stands, and walks into the kitchen to get water. She's always so thirsty when she comes back to me. But now, she's also angry. "Why, Dylan? Why did you force someone out? You know how much I hate that. It's an invasion of privacy. Do you know how hard it is trying to have a private life with three other people constantly in your head? No, of course you wouldn't."

"I'm sorry," I say as I watch her furiously pace back and forth.

"I can't believe you!" She shakes the vampire book at me. You forced Neve out, didn't you? Do you have any idea how draining that can be? How tiring? What the hell is wrong with you? Why couldn't you just ask me to get her? Ugh, you're unbelievable, Dylan, and definitely not in a good way." She storms out of the living room, and heads to our bedroom.

"Molly, will you let me explain?" I plead with her, following behind. Maybe this wasn't a good idea.

"What was so damn important you couldn't ask me to get Neve?" she shouts at me through our closed bedroom door.

"Can I come in?" I place my forehead to the door, and close my eyes. Great. I completely fucked this up.

"No! I'm so angry at you, Dylan."

I get why she's furious. Transitioning between them isn't easy, and it's physically and mentally draining. "Molly," I let out a deep sigh.

She's quiet in the room. God, I hope they haven't told her. I don't think Neve or Kate would, but AJ might. He's always trying to protect Molly. Always there to step in if she's upset or furious at something. And right now, she's livid with me.

"Molly!" I say again. I try the door handle, and I'm surprised to find she hasn't locked the bedroom door. I push the door open, and find Molly sitting on our bed, with her face buried in her hands as she sobs. It breaks my heart that I've done this to her. "Molly." I go to her, kneel before her, and pull her hands into mine.

Her eyes are red, and her cheeks are streaked with tears. "Why did you do that?" her voice is small.

"Because I had to ask them if it was okay with them before I asked you something."

"Ask them what?"

"If they'd accept me as your husband."

She pulls her hands away, tilts her head, and blinks a few times before mumbling an incoherent, "Huh?"

I dig into my pocket and take the little blue box out. "Marry me?"

She looks at the box with the closed lid, then looks back to me. "And you asked them if they'd accept you?" I nod my head. She closes her eyes and rubs at her temple. "I'm sorry."

"You're sorry because?" Dread hits me like a ton of bricks. Is she saying no?

"I'm sorry about how I reacted."

She still hasn't said yes though. "We're not exactly a conventional family. I thought I was doing the right thing, but maybe I shouldn't have done it that way."

"No, no, no." She takes my face between her hands, and peppers kisses all over me.

"Wait, now I'm confused. Remember, I'm just a guy. You're saying no, but you're kissing me. It's screwing with my head, Molly. Please, put me out of my misery. Will you marry me?" my voice breaks with tension.

"Yes!"

Phew.

ACKNOWLEDGEMENTS

I was home one Sunday night, watching a current affairs program, where the most extraordinary story came on. The story was of an incredibly courageous woman, who from a young age was abused in the most heinous of ways by the very person who was supposed to protect her. The abuse was on-going for many years, and as a result of it, she developed over two-thousand personalities in order to help her cope. For many years, the woman chased justice for the inhumane and detrimental acts her father committed. It took a detective believing in her, to start the wheels of justice turning. For the first time in Australian history, her alters were allowed to give evidence against her father, which saw him arrested and thrown in jail for the rest of his natural born life.

It was then I started thinking about the incredible journey this woman bravely took. How something so daunting, and frightening never held her back. It still brings tears to my eyes when I think about the sheer courage she showed.

Of course, Molly's story is completely fictional. I've not based her story on anyone else's, but I'm sure like most my other trauma-driven novels, *Ugly, Mistrust, Drowning, Addiction, Dying Wish and A Life Less Broken,* they're all someone's reality.

Molly's had been brewing for a few months before I started writing Echoes of You. But once I started, the words bled from my fingers and dripped on the page. Even as I write the acknowledgements, Molly still haunts me, gripping my mind making it difficult for me to move on.

There's not one word in Echoes of You I wish I wrote differently. This book is exactly the way it's supposed to be.

As difficult as this may have been for you to read it, it was even harder for me to write. The research I did was extraordinary. Choosing to watch and listen to people who live with DID.

Survivors of trauma, you are my inspiration.

You are exceptional.

But Echoes of You wouldn't be if it wasn't for the people who help me.

Of course, my editor: Debi Orton.

Cover designer: Book Cover by Design, Kellie Dennis.

Formatter: Integrity Formatting, Tami Norman.

Cover reveal and release blitz: Give Me Books, Kylie McDermott.

Proofreaders: Terry, Anna, Mandy, and Sam.

To everyone who always supports me. And of course, to you. The reason why I write.

It's days like today I wish I was dead.

"Lily Anderson, you get your ugly ass out here right this minute. Don't make me come after you," Daddy screams.

He's so angry. I knew the moment I heard him come home from work I was in for it. I was in my bedroom, lying on the floor trying to do my math. He slammed the front door so hard the windows in my room shook.

And then I knew, I knew I was in for it.

"Lily Anderson!" he yells again.

As soon as I heard him yell I ran to my hiding spot. I'm inside the closet in the hallway, wedged as far into the corner as I can get. Mom's old coat hangs in front of me and I can still smell a faint waft of the perfume she used to wear.

"Lily Anderson!" he shouts. I can hear the anger in his voice and I can already feel the pain he's going to inflict on me when he opens the closet door. I know what's coming.

I close my eyes tight, scrunching them up so no light can seep through. I put my hands over my ears so I can't hear him.

"I swear to God; if I have to find you, you will not sit for a month."

My knees are folded into my chest. I'm trying to make myself small, invisible, so he forgets I'm here. I'm rocking myself, trying to block out what he's saying.

School is safe. School is safe. School is safe. I keep repeating the mantra because in a few short hours I'll be back at school. Maybe tomorrow I can go to the library after school, stay there until it closes and then sneak in after Dad's passed out, because he's had too much to drink.

It was never like this before.

I'm twelve years old and I can remember when Mom, Dad, and I were all happy. But that was years ago. It's been a long time since there's been any happiness in this house.

Well, before Mom died, and not a day since.

Mom died when I was nine. I don't remember much about her, except I remember her telling me how ugly I am. How life would be better if I were taken away from them. How I'll never be anything, because I'm stupid and ugly.

Sometimes I dream happy things. Like me, Mom, Dad and a little blond-haired boy all going for a picnic. The sun beamed down on us as we played outside and laughed. We'd eat yummy sandwiches Mom made for us, and we'd drink homemade lemonade. We'd spend hours outside, laughing and talking and just having fun. Mom would tell me how pretty I am, and how much she loved me. She would play with my hair, braid it, and then we'd go and pick bright flowers to take home and put in a vase. Dad would smile and call us "his girls", always kissing Mom and hugging me. Dad would put the little boy on his shoulders and run around the park, trying to catch the clouds.

I love those dreams, and I hold onto them; wishing they were real. But I've never had a mom like that, and my dad doesn't talk much unless it's with his fists, or to tell me how ugly and useless I am.

I feel him walking around the house. The floorboards creak and the vibrations from his footsteps come through the floor to where my bottom is. I close my eyes tighter and try and breathe as quietly as I can.

Please go away, Daddy. Please go away.

My heart is beating so fast. My hands are shaking and I'm trying really hard not to think about what's going to happen the minute he opens the closet door.

Shhh, it's so quiet. The only sound is my heart thrumming in my ears. Nothing else. Not a whisper, not a rattle…nothing.

Maybe Daddy's left. Maybe he's gone to the pub to have a few drinks. Maybe, just maybe, he's left...forever.

I take a deep breath and just relax for a moment. My shoulders drop and I finally stop rocking.

Slowly I take my hands down from my ears, and I'm so happy because I can't hear him yelling at me. I can't hear him at all.

Gradually, I begin to unscrunch my eyes from the way I've tightly closed them. But something's not right. There's light coming into the closet.

I don't even get a chance to open them fully before a rough hand reaches in, latches onto my ponytail and yanks.

"I told you it'd be worse for you if I had to find you," Dad says, as he drags me out of the closet by my hair.

I'm desperately trying to hold onto my head so he doesn't rip my hair out. My feet are trying to find traction on the dirty floorboards.

"Please, Daddy. Please. You're hurting me," I begin sobbing as I plead with him.

"Then your ugly ass should've come when I called you, you stupid bitch. You're fucking worthless, you ugly idiot," he says. But now his voice is calm as he continues to drag me toward the family room.

That's when he's most scary. When his voice is low and his eyes are filled with hate.

He throws me against the side of the sofa and takes a step back to look at me.

I look up and can see he's the angriest I've ever seen him. "You dumb, ugly piece of shit," he says, as he paces back and forth in front of me.

"Sorry, Daddy. Whatever I did, I'm so sorry." I cower into myself, trying to make myself as small as possible.

"You're just too fucking stupid, aren't you?" he spits toward me as he brings his hand up to scratch at his chin.

"I'm sorry," I say again. Tears are falling hot and fast down my cheeks. My head hurts from where he was pulling my hair, but I don't dare try to rub the spot.

"You ugly fuck." He kicks a boot into my leg.

The pain is instant and my leg feels like it's shattered. "Please, Daddy," I beg again, burying my face into my hands.

But 'please' never seems to work.

Nothing does.

I've just got to take the beatings, because that's what stupid, ugly girls do.

Addiction

I CAN STOP ANYTIME I WANT

NEW YORK TIMES BESTSELLING AUTHOR

MARGARET MCHEYZER

Prologue

"Is she dead?"

Groaning, I try to roll over so I can see where the voice is coming from.

"She's moving. We have to help her," someone else says. Their voice is breathy, sounding panicked.

My limbs are heavy, my head is fuzzy, and I swear I can hear my mother's voice.

"Hannah, are you high?" She aggressively holds my chin and stares into my eyes.

"No, Mom," I respond, and giggle.

"Your eyes are bloodshot, and you're barely looking at me."

"I'm just tired," I say and giggle again.

"What's so funny?" she asks as she lets go of my chin and steps backward.

Shrugging, I look around the room.

"We need to call an ambulance," someone says, reminding me that my mother isn't here with me.

My vision is blurry. I can't focus on anything at all. Turning my head, I look straight into the eyes of a girl. She's probably around my age, but I bet she hasn't seen half the stuff I have. She kneels beside me, and behind her are another two girls and three guys. One of them looks bored; he's scrolling on his phone.

"What do you want?" I bark toward her, but my voice comes out broken, and slurry.

"Jasmine, she's a junkie. Look at her. Just leave her. She's not our problem," the bored guy says.

"We can't just leave her," she snarls back at him.

Suddenly, my stomach starts contracting, and my breathing becomes challenged. Gasping for air, my body tightens with spasms, trying to get oxygen into my lungs.

"Shit, she must be overdosing. We gotta get out of here before anyone finds us," bored guy says.

"I'm not leaving her. She's just a kid."

"She ain't my problem. I'm outta here," the bored guy says and takes off, the others going with him.

The girl stays with me, and as I try to focus on her, all I can see is the pretty chain around her neck. It looks like it's worth a lot, I'm sure I could give it to Edgar for some crystals. Man, maybe a few days' worth. I need money big time.

"I'm going to call an ambulance," the girl says as she takes her phone out of her pocket and dials it. "What have you taken?" she asks.

Everything is fuzzy. Her voice sounds disjointed and almost robotic.

Reaching for my pipe, I scream in pain. But she doesn't seem alarmed by my screams, maybe I'm actually not moving. Everything hurts.

"I need an ambulance…" her voice is frantic as she tells the operator where she is.

My eyes keep drifting shut, and she screams at me to open them again.

"She's frothing at the mouth, and she's barely moving."

I try to turn over, but whatever those fuckers gave me was strong. It's weighing me down. I can barely move.

"Her breathing is shallow…"

If I can just get up, I'll find my way back to Edgar's. He'll look after me. He always does. Sometimes he asks me to do stuff for him. "I'm alright," I mumble.

"She's trying to say something," the girl says into the phone. "Okay, I won't touch her." Her eyes are filled with pity and sadness. I stare up at her, and can see how concerned she is. I can see her. Can she see me?

"There's a syringe beside her. I think she might have injected something. There's a pipe, too. Maybe she smoked crack or meth?"

Yeah, baby. Crystal meth. Meth. Crystal. Ice. Tina. Glass. I love it. I love getting iced. It's the best feeling in the world. Being invincible, even when there are a million people in the room. Being free. Floating. That floating is what I love best. Anything can be happening around you, and when you smoke a bit of ice, you're floating above everyone. Free and happy and high.

"I'm here!" The girl jumps up and waves her arms frantically.

"Thank you for calling, we'll take it from here," another woman says to the girl.

The girl steps back and continues to stare at me. I'm being rolled over, and talked at by someone in a uniform. "What's your name?"

"Hannah," I respond.

"She's unresponsive," the woman says as she looks up to someone. She presses into my chest plate with her knuckle, and a shooting pain rips through me. "She's barely coherent. Heart rate is down, pulse is weak. She's overdosing."

"Get me back to Edgar's," I say.

"She's crashing. Administering Narcan."

There's a tightness in my chest. Pain soars through me, every part of me is like someone is stabbing multiple sharp knives into my body.

A darkness overtakes me.

A blanket of warmth is thrown over my entire body. My last breath escapes past my chapped lips.

Suddenly, I feel weightless. This must be what heaven feels like. It's so peaceful.

"We're losing her!" I hear someone yell.

Who's losing who? What's happening?

"ETA sixty seconds," someone else says in a calm voice.

I'm not sure what's happening, all I know is I like the quiet.

"Breathe, damn it, breathe!"

"Great, another dead junkie," someone snickers.

"I haven't lost her yet."

"She's just a junkie, Sally. Who cares if she dies? It's another one off the streets."

"Hey, she's someone's daughter. You want to be the one to knock on her parent's door?"

I hear a grumble from behind me. More like a pained sigh.

Who's talking?

What the hell is happening?

As it turns out, this is far from the end of my story.

Also by Margaret McHeyzer

A Bump in the Road

Pregnant at 15.

These are the words I didn't think I would ever have to live with.

Alex and I thought we were careful.

Becoming accidentally pregnant was obviously written in the stars for me.

I can't know what the future holds, or if Alex will even stick around.

But the one thing I know for sure; I'll turn this hardship into a blessing.

With or without anyone else.

Luna Caged

I often stare at the walls and wonder what's beyond them.

The Elders tell me that nothing but sin, sadness, and disease lie beyond the wall.

Sometimes I hear things, noises that are strange to me. They're often faint, and when I ask the Elders what those sounds are, they tell me they are the tortured souls of thousands of people behind the gates of hell. I don't know what they mean.

I dream of leaving these walls, but the Elders insist this is the only place we're safe. They talk about danger, hatred, and the devil himself waiting just beyond. They tell us the walls were built to keep us safe.

Although I believe the Elders, I want to see the outside world for myself.

But there's no way out.

Or so I thought…

Luna Freed

I often stared at the walls and wondered what was beyond them.

After my first escape, I realized that everything I'd believed, everything the Elders told us, and everything I thought I knew were all calculated lies.

Now I know the truth will set me free.

Addiction

Drugs ruin people's lives.

I should know, they destroyed mine.

I'm Hannah and I got hooked on ice. What started as a trickle, ended with a tsunami washing everything away; my family, my life.

I'm not sure you're ready to read my story, it's real and confronting.

Open the book, read the pages and see how easy it is for anyone to get addicted.

Ice affects all types of people. It doesn't discriminate.

It will SCREW. YOU. UP.

Drowning

I'm a cutter.

I cut because I find solace in it.

I cut because it helps calm my frantic mind.

I cut because the voice inside my head tells me to.

I cut because this is the only way I know how to handle life.

The Gift

I have something people want. I have something they cannot take or steal. I have something they'd kill for.

The something I have, isn't a possession, it's more.

Much, much more.

It's a gift.

It's part of me.

The Curse

It's been the butterfly effect.

I changed the course of my life because I warned a man.

I thought what I had was a gift, but it's quickly turning into my curse.

Now I realize I'm much more than a girl with an ability.

Because now... I'm becoming a weapon.

Dying Wish

I have three major loves in my life: my family, my best friend Becky, and ballet. Elijah Turner is quickly becoming the fourth.

He's been around as long as I can remember. But now he's much more than just the annoying guy at school.

My life was working out perfectly...until it got turned upside down.

Mistrust

I'm the popular girl at school.

The one everyone wants to be friends with.

I have the best boyfriend in the world, who's on the basketball team.

My parents adore me, and I absolutely love them. My sister and I have a great relationship too.

I'm a cheerleader, I have a high GPA and I'm liked even by the teachers.

It was a night which promised to be filled with love and fun until...something happened which changed everything.

Ugly

This is a dark YA/NA standalone, full-length novel. Contains violence and some explicit language

If I were dead, I wouldn't be able to see.

If I were dead, I wouldn't be able to feel.

If I were dead, he'd never raise his hand to me again.

If I were dead, his words wouldn't cut as deep as they do.

If I were dead, I'd be beautiful and I wouldn't be so...ugly.

I'm not dead...but I wish I was.

Chef Pierre

Holly Walker had everything she'd ever dreamed about - a happy marriage and being mum to beautiful brown-eyed Emma - until an accident nineteen months ago tore her world apart. Now she's a widow and single mother to a boisterous little 7-year-old girl, looking for a new start. Ready to take the next step, Holly has found herself a job as a maître d' at Table One, a once-acclaimed restaurant in the heart of Sydney. But one extremely arrogant Frenchman isn't going to be easy to work with...

Twenty years ago, Pierre LeRoux came to Australia, following the stunning Aussie girl he'd fallen in love with and married. He and his wife put their personal lives on hold, determined for Pierre to take Sydney's culinary society by storm. Just as his bright star was on the upswing, tragedy claimed the woman he was hopelessly in love with. He had been known as a Master Chef, but since his wife's death he has become known as a monster chef.

Can two broken people rebuild their lives and find happiness once more?

Smoke and Mirrors

Words can trick us.

Smoke obscures objects on the edge of our vision.

A mirror may reflect, but the eye sees what it wants.

A delicate scent can evoke another time and place, a memory from the past.

And a sentence can deceive you, even as you read it.

Grit

****Recommended for 18 years and over****

Alpha MC Prez Jaeger Dalton wants the land that was promised to him.

Sassy Phoenix Ward isn't about to let anyone take Freedom Run away from her.

He'll protect what's his.

She'll protect what's hers.

Jaeger is an arrogant ass, but he wants nothing more than Phoenix.

Phoenix is stubborn and headstrong, and she wants Jaeger out of her life.

Her father lost the family farm to gambling debts, but Jaeger isn't the only one who has a claim to the property.

Sometimes it's best to let things go.

But sometimes it's better to fight until the very end.

Yes, Master

***** THIS PROLOGUE CONTAINS DISTRESSING CONTENT. IT IS ONLY SUITED FOR READERS OVER 18. *****

ALSO CONTAINS M/M, M/M/F, M/F AND F/F SCENES.

My uncle abused me.

I was 10 years old when it started.

At 13 he told me I was no longer wanted because I had started to develop.

At 16 I was ready to kill him.

Today, I'm broken.

Today, I only breathe to survive.

My name's Sergeant Major Ryan Jenkins and today, I'm ready to tell you my story.

A Life Less Broken

****CONTAINS DISTRESSING CONTENT. 18+****

On a day like any other, Allyn Sommers went off to work, not knowing that her life was about to be irrevocably and horrifically altered.

Three years later, Allyn is still a prisoner in her own home, held captive by harrowing fear. Broken and damaged, Allyn seeks help from someone that fate put in her path.

Dr. Dominic Shriver is a psychiatrist who's drawn to difficult cases. He must push past his own personal battles to help Allyn fight her monsters and nightmares.

Is Dr. Shriver the answer to her healing?

Can Allyn overcome being broken?

My Life for Yours

He's lived a life of high society and privilege; he chose to follow in his father's footsteps and become a Senator.

She's lived a life surrounded with underworld activity; she had no choice but to follow in her father's footsteps and take on the role of Mob Boss.

He wants to stamp out organized crime and can't be bought off.

She's the ruthless and tough Mob Boss where in her world all lines are blurred.

Their lives are completely different, two walks of life on the opposite ends of the law.

Being together doesn't make sense.

But being apart isn't an option

HiT Series Box Set

HiT 149

Anna Brookes is not your typical teenager. Her walls are not adorned with posters of boy bands or movie stars. Instead posters from Glock, Ruger, and Smith & Wesson grace her bedroom. Anna's mother abandoned her at birth, and her father, St. Cloud Police Chief Henry Brookes, taught her how to shoot and coached her to excellence. On Anna's fifteenth birthday, unwelcome guests join the celebration, and Anna's world is never the same. You'll meet the world's top assassin, 15, and follow her as she discovers the one hit she's not sure she can complete - Ben Pearson, the current St. Cloud Police Chief and a man with whom Anna has explosive sexual chemistry. Enter a world of intrigue, power, and treachery as Anna takes on old and new enemies, while falling in love with the one man with whom she can't have a relationship.

Anna Brookes in Training

Find out what happened to transform the fifteen-year-old Anna Brookes, the Girl with the Golden Aim, into the deadly assassin 15. After her father is killed and her home destroyed, orphan Anna Brookes finds herself homeless in Gulf Breeze, Florida. After she saves Lukas from a deadly attack, he takes her in and begins to train her in the assassin's craft. Learn how Lukas's unconventional training hones Anna's innate skills until she is as deadly as her mentor.

HiT for Freedom

Anna has decided to break off her steamy affair with Ben Pearson and leave St. Cloud, when she suspects a new threat to him. Katsu Vang is rich, powerful, and very interested in Anna. He's also evil to his core. Join Anna as she plays a dangerous game, getting closer to Katsu to discover his real purpose, while trying to keep Ben safe. Secrets are exposed and the future Anna hoped for is snatched from her grasp. Will Ben be able to save her?

HiT to Live

In the conclusion to the Anna Brookes saga, Ben and his sister Emily, with the help of Agent rescue Anna. For Anna and Ben, it's time to settle scores...and a time for the truth between them. From Sydney to the Philippines and back to the States, they take care of business. But a helpful stranger enters Anna's life, revealing more secrets...and a plan that Anna wants no part of. Can Anna and Ben shed their old lives and start a new one together, or will Anna's new-found family ruin their chances at a happily-ever-after?

Binary Law (co-authored)

Ellie Andrews has been receiving tutoring from Blake McCarthy for three years to help her improve her grades so she can get into one of the top universities to study law. And she's had a huge crush on him since she can remember.

Blake McCarthy is the geek at school that's had a crush on Ellie since the day he met her.

In their final tutoring session, Blake and Ellie finally become brave enough to take the leap of faith.

But, life has other plans and rips them apart. Six years later Blake and his best friends Ben and Billy have built a successful internet platform company 3BCubed, while Ellie is a successful and hardworking lawyer specializing in Corporate Law.

3BCubed is being threatened with a devastatingly large plagiarism case and when it lands on their lawyers desk, it's handed to the new Corporate Lawyer to handle and win.

Coincidence or perhaps fate will see Blake and Ellie pushed back together.

Binary Law will have Blake and Ellie propelled into a life that's a whirl wind of catastrophic events and situations where every emotion will be touched. Hurt will be experienced, happiness will be presented and love will be evident. But is that enough for Blake and Ellie be able to live out their own happily ever after?

Printed in Great Britain
by Amazon